Praise for Martha Wells

The
CLOUD
ROADS

The
CLOUD
ROADS

MARTHA WELLS

NIGHT SHADE BOOKS
SAN FRANCISCO

The Cloud Roads
© 2011 by Martha Wells
This edition of
The Cloud Roads
© 2011 by Night Shade Books

Edited by Janna Silverstein
Cover art by Matthew Stewart
Cover design by Rebecca Silvers
Interior layout and design by Michael Lee

First Printing

ISBN: 978-1-59780-216-1

Printed In Canada

Night Shade Books
Please visit us on the web at
http://www.nightshadebooks.com

To Jennifer Jackson
for believing in this book

CHAPTER
ONE

෮

Moon had been thrown out of a lot of groundling settlements and camps, but he hadn't expected it from the Cordans.

The day started out normal enough. Moon had been hunting alone as usual, following the vargit, the big flightless birds common to this river valley. He had killed one for himself, then taken a nap on a sun-warmed rock and slept a little too long. By the time he found a second vargit for the camp, killed it, dressed it, and hauled it back, the sky was darkening. The gate in the rickety fence of woven sticks was closed, and he shook it, shifting the heavy dead bird on his shoulder. "Open up, it's me."

The gate and the entire fence were mostly a formality. The camp was built on a field leading down to the wide bed of the river, and the fence didn't even go

1

all the way around. The jungle lay just outside it, climbing up the hills toward the steep cliffs and gorges to the east. The dense leaves of the tall trees, wreathed with vines and hung with heavy moss, formed a spreading canopy that kept the ground beneath in perpetual twilight. Anything could come out of there at the camp, and the weak fence wouldn't stop it. The Cordans knew that, but Moon still felt it gave a false sense of security that made everyone careless, especially the children. But the fence had sentimental value, reminding the Cordans of the walled towns in their old land in Kiaspur, before it had been taken by the Fell. Plans to take it down and use it for firewood always came to nothing.

After more shaking, something moved just inside the gate, and Hac's dull voice said, "Me who?" Then Hac laughed, a low noise that ended in a gurgling cough.

Moon looked away, letting out an exasperated breath. The fence wasn't made any more effective by letting the most mentally deficient member of the group guard it, but there weren't a lot of jobs Hac could do.

Sunset beyond the distant mountains cast the lush, forested hills with orange and yellow light. It also framed a sky-island, floating sedately high in the air over the far end of the valley. It had been drifting into the area for some days, traveling with the vagaries of the wind. Heavy vegetation overflowed the island's surface and hung down the sides. Moon could just make out the shapes of ruined towers and walls nearly covered by encroaching greenery. A flock of birds with long white bodies, each big enough to seize a grazing herdbeast in its talons, flew past it, and Moon felt a surge of pure envy. *Tonight,* he promised himself. *It's been long enough.*

But for now he had to get into the damn camp. He tried to make his voice flat and not betray his irritation. Showing Hac you were annoyed just made him worse. "The meat's spoiling, Hac."

Hac laughed again, coughed again, and finally unlatched the gate.

Moon hauled the bird inside. Hac crouched on the ground beside the fence, watching him with malicious glee. Hac looked like a typical Cordan: short and stocky, with pale gray-green skin and dull green hair. Most Cordans had patches of small glittering scales on their faces or arms, legacy of an alliance with a sea realm sometime in the history of their dead empire. On some of the others, especially the young, the effect was like glittering skin-jewelry. On Hac, it just looked slimy.

Hac, who held a similar opinion of Moon, said, "Hello, ugly."

A few other outsiders lived with the Cordans, but Moon tended to stand out. A good head taller than most of them, he was lean and rawboned where they were heavyset. He had dark bronze skin that never burned no matter how bright the sun, dark hair. The only thing green about him was his eyes.

"Keep up the good work, Hac," Moon said, and resisted the urge to kick Hac in the head as he carried the carcass past.

Tents were scattered across the compound, conical structures made of woven cable-rushes, dried and pressed and faintly sweet-smelling. They stretched down to the greenroot plantings at the edge of the broad river bed. At the moment, most of the inhabitants were gathered around the common area in the camp's center, portioning out the meat the hunters had brought back. People down at the river washed and filled big clay water jars. A few women worked at the cooking fires outside the tents. As Moon walked up the packed dirt path toward the central area, an excited band of children greeted him, hurrying along beside him and staring curiously at the vargit. Their enthusiastic welcome went a long way to make up for Hac.

The elders and other hunters all sat around on straw mats in front of the elders' tent, and some of the women and older kids were busy cutting and wrapping the kills brought back earlier. Moon dropped the vargit carcass on the muddy straw mat with the others, and set aside the bow and quiver of arrows he hadn't used. He had gotten very good at dressing his game in such a way that it was impossible to tell exactly how it had been killed. Dargan the headman leaned forward to look at it and nodded approval. "You had a good day after all, then. When you were late, we worried."

"I had to track them down the valley. It just took a little longer than I thought." Moon sat on his heels at the edge of the mat, stifling a yawn. He was still full from his first kill, which had been a much bigger vargit. Most of his time had gone to finding a more medium-sized one that he could carry back without help. But the novelty of coming home to people who worried that something might have happened to him had never paled.

Ildras, the chief hunter, gave him a friendly nod. "We never saw you, and thought perhaps you'd gone toward the west."

Moon made a mental note to make certain he crossed paths with Ildras' group tomorrow, and to make certain it happened more frequently from now on. He was comfortable here, and it was making him a little careless. He knew from long experience that elaborate lies were a bad idea, so he just said, "I didn't see anybody either."

Dargan waved for one of the boys to come over to cut up Moon's kill. Dargan and the other male elders kept track of all the provisions, portioning them out to the rest of the camp. It made sense, but the way they did it had always bothered Moon. He thought the others might resent it sometimes, but it was hard to tell since nobody talked about it.

Then Ildras nudged Dargan and said, "Tell him the news."

"Oh, the news." Dargan's expression turned briefly sardonic. He told Moon, "The Fell have come to the valley."

Moon stared. But Ildras's expression was wry, and the others looked, variously, amused, bored, and annoyed. Two of the boys skinning a herdbeast carcass collapsed into muffled giggling and were shushed by one of the women. Moon decided this was one of those times when he just didn't understand the Cordans' sense of humor. He discarded the first few responses that occurred to him and went with, "Why do you say that?"

Dargan nodded toward another elder. "Tacras saw it."

Tacras, whose eyes were too wide in a way that made him look a little crazy, nodded. "One of the harbingers, a big one."

Moon bit his lip to control his expression and tried to look thoughtful. Obviously the group had decided to humor Tacras. The creatures the Cordans knew as harbingers were actually called major kethel, the largest of all Fell. If one had been near the camp, Moon would have scented it. It would be in the air, in the river water. The things gave off an unbelievable stench. But he couldn't exactly tell the Cordans that. Also, if Tacras had been close enough to see a major kethel, it would have eaten him. "Where?"

Tacras pointed off to the west. "From the cliff on the edge of the forest, where it looks down into the gorge."

"Did it speak to you?" Vardin asked in wide-eyed mockery.

"Vardin," Dargan said in reproof, but it was a little too late.

Tacras glared. "You disrespect your elder!" He shoved to his feet. "Be fools then. I know what I saw."

He stamped away, off between the tents, and everybody sighed. Ildras reached over and gave Vardin a shove on the shoulder, apparently as punishment. Moon kept his mouth shut and did not wince in annoyance. They had all been making fun of the old man anyway. Vardin had just brought it out in the open. If Dargan hadn't wanted that to happen, he shouldn't have made his own derision so clear.

"He's crazy," Kavath said, sounding sour and worried as he watched Tacras walk away. He was another outsider, though he had been here much longer than Moon. He had shiny pale blue skin, a long narrow face, and a crest of gray feathers down the middle of his skull. "He's going to cause a panic."

The Cordans all just shrugged, looking unlikely to panic. Dargan added, "Everyone knows he's a little touched. They won't listen. But do not contradict him. It's disrespectful to his age." With the air of being done with the whole subject, he turned to Moon and said, "Now tell us if you saw any bando-hoppers down in that end of the valley. I think it must be the season for them soon."

When Moon had first found the Cordans and been accepted into their group, Dargan had presented him with a tent, and with Selis and Ilane. Moon had been very much looking forward to the tent; in fact, it was the whole reason he had wanted to join the Cordans in the first place. He had been traveling alone a long time at that point, and the idea of sleeping warm and dry, without having to worry about something coming along and eating him, had been too attractive to pass up. The reality was every bit as good as he had hoped. Selis and Ilane, however, had taken some getting used to.

It was twilight by the time he reached his tent, shadows gathering. He met Selis coming out with the waterskin.

"You took long enough," she snapped, and snatched the packet of meat away.

"Tell that to Dargan," Moon snapped back. She knew damn well that he had to wait for the elders to divide up the kill, but he had given up trying to reason with her about three days after being accepted into the Cordan camp. He took the waterskin away from her and went to fill it at the troughs.

When the Cordans had fled their last town, many of their young men had been killed covering their escape. It had left them with a surplus of young women. The Cordans believed the women needed men to provide for them; Moon had no idea why. He knew that Selis in particular was perfectly capable of chasing down any number of grasseaters and beating them to death with a club, so he didn't see why she couldn't hunt for herself. But it was the way the Cordans lived, and he wasn't going to argue. And he liked Ilane.

By the time he got back, Selis had the meat laid out on a flat stone and was cutting it up into portions. Ilane sat on a mat beside the fire.

Ilane was beautiful, though the other Cordans didn't think so, and their lack of regard had made her quiet and timid. She was too tall, too slender, with a pearlescent quality to her pale green skin. Moon had tried to tell her that in most of the places he had lived, she would be considered lovely, that it was just a matter of perception. But he wasn't certain he had ever been able to make her understand. Selis looked more typically Cordan, stocky and strong, with iridescent patches on her cheeks and forehead. He wasn't sure why she had been stuck with him, but suspected her personality had a lot to do with it.

Moon stowed his weapons in the tent and dropped down onto the mat next to Ilane. She was peeling a greenroot, the big, melon-like staple that the Cordans ate with everything, fried, mashed, or raw. After the kill earlier in the day, Moon wasn't hungry and wouldn't be for the next day or so. But not eating in front of other people was one of the first mistakes he had ever made, and he didn't intend to make it again. It had gotten him chased out of the nice silk-weaving town of Var-tilth, and the memory still stung.

"Moon." Ilane's voice was always quiet, but this time it held a note of painful hesitancy. "Do you think the Fell are here?"

Tacras' story had, of course, spread all over camp. Moon knew he should say what Dargan had said, but looking at Ilane, her pale green skin ashy-gray with fear, he just couldn't. "No. I've been hunting in the open all up and down the valley and I haven't seen anything. Neither have the others."

As she wrapped the meat up in bandan leaves to put into the coals, Selis said, "So Tacras lies because he wants to frighten us to death for his amusement."

Moon pretended to consider it. "Probably not. Not everybody's like you."

She gave him a sour grimace. Forced into actually asking a question, she said, "Then what?"

Ilane was having trouble getting the knife through the tough greenroot skin. Moon took it and sawed the hard ends off. He squinted at Selis. "Do you know how many things there are that fly besides Fell?"

Selis' jaw set. She did know, but she didn't want to admit it. All the Cordans knew that further up in the hills, there were birds, flighted and not, that were nearly as large as the small Fell, and nearly as dangerous.

"So Tacras was wrong?" Ilane said, her perfect brow creased in a frown.

Moon finished stripping the greenroot's outer husk and started to slice it. "He saw it with the sun in his eyes, and made a mistake."

"We should all be so lucky," Selis said, but Moon knew enough Selis-speak to hear it as a grudging admission that he was probably right.

He hoped he was right. Investigating it gave him yet another reason to go out tonight.

"You're cutting the greenroot wrong," Selis snapped.

Moon waited until late into the night, lying on his back and staring at the shadows on the tent's curved supports, listening to the camp go gradually quiet around him. The air was close and damp, and it seemed to take a long time for everyone to settle down. It would never go silent; there were too many people. But it had been a while since he had heard a voice nearby, or the low wail of a fretful baby.

Moon slid away from Ilane. She stirred, making a sleepy sound of inquiry. He whispered, "It's too warm. I'm going to take a walk, maybe sleep outside."

She hummed under her breath and rolled over. Moon eased to his feet, found his shirt, and made a wide circle around Selis' pallet as he slipped outside.

He and Ilane had been sleeping together since the second month Moon had been here. She had made the first overtures to him before that, apparently, but Moon hadn't understood what she wanted. Ilane hadn't understood what she had interpreted as his refusal, either, and had been very unhappy. Moon had had no idea what was going on and had seriously considered a strategic retreat—right out of the camp—until one night Selis had thrown her hands in the air in frustration and explained to him what Ilane wanted.

Ilane was sweet-tempered, but her lack of understanding was sometimes frustrating. Several days ago, she had said she wanted to have a baby, and Moon had had to tell her he didn't think it was possible. That had been a hard conversation.

She had just stared tragically at him, her eyes huge, as if this was something he was deliberately withholding. "We're too different," he told her, feeling helpless. "I'm not a Cordan." He thought that if there had been any chance of it, it would have happened already.

Ilane blinked and her silver brows drew together. "You want Selis instead."

Selis, sitting across the fire and mending the ripped sleeve of a shirt, shook her head in weary resignation. "Just give up," she told Moon.

Moon threw her a grim look and persisted, telling Ilane, "No, no, I don't think…I can't give you a baby. It just won't happen." He added hopefully, "You could have babies with somebody else and bring them to live with us." Now that he thought about it, it wasn't a bad idea. He knew he could bring in enough food for a larger group, even with the elders taking their share.

Ilane had just continued to stare. Selis had muttered to Moon, "You are so stupid."

He stepped outside. The air was cool compared to the close interior of the tent, with just enough movement to lift the damp a little. The full moon was bright, almost bright enough to see the groundling woman that supposedly lived in it. The sky was crowded with stars; it was hard not to just leap into the air.

Moon stood beside the tent for a moment, pretending to stretch. Across the width of the camp, two sentries stood at the gate with torches, but the cooking fires were out or banked. He carried Ilane's scent on his skin, and the whole camp smelled of Cordan, so it was tricky to sense anyone nearby. But he wasn't going to get a better chance.

His bare feet were silent on the packed ground between the tents. He didn't see anyone else, but he could hear deep breathing, the occasional sleepy mutter as he passed. He stopped at the latrine ditches, pissed into one, then wandered off, tying the drawstring on his pants again.

He went toward the far end of the camp, where the fence ran down toward edge of the river channel. Made of bundles of saplings roped together, the fence wasn't very secure at the best of times but here, where it cut across the slope of the bank, there were gaps under the bottom. Moon dropped to the ground and wiggled under one.

Once through the fence, he loped across the field and reached the fringe of the jungle. There, in the deep shadow, he shifted.

Moon didn't know what he was, just that he could do this. His body got taller, his shoulders broader. He was stronger but much lighter, as if his bones weren't made of the same stuff anymore. His skin hardened, darkened, grew an armor of little scales, overlapping almost like solid feathers. In this shadow it made him nearly invisible; in bright sunlight the scales would be black with an under sheen of bronze. He grew retractable claws on his hands and feet and a long flexible tail, good for hanging upside down off tree branches. He also had a mane of flexible frills and spines around his head, running down to his lower back; in a fight they could be flared out into rigid spikes to protect his head and back.

Now he unfolded his wings and leapt into the air, hard flaps carrying him higher and higher until he caught the wind.

It was cooler up here, the wind hard and strong. He did a long sweep of the valley first, just in case Tacras was right, but didn't see or catch scent of anything unusual. Past the jungle, the broad grassy river plain was empty except for the giant lumpy forms of the big armored grasseaters that the Cordans called kras. He flew up into the hills, passing over narrow gorges and dozens of small waterfalls. The wind was rougher here, and he controlled his wing curvature with delicate movements, playing the air along his joints and scales.

There was no sign of Fell, no strange groundling tribes, nothing the Cordans needed to worry about.

Moon turned back toward the sky-island where it floated in isolation over the plain. He pushed himself higher until he was well above it.

He circled over the island. Its shape was irregular, with jagged edges. It had been hard to tell how large it was from the ground; from above he could see it was barely four hundred paces across, smaller than the Cordans' camp. It was covered with vegetation, trees with narrow trunks winding up into spirals, heavy falls of vines and white, night-blooming flowers. But he could still make out the round shape of a tower, and a building that was a series of stacked squares of vine-covered stone. There were broken sections of walls, choked pools and fountains.

He spotted a balcony jutting out of curtains of foliage and dropped down toward it. He landed lightly on the railing; his claws gripped the pocked stone. Folding his wings, he stepped down onto the cracked tiles, parting the vines to find the door. It was oblong and narrow, and he shifted back to groundling form to step through.

Fragments of moonlight fell through the cracks and the heavy shrouds of vegetation. The room smelled strongly of earth and must. Moon sneezed, then picked his way carefully forward.

He still wore his clothes; it was a little magic, to make the shift and take any loose fabric attached to his body with him, but it had taken practice to be able to do it. His mother had taught him, the way she had taught him to fly. He had never gotten the trick of shifting with boots on. His feet had a heavy layer of extra skin on the sole, thick as scar tissue, so he usually went barefoot.

When he was a boy, after being hounded out of yet another settlement, Moon had tried to make his groundling form look more like theirs, hoping it would make him fit in better. His mother had never mentioned that ability, but he thought it was worth a try. He might as well have tried to turn himself into a rock or a tree, and after a time he had concluded that the magic just didn't work that way. There was this him, and the scaly winged version, and that was it.

He made his way to the door, startling a little flock of flighted lizards, all brilliant greens and blues. They fluttered away, hissing harmlessly, and he stepped into the next room. The ceiling was several levels above him, and the room had tall doorways and windows that looked into an atrium shaped like a six-pointed star. Shafts of moonlight pierced the darkness, illuminating a mosaic tile floor strewn with debris and a shallow pool filled with bright blue flowers. Doorways led off into more shadowed spaces.

He made his way from one room to another, the tile gritty under his feet. He poked at broken fragments of pottery and glass, pushed vines away from faded wall murals. It was hard to tell in this bad light, but the people in the murals seemed to be tall and willowy, with long flowing hair and little bundles of tentacles where their mouths should be. There was something to do with a sea realm, but he couldn't tell if it was a battle, an alliance, or just a myth.

Moon had been very young when his mother and siblings had been killed, and she had never told him where they had come from. For a long time he had searched sky-islands looking for some trace of his own people. The islands flew; it stood to reason that the inhabitants might be shifters who could fly. But he had never found anything, and now he just explored because it gave him something to do.

When Moon had first joined the Cordans, he hadn't thought of staying this long. He had lived with other people he had liked—most recently the Jandin, who had lived in cliff caves above a waterfall, and the Hassi, with their wooden city high in the air atop a thick mat of link-trees—but something always happened. The Fell came or someone got suspicious of him and he had to move on. He had never lived with anyone long enough to truly trust them, to tell them what he was. But living alone, even with the freedom to shift whenever he felt like it or needed to, wore on him. It seemed pointless and, worst of all, it was lonely. Lost in thought, he said, "You're never satisfied," not realizing he had spoken aloud until the words broke the stillness.

In the next room, he found a filigreed metal cabinet built into the wall stuffed with books. Digging down through a layer of moldy, disintegrating lumps of paper and leather, he found some still intact. These were folded into neat packets and made of thin, stiff sheets of either very supple metal or thin reptile hide. Moon carried a pile back out to the atrium, sat on the gritty tile in a patch of moonlight near the flower-filled fountain, and tried to read.

The text was similar to Altanic, which was a common language in the Three Worlds, though this version was different enough that Moon couldn't get much sense out of it. But there were drawings with delicate colors, pictures of the people with the tentacle faces. They rode strange horned beasts like bando-hoppers and flew in carriages built on the backs of giant birds.

It was so absorbing, he didn't realize he was being watched until he happened to glance up.

He must have heard something, smelled something, or just sensed another living presence. He looked up the open shaft of the atrium, noticing broad balconies, easy pathways to other interior rooms if he shifted and used his claws to climb to them. Then he found a shadow on one of the balconies, a shadow in the wrong place.

At first he tried to see it as a statue, it was so still. Then moonlight caught the gleam of scales on sinuous limbs, claws gripping the stone railing, the curve of a wing ending in a pointed tip.

Moon's breath caught and his blood froze. He thought, *You idiot.* Then he flung himself through the nearest doorway.

He scrambled back through the debris, then crouched, listening. He heard the creature move, a rasp of scales as it uncoiled, clink of claws on stone. He thought it was too big to come further in, that it would go up, and out. Moon bolted back through the inner rooms.

He couldn't afford to be trapped in here; he had one chance to get past that thing and he had to take it now. He skidded around the corner, his bare feet slipping on mossy tile, and scrabbled up a pile of broken stone to a vine-draped window. He jumped through, already shifting.

He felt movement in the air before he saw the claws reaching for him. Moon jerked away with a sharp twist that wrenched his back. He swiped at the dark shape suddenly right on top of him. He swung wildly, catching it a glancing blow across the face, feeling his claws catch on tough scales. It pulled back, big wings knocking tiles and fragments of greenery off the sides of the ruin.

Moon tumbled in midair toward the cracked pavement below, caught himself on a ledge around a half-destroyed tower, and clung to the stone. He looked back just as the creature flapped upward in a spray of rock chips and dead leaves. *Oh, it's big,* Moon thought, his heart pounding. Not big enough to eat him in one bite, maybe. But it was three times his size if not more. Moon's wingspan was close to twenty paces, fully extended; this creature's span was more than forty. *So two bites, maybe three.* And it wasn't an animal. It had known it was looking at a shifter. It had expected him to fly out of an upper window, not walk or climb out.

As the creature flapped powerful wings, positioning itself to dive at him, Moon shoved off from the tower, sending himself out and down, over the edge of the sky-island. He angled his wings, diving in close past the jagged rock and the waterfalls of heavy greenery. He landed on a spur of rock and clung like a lizard. Digging his claws in, he climbed down and under, folding and tucking his wings and tail in, making himself as small as possible.

He kept his breath slow and shallow, hoping he didn't have to cling here too long. His claws were meant for fastening onto wooden branches, not rock, and this was already starting to hurt. He couldn't hear the creature, but he wasn't surprised when a great dark shape dove past. It circled below the island, one slow circuit to try to spot Moon. He hoped it was looking down toward the jungle.

It made another circuit, then headed upward to pass back over the top of the island.

Here goes, Moon thought. He aimed himself for the deep part of the river, flexed his claws, and let go.

Tilting his wings for the least wind resistance, he fell like a rock. The air rushed past him and he counted heartbeats, gauging how long it would take the creature to make a slow sweep over the sky-island. Then he rolled over to look up, just in time to see the dark shape appear at the western end of the island.

It saw him instantly. It didn't howl with rage, it just dove for him.

Uh oh. Moon twisted back around, arrowing straight down. The rapidly approaching ground was a green blur, broken by the dark expanse of the river.

At the last instant, he cupped his wings and slowed just enough before he slammed into the river. He plunged deep into the cold water, down until he scraped the bottom. Folding his wings in tightly, he kicked to stay below the surface, the rushing current carrying him along.

Moon wasn't as fast in the water as he was in the air, but he was faster in this form than as a groundling. Swimming close to the sandy bottom, Moon stayed under until his lungs were about to burst, then headed for the bank and the thick stands of reeds. The reeds were topped with large, wheel-shaped fronds that made a good screen from above. Moon let his face break the surface, just enough to get a breath. The fronds made a good screen from below, too, but after a few moments, Moon saw the creature make a lazy circle high above the river. He had been hoping it would slam into the bank and snap its neck, but no such luck. But he knew the water would keep it from following his scent. It probably knew that, too. He filled his lungs, sunk down again, and kicked off.

He surfaced twice more, and the second time, he couldn't spot the creature. Still careful, he stayed under, following the river all the way back to camp. Once there, he shifted back to groundling underwater, then swam toward the shore, until it was shallow enough that he could walk up the sloping bank.

He sat down on the sparse grass above the water, his clothes dripping, letting his breath out in a long sigh. His back and shoulder were sore, pain carried over from nearly twisting himself in half to avoid the creature's first grab. He still hadn't gotten a good look at it. *This is going to be a problem.* And he and all the Cordans owed Tacras an apology.

But that thing wasn't Fell—he knew that from its lack of scent. It might live on the island, drifting with it, and just hadn't needed to hunt yet. Or it might just be passing through, and had used the island as a place to shelter and sleep.

He thought it must have been sleeping when he had reached the ruins, or he would have heard it moving around. *Idiot, you could have been dinner.* If it had snatched him in his groundling form, it could have snapped him in half before he had a chance to shift.

If it attacked the camp, what it was or why it had come here wouldn't matter much; it could still kill most of the Cordans before they had a chance to take cover in the jungle. Moon was going to have to warn them.

Except he couldn't exactly run into the center of the camp yelling an alarm. If he said he had seen it tonight, while sitting out by the river…No, he could hear that the camp wasn't as quiet as it had been when he left. It was a warm night, and there must be others sitting or sleeping outside, who would say they hadn't seen anything. He would look as unreliable as Tacras and no one would listen to him. He would have to wait until tomorrow.

When he went hunting, he would walk down the valley toward the sky-island. That would give him a chance to scout the island by air again, to see if the creature was still there, if it would come out in the daylight. *Cautiously scout*, he reminded himself. He didn't want to get eaten before he could warn the Cordans. But when he told them he had seen the same creature as Tacras at that end of the valley, they would have to take it seriously.

Moon pushed wearily to his feet and wrung out the front of his shirt. As he started back up the long slope of the bank, he considered the other problem: what the Cordans were going to do once they were warned.

Moon didn't have any answers for that one. The creature would either drive them out of the valley or it wouldn't. He knew he couldn't take it in an open fight. But if he could think of a way to trap it… He had killed a few of the smaller major kethel that way, but they weren't exactly the cleverest fighters; he had the feeling this thing… was different.

Moon took the long way back through the camp, which let him pass the fewest number of tents. Still thinking about traps and tactics, he came in sight of his tent and halted abruptly. The banked fire had been stirred up, and the coals were glowing. In its light he could see a figure sitting in front of the doorway. A heartbeat later he recognized Ilane, and relaxed.

He walked up to the tent, dropping down to sit next to her on the straw mat. "Sorry I woke you. I went down to the river." That part was obvious; he was still dripping.

She shook her head. "I couldn't sleep." It was too dark to read her expression, but she sounded the same as she always did. She wore a light shift, and used a fold of her skirt to lift a small kettle off the fire. "I'm making a tisane. Do you want some?"

He didn't; the Cordans supposedly used herbs to make it but it just tasted like water reed to him. But it was habit to accept any food offered to him, just to look normal. And Ilane hardly ever cooked; he felt he owed it to Selis to encourage it when she did.

She poured the steaming water into a red-glazed ceramic pot that belonged to Selis and handed Moon a cup.

Selis poked her head out of the tent, her hair tumbled around her face. "What are you—" She saw Moon and swore, then added belatedly, "Oh, it's you."

"Do you want a cup of tisane?" Ilane asked, unperturbed.

"No, I want to sleep," Selis said pointedly, and vanished back into the tent.

The tisane tasted more reedy than usual, but Moon sat and drank it with Ilane. He listened to her detail the love affairs of nearly everybody else in camp while he nodded at the right moments and mostly thought about what he was going to say to Dargan tomorrow. Though he was a little surprised to hear that Kavath was sleeping with Selis' cousin Denira.

He didn't remember falling asleep.

CHAPTER TWO

Moon didn't so much wake up as drift slowly toward consciousness. It seemed like a dream, one of those in which he thought he was awake, trying to move his sluggish still-sleeping body, until he finally succeeded in making some jerky motion and startling himself conscious. Except he didn't succeed.

He finally woke enough to realize he lay on his stomach, face half-buried in a thick, felted blanket that smelled like the herbs Selis used to wash everything. His throat was dry and his body ached in ways it never had before, little arcs of pain running up his spine and out through the nerves in his arms and legs. In panicked reflex he tried to shift, realizing his mistake an instant later. If he was ill now, he would be ill in his other form. And he could see daylight on the tent wall; someone might be just outside.

But nothing happened. He was still in groundling form.

Nothing. I can't— He tried again. Still nothing. His heart started to pound in panic. He was sick, or it was a magical trap, some lingering taint from whatever had killed the inhabitants of the sky-island.

He heard voices just outside—Selis, Dargan, some of the others, not Ilane. With an effort that made his head spin, he shoved himself up on his elbows. More pain stabbed down his spine, taking his breath away. He tried to speak, coughed, and managed to croak, "Ilane?"

Footsteps, then someone grabbed his shoulder and shoved him over. Dargan leaned over him, then recoiled, his face appalled, disgusted.

"What—" Moon gasped, confused. He knew he hadn't shifted. Half a dozen hunters pushed into the tent, Garin, Kavath, Ildras. Someone grabbed his wrists and dragged him outside onto the packed dirt of the path. Morning light stung his eyes. People surrounded him, staring in condemnation and horror.

I'm sick and they're going to kill me, Moon thought, baffled. It didn't make any sense, but he felt the answer looming over him like a club. He managed to push himself up into a sitting position. They scrambled away from him. *Oh. Oh, no.* It couldn't be what it seemed like. *They know. They have to know.*

Dargan stepped into view again. His face was hard but he wouldn't meet Moon's eyes. Dargan said, "The girl saw you. You're a Fell, a demon."

Except a club would have been quick—one brief instant of stunned agony, then nothing. "I'm not." Moon choked on a breath and had to stop and pant for air. Ilane had done this. "I don't know what I am." Desperate, he tried to shift again, and felt nothing.

"The poison only works on Fell." Dargan stepped back, signaling to someone.

Poison. Ilane had seen him shift, then gone back and readied the poison, and waited calmly for him to return.

He heard running footsteps and suddenly Selis landed on her knees beside him. Her voice low and desperate, she said, "She followed you, saw you change. She probably thought you were going to another woman, the stupid little bitch." The others shouted at her to come away.

With everything else, Moon barely felt this shock. "You knew."

"I followed you the first time you left at night, months ago. But you never hurt anyone and you were good to us." Selis' face twisted in grief and anger. "She ruined everything. I just wanted my own home."

Moon felt something wrench inside him. "Me too."

Kavath darted forward, grabbed Selis' arm, and dragged her to her feet. Selis twisted in his grip and punched him in the face. Moon had just enough time to be bitterly glad for it. Then the others jumped him, slamming him to the ground.

One arm was dragged up over his head, the other pinned under someone's knee. Moon bucked and twisted, too weak to dislodge them. Someone grabbed his hair, yanked his head back, and covered his nose, cutting off his air. He bit the first hand that tried to pry at his mouth, but pressure on his jaw hinge forced it open. One of them punched him in the stomach at the right moment and his involuntary gasp drew the liquid in. Most of it went into his lungs, but they released him, shoving to their feet.

Moon rolled over, coughing and choking, trying to spit the stuff out. Then darkness fell over him like a blanket.

Moon drifted in and out. He felt himself being carried and heard a babble of confused voices, fading in the distance. The sunlight was blinding and he could only see shapes outlined against it. He heard wind moving through trees, the hum of insects, squawks from treelings, birdcalls. His throat was scratchy and painfully dry. Swallowing hurt, and there was a metallic tang in his mouth, the aftertaste of the poison. It tasted a little like Fell blood.

Whoever carried him dumped him abruptly; stony ground and dry grass came up and slapped him in the back of the head. The jolt knocked him closer to consciousness. They were in a big clearing, a rocky field surrounded by the tall, thin plume trees of the upper slopes of the valley. He rolled over to try to sit up; somebody stepped on his back, shoving him down again.

Enough of this. Rage gave him strength and he shot out an arm, grabbed an ankle, and yanked. A heavy form hit the ground with a thump and a grunt, and the weight was off him. Moon tried to shove to his feet but only made it to his hands and knees before the world swayed erratically. He slumped to the ground, barely managing to hold himself half upright. Desperately, he tried to shift. Again, nothing happened.

A kick caught him in the stomach. He fell sideways and curled around the pain, gasping.

Someone grabbed his right arm and dragged him around, then clamped something metal and painful around his wrist. Moon opened his bleary eyes to see it was a manacle and a chain. He hadn't even known that the Cordans had chains. They hadn't even had enough big water kettles to go around, and they had wasted metal on chains?

Moon lay on his back in the dirt, his shirt shoved up under his armpits, pebbles digging painfully into his skin. By the sun, it was mid-morning, maybe a little later. He felt a hard jerk on the manacle, turned his head to see Garin and Vergan pounding a big metal stake into the ground. Moon took an uneven raspy breath and forced the words out: "I never did anything to you."

Vergan faltered, but Garin shook his head and kept pounding. After a moment,

Vergan started again.

Finally Vergan stepped back and Garin tugged one more time on the chain, making certain it was secure. They backed away, then hurried across the clearing. Moon saw them join more Cordans waiting under the trees, then the whole group retreated out of sight.

Still alive, Moon reminded himself, but at the moment it was hard to muster enthusiasm for it. He shoved himself up, rolling over—and froze, staring at the back of his hand.

There was a ghost pattern of scales, his scales, on his hands, his arms. He sat up and looked down the open neck of his shirt. It was everywhere, a faint, dark outline just under the upper layer of his skin, obscured by the dusting of dark hair on his chest, his forearms. He rubbed at his hands, his arms, but couldn't feel anything. *Oh, that's... bizarre.* This had to be an effect of the poison. Suddenly uncomfortable in his own skin, he twitched uneasily, running hands over his face, through his hair, but everything else seemed normal.

At least now he knew why they had been so certain. They weren't just taking Ilane's word for it.

Ilane. He couldn't afford to think about her right now. *Later.* He pried at the manacle on his wrist and tugged at the chain, looking for weak spots.

The sun beat down on his head, heat radiating up from the ground. The tall plume trees and underbrush around the clearing shielded him from any cool breeze, making it hot enough to torture a real groundling. Testing each link for weakness, Moon kept one uneasy eye on the green shadows under the trees. The Cordans were still out there somewhere, watching.

The chain wasn't well made, but it didn't yield, even when he braced his foot against the stake and leaned his whole weight on it. He gave that up and started digging around the stake itself. The dirt was hard and packed with broken rock, and it was slow going. And he had to worry that the Cordans might decide he was too close to escape and come out to knock him in the head. Instinctively he kept trying to shift, snarling impatiently at himself when nothing happened. This poison had to wear off sometime.

If it isn't permanent. The thought had been hovering but articulating it was worse. It formed a cold, tight lump in his throat, threatening to choke him. He couldn't live only as a groundling. It wasn't what he was. He was some weird combination of both. To lose one form or the other would cripple him as surely as losing his legs.

He hadn't even known a poison like this existed. The Cordans had been driven out of their old territory in Kiaspur by the Fell, and the elders had told stories of battles against them, but nobody had ever mentioned this poison, or the fact that they had brought it with them into exile. *But even if you'd known, you wouldn't have thought it would do this to you,* he reminded himself grimly. He knew he wasn't a Fell.

He wouldn't have thought that Ilane would do this to him.

His fingers were already sore and bleeding, and the hollow in the hard ground around the stake wasn't very deep. Moon dug up a couple of fist-sized rocks and set them aside, but those were the only weapons he had. He stood, putting his full weight on the chain again, working it back and forth. Abruptly he realized the birdsong had gone quiet. He jerked his head up and scanned the trees, pivoting slowly.

On the far side of the clearing something rustled in the undergrowth, movement deep in the shadows. Moon hissed in dismay. *And this is when it gets worse.* He dropped to the ground again and dug frantically, gritting his teeth. There wasn't much else he could do. He had two rocks and he was still chained to this stake. This wasn't going to be good.

A giant vargit walked out of the jungle. It wasn't like the smaller ones down in the river valley that the Cordans hunted for food. It was a good twelve paces high at least, its beak long and sharp, its bright, greedy eyes fixed on Moon. Dark green feathers shaded to brown on its belly, and its wings were stunted, shaped almost like hooks, but it could stretch them out to snatch at prey.

Moon eased up into a crouch and picked up his first rock. He knew he could take a giant vargit—from the air, in his other form. Like this, unarmed, chained to the stake, all he could do was make sure the vargit had to work for its meal.

It cocked its head, sensing resistance, stalking toward him. Moon waited until it was barely ten paces away, then flung his first rock.

The rock bounced off its head, and the vargit jerked back with a shrill cry. But he hadn't managed to crack its tough skull or, if he had, it just didn't care. It crouched, its neck weaving, wings stretching as it readied itself for a lunge.

Then something big and dark struck the ground. A rush of air threw the vargit sideways and knocked Moon flat on his back.

He looked up, and up, at the creature from the sky-island.

It looked bigger from this angle, more than three times his size, but it was hard to focus on. He got an impression of sinuous movement from a long tail, spines or tentacles bristling around its head, a long narrow body standing upright, with a broad chest to support the giant wings. Then it moved, fast.

One big-clawed hand reached past Moon, caught the chain, and snapped it in half. *Run,* Moon thought in shock, scrambling to his feet to bolt away.

A blow to his back slammed him to the ground, a weight held him there. He struggled, twisting around; the creature had one clawed hand pinning him to the dirt. The other hand wrapped around the stunned vargit's torso, gripping it securely.

From the trees, Dargan shouted, and half a dozen arrows struck the creature's scales. It lifted the struggling vargit and tossed it toward the jungle. Moon couldn't see where it landed but the startled screams of the Cordans and the broken crashing of underbrush were a good indication. Moon had a moment to wonder if the creature was going to throw him, too, and if he could survive it as well as the vargit evidently had. Then the hand pinning him adjusted its grip, wrapping firmly around his waist. Moon wrenched at its claws in desperation, knowing it was going to snap him in half.

Then it snatched him up off the ground and dragged him up against its chest. He felt the big muscles in its body gather, then it leapt into the air.

Moon yelled in pure, frightened reflex, muffled against the creature's scales. Air rushed past him, cold and harsh; when he twisted his head, he could only get a view of the joins where the creature's wings met its body. He knew they were high in the air, and it was terrifying. He had never flown except under his own power, and he had to fight down nausea.

They flew a long time, at least long enough to leave the valley, though it was hard for Moon to judge. The air was freezing. He tried to concentrate on breathing, not what was going to happen when the creature landed. Its scales were thick but overlapped smoothly, not unlike Moon's other form. It was hard to tell how tough they were. Moon growled silently and wished for his claws.

He was shivering and nearly numb from the cold when the creature slowed, and he recognized from its change in angle that it was cupping its wings, getting ready to land. It adjusted its grip on him, and Moon twisted his head, squinting against the wind. He caught a glimpse of a square stone tower with sloping sides, perched on the edge of a river gorge. Then they dipped down toward it.

The creature landed on the tower's broad, flat roof, and released Moon onto dirty stone flags. His shaky legs gave way and he sat down hard. It loomed over him, dark and sinuous and still hard to focus on, even this close. Moon dug his heels into the paving, scrambled away from it, and hissed in defiant reflex. It had brought him up here to tear him apart, but he wasn't going down easy.

His vision flickered, as if the dark form was suddenly made of mist and smoke. Then it was gone and a man stood in its place, a tall, lean man with gray hair and strong features, his face lined and weathered. He was dressed in gray.

Moon stared, breathing hard. Then he lunged for the man's throat. The burst of renewed fury only got him to his feet; the man stepped back out of reach and Moon collapsed to his hands and knees.

Between one heartbeat and the next, the man shifted. The great dark form crouched, spreading its wings. Moon flinched back, but it jumped into the air. Wincing against the sudden windstorm of dirt, he saw it soar out and down, vanishing over the side of the battlement.

Another shifter. Moon swore and sat back, rubbing sweat and dirt out of his eyes. The manacle was still on his wrist, the chain dangling. *I can't believe this.*

He looked around. The tower was a ruin, cold wind tearing across it. The stone was cracked and dirt filled the chinks, weeds sprouted everywhere. He didn't see any way down, no doorway into the structure below.

The battlement had rounded crenellations, blocking his view. He stumbled awkwardly to his feet; lingering weakness from the poison made him dizzy. Weaving from side to side, he made it to the battlement, aiming for a spot where one of the crenellations had broken and fallen away. Digging sore fingers into the crumbling rock, he dragged himself up enough to see. The tower stood on the edge of a gorge, surrounded by rock-clinging trees and vegetation, mountains rising all around. Then he looked down.

A long way down. The tower was hundreds of paces high, and though the sides were slanted, they were still far too steep to climb. If Moon had had his claws and wasn't half dead, he could have done it. Of course, if he had his claws, he would have his wings and this wouldn't be a problem. He tried to shift again, just in case the poison had miraculously worn off in the last few moments.

"Don't fall."

Moon's lips curled into a snarl. He looked back, leaning into the wall to support himself. The shifter stood behind him. His voice a dry croak, Moon said, "You think that's funny."

The shifter just held out a small waterskin made of some bright blue hide. It took Moon a moment to realize the shifter expected him to drink from it. He shook his head. "That's how I got into this."

The shifter lifted gray brows, then shrugged. He tilted the skin back and took a drink. "It's just water."

Piss in your water, Moon started to say, then realized the words weren't coming out in Altanic or Kedaic, or in any of the other common groundling languages. They were both speaking a language Moon knew in his bones, but hadn't heard since he was a boy. It was too strange, another shock on top of everything else. He just said, "What do you want?"

The shifter watched him, his expression opaque. His eyes were blue, but the right one was clouded and its pupil didn't focus. "Just trying to help," he said. The even tone of his voice gave nothing away.

Moon grimaced, unimpressed. "You tried to kill me on the sky-island."

"I tried to catch you," the shifter corrected pointedly. "I just wanted a closer look." His gaze flicked over Moon, assessing. *He's old,* Moon thought, not sure what it was about the man that gave it away. Far older than his groundling form looked. Everything about him was faded to gray, skin, hair, clothes. He wore a loose shirt with the sleeves rolled up, pants of some tougher material, a heavy leather belt with a pouch and knife sheath. The man said, "I'm Stone, of the Indigo Cloud Court."

Moon pushed away from the battlement, still weaving on his feet. He had never heard of the place, if it was a place. "Are you going to kill me, or just leave me up here?"

"I thought neither." Stone stepped away, turning to cross back over the roof. A heavy leather pack lay on the dirty paving, and a pile of broken branches and chunks of log. Stone must have had the pack stashed somewhere lower in the tower, and that casually spectacular shift and dive had been to retrieve it and the wood. "What did they give you?"

"They said it was a poison that only works on Fell." Moon followed him warily. He had met other shifters before. He had run into a group in Cient that could shift into big lupine predators; they had tried to eat him, too. He had never found or heard of any shifters who could fly. Except the Fell. But Stone wasn't Fell. *You didn't think he was a shifter, either,* he reminded himself. "I'm not a Fell."

Stone's brows quirked. "I noticed." He sat on his heels, breaking up the wood to lay a fire. He was barefoot, like Moon. "Poison for Fell? I've never heard of that before."

Moon eased himself down to sit a few paces away, wincing at the tug of pain in his back and shoulder. The battlement provided a little protection from the cold wind, but the thin fabric of his sweat-soaked clothes, fine for the warmer valley, was worse than inadequate here. If Stone didn't kill him before the poison wore off—if the poison wore off… Brows knit, Moon looked down at his arms, still showing the ghost-pattern of scales just under the bronze tint of his skin. *Oh, I get it now,* he thought sourly. *Just trying to help. Right.*

"Why did they stake you out?" Stone broke up twigs for tinder. "Catch you stealing their cattle?"

Moon thought over possible replies, trying not to huddle in on himself against the wind. He could sit here and say nothing, but talking might distract Stone. He tried to answer, and had to clear his throat. "I was living with them. They found out what I was."

Stone flicked a look at him and held out the waterskin again. The slosh of the water inside made Moon's dry throat burn. He gave in and, without taking his eyes off Stone, took a long drink, then coughed and wiped his mouth. The lukewarm water soothed his throat a little. He tied the bone cap back on and set it aside.

Stone tried to light the fire. He shielded the tinder with larger pieces of wood, striking sparks off a set of flints, just like anyone else. Moon tried to reconcile this picture with the creature that had tossed the giant vargit into the Cordans. Frustrated curiosity getting the better of caution, he asked, "What are you?"

Stone glanced at him from under skeptical brows. "Did you get hit on the head?" Moon didn't respond, and after a moment Stone's expression turned thoughtful. He said, "I'm a Raksura. So are you."

"I'm—" Moon started, then realized he had no way to finish that sentence. He had never known where he came from or what his people were called. *And he speaks the language your mother taught you.* Moon didn't want to believe it. But if it was a ploy, it was a patently bizarre one. *He's trying to make me think he didn't bring me up here to kill me, or…* He had no idea. Moon settled for saying skeptically, "Then why are you so much bigger than me?"

"I'm old." Stone frowned at him, as if Moon was the one who sounded crazy. "What court are you from? Where's your colony?"

Moon debated a moment, weighing the tactic of implying that there were others who would come to his aid versus the possibility of being tortured to reveal their location. No, it wasn't worth it. He admitted, "It was just my mother, and my brothers and sister. Dead, a long time ago."

Stone winced, and turned his attention back to the fire. Once the tinder and the smaller twigs had caught, he sat back, carefully feeding in broken branches. "This happened somewhere further east? Around the curve of the gulf of Abascene?"

It had to be a guess. It was just a very good guess. "Further than that."

"There were a few courts that went that far east. I thought they all failed and went back into the reaches, but maybe not." Stone poked at the tinder thoughtfully. "This woman you call your mother. She was the reigning queen?"

Moon eyed him. "No," he said, slowly, not trying to conceal his opinion that this was a crazy question. "We lived in a tree."

Stone just looked annoyed. "What did she look like?"

Does he think he knew her? Moon thought, incredulous. At least trying to see where this was going helped take his mind off the cold and his impending death. "Like me." He remembered he was a groundling at the moment with a scale pattern under his skin, and clarified, "When she shifted, she was like my other… me. With wings. And she was dark brown, with red under her scales."

Stone shook his head, leaning over to untie the pack's laces and rummage in it. "She wasn't your mother."

Moon pressed his lips together to hold back his first knee-jerk response, then looked away. It was stupid to get into a pointless argument with someone who was planning to kill you.

Stone pulled out a small cooking pot, battered but embossed with figures in a lighter metal around the rim. "Flighted females with those colors are warriors, and they can't breed. Only queens and Arbora females are fertile." Moon's face must have reflected extreme doubt, because Stone added with a trace of exasperation, "Don't look at me. We're Raksura. That's how it works."

Moon stared at the fire, trying to keep his expression noncommittal. He couldn't tell if Stone really did believe that Moon was a Raksura, or if he was just trying to get his confidence. The first option made his skin creep. The second… at least made sense. *He wants you to sit here, thinking nothing's going to happen, until the poison wears off.*

Stone filled the pot from the waterskin and put it at the edge of the fire to warm. "This warrior, she didn't say where you came from?"

"No."

Stone's gaze sharpened. "She didn't tell you anything?"

Moon folded his arms and looked away. Talking had been a bad idea.

"She probably stole you."

Moon set his jaw. *It's not enough that he's going to eat you; he's got to insult your dead mother.*

With more heat, Stone added, "She didn't even tell you how to reproduce, that's—"

That stung him to a reply. "I was a child. Reproducing wasn't exactly a concern."

Stone watched him a moment, then turned to rummage in his pack again. "Oh, that young." He pulled out a leather-wrapped packet. "There were four others? Younger than you?"

Moon eyed him narrowly, not sure how Stone knew that. "Yes."

Stone heard his unspoken question. "It was a guess. There's usually five in a clutch. They had wings?"

"No." Through the first long turns alone, finding places to shelter, hunting for food, trying not to become prey for something else, all Moon could think about was how much better it would have been if the others were still with him. The isolation had driven him to seek out groundling settlements—disastrously, at first. He had gotten better at that. He had thought he had gotten better at it. The events of the last day or so would suggest otherwise. He let out his breath in resignation. "Just me."

Stone nodded. He opened the leather packet, took out a dark cake of pressed tea, and scraped off a portion into the steaming water. "Raksura without wings are called Arbora. The females are fertile, and they can give birth to both Arbora and warriors." He shook his head, admitting, "I don't know how that works. A mentor explained it to me once but that was turns ago and it's complicated. But Arbora are divided up into soldiers, hunters, and teachers. They take care of the colony, raise the children, find food, guard the ground." He shrugged. "Run the place. They're also mentors, but you have to be born with a special talent to be a mentor." He glanced up, meeting Moon's eyes. "We're Aeriat. We protect the colony."

Moon couldn't stop a bitter snort. "Stop saying 'we.'"

Stone ignored that. He dug a cup out of the pack and said, "You want some of this?"

Moon stared in disbelief. He shook his head incredulously. "How stupid do you think I am?"

"What?" Stone waved the cup in exasperation. "It's tea. You watched me make it."

Moon had thought he could play this game, but he just couldn't stand it. He pushed away from Stone, stumbled to his feet. "You know, I'd rather you just kill me than talk me to death."

Stone grimaced in frustration. "If I wanted to kill you—"

"You're just waiting until the poison wears off. If you eat me while it's still in me, you won't be able to shift either."

Stone slammed the pack down, stood, and shifted.

Moon dodged back, but Stone leapt into the air, caught the wind, banked, and dove away. Moon lost sight of him and pivoted, trying to watch the sky and all sides of the tower at once.

He waited, but Stone didn't reappear.

Warily, tension making his nerves jump, Moon searched the roof again, looking for another way down. He found what might have originally been a trap door, but the shaft was filled in with rocks and mortar, as if intentionally blocked from below. As if the original inhabitants had tried to wall themselves in. He wondered if any of them had survived, or if the tower was a giant tomb.

Finally, shoulders hunched against the cold, he went back to the fire. He fed in more wood, building it up again. Then he looked through Stone's pack.

It contained no weapons except for a small, dull fruit-peeling knife. There was another cup with the same design as the kettle, a couple of empty waterskins, and leather packets all of which contained food. And they weren't even staples, just dried limes, nuts, two more pressed tea cakes, and some broken pieces of sugar cane. Opening a last packet of dark leather, expecting it to be more food, Moon found a heavy bracelet of red gold. Holding it up to the light, he could see designs etched on it, a fluid image like interlinked snakes.

Moon shook his head, baffled at the collection. He wrapped the bracelet up again and tucked it back in with the rest. Whatever Stone was, he didn't have to pretend to be a groundling; he had few useful supplies for traveling or camping on the ground. And he must be strong enough to stay in his other form for a long time. *Is that what he wanted you to see?* Stone must have known that Moon would go through the pack or he wouldn't have left it here. *So he's not lying about coming from some kind of shifter enclave.* He had never heard of one, but the Three Worlds was a big place. Though Moon traveled faster and further than a groundling could have, he had only seen a tiny part of it.

Moon sat back and rubbed at the manacle where it chafed his wrist. The wind gusted, scattering sparks from the fire. It was only late afternoon, but it was getting colder. Even if he managed to get away from Stone, he could only fly so far in one day, only stay in his other form so long. His oiled skin coat and hood were back at his tent in the Cordans' camp, with everything else he owned, like the good steel hunting and skinning knives he had traded for at the Carthas forge. Not counting the things he had gotten from the Cordans, there were his flints, his waterskins, blankets, and the bow and quiver he kept for show, to explain his success at hunting. Some of it he didn't need when he wasn't living as a groundling. But he would have to make his way through these mountains with nothing.

The whoosh of air warned him; Moon looked up to see Stone high in the air, drawing nearer to the tower. Moon just had time to stand and back away from the fire. Stone swooped in and dropped a carcass on the paving, a creature nearly as big as a kras, with thick oily skin and flippers instead of hooves.

Stone landed lightly on his feet, then shifted back to groundling. He waved toward the dead creature, still exasperated. "That's what I'm planning to eat. You? From what I can see, you're mostly skin and bones."

He had a point there, but Moon demanded, "Then what do you want from me?"

Stone paced toward the fire, frowning down at it. The impatience was gone from his voice when he said, "I want you to come with me, back to my court."

That... wasn't what Moon was expecting. It took him a moment to realize he had heard Stone right. "What for?"

His gaze still on the fire, Stone said, "I've been looking for warriors to join us. Our last generation... didn't produce enough. I've been at a colony to the east, the Star Aster Court. But I couldn't talk any of them into coming back with me." He glanced up, his face a little wry. "You've got somewhere else you want to go?"

Moon woke slowly, his body sluggish and his brain reluctant to face whatever was going to happen next. He couldn't hear Ilane or Selis' deep breathing, or the camp waking up around him. He was curled on his side, head pillowed on his arm, stiff and aching from lying on dirt-encrusted paving, but it was pleasantly warm. He rubbed his face and squinted up at the tent stretching over him—He went still, suddenly wide awake. *Not a tent.* It was a wing. Stone's wing. *That's right. Yesterday your friends tried to murder you.* The manacle was still around his wrist, the skin under it rubbed raw.

Moon rolled onto his back and stared up at Stone's wing. With the morning light glowing through it, the dark, scaly membrane shone with a faint red tint. He hadn't seen anybody else's wings since his mother had been killed. This close he could see scars, old healed-over rents where the scales had been torn. The front edge of the wing still looked razor-sharp, but the skin folded over the joints was hard and gnarled where Moon's was still smooth. Hopefully still smooth, if he could shift.

They had spent the night on top of the tower, not talking very much. Moon still had no idea how to reply to Stone's offer, if Stone was even serious about it. Stone had stated that he was tired of arguing and they would talk about it in the morning when he hoped Moon would be less crazy. After some sleep, Moon was willing to admit that he had been a little hysterical, but it had been a hard day.

But it's over. I hope. Moon bit his lip and looked at his hands. The faint outline of scales wasn't visible, at least in this light. He pressed a thumb to the skin of his forearm, forcing the blood away, but still couldn't see anything. *All right. That's good.* He knew why he was reluctant. If he tried and nothing happened… Putting it off wasn't helping. He took a deep breath, and tried to shift.

He felt the change gather in his chest. There might have been a hesitation or it might have been his fear. Then he felt his bones lighten and his scales scrape against the paving, the weight of his folded wings, his tail. He curled up on himself for a moment, relief washing over him in a heady wave.

From the deep, steady breathing, Stone was still asleep, or doing a good imitation of it. Moon crawled to the edge of the big wing, then wriggled out from under it.

Once free, he stood and stretched, shaking out his spines and frills. The morning light was bright on the snow-capped mountains, the air chill and crisp. Nothing had disturbed the roof of the tower while they slept except a few brave carrion birds picking at the remnants of the riverbeast carcass.

The manacle was still on Moon's wrist. He hooked his claws under the lock, wincing as the metal ground into his scales. He exerted careful pressure until the lock snapped and fell away.

Moon crossed the pavement and leapt to the battlement, digging his claws into the crumbling stone. He looked down at the dizzyingly steep drop to the rock below. Then he unfolded his wings and dove.

He flew up and down the gorge, stretching his wings, fighting the gusty wind and feeling the sun heat his scales. The exercise made him hungry.

He rode the air currents down to the river, which rushed over tumbled rocks in its shallow stretches, then turned calm where the channel was wide and deep. Moon plunged into water that would have been shockingly cold in his groundling form, and swam along the bottom. He found a slow-moving school of fish, each nearly three paces long with thick, heavy bodies and trailing iridescent fins. He snatched one and shot up into the air again.

There hadn't been much point in seriously considering Stone's offer when he hadn't known whether the poison had ruined him permanently or not. Now… Moon found himself thinking about it. Long ago he had given up looking for his own people, assuming if there were any others, they were lost somewhere in the vastness of the Three Worlds, not to be found except by wild accident. Now the wild accident had actually happened.

But going with Stone meant trusting him. Moon would be putting himself in the middle of a large group of shifters, and while he might be a Raksura, he knew nothing about what they were like. If they turned out to be as murderous and violent as the Fell, he could find himself trapped and fighting for his life.

Another option was to look for another groundling settlement to join, which meant starting over again, with all new pitfalls and hazards. What he wanted most at the moment was to fly off alone to hunt and explore, with no other people to make him constantly wary. He was sick of growing to like and trust groundlings like the Cordans, and knowing it all meant nothing if they found out what he was.

But he was sick of being alone, too. He had done this all before, resolving to live alone only to become desperate for company, any company, after a few changes of the month.

He was on his fifth fish when he surfaced and saw he wasn't alone. Stone, in groundling form, sat on a big flat rock by the bank. He leaned back, propped on his arms, face tipped up to the sun. Deliberate and unhurried, Moon slapped his fish against a rock to kill it, finished eating, then went back in the water to wash the guts off his scales. He surfaced again in the shallows, below where Stone sat, and used the sandy bottom to clean his claws.

Still sunning himself, Stone said, "You're not supposed to do that, you know. Raksura don't."

"Raksura don't bathe?" Moon said dryly, deliberately misunderstanding. He shook water out of his wings, spraying the bank. "That's going to be a problem."

Stone sat up to give him an ironic look. "Yes, we bathe. We don't fish. Not like that."

Moon climbed up onto the rock and sat to the side so he could keep his wings unfolded and let them dry. The sun was warm but the wind was still cold, and if he switched back to groundling form now, the water still on his scales would soak his clothes. "Why don't you fish?"

"I don't know. Probably never had a good place for it." Stone squinted at him. "So. I've got one other court to visit before I head home. Are you coming with me?"

Moon looked across the river. Small swimming lizards stretched out on the rocks across the bank, waiting for them to leave so they could go after the remains of Moon's fish. "If you were looking for Raksura, why did you come to the valley?"

Stone didn't seem disconcerted by the question. "It was on my way back. I stopped to rest, caught a scent of something that turned out to be you. It was faint because you were in groundling form." He shrugged. "Thought I'd stay on a few days to look around, see if there was a small colony there that I hadn't heard about."

Moon hadn't been able to scent Stone. But that might just mean that Stone's senses, like his shifted form, were stronger and more powerful. And it was beyond strange, talking to someone while Moon was in his other form; he had forgotten how different his own voice sounded, deeper and more raspy. He liked not having to hide.

He let his breath out, frustrated. Agreeing to go with Stone wasn't a commitment to stay in his colony. If Moon let this chance go by, he knew he would regret it. He said, "I'll come with you."

Moon couldn't tell if Stone was relieved. Stone just nodded, and said, "Good."

CHAPTER
THREE

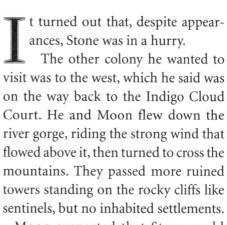

I t turned out that, despite appearances, Stone was in a hurry.

The other colony he wanted to visit was to the west, which he said was on the way back to the Indigo Cloud Court. He and Moon flew down the river gorge, riding the strong wind that flowed above it, then turned to cross the mountains. They passed more ruined towers standing on the rocky cliffs like sentinels, but no inhabited settlements.

Moon suspected that Stone could have easily made twice the distance, but he seemed content to glide along at Moon's fastest pace. Moon was just glad Stone didn't press to go faster; he was used to spending most of the day as a groundling, and it had been more than half a turn since he had stayed in his other form so long, or flown this far at one time. By afternoon, his back ached as if he had been hauling rocks all day. At least it distracted him from thinking about the Cordans. Every thought of

Ilane was like poking an open wound, but he hoped Selis was all right, that she had found a home or at least someone to live with whom she could tolerate.

As the sun set, they finally stopped to rest in a ridge where the rock formed a sheltered hollow. Heavily overhung by trees on the rise above, it looked down on the terraced steps of the forest below. Moon climbed in, shifted back to groundling, and collapsed in an exhausted heap.

Stone landed on the ledge, shifted, ducked inside, and dropped his pack. He stretched, not looking any more fatigued than he had this morning. "It's a little chilly in here."

Moon snorted. "A little." The hollow was screened from the wind bending the tops of the spiny trees, but the sun had never penetrated back here, and the rock radiated cold like a block of ice. It was also small. "There's not much room for a fire." Not that he was eager to get up and look for a better spot.

Stone sat on his heels to rummage through his pack. "We're not staying that long. I want to get moving again soon."

Moon growled under his breath but didn't argue; if Stone wanted to test him, fine. And he didn't want to stay in these mountains any longer than they had to, either. He curled up into a huddle, trying to keep his teeth from chattering. To distract himself, and to try to get some understanding of Stone's route, he asked, "Why didn't you stop at the other colony on the way east?"

"Sky Copper has always been small. I knew they weren't likely to have any spare warriors. I need to talk to them about something else." Stone found a ratty, dark-colored bundle in his pack that Moon had assumed was just cushioning for the kettle. Apparently it was a blanket. "And the mentors said the best chance was to go to Star Aster." His expression turned preoccupied. "Or toward Star Aster. Maybe they said 'toward.'"

Moon put that together with Stone's earlier comment, that it took special talent to be a mentor. "The mentors are shamen?" He had often had bad luck with shamen. They were either worthless or immediately suspicious of him.

"Augurs, mostly, and healers," Stone corrected, still preoccupied as he spread out the blanket. He lay down and shoved his pack into place as a pillow. "Come on, get some rest." He patted the other half of the blanket, offering it to Moon.

Moon didn't move. He still found Stone nearly impossible to read. Not that he had been able to read Ilane, either. "I'm not sleeping with you." If this was going to be a problem, he wanted to find out now, before he spent any more long, miserable days fighting headwinds.

Stone lifted a brow, deeply amused. "I have great-grandchildren older than you." He pointed to a white seam on his elbow. "You see this scar? That's older than you."

Moon's eyes narrowed in annoyance, but he wondered if that was true. He hadn't been keeping close track, but he knew roughly that it had been around thirty-five turns of the seasonal cycle since his family had been killed. That made him old for some groundling races and young for others. If Stone was really that old, and Moon was really the same species…*If this doesn't work out, you're going to be spending a lot of time alone.*

He edged over and eased down next to Stone. The blanket looked shabby but it was thick and well made; it didn't soften the rock but it kept the cold at bay. Rolling on his side, facing away from Moon, Stone said, "I'll try not to molest you in my sleep."

"Bastard," Moon muttered. He would have retreated to the other end of the cleft in a huff, but Stone seemed to put out almost as much body heat as a groundling as he did in his other form. Still annoyed, Moon fell asleep.

It was deep into the night and Moon was curled against Stone's back, when Stone thumped him with an elbow and said it was time to go.

The mountains stretched on and on, but even when the clouds gathered and they flew through cold mist that was like breathing wet wool, there was no question of getting lost. Moon had always known which way due south was, could feel it as if it pulled at his bones. From the way Stone confidently soared through the thick clouds, never veering from their course, Moon thought he must have a similar ability.

For the next few days, they flew by day and by night, stopping only briefly to sleep and hunt the sparse game. Moon had seen several different breeds of mountain grasseaters but they were all boney and lean, and didn't make for satisfying meals. Though the long flights were exhausting, Moon quickly gained stamina. But the part of the day he looked forward to the most was before they slept, when Stone asked him questions about where he had lived, how far he had traveled, what he had seen. With more tact than Moon would have given him credit for, he didn't mention the Cordans.

It was strange to talk about the places Moon had been without having to carefully avoid anything that had to do with flying or shifting. In return, Stone talked about flying over the sea realms, seeing the shapes of white coral towers just below the waves, the flickering tails of merrow-people and waterlings as they fled his shadow. It was dangerous to go out over the seas, with nowhere to land if you ran into a storm or grew too tired to go on; it was even more risky to swim in the deeps, where creatures far larger than the biggest land predators lived. Moon had never ventured much past the coastal islands to the south, and found it fascinating to hear what lay further out.

By twilight on the fifth day, they came to the fringes of the mountains, where the sharp peaks tumbled gradually down into green hills and rocky outcrops were cut through with narrow, rushing streams. This time Stone picked out a grassy ledge wide enough for a fire, though it was warmer down here than on the upper slopes. Moon suspected he just wanted to make tea. When Moon brought back a bundle of deadfall collected from the brush in the ravines, he found Stone shifted to groundling, with a big, woolly grasseater carcass steaming in the cool air and a rock hearth already built.

After they ate, Moon stretched out on his stomach, basking in the warm fire-light, the cool turf soft against his groundling skin, comfortably full of grasseater and tea. From somewhere distant, he heard a roar, edged like a bell and so far away it almost blended with the wind. He slanted a look at Stone to see if they had to worry.

"Skylings, mountain wind-walkers." Stone sat by the fire, breaking sticks up into small pieces and absently tossing them into the flames. "They live too far up in the air to notice us."

Moon rolled onto his side to squint suspiciously up at the sky. The stars were bright, streaked with clouds. "Then what do they eat?"

"Other skylings, tiny ones, no bigger than gnats. They make swarms big enough to mistake for clouds." As Moon tried to picture that, Stone asked, "Did you ever look for other shifters?"

Stone hadn't asked about this before, and Moon wanted to avoid the subject. Looking for his own people had led him into more trouble than anything else. "For a while. Then I stopped." He shrugged, as if it was nothing. "I couldn't search the whole Three Worlds."

"And the warrior you were with didn't tell you which court, or the name of the queen, or anyone in your line?" Stone sounded distinctly irritated. "She didn't even give you a hint?"

Moon corrected him pointedly, "No, my mother didn't tell me anything."

Stone sighed, poking at the fire. Moon got ready for an argument, but instead Stone asked, "How did she and the Arbora die?"

That wasn't a welcome subject either. It was like an old wound that had never quite stopped bleeding. Moon didn't want to talk about the details, but he owed Stone some kind of an answer. He propped his chin on his arms and looked out into the dark. "Tath killed them."

Tath were reptilian groundlings, predators, and they had surrounded the tree Moon's family had been sleeping in. He remembered waking, confused and ter-rified, as his mother tossed him out of the nest. He had realized later that she had picked him because he was the only other one who could fly, the only one who had a chance to escape while she stayed to defend the others.

He had been too young to fly well, and had crashed down through the branches, tumbling nearly to the ground, within reach of the Tath waiting below. One had snatched at him and Moon had clawed its eyes, struggling away. He had half-flown, half-climbed through the trees back up to the nest. But his mother and the others were all dead, torn to pieces.

If he had realized how hard living without them would be, he would have let the Tath catch him. He just said, "It happened… fast."

They were both silent for a time, listening to the fire crackle. Moon had the feeling that Stone was as uncomfortable offering sympathy as Moon was reluctant to accept it. He wasn't surprised when Stone tossed a last stick into the fire, dusted his hands, and veered off the subject completely. "Do you know why it's called the Three Worlds?"

Moon relaxed again, settling down into the turf, relieved to be on safer ground. "Three continents." It was a wild guess. Moon had never seen a map big enough to show more than the immediate area.

"Three realms: sea, earth, and sky. Everyone remembers the sea realms, but they've forgotten the sky realms. It's been so many generations since the island peoples fought among themselves. They're mostly gone now, with no one left to tell the stories."

Moon wondered if he had been right about the sky-islands all along. "Is that where we're from?"

His gaze distant, Stone said, "No. We've always come from the earth."

At dawn they flew out across the grassland, where old pillars stuck up out of the ground, part of an ancient scattered roadway or aqueduct. So many peoples had come and gone from the Three Worlds that it was littered with their remnants.

By afternoon they found an intact road, cutting through the ocean of tall green grass, more than a hundred paces wide and built of the same white stone as the broken pillars. As the day darkened toward evening, they spotted a groundling caravan traveling upon it.

The caravan included box wagons, heavily carved of dark wood, pulled by large, shaggy draughtbeasts with substantial horns. It had stopped and was preparing to camp for the night, with the groundlings unharnessing the beasts, putting up tents, building cook fires.

Moon and Stone flew high enough that the groundlings hadn't noticed them. They both blended in with the twilight sky, but Moon banked to give the camp wide berth anyway. He doubted the caravan had weapons that could do any damage at this distance, but there was no point in frightening them. Then he saw Stone circling down, heading for a landing in the tall grass some distance from the edge of the road. *Is he out of his mind?* he thought, startled.

Stone dropped into a low spot at an angle to the road, so swift and silent the groundlings probably hadn't seen him.

Moon went down as fast as he could, alighting in the flattened grass that marked Stone's landing site. Stone had already shifted to groundling and stretched extravagantly, rolling his shoulders. The grass around them was as tall as a small tree, standing well above their heads. Moon shifted, demanding, "What are you doing?"

Stone gave him a pointed look, as if the answer was obvious. "I want the news. They're Sericans, probably coming from Kish."

"What, you're just going to walk up to them?" Moon had trouble believing he was serious.

Stone lifted a brow. "I could stand on the roadside and try to signal, but—"

Moon shook his head incredulously. "They're going to know what we are. How many groundlings do you see wandering around out here?"

"Maybe fifty or sixty, judging by the wagons." Stone shouldered his pack and explained patiently, "These people travel long distances, and they see a lot of strange things. Some of them will suspect we're different. As long as they don't feel threatened, they won't act on it."

It still sounded crazy. Moon had approached groundlings like this before, but only after making certain he didn't look like anything but another traveler, even if it meant landing a day's walk or more away. "What if you're wrong?"

Stone started away through the grass. "I've been wrong before," he admitted, not helpfully.

Moon reluctantly trailed him to the edge of the road. It was built up more than ten paces high, more of a causeway through the grassland, something that hadn't been apparent from the air. Crumbling sets of steps had been built at intervals, half-buried in the grass; whatever they led to was long vanished. Stone climbed the nearest and started across toward the camp. Still expecting disaster, Moon crouched uneasily at the edge of the road.

The wagons were arranged in a half-circle, and the camp smelled of wood smoke, incense, and onion roots frying in nut oil. The groundlings had blue skin, a much darker blue than Kavath's, and their hair was black. They wore bright colors, long coats and pantaloons of red or blue or dark green, embroidered and trimmed with gold or black braid. They had spears, and short bows that looked as if they were made of horn. The furry draughtbeasts shook their hides and lowed as Stone approached.

Several men came out to greet him, warily at first, but they seemed to grow easier as he spoke to them. The wind carried their voices away but Moon could hear fragments. The head drover, speaking Altanic, asked if they were from Kaupi or Loros, and Stone replied only that they were travelers, heading west. Finally they took Stone into the camp to sit by the fire with an older man who was probably their leader. Moon saw the man's sharp eyes glance his way, and heard him say, "The young one is skittish?"

"That's putting it mildly," Stone answered.

Moon noticed he didn't accept the caravaners' offers of food and drink. In turn, the caravaners refused Stone's offer of a pressed tea cake from his pack. Moon watched the old man watch Stone. *He knows,* and the thought made Moon's nerves itch. Only two of them out here, Moon without even a bag to carry food, fighting their way through the grass rather than walking on the road. The groundling knew he was sitting there at his fire with something strange, not just a man from a different race. But he seemed to be intrigued rather than frightened. How Stone could do this, Moon didn't understand.

He hasn't been alone forever, hasn't been hunted, Moon thought. Maybe the caravaners felt it, and it made them unafraid. Of course, Stone could shift in an eye blink, and those arrows would do little damage to his hide.

Maybe Moon had just been doing it wrong all this time. Living in the wrong part of the Three Worlds, approaching groundlings in the wrong way, living a deception he couldn't maintain. After a time, people sensed he was lying, and assumed he meant them harm. *I don't know.* He sighed and rubbed his gritty eyes and wished Stone would hurry.

The women came over to sit by the fire and join the conversation. They wore the same clothes as the men, their breasts bare under the open coats, their hair worn straight and unbound to the waist. After a time, some of the younger girls even ventured to the edge of the camp, trying to coax Moon over. He sidled away along the wall when they came closer than twenty paces. Someone called them back and they retreated, giggling, the bells sewn into their clothes chiming as they ran.

Stone left them not long after night fell, coming back to the wall where Moon waited. "Was there news?" Moon asked, sounding deliberately skeptical. He unfolded his legs and jumped down off the road.

Stone took the steps. "There are rumors of Fell along the inland sea. They haven't seen any, but they know caravaners and shipmasters who won't go any further east than Demi now." He sounded thoughtful. "For a couple of generations it seemed like they were dying out up this way. But now they're moving around again, more active than they've been for twenty turns."

Moon had never heard of Demi, which just told him how well and truly lost he was. He shrugged uncomfortably. "There's Fell everywhere," he said, as they walked away into the grass.

A few days later, Moon broke down and asked why Stone thought his mother had stolen him.

They sat on top of a broken pillar at least a hundred paces high and wider than one of the Sericans' big wagons, listening to the wind rustle the tall grass. It was a comfortable perch for the night; dirt and grass had collected on the rough surface, making a soft carpet to sleep on. Moon could see hills in the distance, dark outlines against the star-filled sky; Stone had said Sky Copper lay among them and that they would reach it in another day or so.

Stone said slowly, "There's what's called a royal clutch. Five female Aeriat, born at the same time. As they grow into fledglings, one or two or three turn into queens and the rest become warriors. Sometimes the ones that turn out to be warriors... don't get over the disappointment. It makes them do crazy things, sometimes. Like leave their court, steal clutches, or... other things." He stirred a little uncomfortably, admitting, "It might have been something else. Sometimes colonies fail, and there were never many Raksura that far east where you were living. She could have been a survivor, trying to find somewhere to go."

Moon thought it over, looking off across the plain. Insects sang in the dark, and the day's heat still hung in the air. Further away, he could hear movement in the grass, low growls, carrion hunters coming for the carcass of the big furry grasseater they had eaten earlier. He had noticed that the big predators kept their distance; he thought there was something about Stone, even in groundling form, that warned them off.

Moon tried to remember if there had been any hint that his mother was running from something, or to something. It was long ago, and as a boy he hadn't paid much attention to anything but playing and learning to fly and hunt. But he knew she hadn't been crazy. And talking about it any more was pointless. "What makes queens so different?"

Stone stretched out on the grass and folded his hands on his chest, seeming content with the change of subject. "They have a color pattern to their scales, and their spines are longer. When they shift, they lose their wings, but they look more like Arbora than groundlings. They keep their claws, tails, some of their spines."

That was a strange thought, not being able to shift all the way to groundling. But it didn't sound like queens could do much more than female warriors, except make more queens. "So what makes them special?" he asked, just to provoke Stone.

"Queens hold the court together. And they have a power that mentors don't," Stone explained patiently. "If you're close enough to her, a queen can keep you from shifting."

Is he serious? Moon thought, appalled. He stirred uneasily, scratching at the gnat bites on his thigh, trying to conceal his reaction. "Even you?"

Stone lifted his brows. "Even me."

He was serious. "Are there a lot of them?"

Stone frowned, as if this question was somehow loaded with meaning. "In Indigo Cloud, just the two. The reigning queen and the young one. There should be more, at least a clutch of sister queens to support the reigning queen. But we've had bad luck."

Two. That didn't sound so bad. Moon should be able to avoid them. If he couldn't, he wouldn't stay at the colony. But he was getting used to being with Stone, flying with him, hunting as a team, talking without having to conceal anything. Used enough to it that he would miss it when it was gone.

Stone was watching him again, his gaze opaque, and not just because of his bad eye. Moon wondered if his own thoughts had shown on his face. But Stone just asked, "What was her name, the warrior who said she was your mother?"

Moon hesitated. He didn't see a reason not to tell. "Sorrow."

Stone sighed in that particular tone Moon was beginning to recognize. "What?" Moon demanded.

"Nothing," Stone told him with a shrug. "I just wouldn't give one of my kids a name like that. It's asking for trouble."

"You really have kids." He was a little surprised. Stone had made that crack about great-grandchildren earlier, but Moon had thought he was making it up.

"Quite a few, over the turns." Stone fixed his gaze on the sky, narrowing his eyes. "I'm bringing my great-great-granddaughter a present."

He must mean the gold bracelet in his pack. Moon had assumed he had brought it along to trade in case he needed something from a groundling settlement, but this made more sense. Moon started to ask another question, but noticed Stone's eyes were closed.

Frustrated, Moon stretched out in the grass and looked up at the night, crowded with stars. At least seeing the Sky Copper Court would give him some idea of what to expect at Indigo Cloud, though Stone had said it was smaller. *You won't know what it's like until you get there. Worrying about it won't help.* Telling himself that didn't help either.

It was late the next afternoon when they reached the end of the plain, where big rolling hills were covered with scrubby brush and short wind-twisted trees turned red and gold by the sunset. Their shadows startled herds of large, horned grasseaters with brown fur. When Stone stopped abruptly, flaring his wings out, Moon overshot him.

By the time he banked and returned, Stone had landed on the rocky crest of a hill. Moon landed beside him, breathing hard. It had been a long flight, and the wind hadn't been with them until they reached the hills. "What is it?"

Stone shifted to groundling. He never spoke in his other form. Moon wasn't certain he could. Stone stared into the distance, eyes narrowed, and said, "Something's wrong. Their sentries should have come out to meet us."

Moon turned to squint into the sunset, trying to spot which distant, rounded hill was the colony. "What does—" The rush of air sent him staggering as Stone shifted and surged into flight.

Swearing, Moon leapt after him.

Moon didn't see the colony until he was almost on top of it. The sun sank in the distance, shadows pooling at the hills' feet. The mound was buried among the other hills, but the shape gave it away. It was too even, and the trees formed a series of terraced rings all the way to the top. Closer, and he could see openings carved out of the rock and dirt. What he couldn't see was any movement, except for a lazy circle of dark green carrion birds that fled as they drew near.

Moon followed as Stone circled the mound. Glowing in the golden light of the sunset, the back side was a collapsed jumble of rock and dirt and uprooted trees. No smoke drifted up from it, but he could smell charred wood and flesh.

Stone landed on a terrace below the collapse, folded his wings back, and just stood there. Moon landed a moment later. The sun baked off the rock and bare dirt; the sweet smell of the white blossoms on the gnarled trees couldn't disguise the stench of death. Moon paced carefully along the edge, digging his claws into the loose dirt, shaking his head in disbelief. He had expected a hundred different things, but he hadn't expected this.

Big broken logs were jammed into the dirt in all different directions. Moon stopped at one, retracting his claws to run his hand over the smooth polished surface. The wood must have been brought from the mountain forests to build the framework that supported the mound. Had supported it. He couldn't see any corpses buried in the dirt, but the stink of decay and the hum of flies told him they were here somewhere.

It obviously wasn't a natural collapse: the uprooted trees and most of the dirt had slid down the outside of the mound. *Something dug through from out here,* Moon thought uneasily. Possibly several somethings, all Stone's size, or larger. He knew what that meant.

Stone turned and walked along the terrace past Moon, toward the nearest intact opening. Distracted, Moon moved to follow.

The slap from Stone's tail caught him in the shoulder and knocked him down the side of the mound. He tumbled over rocks and slammed painfully into a tree. Dizzy, he looked up in time to see Stone tuck his wings back and slip into the opening.

Damn it, ow. Moon extracted himself from the broken branches of the tree, shook the dirt off, and jumped into the air.

He glided down to the next hill and landed on a big flat rock at the summit. His claws scored the sandy surface, and he saw the whole top of the rock was covered with similar marks; the inhabitants of the colony must have used it as a frequent perch. He tried to imagine this place as it must have been only a short time ago, with dozens of people like him flying in and out of the mound, landing on this rock to watch the sunset. *Not anymore.*

Weary to the bone, he shifted to groundling. He sat down with a groan and wrapped his arms around his knees, trying to ease the dull ache in his back and shoulders. *Well, that's that,* he thought sourly.

Stone's rebuff hadn't been necessary; he didn't need to see whatever carnage lay inside the mound to know this had been done by Fell. There were predators big enough to make that hole in the hillside, but they were just animals, and he was certain a group of shifters could have driven one off or killed it.

Moon had suspected the Fell were a factor ever since Stone had said he was looking for more warriors to protect his colony. But suspecting it was one thing; now he was certain.

The rock was still warm from the day's heat and the wind was strong and cool. Far to the west a small storm was gathering, boiling clouds dyed purple by the growing twilight, something else to worry about. Part of Moon wanted to hunt and look for a spring so Stone wouldn't have to do it when he came out, to pretend that nothing had changed so they could go on as they had before, at least until they reached Indigo Cloud. He couldn't believe part of him was that stupid.

He should get out of here before Stone came for him, if he came for him. It would be days and days of travel before he could get back to more familiar territory. Once there, he had no idea. But there were plenty of groundling cities he hadn't been hounded out of yet.

Then the wind changed, and Moon froze.

The Fell were still here.

He pushed to his feet, tasting the air. No, it wasn't his imagination. He snarled under his breath. *This day just keeps getting worse.*

Moon shifted and jumped off the rock, snapping his wings out to catch the wind.

He circled the mound, studying it more closely. There were more entrances like the one that Stone had vanished through. He landed at one near the top of the mound, across from the collapsed area. The passage slanted down at a near vertical angle, lined with rock. Not far below the edge, a tangle of rope was secured to the side by metal pegs, hanging down until it vanished into the darkness below—a rope ladder, meant for the Arbora, the Raksura who had no wings.

Moon crouched low, tasting the cool air flowing up from deep inside the mound. It carried Stone's now familiar scent, mingled with death and rot and charred wood, all blended with the stench of Fell. Live Fell, not corpses from the battle that must have raged inside. Moon felt his whole body tighten, felt a growl gather in his chest.

He folded his wings back and slid into the passage to catch the ropes and climbed rapidly down.

The rope was made of something like braided hair or silk, not plant fiber. Whatever it was, it was tough enough to resist his claws. Faint light glowed ahead, just enough to change the shade of the darkness and show that the passage opened into a larger chamber. Through his grip on the rope, Moon felt the rock and dirt tremble, as if somewhere deep in the mound, something heavy slammed into the supporting walls. *Idiot,* Moon snarled, not sure if he meant himself or Stone or both.

He swung out of the passage, hanging onto the tangle of rope. There was just enough light to make out glimpses of the heavy carved logs braced against the curving walls, supporting a structure of delicate wooden balconies, bridges, galleries, many with tents of some slick material pitched atop them, the colors leached away by the dark. Some galleries were collapsed or hanging drunkenly, with the rope netting that connected them in confused tangles. Wan, yellow illumination came from hanging baskets, too small and faint to provide much light. Moon had seen magic used for light before, objects like bones or wood spelled to glow, though it usually didn't last long, and these must be fading.

He heard rustling, something moving. The sound came from an intact balcony occupied by a half-collapsed tent. Moon spread his wings, half-leaping, half-gliding down to the balcony. He landed amid a mess of broken crockery, uprooted plants, scattered cushions. The tent fabric fluttered as something moved inside. A flap flew up and a Fell leapt out.

It was only a small one, a little shorter than Moon, a minor dakti. It did look somewhat like Moon; he had always understood how terrified groundlings might be confused. But instead of scales it had thicker armored plates on its back and shoulders, and its face was distorted, with a long, animal jaw and a double row of fangs. Its less flexible wings were webbed and leathery, with fewer joints. It had a severed arm clutched in its teeth, a dark limb that made Moon think *groundling* before he saw the claws on the rigid hand.

The dakti stared at him in blank astonishment, the red-rimmed dark-adapted eyes going wide. Moon grinned and lunged.

It turned to jump off the platform and spat the arm out so it could shriek a warning to the others. Moon was on it before it managed either, landing on its back and slamming it to the wooden floor. It grabbed at his arm, its claws ripping at his scales before he wrenched its head around, snapping its neck. Moon bounced to his feet, listening, but he didn't hear any more movement nearby.

There were three main breeds of Fell, dakti, kethel, and rulers. The rulers were the only ones with the brains to plan a trap; all the others did was follow orders. *There had better not be a ruler here*, Moon thought, still grimly angry. He stepped to the edge of the balcony and left the minor dakti twitching in its death throes. *Or we're already dead.*

He leapt off the balcony and down to a bridge, then down again to a curtain of netting, swinging along it to another passage in the floor.

This tunnel was wider, and halfway through it the massive thumping grew louder, shaking the walls, knocking dirt loose from every crack and cranny. Somewhere below, someone growled, a voice he didn't recognize.

Moon dropped out of the passage into a chamber mostly lost in shadow, only a few of the baskets still lit. The stink of charred flesh and wood was suffocating, but it didn't disguise the Fell taint. Moon sensed bodies moving in the dark, frantic motion. He caught the netting with his feet and hung upside down, letting his eyes adjust, trying to pinpoint the movement by sound.

Midway down, a complex grid of log bridges and platforms was strung with rope ladders and trailing fabric. Far below it, in the bottom of the chamber, massive bodies struggled. After a moment he caught the reflected glints off scales, and recognized the pointed spade-shape on the end of Stone's tail whipping up to smash into the wall. Stone was fighting a Fell nearly as big as he was, a major kethel, but Moon had expected that. He couldn't see what the other Fell were doing.

At least half a dozen minor dakti, Moon's size or a little bigger, clustered on two of the supporting logs. It looked like they were working at the join, gnawing and tearing with teeth and claws at the thick ropes that still held it together. The structure was already precarious, broken in enough places to hang drunkenly over... over the bottom well of the chamber, where Stone was occupied by the fight with the big kethel. *Good idea,* Moon thought.

He meant to just hang here and wait for the right moment, but one of the dakti must have seen him; its warning-shriek hurt his ears. Moon grimaced, annoyed. He didn't want them to stop what they were doing to come up here after him. *Fine. We'll do it the hard way,* he thought, and dropped for the platform.

He struck one dakti square on the head, knocking it flat, and used it as a springboard to leap on the one that swung to face him. Moon landed on it, bowling it over backwards. It tried to sink its claws into his shoulders and Moon flared his spines to keep it off. He grabbed its wrists, using his feet to rip from its chest down, disemboweling it. He threw the body at the next dakti waiting to leap on him, knocking it off the platform. He rolled to his feet, then staggered as the surface under him jerked. The other three dakti had kept to their job, tearing at the ropes holding the logs in place. The join was giving way. At the top of his lungs, Moon yelled, "Stone, get out of there!"

The dakti spun to face him, snarling, but the logs shifted, creaking and groaning as the whole structure started to lean. Moon braced to leap, then a sudden whish of air warned him. He flung himself forward, but something hit him from behind, the jolt knocking him flat on the platform.

Moon rolled over to see a major kethel loom over him, glaring down, its breath stinking of old blood and overripe corpses. It looked like the minor dakti but was as big as Stone, and an array of horns stood out around its head. A heavy collar around its neck was hung with groundling skulls. Deep ragged claw marks across its face dripped black ichor. *Uh oh,* Moon had time to think frantically, digging his claws in to scramble away from it. This wasn't exactly working out the way he had planned.

Then Stone shot up behind the kethel and landed on its back, claws digging into the joints in its armor to yank it backward. Moon leapt up as the platform gave way under their weight, logs flipped upward, and the whole structure collapsed.

Moon jumped off, snapped out his wings, and beat hard to get high enough to reach another dangling rope net. Clinging to it, he looked back to see the kethel going down under the heavy logs. Stone perched on the wall, sweeping his tail around to knock more logs and debris down after it.

The kethel shrieked one last time, its body twisting in death throes. Moon breathed out in relief and started to climb.

Then from below, he heard a voice, raspy and thick, but still loud enough to carry. "Stone, absent elder of Indigo Cloud!"

His claws hooked in the net, Moon looked back. A dakti was trapped in the broken remnant of the platform, crushed between two logs. Its mouth was open, the voice echoing out from the distended throat. It said, "Is that your get? We thought you too feeble now to breed."

It was the voice of a Fell ruler, speaking in the Raksuran language through the dying dakti. *It knows we're here. It knows Stone's name,* Moon thought, a chill running through his blood. *It's seen me.*

Stone made a noise, a reverberating growl that was more weary annoyance than anger. He reached up and closed his fist around the dakti, crushing it.

Moon twitched to settle his spines, and started to climb again. The instant of panic was gone, and he told himself to be rational. The groundlings said that what one ruler knew, they all knew, but that couldn't be entirely true. There were different flights of Fell, and they fought each other for territory; surely they wouldn't share knowledge. And yes, a ruler might have seen him through a dakti, but it had been more interested in Stone. It would think Moon was just another Raksura.

On his way back up through the mound he found a wounded dakti taking the same route, caught it, and tore its throat out. At least it didn't try to talk to him.

He climbed out of the top passage into fresh, cool air and twilight, the stars coming out in a sky turning from blue to deep purple. Moon flew back to the rocky perch on the next hill. He was covered with dust and Fell blood, scratched and sore.

The sudden whoosh startled him. Moon hissed and scrambled away, tumbling down the hill. He landed in a clumsy crouch, but when he looked back, Stone was standing on the rock in groundling form. Stone said, "Come here."

Moon hesitated, all too aware that if he wanted to run, he should have done it before now. He couldn't outfly Stone without a good head start, even when he wasn't already exhausted from a long day's flight. The worse part was that he didn't want to run.

Tense and reluctant, he climbed back up to the rock. He shifted to groundling, facing Stone.

"Sorry," Stone said, which wasn't what Moon was expecting. "You all right?"

He reached out to brush the dirt off Moon's forehead.

Moon shied away, startled and self-conscious. "Yes."

Stone watched him for a moment, then let his breath out. "Will you still come with me to Indigo Cloud?"

Moon hesitated. He had always thought that he was flying into a fight; not talking about it had just let him ignore it until they got there. And he was going to have to deal with the Fell sometime. "You think the Fell are already there."

"Yes, they could be there now. They know we're weak, ready to be hit. I don't know how much time we've got." Stone winced, as if it hurt to admit it. "It'll take three days at the speed we've been traveling. I can make it in one."

Moon nodded. That would give him more time to think, at least. "Show me which way to go and I'll follow—"

"Or I could take you with me. Now."

Moon eyed him. After Stone's rescue, he knew what being carried was like. He would have to be in his other form most of the time to stand the cold and the wind, and he had already spent more than a day that way. It was one thing to keep flying on the edge of exhaustion when you knew you could land and collapse when you couldn't take it anymore; it was another to know he wouldn't have any control. He said, warily, "I don't understand why I can't just follow you."

"Because I need to get there in a hurry," Stone said, every word pointed, "and I need you with me. Look, you either trust me or you don't—"

"I don't," Moon said, frustrated.

"You're such a cynical bastard. You're going to fit right in at home." Stone lifted his brows. "Well?"

"Why do you need me with you?"

"I don't want you changing your mind along the way." Stone shook his head, exasperated. "I haven't given you a lot of reasons why coming to Indigo Cloud is a good thing for you. That's because I've been gone for half a season, most of which I wasted talking while those worthless asses in Star Aster strung me along. I don't know what I'm going to find when I get back. I don't know what I'll be up against. And I'm not going to make empty promises."

Moon set his jaw to keep from growling. The sun was dying into the distance, only the bare rim still visible above the hills, and the glow on the black wound in the side of the mound was fading. "All right, I'll go."

For once, he could tell Stone was relieved. "Good."

Moon looked away, uncomfortable. "But we need food and water first. The damn Fell aren't any good to eat." Stone lifted a brow. Moon added belatedly, "Not that I ever tried."

CHAPTER
FOUR

&ofs;

"**W**e're here."

Moon opened bleary eyes to see Stone leaning over him. "Uh?"

Stone patted his chest. "Still with me?"

"I think…" Moon was cold and sick and didn't remember shifting to groundling. He lay on hard ground with sparse grass poking him everywhere. He winced. "Maybe."

"I'll get some water." Stone retreated and Moon blinked up at a gray sky, heavy with rain clouds. *Did he say we were there?*

The past night and day of flying was mostly a painful blur. They had stayed at Sky Copper only long enough for Moon to hunt down one of the big grasseaters while Stone checked what was left of the colony for survivors. It was well after dark, and Moon sat at the edge of a small spring a little distance away when Stone came out again. He landed near Moon, shook the dirt off, and shifted to groundling.

"Nothing?" Moon asked, not expecting an answer. Over the scent of wet earth from the spring, Moon could still smell the stink of death radiating off Stone. He thought if there had been anybody alive in there, they would have come out by now.

"I had to dig down to the nurseries." Stone wiped the gritty dirt off his forehead and crouched next to Moon, scooping up a double handful of water to drink. He shook the drops off his hands, looking away. "I found what was left of the Arbora clutches, but no royal Aeriat. I know they had at least one fledgling queen. They brought her out to show me the last time I was here."

Moon felt a sick chill settle into his gut. "They took them alive."

Stone let his breath out, weary and resigned. "I hope not."

There wasn't much else to say, and nothing they could do. Since the Fell would have eaten most of the dead, it was impossible to tell if any Raksura had escaped. Moon wondered if this was what had happened to the colony he had been born in, if Sorrow had been fleeing a disaster like this and had found herself with nowhere to go.

After they ate Moon's kill and drank from the spring, they were as ready as they were going to get. Stone had told him, "If it gets too much for you, let me know."

Trying to hide how little he wanted to do this, Moon had said mock-earnestly, "I'll bite a hole in your chest."

Being carried was at best uncomfortable; when he was already weary from being in his other form all day, it soon became an active torment. It helped somewhat that Moon didn't have to expend any effort. Stone held him around the waist, tucked into his chest, so Moon didn't even have to hook his claws into Stone's scales to hold on, though for a while he did it anyway. About midway through the night, he finally had to shift to groundling to sleep, but he could only stand the wind so long before having to shift back. By morning he was miserable and exhausted and half-conscious. If Stone had ever stopped to rest, Moon had been unaware of it.

"Did you say we were—" Squinting, Moon rolled over and pushed himself up on his arms. "There."

They were on a low bluff in a hilly jungle, looking out over a narrow river valley. Built across the shallow river was a huge structure, a gray stone step pyramid. It was big, bigger than the tower where they had spent the night back in the mountains. Heavy square pillars crossed the river banks, supporting the pyramid and the several levels of stone platforms at its feet. Tall trees covered the hills rising up around it, and greenery ate into the edges of the gray paving.

Some of the lower hills were terraced into gardens, with rambling rows of tall leafy plants. Unlike Sky Copper, it was occupied.

Figures moved across the platforms, standing and talking, or carrying baskets up from the gardens. Some looked like groundlings, some like Moon's other form, but smaller, and without wings. Their scales were all different colors, warm browns and metallic blues and reds and greens, and somehow he hadn't expected that at all. Then he saw one of the groundlings shift and fly up to an opening high in the face of the pyramid.

Moon couldn't stop staring. Somewhere in the back of his mind he had thought he would never see this, that when they got here the place would be as dead as Sky Copper. And seeing that pitiful ruin hadn't prepared him for this. There had to be a few hundred people in there. People like him. It was wonderful and terrifying.

And seeing it let him articulate the thought that had been plaguing him since Stone had asked him to come to a shifter settlement: *If you can't fit in here, it's not them; it's you.*

Stone sat on his heels and handed him the waterskin. Moon took it, still overwhelmed. "Did you build this place?" he managed to ask.

Stone eyed the complex as if he thought it unsatisfactory at best. "No. Found it, a long time ago."

It was so different from Sky Copper's mound. "Is it a good place to live?"

Stone shrugged. "It's all right." He prodded Moon in the ribs. "Drink that."

Reminded of the waterskin, Moon lifted it and drank. He didn't realize how thirsty he was until the lukewarm water hit his dry throat. He coughed, sputtered, and tried again, keeping it down this time. It cleared his head a little, and when he lowered the skin and wiped his mouth, he asked Stone, "What's wrong?"

Stone rubbed his face wearily. "Fell. Somewhere inside."

Moon stared at the building, the people moving with unhurried calm along the terraces. It didn't seem possible. And if Stone could scent Fell up here, the Raksura down there couldn't miss it. "Are you sure—" Stone gave him a withering look, so he said instead, "Then why does everybody look so normal?"

"I don't know. The possibilities aren't encouraging." Stone took the waterskin and stuffed it back into his pack. "Come on."

Before Moon could stand, Stone shifted, grabbed him around the waist, and they were in the air, flying toward the pyramid. Tucked into Stone's chest, Moon missed his first entrance into Indigo Cloud. He felt Stone tilt his wings to land, and then they passed into cool shadow.

Stone released him, and Moon stumbled sideways before catching his balance. They had landed in a wide high-ceiling room, easily large enough for Stone's other form. The slanted outer wall was open to the outside and vines had crept in, curling around the blocky, rectangular designs carved into the walls. Gray and blue paving stones lined the floor, and wide square doorways with heavy, carved lintels led further into the structure. People hurried in through those doorways, some in groundling form, some not. A few had wings folded behind their backs, but most didn't. *Arbora,* Moon remembered. He and the few others with wings were Aeriat.

Moon could barely take it all in, overwhelmed by scent more than anything else. The air was laden with strange people—strange Raksura—and sweet floral scents and clean sweat. But under it all was a trace of Fell taint. Stone was right, not that Moon had doubted it.

Stone shifted to groundling, and everyone in the room instantly followed suit. It belatedly dawned on Moon that it might be a courtesy, or a gesture of respect toward Stone's age and potential threat. Moon had been doing it, most of the time, but only because it was easier to talk when they were both the same size.

Caught up in trying to absorb detail, Moon belatedly realized that everybody was staring at him. He kept his expression blank, made himself stand still when his first impulse was to dive out the doorway behind him. He had always tried to keep a low profile when he arrived at any new place; apparently that wasn't going to be an option here. And everyone was dressed better than he was, in silky garments in dark rich colors, robes or jackets and loose trousers. Moon's thin shirt and drawstring pants were torn and dirty after days of sleeping on grass or bare ground with no chance to wash, and he was suddenly intensely conscious of it.

Everybody looked different, too: short, tall, hair every shade between light and dark, skin all different tints, though that tended toward dark, warm colors, and there were no greens or blues like some groundling races. Not that Moon had been expecting their groundling forms to resemble him or Stone, but... All right, he had been expecting everyone to look like him or Stone.

One of the men stepped forward. He was short and stocky, with dark-tinted skin and red-brown hair.

"Stone," he said, sounding both wary and relieved. "We thought it would take you longer to get back." He jerked his head toward Moon. "He's from the Star Aster Court?"

Stone didn't reply immediately. His gaze swept the crowd, giving nothing away. He said, "No. None of them would agree to come. I found him along the way." He fixed his attention on the group spokesman. "There are Fell here."

An uneasy ripple traveled through the room. Most of the men dropped their gaze. One of the women said, "Pearl let them in. They were here for two days and left this morning."

Stone cocked his head. The room seemed to grow colder, as if his anger drew the warmth out of the air. "Did they happen to mention they destroyed the Sky Copper Court no more than two days ago?"

Someone gasped, and everyone went still.

Shocked, the woman said, "They asked Pearl for a treaty."

A treaty with Fell. Moon managed to choke back a derisive snort. The ground-lings fell for that, too. The Fell rulers came in and pretended to be reasonable, and the groundlings thought they could somehow appease them with land or goods or promises.

Stone absorbed that information in a silence tinged with threat. He told Moon, "You stay down here," and strode forward. The crowd hastily parted for him, and he vanished through the farther doorway.

What? Moon thought, startled. The others went after Stone, or hurried off in different directions. Moon followed, trailing behind. He had no idea how this place was laid out, where to go, how to behave. At least in groundling cities, he had some idea of how to act.

And from what he had seen outside, there were a lot of people here. It was impossible to take note of how many had wings, and maybe there was a shortage of warriors. But Moon found it increasingly hard to believe that one extra was going to make that big a difference. There was something Stone wasn't telling him. Not that he was particularly surprised by that. *And there's the Fell.*

He sighed and ran both hands through his hair, scratching his head. He itched all over with dirt and sweat. He needed food and a bath; he needed rest. *Worry about the Fell later,* he thought, and wandered into the next room, following the sound and scent of running water.

He found a wide corridor with a shallow pool running down one side, fed by water falling out of a channel in the wall and down a series of square stone blocks. The other walls were ornamented with deep carvings, bas-reliefs all showing giant groundlings in strange, square-plated armor, towering over trees and hills and other fleeing groundling tribes. The corridor led to another large room with an outer doorway, letting in a cool, rain-scented breeze. It looked out onto the jungle climbing the cliff and the river below the pyramid.

This area was more temperate than the Cordans' river valley. The trees were taller with heavier trunks, with dark gray bark and wide spreading canopies. Many of them had to be at least a hundred paces tall. They fought for space with fern-trees nearly as large, with deceptively delicate foliage, more familiar plume and spiral trees. The river was shallow and clear enough that Moon could see the bottom, lined with flat stones and gravel. Like Stone had said, it wasn't deep enough for good fishing.

Moon drifted back toward an interior doorway, following the sound of voices. He passed through a couple of blocky connecting passages into a big airy chamber that had to be at the center of the building. A shaft was open to the floors above and below, daylight falling through from some opening high above. Green plants hung down from the upper levels, vines heavy with small yellow fruit. A few people stood across the room in an anxious group, talking. Several children ran past, boys and girls, none taller than Moon's elbow, all shifting apparently at random.

Moon stared after them, having a sudden, vivid memory of playing with his brothers and sister, of being able to make them shift just by startling them. None of these children seemed to have wings. Watching everyone shift was strange, too. He had forgotten how it looked, the blurring of vision, the illusion of dark mist in the instant of change. It wasn't as impressive as when Stone did it, but it still took some getting used to again.

"What do you think you're doing here?"

Moon turned slowly. Confronting him were two young men, both shorter than him, but heavyset and powerfully muscled. The leather vests and pants they wore were scratched and stained from hard use. Long machete-like blades with carved bone handles hung from their belts. Both men looked hostile and cocky. Since Moon wasn't going to say *I don't know what I'm doing here,* he said nothing, just studied them with narrowed eyes.

When Moon failed to respond, one man said to the other, "He's the feral solitary Stone brought."

"Solitary" might be accurate, but "feral" just wasn't fair. Moon said, "So?"

The second one bared his teeth. "You need to leave."

Moon let out an annoyed breath. He needed a fight right now like he needed a kick to the head. Then another man strode in through the archway behind them. He was taller than the first two, though not quite Moon's height. He had dark bronze skin, fluffy brown hair, and a belligerent jaw. With an irritated glare, he said, "Leave him alone."

Being defended by a stranger was new and diverting for Moon, but the two men didn't seem impressed. The first one made his voice deliberately bored, saying, "This isn't your concern, Chime."

Chime didn't back down. "I think it is. Who told you to do this?"

The second one shot him a sideways glance, growling, "No one told us to do anything."

"Really?" Chime's mouth set in a skeptical line. "Because you two have never had a thought in your heads that someone else didn't put there."

Both men shifted. They were both Arbora, and while one had copper scales, the other was a dark green. Both bared fangs at Chime, crouching as if preparing to leap at him. Chime shifted in response, falling back a step. He was a dark reflective blue, with a gold sheen under his scales and wings folded against his back.

That they had all shifted seemed to indicate that the fight was on. *Here we go,* Moon thought wearily. He hadn't even been here long enough to find a place to sit down. He shifted, flaring his wings, spines, and tail to look bigger.

The response wasn't exactly what he had anticipated. Both the Arbora leapt backward out of reach, badly startled, shifting back to groundling almost in tandem.

The first one muttered, "Sorry," and they both backed away, turning only to slip out through the nearest doorway.

Chime shifted back to groundling, and he looked startled, too. "Oh, I didn't—"

"You handled that well," a woman said, sounding amused. She stood barely three paces away, watching them, and somehow Moon hadn't noticed her before. Her groundling form was small, with unkempt, ragged white-blonde hair, and very pale, nearly colorless skin. Her face was thin, making her look older than she should, and her dress was a loose red smock with a torn hem. "Shell and Grain have been effectively embarrassed, but they know it's their own fault."

Moon shifted back to groundling too, since he was the only one who hadn't. He shrugged one shoulder, uncomfortable with the woman's scrutiny.

"Can you talk?" Chime demanded.

The woman lifted her brows at him in reproof. "Chime."

Chime waved a hand in exasperation. "Well, he hasn't said anything!"

Moon folded his arms, even more uncomfortable. He knew he probably looked surly, but there wasn't much he could do about that. "I can talk."

"Ah." Smiling, the woman inclined her head to him. "I'm Flower, and this is Chime."

"I'm Moon," he admitted warily.

Flower asked, "Will you come with us?"

Moon's first impulse was to say yes. Then it occurred to him that going off with Stone just because he asked him to had gotten Moon far across the Three Worlds in the middle of a situation where he had no idea of the dangers or what anyone's motive was. "Where?"

"Just down to the bowers." After a moment, she clarified, "The living quarters."

It wasn't as if Moon had anywhere else to go just now, but he still hesitated. "Do you have food?"

Chime looked puzzled and a little suspicious. "Why wouldn't we have food?"

Flower nodded seriously. "Yes. It's nearly time for the second day-meal, and we have plenty to share."

That did it. "Then I'll go with you," Moon said.

Flower led the way to the next chamber, to a narrow stairwell. It had more of the blocky carvings standing out from the walls and, as they descended, Moon noticed the steps were a little too tall for his comfort. They weren't nearly tall enough for the giant stature of the groundlings in the wall carvings; either the artists had been exaggerating for flattery or for some ritual purpose, or they had had a wildly disproportionate view of themselves.

"There are other ways down," Flower explained, glancing back at Moon, "but this is the quickest and we don't have to shift. Well, the quickest for me. I don't have wings."

"We're both mentors," Chime added firmly, as if Moon might argue.

Moon was glad most of their attention was focused on not stumbling on the awkward stairs; it gave him a chance to adjust to the fact that he was with two shamen without betraying any dismay. Except... hadn't Stone said that mentors were a caste of the Arbora? He slid a look at Chime. "You've got wings."

"I know that," Chime said, pointedly.

All right, fine, Moon thought, and dropped the subject.

Several levels down, low enough to hear the rush of the river somewhere below them, they turned into a maze of small rooms with ceilings streaked with old soot. Niches were carved out of the walls, probably meant for lamps but now stuffed with glowing moss, like the light-baskets Moon had seen in Sky Copper. So far, that seemed the only similarity; this place felt cramped and closed-in compared to what he had seen of the ruined mound. Remembering Stone's answer on this subject hadn't been very informative either, he asked, "Why did you pick this place to live?"

"We didn't," Chime said, sounding resigned. "The court has been here at least seven generations."

"Many of us think we should go back to the west, where we came from in the first place," Flower said as she stopped at a doorway. She looked up at Moon, her face thoughtful and a little worried. "It's why Stone went to the Star Aster Court for help. Didn't he tell you?"

Moon hesitated, then found himself answering honestly. "Sort of."

"Hmm," Flower said to herself, and stepped into the room. "This is the teachers' court. The mentors use it too, but there aren't nearly as many of us." The lintel was low and both Chime and Moon had to duck under it. Inside, the ceiling was just high enough to stand comfortably, but this room didn't feel cramped; one wall looked out into an open atrium lined with pillared porticos, and heavily planted with fruit vines and white and yellow flowers. Three low doorways led off into other rooms, and cushions and woven straw mats were scattered on the floor. Moon smelled baking bread, and his stomach cramped in pure lust.

A young man ducked out another doorway, startled to see them, or maybe just startled by Moon's strange presence. He had dark hair and bronze skin, and a stocky, strong build. Flower told him, "Bell, this is Moon. He's been traveling with Stone for days, and he's starving."

Moon knew he should have been trying to get more details about the situation, like why the Fell had been allowed in, and what was likely to come of it. And he

needed to find a casual way to ask the direction of the nearest groundling territory in case he had to leave here in a hurry. But Moon was thoroughly distracted
by the food and the number of people who kept coming in to be introduced
by Flower. Bell, with helpers Rill, Petal, and Weave, brought big wooden plates
with cuts of raw red meat, pieces of yellow and green fruit, crispy bread, and
lumpy white things that turned out to be root vegetables baked in sweet spices.
It was a surprise, and a relief, that except for not cooking the meat, they ate like
groundlings, and didn't just hunt for big kills. Moon had started to miss bread,
cooked roots, and fruit.

By the time he made it through the first helpings of everything, he had an
audience of more than twenty people. They were all in groundling form, and
all seemed to be half a head or so shorter than he and Chime.

When most of the people in the room were finished eating, Bell and his helpers brought out brown glazed clay pots and cups, and Flower poured tea for
Moon. Watching him, her face serious, she asked, "Were you with Stone when
he stopped at Sky Copper?"

Everyone went quiet, hanging on his answer, and Moon tried not to twitch
uncomfortably. "Yes."

"Is it true?" Petal asked worriedly. She had dark hair and warm brown skin,
and a serious set to her expression. "The Fell killed them?"

Moon knew the kind of lies and distortions the Fell were capable of, and that
if there were any possible way to make Stone out a liar, they would try it. He
said, "Some dakti and a kethel were still there. If Stone had known he needed to
prove it, he could have brought their heads back." Not that Moon would have
enjoyed traveling with even dead dakti.

Chime looked at Flower, his jaw set stubbornly. "Pearl can't ignore this. She'll
have to admit that the Fell are too dangerous to ally with."

"She doesn't have to admit anything. That's the problem," Flower said with
irony. She glanced at Moon, who thought he was keeping his expression noncommittal. She smiled in apology and explained, "Pearl is our reigning queen.
She allowed the Fell to enter the colony to 'negotiate.'"

"How many Fell?" Moon asked cautiously.

Bell settled on a mat next to Flower, saying ruefully, "It was only one ruler and
two minor dakti. We didn't really get a close look at them."

Moon nodded, folding another square of bread around several syrupy root
slices. "It always starts with one."

Chime, who picked at the fruit with a depressed expression, looked up, frowning. "What do you mean?"

Moon managed to swallow a large bite without choking himself. "When they
take groundling cities."

Everyone absorbed that in worried silence. Petal wrapped her arms around her knees as if she were cold. "I wonder if Pearl realizes that."

"She does." Flower's mouth was a grim line, as if the yellow fruit she was slicing presented some desperate problem. "Our histories have chronicled the Fell's advances in the larger groundling capitals around the Crescent Sea, and in the Star Isles. Some of the mentors of the last generation made a study of it."

Bell asked Moon, "You lived with groundlings?"

Moon just answered with a combination shrug and nod. He realized he was still having trouble getting his mind around the fact that these people knew what he was.

Flower wasn't deterred by his failure to answer. She passed the new plate of fruit to the newcomers in the back and asked Moon, "What court did you come from? I know you were living alone, but where were you born?"

Moon hesitated over that. He could lie, but if he did, this was going to turn into that conversation, the one where he was asked ordinary, innocuous questions he had no way to answer. Pretending to be a groundling had trapped him into it time after time. And it would be for nothing, if anybody bothered to ask Stone. "I don't know."

Flower lifted her brows at that, started to speak, then hesitated. Puzzled, Chime asked, "Were you living near the Star Aster Court?"

"I don't think so. I'm not sure where it is." Moon decided to get it over with and admitted, "I hadn't seen another Raksura in a long time."

Petal frowned doubtfully. "How long?"

Moon shrugged. "About thirty-five turns. I think."

Flower watched him with a particular concentration. Bell and Chime stared at Moon, then at each other. Petal shook her head slightly, almost in disbelief, and said, "But you must have been a fledgling, then."

Moon shrugged again, trying to think of a way to change the subject. Saying, *Hey, do you think a Fell flight will show up in the next few days?* might do it.

"But why?" Chime asked. He made a vague gesture, taking in the room, the group of teachers and mentors. "Why avoid other Raksura?"

Moon couldn't help betraying a little exasperation. After all, he had looked for these people for at least fifteen damn turns before giving up. "I wasn't avoiding anybody. I didn't know where I came from, what my people were called. My—The others died before they could tell me."

"Who were—" Chime began, and Flower held up a hand for him to be silent. She said slowly, "I have a terrible feeling…" She wiped the fruit syrup off her hands, watching Moon. "Did Stone tell you why he wanted you to come here, to the Indigo Cloud Court?"

Moon was getting a terrible feeling too. By habit he had taken a seat near the open wall into the atrium, and no one was behind him. "He said you needed warriors to help defend the colony."

"That's partly true." Chime looked dubious. "He was going to try to get the Star Aster Court to send at least a couple of clutches of warriors, but—"

Flower said deliberately, "Stone went to look for a consort. He didn't say he had succeeded, and the two soldiers who challenged you earlier obviously didn't realize what you were. You aren't wearing the token that Jade sent with Stone, and it's not easy to tell a young consort from a warrior in groundling form."

Everybody was looking at him expectantly. Confused and wary, Moon asked, "What's a consort?"

Now everybody was looking at him as if he had said something crazy. Petal put a hand over her mouth. Chime's jaw dropped.

Flower bit her lip. "Yes, that's what I was afraid of." Hesitating, as if choosing her words carefully, she said, "A consort is a male warrior. A fertile male warrior, who can breed with a queen."

What? Moon shook his head. "But I'm not—"

Flower nodded. "You are."

Moon kept shaking his head. "No. How could you possibly—"

Anxiously, Chime put in, "Your scales are black. Only consorts are that color. You didn't know? You really didn't know that?"

I really didn't know, Moon thought blankly. *I really didn't know a lot of things.* "But Stone is—" *that color.* Stone who had said he had children, grandchildren.

Flower leaned forward, carefully explaining, "Stone is a consort. Or was, turns ago. Pearl, the reigning queen, is one of his line. Jade is her daughter, the only surviving queen from her last royal clutch."

"He didn't tell me that," Moon managed to say. He pushed to his feet, turned, and took a couple of long strides outside to the atrium, where the grass and plants were green under the wan cloudy daylight. He shifted and jumped straight up the wall.

He caught the ledge above and climbed. Using the clinging vines and the cracks and chinks in the old stone to get up out of the atrium, he made it to the broad ledge of the next level.

He needed more of a drop to clear the side of the pyramid, so he followed the ledge around to where it hung out over the river. A woman sat there, glumly surveying the water and the hilly gardens. Her scales were a soft but vivid blue, with a silver-gray pattern overlaying them like a web. Her wings were folded, and the frills and spines behind her head formed an elaborate mane, reaching all the way down her back to her tail. They flared out as she sat up, startled.

"Sorry," Moon muttered, and dove off the ledge.

The sky threatened rain, though the air was warm and close. Moon flew upriver a short distance, far enough to get past the terraced gardens, but still in sight of the pyramid. The river was wider here, with pools all along the banks. A small stream trickled down from the hill, turning into a waterfall where it tumbled over the rocky bank and into a pool. Its edges were overhung by trees with broad leaves longer than Moon was tall, forming drooping curtains. He landed on a flat rock that jutted up from the shallow water, and shifted back to groundling to conserve his strength.

He sat down and put his feet in the cool clear pool. This was his fault. He should have pushed Stone for more information, asked more questions, but it was another engrained habit from turns of hiding what he was. In most groundling societies he had lived in, if you asked questions, it was an invitation for others to ask questions back, necessitating more complicated lies. It was less dangerous just to listen and try to glean information that way. *Idiot,* he told himself again.

Tiny little fish, blue-gray to blend in with the river bottom, came to investigate his feet. They scattered as Moon climbed down the rock and waded to the waterfall. He stood under the spray, hoping it would clear his head. It didn't, but at least it washed several days worth of dust and grime out of his skin and hair and ragged clothes.

He stepped out of the fall, shaking water out of his hair, and sensed movement above him. He squinted up to see a winged form against the gray sky. The scales were dark blue, the vivid color dimmed by the rain clouds.

It didn't surprise him that they had sent someone after him. That was part of the reason he had come out here, to see who they would send, and if they would come to talk or to try to drag him back. Moon wrung the water out of his shirt and watched as whoever it was spiraled down. As the figure drew closer, he realized it was an indigo blue warrior carrying someone still in groundling form: Chime and Flower. They landed on the flat rocks above the bank, and Chime set Flower on her feet as he shifted to groundling.

"There's no reason to be upset," Flower said immediately. She waved her hands in helpless frustration. "It's an honor, and a responsibility too, of course. Like being born a queen, or a mentor."

Chime added rapidly, "Stone is the only other consort in the court now. The ones in Pearl's clutches didn't live, and her sister queen Amber died, and Rain, who was Pearl's consort, and the younger consorts, Dust and Burn and all the others—all died in fighting with the Sardis, or the Gathen, or went to other courts, and then there was a bad outbreak of lung disease, we're susceptible to that, you know, or maybe you didn't know, and—"

"I'm …" Moon made a broad gesture, taking in the whole valley. "Not ready for this."

"For what?" Flower looked a little desperate.

"I don't know." If he couldn't explain it to himself, he couldn't explain it to them. He had come here thinking he would do what he always did: try to fit in. Not that it had worked out so far, but he had never found a better alternative.

Flower spread her hands. "Just come back and rest, and talk to Stone. You've come all this way, and you have nothing to lose."

Moon wearily scrubbed his hands through his hair. Of course, she was right about that. But it still felt like he was giving something up when he said, "I'll come back."

CHAPTER
FIVE

ᥫ᭡

Moon reluctantly followed Flower and Chime back to the colony, alighting in the teachers' court again. The food and the cold water had helped, but Moon's exhaustion had settled in his back as long lines of sore muscle, and he knew he had reached the limit of his endurance. When he shifted back to groundling, he almost stumbled into a shallow pool of water half-concealed by trailing vines. He said, "Where's Stone?"

"He's still with Pearl," Chime said, watching him anxiously. "You know, the reigning queen."

Flower took Chime's arm and gave him a gentle push toward the door into the common room. "Go and tell the others not to worry." She turned back to Moon. "Stone is the only one who has any chance of convincing Pearl not to treat with the Fell." Her hair was tangled from the flight and she smoothed it back. In the daylight her skin was milky pale, almost translucent; it made her seem absurdly delicate. The shadows under her eyes looked like bruises. "We've all tried, and he's our last hope."

Moon had to admit that was more important than his problems. If the Fell came at this place the way they had attacked Sky Copper, hope wouldn't be an issue. He looked around the court; maybe the rain would hold off and he could at least get some sleep. "I'll wait here."

Flower gave him a rueful look. "Come inside to the bowers. There's plenty of room and you can get some rest. And we'll find you some new clothes."

Moon shook his head. He didn't want to accept gifts from these people. "No, I don't need—"

"Moon," Flower said, with a trace of exasperation, "Yours are about to fall off. And you're a guest here; we owe you that much, at least."

When she put it that way, it was hard to argue. And the lure of a comfortable place to sleep was impossible to resist.

The first part of the living quarters Moon saw was the baths. Petal and Bell led him down the stairs from the common room to a series of vaulted, half-lit chambers, where pools were filled by the water wheels that fed the fountains throughout the pyramid. Some were as cold as the river while others were warmed by hot stones, fueled by the same magic that made the glowing moss.

Once Petal and Bell left, the place was almost empty. Only one chamber at the far end of the space was currently occupied. It held two young men and a woman, presumably teachers, who all struggled to bathe five small children. With all the splashing and shrieking, no one paid attention to Moon. Hot water and oil soap were a luxury he hadn't experienced in more than a turn.

He spent the time just lying in a hot pool, soaking the aches out of his skin. His clothes were mostly dry by the time Petal returned, but she brought him a robe of heavy, silky material, dark blue lined with black.

He followed her up another level to a long open hall. It had many tall door-ways, some opening to narrow stairways, some to rooms curtained off with long drapes of fabric. A shallow pool of water stretched down the center, and air shafts wreathed with vines pierced the outer wall.

"It's all teachers in these bowers," Petal said, pointing him to one of the door-ways. It had a little set of stairs leading up to a small room. "There's an extra bed up there. No one will bother you." He hesitated. Smiling, she gave him a little push. "Go on. You need to rest."

Moon went up the stairs to the little room at the top. He had thought it would be too closed-in for comfort, but it was only partially walled off, with a large gap between the tops of the blocky walls and the ceiling. It took him a moment to realize the big straw basket thing suspended in the middle of it was the bed.

It was curved, made of woven reeds, and hung from a heavy wooden beam placed across the walls. Wide enough for at least four people, it was stuffed with a random collection of blankets and cushions. A few more tightly-woven storage baskets were stacked around. Moon lifted the lids and saw they held soft folded cloth, packed with sweet herbs. He wondered if they traded it to anybody. There were plenty of places where bolts of good strong cloth would be highly-prized items.

By that point, he could hear that Petal had left the room below, and he went back down to do a little exploring. A few other people remained, all of them occupied with chores; no one paid much attention to him. He prowled around the long central hall to find other ways in and out, exploring the air shafts, making certain he could get out in a hurry if he had to. He went up a stairway, finding three levels of similar halls above this one, all of which seemed to be occupied by Arbora. It was all open, nearly indefensible. When the Fell came, the stone walls might keep out the major kethel, but the minor dakti would come through here in swarms, killing everything in their path.

When Moon returned to his room or bower or whatever it was called, he faced the swaying basket bed, regarding it with weary doubt. He had slept on the ground, on rocks, and occasionally hanging upside down by his tail from a tree branch, so he supposed he could manage this. At least the basket was more than long enough for him; he had spent time in the enclaves of short-statured groundling races where all the beds were a pace or two shorter than he was.

He shifted to use his claws to climb the wall, belly-flopped into the basket, and shifted back. It took his weight, only swaying a little, and he sprawled in relief.

Whether it was the soft cushions or the fact that the basket was suspended in the air through no effort of his own, it was the most comfortable bed he had ever been in.

He slept soundly, only cracking an eyelid suspiciously when he heard quiet footsteps on the stairs. But it was only Petal, who left a bundle of clothing on the top step and retreated.

He woke sometime later, aware that somewhere past the heavy stone walls, the sun had set. His stomach was empty again, and he realized he had no idea if they had an evening meal here. Add one more to the long list of things he still don't know.

With a groan, he climbed out of the bed and dropped to the floor. He picked up the bundle of clothes Petal had left, still debating whether or not to accept them. The fabric was dyed dark, the weaving of the shirt so fine it caught on the callous on his fingers. The pants were of a tougher and probably more durable material. A draft came up the open stair raising a chill on his groundling skin and reminding him it would be cooler here, especially at night; he decided not to be stupid.

He pulled on the shirt and pants, leaving the robe Petal had loaned him on the basket next to the bundle of his old clothes. He started to go down the steps, but hesitated in the doorway.

The scent in the air was different than it had been earlier. He couldn't hear any casual movement, but instinct told him someone waited silently nearby, maybe more than one someone. The others who lived in this hall would be talking or sleeping or doing some task, not just watching. *Stalking*, Moon thought, putting a name to that change in the air. It might be the two soldiers again, back for another try at him. If he was going to be attacked, he might as well get it over with.

He went down the steps and into the apparently empty hall. To draw them out, he stopped at the pool and sat on his heels to scoop up a handful of water and drink.

Two male warriors dropped out of the shadows in the high ceiling and landed lightly on the floor not ten paces away. Moon didn't twitch, didn't glance up at them.

One said, "Solitary." His voice had the extra resonance of his shifted form, rough and threatening.

Moon slid a look at him, slow and deliberate. "That's not my name." The first warrior was a vivid green, with a blue tone under his scales. The other was copper with a gold tone. Both were big, at least as tall and as broad as Moon's shifted form.

The green one tilted his head with predatory intent. "I'm River and that's Drift. We don't care what your name is."

Moon shook the water off his hand and pushed to his feet, making the movement casual and easy, as if they were no more threatening than a couple of noisy groundling kids. "How long were you waiting to tell me that?" He didn't shift; they wanted a fight, and he wanted to make them work for it.

River didn't make the mistake of trying to answer the question. He gave an amused growl. "You thought no one would notice you hiding down here with the Arbora?"

"No. I thought even you two could find me." There was a certain freedom in not having to be unobtrusive; Moon could be as big an ass as he wanted to these two.

Drift, the copper warrior, bared his fangs in a derisive grin. "Oh, we found you. And this court doesn't need a consort so badly that we have to take in a crazy solitary."

Moon folded his arms, another sign he didn't consider them a threat. "I heard you did, since Star Aster wouldn't bother to piss on you."

That one hit the target. Drift hissed, and River snarled, "If you want to leave here alive, then you leave tonight."

Moon moved forward, shifting in mid-step and closing the distance between them in a sudden blur of motion. The next instant he was barely a hand span away, wings half-extended and spines flared. "Make me leave."

Drift jerked back, but River didn't flinch. His spines flared, but voices from the far end of the hall interrupted. A group of men and women were coming in through the passage, some of them in Arbora form. One of them said, loud enough to carry, "What are River and Drift doing here? I thought they were too good for us."

In a hushed tone, someone else said, "And who's that?"

Drift fell back another step. "River. Not in front of them."

Moon didn't move. River hissed again, low and furious, then he leapt up the nearest partition. Drift was barely a pace behind him, and they both vanished into the darkness of the ceiling near the air shafts. The Arbora watched them go, with a babble of hushed comment.

Feeling suddenly far too conspicuous, Moon shifted back to groundling and turned away. He didn't really have anywhere else to go, so he went to the doorway on this end of the hall, descending the steps toward the teachers' court.

He was at the bend of the stairs when he heard Stone's voice. On impulse, he stopped just out of sight of the room below. He couldn't see anything except glowing moss crammed into a niche on the opposite wall, but he could hear a dozen or so people, breathing, stirring uneasily.

He heard Stone say, "I'm telling you, I want to leave here."

Sounding startled, someone said, "But you just got back."

There was grim exasperation in Stone's voice. "I meant the colony. Is there any one of you who won't admit that there's something wrong here? That there has been for the past forty turns? We've had dead clutches, fewer births —"

"But that just happens—" another voice protested.

"That doesn't just happen," Stone snapped. "You're all too young to remember how it should be. We're a strong court with good bloodlines. We should have as many Aeriat as we have Arbora, and enough consorts that each sister queen could take three or four and go off to build her own court. That's what they're doing at Star Aster. Why do you think none of them would come with me?"

Someone said, "If their mentors told them this place was ill-omened, they were—"

"Pearl's thinking of treating with the Fell," Chime pointed out, his voice dry. "I'd call that ill-omened."

Flower spoke, and she just sounded tired. "Stone, I've looked and looked. All the mentors have looked, alone and in concert. We can't find anything wrong, no matter what we try."

There was a pause, and Stone prompted, "And?"

"And I think it means that whatever it is... is hidden very carefully," she admitted.

There was an uneasy murmur from the others. Petal said, "There's nothing wrong with your augury; we know that."

A new voice, male, low and rough, said, "Speaking for the soldiers, I'm not against leaving. Whether it's some kind of bad omen working here or not, this place hasn't been good for us for a long time. But what is Pearl going to say?"

"The fact that we're having this talk without her says a lot, doesn't it?" Chime said uneasily.

Stone didn't seem disturbed by the objection. "I'll handle Pearl."

Flower sighed. "I know you want her to give way to Jade. I do, too. But Jade has to take that responsibility for herself. You can't do it for her."

There was another uncomfortable pause. The man who had said he spoke for the soldiers broke it with, "I think we all agree that if Jade takes the court, it would be a good thing. But not with a consort we don't know."

There was an edge to Stone's voice. "What exactly did you think I was going to Star Aster for, Knell?"

Knell replied, "He's not from Star Aster. He's a wild solitary you picked up along the way."

Petal's voice was pointed. "If he was wild, he wouldn't have been living with groundlings; he would have been eating them—"

"How do we know he wasn't?" Knell said. "Besides, living with groundlings isn't exactly a point in his favor either—"

Flower cut him off sharply. "Knell, the mentors and teachers in this room have spoken to him. You haven't. You may want to reserve your opinion until you have something to base it on."

There was another glum pause. Then Chime said, "And how do you know Pearl isn't going to want him herself? I mean, he's beautiful, and if she takes a new consort—"

Stone interrupted, "She's three times his age, and she's not so lost to sense that she'd try to take a young consort against his will."

Flower cleared her throat suddenly. "And he's here."

She must have caught Moon's scent. He didn't hesitate, pushing away from the wall and taking the last few steps down into the room. The space was more crowded than he had realized, with people seated all around on the floor, standing in the other doorways. All of them stared, flustered by his sudden appearance; for most of them, this would be their first look at the feral solitary. Moon ignored it all to face Stone. "Something you forgot to tell me?"

His voice came out more choked than he had intended, and his jaw was so tight it almost hurt to talk. It was ridiculous to feel this way; Stone didn't owe him anything. Moon had been the one in debt, and helping Stone against the Fell in Sky Copper had made them even.

Stone watched him a long moment. His blue eyes, clear and clouded, were as unreadable as ever. He said, "We need to talk in private."

There was a confused stir as some of their audience took that as a dismissal, but Stone turned and walked outside to the atrium. Moon went after him, stepping out of the light of the glow-moss into the dark garden space and the heavy scent of wet earth and recent rain. His shoulders twitched in relief; it was enough for the moment just to be out of reach of all those unfriendly and curious eyes.

Stone didn't speak; he just shifted and jumped straight up and climbed the side of the building, a great dark shape, big wings half-furled and tail lashing.

Moon waited until Stone leapt off the building into the air. He shifted and followed, climbing up until he could drop off a ledge and catch the breeze with his wings. The crescent moon was mostly shrouded by clouds, but he could see Stone had already crossed the dark stretch of the river and the terraced fields. Stone landed on one of the higher hills, treeless and unoccupied by anything except a few flat rocks arranged in a rough circle. Moon banked around and landed a careful distance away, well out of the reach of a sudden lunge.

Stone shifted back to groundling, then sat down on one of the rocks, facing toward the dark shape of the colony. He moved slowly, like his body ached, like old groundlings with bad joints moved.

Moon hesitated then shifted, too. The wind was cool enough to make him glad he had accepted the new clothes. He could scent other Raksura in the air, probably sentries, but none were close. Stone didn't move, and after a moment Moon walked up through the wet grass to stand near him.

The pyramid was studded with light from doorways, openings, and air shafts, shining down to reflect off the dark surface of the river. In the night the whole structure looked vulnerable—too open, indefensible.

Up here, the only sound was the wind moving through leaves. Into the quiet, Stone said, "I meant to tell you at Sky Copper, but I changed my mind. If you knew, you might not have come here with me. And I needed you to come here with me."

Moon felt a little of the tension go out of his back. At least Stone wasn't trying to pretend it had been some kind of mistake and not a deliberate omission. Moon folded his arms, looking down the dark river. His own thoughts weren't so easy to sort out.

Becoming one of the warriors who defended the colony from Fell and other threats was one thing, but this… was something else. And he hadn't forgotten that a queen's power wasn't just theoretical; a queen could keep him from shifting, keep him grounded, as long as he was close to her. He wasn't sure what he was going to say, and was a little surprised when it was, "The last woman I was with poisoned me so her people could drag me off to be killed by giant vargits."

It was hard to tell in the dark, but Stone seemed to take that in thoughtfully.

He shrugged. "Most groundlings think consorts look like Fell."

Moon's grimace was bitter. "I'd been with her for months. She said she wanted a baby. My baby."

"Oh." Stone apparently felt he couldn't argue with that. "Are you going to leave?"

Moon took a sharp breath, swallowing back the first impulsive reply. He paced away, looking down on the terraced fields, the plants moving gently in the breeze, the moonlight catching a glint of water between the rows. It would help if he knew what he wanted. "What, are you saying you wouldn't keep me here?"

Stone snorted. His voice dry, he said, "We both know you can get away from me if you put your mind to it." He sat up straight and stretched extravagantly, rubbing the back of his neck. "Even if I was that stupid, the Arbora wouldn't stand for it, especially the mentors. Besides, the court doesn't need a prisoner, it needs consorts."

From what Moon had seen, the court apparently differed in that opinion and didn't feel it needed either. Moon said, "I've already been told to leave."

"By a warrior called River?"

Moon rolled his shoulders and didn't answer, staring stubbornly at the dark fields. Stone's occasional ability to read minds was only one of his annoying qualities.

"That was a guess," Stone said. "I told you about royal clutches. Sometimes they're all male, and the fledglings who don't develop into consorts become ordinary warriors. Amber was Pearl's sister queen, and River came from one of her royal clutches." He added, with a trace of acid, "I don't solicit River's opinion, no matter how much he thinks I ought to."

That might be true, but it didn't change anything. River wasn't the only one who wanted Moon gone.

Moon realized he could hear sound rising from across the river, a chorus of notes, high and low, blending in harmony and mingled with the wind and the gentle rush of the river. He went still, staring toward the colony, the breath catching in his throat. He couldn't make out words, but the sound seemed to gather in his body, resonating off his bones, as if it were playing him like an instrument.

Stone lifted his head, listening. "They're singing, Arbora to Aeriat, and back again." A single voice, high and pure, lifted to weave through the others, then died away. Moon felt sweat break out all over his body, prickling on his skin in the cool air. Apparently unaffected, Stone said, "That was Jade. Pearl never sings anymore."

Moon turned half away, suppressing the urge to shiver and twitch. The singing felt... alien, and he resented the way it seemed to pull at him. It could pull all it wanted; whatever that was, he wasn't a part of it.

He wondered just how close the Cordans' camp had been to the Star Aster

Court, how close he had been to finding other Raksura. Or how close they had been to finding him. Not that that would have left him any better off than he was now. It sounded as though Star Aster had no need for extra consorts; having seen the prevailing opinion of feral solitaries here, he knew they would have driven him off. He spoke the thought that had become increasingly obvious all day long, with every interaction he had had. "I don't belong here." Maybe if he had been younger, there would have been a chance, but not now.

Stone made a derisive noise. "You're afraid you don't belong here. There's a difference."

Moon seethed inwardly but held his temper, knowing it would give Stone a victory if he lost it. "I've been walking into new places all my life. I know when I don't belong."

Stone sounded wry. "You've been here half a day, and for most of that you were asleep."

Moon said sourly, "I like to make quick decisions."

Stone pushed to his feet with a groan, looking across at the pyramid. If Flower was right, Stone had been with Pearl all afternoon trying to convince her of things she apparently didn't want to hear. "All I'm going to ask is that you stay until I convince Pearl to give way. I want the court to leave this colony and go back to the west, to the home forest. They won't even consider it unless we have a consort—at least a prospective consort—for Jade. Once we have a secure colony, we'll be in a better position to get a consort to come over from another court." He added, his voice grim, "It won't take long. Things will come to a head soon."

Moon wished he could find an objection to it, but it just didn't seem that much to ask. Staying here for a short time, even if he was threatened, stared at, and talked about, wouldn't hurt him. Not much. But there was the other problem. "What about the Fell?"

"The place of the Raksura in the Three Worlds is to kill Fell."

Moon looked at Stone, not certain he was serious.

Stone shrugged, as if he wasn't saying anything particularly odd. "They're predators, just like Tath, Ghobin, a hundred others. We should be hunting them, not the other way around." He shook his head. "After Pearl's reign, we don't have a lot of allies except for Sky Copper. I'd been talking to their reigning queen about combining with us."

Moon thought Stone wasn't the only one in the Indigo Cloud Court who had been talking. "Then someone warned the Fell you wanted to join with Sky Copper. Someone here."

"I thought of that, too." Stone's voice held an edge now. "You staying?"

Moon looked at the colony; all those people, so vulnerable in the dark. "I'll stay, and I'll let you use me for this. But I won't promise anything afterward."

"We'll see," Stone said, amused rather than grateful. "Maybe you'll make another quick decision."

Moon hissed at him, shifted, and leapt into the air.

Flying back across the river to the colony, he avoided the teachers' court and the other lighted areas. The voices still rose and fell, but the effect wasn't as loud or as penetrating, as if many of the singers had lapsed into silence.

Moon landed on a ledge and went to one of the air shafts he had found earlier, climbing down, taking the back way into the living quarters. He hoped that if anyone detected his presence, they would take the hint and leave him alone. The hall was empty, and he went back to the bower Petal had shown him. He had a warm place to sleep, at least, and he should take advantage of it while he could.

But as he climbed the steps to the little room, he paused. Someone else had been up here, and it hadn't been Petal or Bell, or even River or Drift; the unfamiliar scent still hung in the air.

Moon had left his old clothes on a basket next to the robe Petal had loaned him. There was now something on top of them, a roll of blue fabric. He poked it warily, and when nothing leapt out at him, unwrapped it. Inside was a belt, of dark butter-soft leather, tooled with red in a serpentine pattern, the round buckles of red gold. Attached to it was a sheathed knife. He drew it, finding the hilt was carved horn, and the blade was something's tooth, sharp as glass with a tensile strength like fine metal.

He thought of the bracelet he had found in Stone's pack, made of the same rich red gold as these buckles, and how Flower had said something about a token Jade had sent, to be given to the consort Stone might bring back from the Star Aster court. And he recalled Stone's comment: *I'm bringing a present back for my great-great-granddaughter.* Moon let his breath out in a bitter hiss. *Very funny.*

Moon sheathed the knife and re-wrapped it and the belt, and left the bundle halfway down the steps of the bower. Hopefully that made it clear that he wasn't accepting the gift, bribe, wage for selling himself into servitude, or whatever it was. Hopefully Stone would tell Jade or whoever had left it that Moon had said he would cooperate, that this wasn't necessary.

He climbed into the bed, listening to the court's song as it gradually diminished and finally faded away.

When Moon woke the next morning, he lay still for a while, watching dust drift in a ray of light from an air shaft. He wasn't looking forward to the day, mostly because he had no place here and no idea what to do.

He had slept badly; even if he hadn't been half-expecting River to return for another try at him, the noise had kept him awake. The openings between the thick walls and the ceiling allowed sound to travel from the other bowers, making him even more hyper-aware of quiet voices, deep breathing, and the soft sounds of sex. It hadn't been any different at the Cordans' camp, and he knew his nerves were only on edge because these were strangers, some of them actively hostile.

The noise hadn't seemed to bother anyone else. Though if there had been two or three friendly bodies in this bed like there obviously were in some of the other bowers, Moon wouldn't have noticed it either.

He decided to do what he would usually do anywhere else and go hunting. It would give him some space to think and also make it clear he wasn't depending on the court's generosity for food.

When he climbed out of the bed, he saw the wrapped knife and belt still lay where he had left them, undisturbed. But on the step below it was another bundle, a bigger one. Unrolling it, he saw it was a fur blanket, the long soft hair dyed a shade of purple close to the haze of twilight.

With an annoyed grimace, Moon rolled it back up and left it on the step. If this went on, he was going to have to climb over a pile just to get out the door.

He went through the hall and down to the common room. As he stepped out of the stairwell, there was a sudden flurry of movement and a flash of blue and silver-gray disappeared through the outer door. The people left in the room, including Chime, Bell, and a few he didn't know, all tried to pretend that nothing had happened, with varying degrees of flustered confusion.

Moon had the feeling he knew who that blue and gray figure was: the woman he had seen on the ledge of the pyramid yesterday with a slim build and a mane shape and scale color different from anyone else. If that was Jade, then the best thing he could do was follow her example and make himself scarce. At least the atrium was bright with sunlight, promising a good flying day. He cleared his throat and said, "I'm going hunting. Is there any place I should stay away from?"

They stared blankly at him. Puzzled, Bell asked, "What do you mean?"

"Territories? Preserves? Places that are reserved for other people, or where you're letting the game increase?" He wished they would stop looking at him like that. This was a perfectly rational question.

One of the women he hadn't met yet said, "Aeriat don't… don't usually hunt, not when they're in the colony." She must be a warrior herself. She had a slim but strong build, with dark skin and curly honey-colored hair tied back from a sharp-featured face. "That's what the hunters do."

Moon set his jaw, trying to control his annoyance. *Yes, even I figured that one out.* "Where I come from, if Aeriat don't hunt, they don't eat."

Chime stood hastily. "I'll go with you."

Flustered, the woman followed him a moment later. There was something just a little awkward about her that made Moon think she was young, maybe not that far from girlhood. She said, "I'm Balm. I'll go, too."

Moon kept his expression noncommittal. He had meant to go alone for a chance to explore the area and to think, but if he was going to be saddled with guards, he wasn't going to let his irritation show. He just turned and walked out to the atrium, leaving them to follow or not. The sky was a clear blue vault, no clouds in sight.

They did follow, Balm saying, "The hunters have the forest portioned off so they don't over-hunt any one area, as you said. But they don't go much more than four or five ells from the valley."

Ells? Moon thought. They must have a system of measures that he had no idea how to translate. That was all he needed. *I'm getting tired of feeling like an idiot. A feral idiot.*

Fortunately, Balm continued, "So if we fly toward the east, past those hills, we'll be well out of their range."

Moon shielded his eyes to look in that direction and nodded. "Good, let's go."

Balm's directions weren't wrong. Past the edge of the jungle, the hills gave way to a grassy plain with a deep clear lake in the center. Moon spotted at least five different breeds of grasseater on the first sweep, from small red lopers with high racks of horns to big shaggy beasts with blunt heads and hooves like tree trunks. But that wasn't the valley's most striking feature.

A series of large statues made of some grayish-blue stone half-circled the plain, pitted and worn by the weather. Each had to be at least eighty paces tall and twice that wide. Moon circled one but couldn't tell just what kind of creature it was meant to depict. It seemed to be a crouched bipedal figure with a beak, but any other detail had long been worn away.

Flying closer, he saw that at some time the figures had been connected by arched bridges, but most of that structure had fallen away and lay half-buried in the tall grass. He landed on the flat top of a statue's head, the warm stone pleasant under his feet, and turned for a view of the valley. Traveling across the Three Worlds, he had seen plenty of ruins, but there was something about the way the statues were placed, the way the plain swept up to them, framed against the hills. Whoever had done this had seen the entire valley as a work of art.

Chime landed beside him, furling his wings. "Impressive, isn't it?" He managed to sound as if he had personally constructed it.

Moon thought impressive was a good word for it. "Is it part of the same city as the colony?"

Chime nodded. "Probably. The stone is worked in the same way."

Balm circled overhead, waiting impatiently, and Moon was hungry. He jumped off the statue, catching the air again.

They split up to hunt, but as Moon made his first pass, he heard a yelp. He pulled out of his dive and banked back around, startled to see Chime on the ground. He huddled over his wing. It didn't look broken but it was crumpled, as if he had landed badly and fouled it.

Moon hit the ground nearby with a dust-raising thump and started toward him. Chime snapped, "No, leave me alone!" and half-turned away.

Moon stopped, but he wasn't going to leave with Chime helpless on the ground, even if he was only winded from a bad impact. The high grass didn't allow for much visibility and the herds of grasseaters would draw predators.

A wing injury could be bad, and shifting to groundling would just transfer a break to Chime's arm or back, where it could be much worse. Moon knew he healed faster when he wasn't in groundling form, and assumed that was normal for all Raksura. He hoped it was normal.

Even if Chime was hurt, he was still lucky; Moon could carry him back to the colony, or send Balm for help if the wing was too damaged to move without splints. Moon had broken a small bone in his wing once, slamming into a rock wall while trying to avoid being eaten by the biggest branchspider he had ever seen. He had spent three days curled in a hollow tree, sick and shivering, waiting for it to heal enough that he could shift without crippling himself.

And he needed to get it straight in his head whether he wanted to leave the Indigo Cloud Court because he thought it was too late for him to belong here, or because he just bitterly resented the fact that nobody had found him before.

Balm landed beside him, calling out, "Chime? Are you all right?"

"Yes. Ow." Sounding more disgruntled than hurt, Chime pushed to his feet, stumbled a little, and carefully extended the crumpled wing. His tail dragged along the ground in complete dejection. "I think it's just… bruised."

Moon looked down, distractedly digging his claws into the dirt, trying to conceal his expression. Bitter resentment or not, it was a relief that Chime wasn't injured.

Balm must have misinterpreted his relief as something else. "Chime didn't learn to fly until a couple of turns ago," she said, a little embarrassed, apparently feeling she needed to excuse Chime's behavior.

Moon was trying to stay out of this, but that was so odd he had to ask, "Why not?" He had thought Chime was his age. And Chime might be a little uncoordinated in flight, but he didn't look unhealthy.

Still limping and trying to work his wing, Chime growled, "Because I'm a mentor."

"I know that." Moon didn't quite suppress an irritated hiss. "If you don't want to tell me, don't." He wasn't going to be a permanent part of this court, and it wasn't as if he needed to know.

"All right, fine." Chime's voice grated as he carefully extended his wing again. "I was born a mentor. But then three turns ago, I shifted, and—" he gestured helplessly at the wing, "—this happened."

Moon hesitated warily, his first thought that Chime was making it up, or being sarcastic. But Balm's expression was deeply uncomfortable. Suspiciously, he asked, "Are you serious?"

Chime sighed, waved a hand over his head, and almost tangled his claws in his own mane of spines. "Unfortunately, yes. Believe me, I wish it was a bad joke."

Balm folded her arms, betraying some exasperation. "If you'd just make an effort, let Drift or Branch teach you—"

Chime's hiss was pure derision. "I don't need their kind of teaching."

Moon was still stuck on the horror of the initial change. "That must have been…" He couldn't conceive of how strange it would be, to shift and find your other body had changed, that you were different. Feeling inadequate, he finished, "…a shock."

"You have no idea." Chime's shoulders slumped in relief. Moon wondered if too many of the others had reacted by telling him he should just feel grateful for getting wings. Moon couldn't imagine anyone not wanting to fly once they learned what it was like, but that wouldn't make the sudden change any less horrifying. He knew, from shifting to groundling and back, that the weight of his wings, even when folded, drastically changed his balance, that his tail helped to compensate for that. An Arbora's body must be completely different, since it was designed for climbing and leaping. When Chime had first changed, he must have had to re-learn everything, even how to walk in his other form. And all the Arbora Moon had seen were shorter and more heavily built than Chime. *So his groundling form could have changed, too,* Moon thought, feeling the skin under his scales creep in uneasy sympathy. He hadn't known that could happen. He wished he didn't know it now.

Still depressed, Chime added, "Did you know that Aeriat really do have to sleep more than Arbora? I didn't. I thought it was a myth; I thought they were just lazy. In the afternoon, I can't get anything done. All I want to do is nap." He shrugged in unwilling resignation. "Flower thinks it was because of the shortage of warriors in the colony, that it's just something that happens."

"Are you still a shaman?" Moon asked. When Balm ruffled her spines in embarrassment and looked away, he realized it might be an insensitive question.

He was certain of it an instant later, when he could practically see Chime's spine stiffen. "That's not all there is to being a mentor."

"I didn't know mentors existed until—" Moon counted back. "Nine or so days ago."

"Oh, that's right. Sorry, I keep forgetting." Chime relaxed a little. "We're not just augurs and healers, we're historians, physicians. We keep the records of the colony, make sure the other castes have the knowledge they need."

"Then what's wrong with learning what you need to know to be a warrior?" Balm demanded, her tail lashing impatiently.

Chime hissed at her and turned away.

Moon felt he had to say, "She has a point."

Chime didn't respond for a moment, lifting and flexing his bad wing with a cautious wince. He finally said, "You've been alone all this time. How did you teach yourself to fly?" He waved a hand at the plain, the breeze bending the tall grass, the now-distant herds of grasseaters. "How to hunt? How did you know—"

It was Moon's turn to hiss in annoyance, and he paced away from them, lashing his tail. It was turns too late for him to want sympathy from these people. "If you stop asking me about it, I'll show you how to take down a grasseater without breaking your neck."

He had only said it to make Chime angry and to shut him up. He didn't expect him to perk up and say, "All right."

Even as Moon explained the basics—grip the creature with your feet to leave your hands free, rip its throat out quickly before it has a chance to roll over on you, don't attack anything too much bigger than you are—he didn't expect Chime to listen. But Chime did, asking careful questions and prompting Moon to provide more detailed examples and advice, things he had learned for himself the hard way, and other knowledge picked up from the various groundling tribes he had hunted with.

Balm, tactfully, didn't stay to watch or to enjoy being vindicated. She flew off to take a kill from the edge of one of the smaller herds, and then carried it away downwind to bleed it. Chime, after three false starts, managed to follow Moon's example and take down a young loper bull. Moon wondered if Chime's aversion to learning had more to do with being taught by people he had grown up with, who had known him only as a shaman, with abilities they didn't have.

To eat, they took their kills back to the flat-topped head of the statue Moon had first landed on, high above any predators that might stalk the plain. The wind up there was strong enough to keep away the more persistent insects, and the view was still impressive.

When he finished eating, Moon, who had been looking forward to this since he had first seen the valley, leapt high into the air to circle around and dive into the deep part of the lake. Chime and Balm didn't follow his example, but did venture into the shallows, swimming around the tall water grass near the bank. After a while, Chime actually relaxed enough to get into a mock-fight with Balm, both of them splashing and snarling loud enough to drive all the game to the far end of the valley.

When Moon swam back to see if they were really trying to kill each other, Chime tackled him. Since Chime's claws were sheathed, Moon just grabbed him and went under, taking him out of the shallows and all the way down to the weedy bottom, some thirty paces down. He then shot back up. By the time they surfaced, Chime was wrapped around him, wings tightly tucked in, clinging with arms, legs, and tail. "I didn't know we could do that!" he gasped.

"You learn something new every day," Moon told him, grinning. Chime tried unsuccessfully to dunk him, and Balm stood in the shallows, pointing and laughing.

If Moon had been alone, he would have spent the rest of the afternoon sleeping on the warm stone of the statue's head, but he was supposed to be a functioning member of the court and that meant each of them bringing another kill back. After this day, it didn't seem like such an insupportable burden.

They flew back to the herd, and Moon and Balm took their kills with no difficulty. They waited upwind while Chime tried to bleed his without ripping up the meat too much and losing all the organs.

Moon caught a scent on the wind that wasn't blood or viscera. He pivoted, studying the empty sky. "Did you smell that?"

"What?" Balm lifted her head, tasting the air. "No. What was it?"

It had just been a trace, there and gone almost too quickly to mark it. "Fell."

"There's been Fell taint in the air off and on since that ruler came to see Pearl." Balm showed her fangs in a grimace of disgust. "They must still be in the area, watching the court."

The wind came from the south, away from the colony. The Fell must be lurking out there somewhere; maybe this valley wasn't such a good place to nap in the sun after all. Moon asked, "Were you there? When the ruler came?"

Balm shook her head, her spines flaring. "No, I'm not in favor with Pearl. I'm Jade's…" She trailed off, looking up at Moon, suddenly uneasy.

It was the hesitation that did it. *Spy,* Moon thought. *Spy is the word you're looking for.* He had known that Chime and Balm had only come out here to keep an eye on him; that Balm was here specifically on Jade's behalf somehow made it… personal.

Chime landed next to them, dropping a carcass on the dry grass. He panted with exertion, proud and flustered with his success. "There, is that right? Can we go now?"

Moon turned away, picked up his own kill, and leapt into the air. Behind him, he heard Chime asking Balm, "Hey, what's wrong? What did you do?" Moon didn't listen for the answer.

CHAPTER SIX

ᥱᎧ

Moon reached the colony well ahead of Chime and Balm, finding and following the river back up the valley. As he circled the main structure, he identified the pillared terrace that belonged to the hunters by the hides drying on wooden racks. A dozen or so Arbora worked there, skinning something large and furry that had a double set of spiral horns. The place stunk of butchered meat and the acidic tang of whatever they used for tanning.

Moon landed and dumped the carcass on the paving, folded his wings, and shifted. He managed not to twitch when all the Arbora working in the court shifted too. He was going to have to get used to that.

They were all dressed roughly for the messy work, most wearing just ragged cloth smocks or leather kilts. All stopped their work to watch Moon with open curiosity. The one who stepped forward, eyeing the carcass as if he grudged its existence, said, "Well, you killed it. Did you bother to bleed—Oh, you did." He had the heavyset build of most Arbora, and he was old, showing the signs of age that Moon was learning to recognize in Raksura. His hair was white and his bronze-brown skin had an ashy cast. Other than that he looked as tough as a boulder, with heavily muscled shoulders and a ridge of scar tissue circling his neck, as if something had tried to bite his head off. "I'm Bone," he added, and kicked the carcass thoughtfully. "Do you want the hide? You've got first claim on it."

"No. Give it to someone else." It would have come in handy, but Moon hoped to be long gone before they could finish tanning it.

"Huh." Bone looked as if he might argue, then subsided with a scowl.

That seemed to be it. Moon turned away, wanting to get out of there before Chime and Balm arrived. "Hey," one of the hunters called out. Warily, he turned back. A woman, silver-gray threaded through her light-colored hair, sat on the steps and sharpened a skinning knife. She said, "Why are you staying down here in the Arboras' bowers, instead of up there with the Aeriat?"

Moon suppressed an annoyed growl. He had had enough of this from the warriors; he didn't need to hear it here, too. He said, "Do you have a problem with it?"

She snorted with amusement. "Not me."

But Bone, still watching him, said, "That's going to make trouble for you. You should move up there with them. It'd go easier on you."

Moon shook his head, frustrated with all of it. All his turns trying to fit in had come to nothing, over and over again, and he was too weary to start the whole process again here. The Raksura could take him as he was. He said, "No, it wouldn't."

He caught movement overhead, and looked up to see Chime and Balm circling in. Moon shifted and jumped to the terrace roof, then up to the first ledge. He followed it around the outside of the building, to the passage that led to the back entrance into the teachers' hall.

He was looking for somewhere to be alone, but there were more people here than he had expected. The curtains over the doorways and stairs had been lifted back, and a group of men and women at the end of the hall worked with bone spindles and distaffs, spinning masses of beaten plant fiber into yarn. Near the shallow fountain, Petal and a couple of younger Arbora played with five very active babies, all just old enough to toddle on unsteady legs.

Moon headed for his bower, hoping no one would notice him. But Petal greeted him, waving. "Moon, did you have good hunting?"

"It was all right." Reluctantly, he stopped beside her. Before she could ask anything more, two figures, one green and one bright blue, crashed down the nearest stairway. They tumbled out onto the floor, spilling a few empty baskets and knocking over a clay jar.

Petal shouted, "Spring, Snow, stop that! What do you think is going to happen if you hurt your wings?"

It wasn't until the two figures rolled to a halt and separated that Moon realized they were young, half-sized warriors, one male and one female, as wild and awkward as fledgling raptors. They both sat up and shifted, turning into thin and gawky children on the edge of adolescence. They stared wide-eyed at Moon, as startled to see him as he was to see them.

Petal got to her feet, eyeing them with exasperated affection. "The girl is Spring and the boy is Snow," she told Moon. "They're from Amber's last clutch. She was Pearl's sister queen."

Amber was one of the queens who had died, Moon remembered. It seemed like he had heard about more dead Raksura than live ones. He was trying to think of a polite response when something grabbed his leg. He looked down, bemused to see one of the Arbora toddlers had shifted and was now trying to climb him like a tree. The rest of the clutch rolled on the floor in play, keeping the other teachers busy.

"Oh, Speckle, don't." Petal made a grab for her and the little girl ducked away agilely, still climbing.

"Speckle?" Moon caught the baby and lifted her up. She immediately sank her claws into his shirt, looking up at him with big, liquid brown eyes. Her gold-brown scales and tiny spines were still soft, and she smelled like a combination of groundling baby and Raksura. Moon's heart twisted, and he reminded himself he planned to leave eventually.

"It almost makes sense when you know the rest of the clutch is Glint, Glimmer, Pebble, and Shell," Petal said, prying little claws out of Moon's sleeve as she tried to coax the baby to let go. "Most of us like to give our clutches similar names."

"Does that mean you're related to Flower?" Moon asked, still distracted as the baby stubbornly tightened her grip on him.

Petal laughed. "Distantly. She's much older than I am. Chime, though, is clutch-mate to Knell and Bell. Knell is leader of the soldiers, and Bell is a teacher. The other two were mentors, but they died from the lung disease." She hesitated, suddenly self-conscious. "Chime wasn't always a warrior."

"He told me he used to be a mentor." Moon ruffled Speckle's frills. Keeping his attention on the baby, he asked casually, "Who is Balm related to?"

"She's a warrior from a royal clutch, the same one Jade came from." Sighing in exasperation, Petal tried to work her fingers under Speckle's claws. "It's not true, what they say about female warriors who come from royal clutches. They don't all go mad because they think they're failed queens." She frowned a little and added, "It's only happened to a few."

So Jade had sent her clutch-mate to watch him? Or just to find out more about him and report back? Moon wasn't sure what to make of it.

The warrior girl Spring was still watching them with wide eyes. She said suddenly, "There's only two of us. The others died."

"Where's your clutch?" Snow demanded, half-hiding behind her.

Moon hesitated while Speckle gnawed on his knuckles with fortunately still-blunt baby teeth. He could accept the fact that Sorrow hadn't been his mother, and that it was impossible for a consort to come from a clutch of Arbora. But it hadn't changed anything. "They died."

Petal managed to pry Speckle off Moon just as Flower hurried up the stairs from the common room. "Moon, good, you're back." She looked flustered and worried, her gossamer hair frazzled. "Pearl has called for a gathering."

"A gathering?" Petal looked startled, and not a little alarmed, which made Moon's hackles rise. She flicked a quick, worried glance at him. "Everyone?"

Flower gave her a grim nod. "Except the teachers who are watching the children, the soldiers guarding the lower entrances, and the hunters too far out to call back."

Or very fast consorts who make it up to that air shaft when no one is looking, Moon thought, preparing to fade into the crowd.

Flower fixed her gaze on Moon, as if reading his thought, and added firmly, "And you are specifically included."

Flower wanted Moon to come with her immediately, which he suspected meant she thought he might to try to escape in the confusion. She was right, but since she had grabbed his arm and immediately towed him out of the hall to the main stairwell, there wasn't much opportunity for an unobtrusive exit.

People hurried in from the fields outside, and the outer terraces and courts. The crowd grew as they went up the stairs, higher and higher, much further up inside the building than Moon had been before. The steps were taller up here, almost too tall for the Arbora. It just confirmed Moon's growing belief that the groundlings who had built this place had greatly exaggerated views of their physical size. Some of the Arbora shifted and skittered along the walls, using their claws on the reliefs and chinks in the stone. Flower stayed in her groundling form, and Moon found himself reaching down to take her hand and steady her as she climbed.

"Thank you," she said, a little breathless. She glanced up at him, her brows quirking. "There's no need to be nervous."

Moon had thought he had kept his expression laconic, but maybe not. And he wasn't the only one who was nervous; her hands were cold as ice. "Unlike you?"

She gave him a thin-lipped smile. "Very unlike me."

The stairs took another turn, ending in a broad landing, and Moon was surprised to see Stone waiting there. As they reached him, Stone leaned down to take Flower's other hand, and he and Moon lifted her up the last step. "I hate this damn place," Stone muttered.

"Really?" Flower pretended to look startled. "And you've kept your views to yourself all this time?"

"Why do you hate it?" Moon asked, ready for any distraction. Only one archway led off the landing, opening into a narrow passage lined with glow-moss. The Arbora crowded down into it, talking in whispers, nervously jostling each other. At least the closed-in feeling was alleviated by the high ceiling, nearly three times Moon's height.

Stone growled under his breath, causing several Arbora to give him wide berth. "It's a dead shell. It's not Raksura."

"No one knows what that means except you," Flower said, with the air of someone who had heard it all before. She turned to lead the way down the passage.

"That's the problem," Stone said after her.

As Moon followed her, Stone caught his arm. Twitchy already, Moon managed not to slam himself into the wall flinching away. As the Arbora flowed past them, Stone said softly, "Pearl is old, and she's ill, and she's stubborn."

Moon nodded, thinking what Stone was mainly telling him was, *Don't panic.*

Flower waited at the end of the passage where it opened into a larger chamber, and stood to one side so the others still filing in could get past her. "This is going to depend on a number of things that we have no control over," she said softly, as Moon and Stone reached her.

Stone grunted agreement and stepped past her into the room. Moon fought down one last urge to escape and followed as the other Arbora made way for them.

The place was large and cave-like, with no openings to the outside except for a shaft in the center of the high roof. Sometime in the past, when the pyramid had first been built, this could have been a throne room, or the central mystery chamber of a temple. Vines had crept down through the open shaft, but they were discolored by a creeping white moss.

Everyone here was in groundling form, and the Arbora still crowded in, filling in the floor space near the door. The Aeriat were already here, standing on two broad stone ledges above the doorway and to the right. They were as distinctive as the Arbora; all tall, the women slim, small-breasted, the men lean. *Is that all the warriors?* Moon wondered, a little shocked. Stone had said the colony didn't have enough Aeriat, but there were only a third as many here as the Arbora. And there were still more soldiers, teachers, and hunters who weren't free to be here.

Moon saw Balm up on the ledge with the other warriors, pacing anxiously. Many of the warriors stared at him, and one dark-haired man glared with a familiar, angry intensity. That had to be River in his groundling form, and Moon was willing to bet the man next to him was Drift.

Chime stood on the floor with the Arbora, further down the wall with Petal and Bell, easily visible since he was nearly a head taller than most of them. Chime spotted Flower and made his way toward her, shouldering people aside, ignoring their objections.

The room went quiet, the murmur dying away. Moon scanned the shadows, trying to see what had caught the others' attention. Scent didn't tell him anything, since the whole place smelled of anxious Raksura.

Then, on a stone platform across the back of the room, a shadow moved. It spilled down the steps to the floor until a tall form stepped out of it into the light.

Her scales were brilliant gold, overlaid with a webbed pattern of deepest indigo blue. The frilled mane behind her head was like a golden sunburst, and there were more frills on the tips of her folded wings, on the triangle-shape at the end of her tail. She was a head taller than the tallest Aeriat, and wore only jewelry, a broad necklace with gold chains linking polished blue stones. As she moved into the center of the room, the air grew heavier. A stir rippled through all the assembled Raksura, an almost unconscious movement toward her. For the first time, Moon understood why Stone had said that queens had power over all of them; feeling the pull of it in himself turned him cold. *I'm not one of them. I shouldn't be here.*

In a voice soft and deep as night, she said, "Where is he?"

Moon's breath caught in his chest. *Leaving,* he thought, turning for the door. He would have made it, but Stone was fast even as a groundling, and caught his wrist.

Rather than be hauled forward like a criminal, Moon didn't resist. He let Stone pull him to the front of the crowd, to the empty space in front of Pearl. As Stone let him go, Moon tried to shift, meaning to fly straight up the air shaft.

Nothing happened.

Moon's mouth went dry. So Stone hadn't exaggerated; she could keep them from shifting. He wished he knew if she was doing it to everyone, or just him.

Stone's voice was neutral, his tone giving nothing away. "Pearl, this is Moon."

She beckoned him forward with one deceptively delicate hand. Her claws were longer than his, and she wore rings on each finger, thick bands of gold woven with copper and silver.

It wasn't until the back of her hand brushed his cheek that Moon realized he had taken two steps toward her, that he was within her reach. Her claws moved through his hair, the touch too light to scratch, and she cupped the back of his head, drawing him closer.

Moon looked into her eyes, heavy-lidded, sea-blue, and fathoms-deep, drawing him in. Her scent was strong and musky, but there was a trace of bitterness under it, too faint for him to place. It brought him back to his senses abruptly, and he tried to pull away from her. But sudden heat warmed his body, the tension flowing out of his spine.

That she could keep them all from shifting meant she was connected to them somehow, through mind or heart or something else, and Moon should have realized that. Should have realized the connection could go both ways. For a moment it was as if he was part of every other Raksura in the room, and he leaned toward her.

Then, as if she had judged it for the exact moment she felt his resistance fade, she said, "This was the best you could do."

Her tone was calm, the warm purr of her voice unchanged. Moon blinked, so caught in her spell that for a heartbeat he didn't understand. The whole room seemed to take a startled breath.

In that same tone, she continued, "A solitary, with no bloodline."

Understanding hit him like a sudden slap. He jerked backward, but her hold on him tightened, her claws digging into his skin. Moon twisted out of her grip, the claws opening cuts across the back of his neck, snagging in the collar of his shirt. He fell back a few steps, out of her reach, baring his teeth.

Her lip curled, showing her fangs, and her tail lashed; growls echoed from the assembled warriors perched on the ledges, as if she was the one who had been insulted.

Moon spun on his heel, hissing up at them, furious and humiliated and ready to fight everybody in the room. The growls stopped as the warriors stirred uneasily. Apparently nobody wanted to fight, at least not while they were all trapped in groundling form.

"I didn't bring him for you," Stone said, his voice dry and acid in the silence.

The words broke the spell. Moon took a sharp breath, trying to clear his head and make himself think. He couldn't feel that pull toward Pearl anymore, that connection to the others. There and gone so briefly, it had still left an empty place in his chest, as if something had been torn out of him. It was pure cruelty to let him feel that, to draw him into that, just to rip him away.

Pearl paced, her tail still lashing, her mane rippling with agitation. Cold edged her voice as she told Stone, "Solitaries live the way they do for a reason."

Stone watched her, unmoved and unimpressed. "He wasn't a solitary by choice. I told you how I found him."

"And you have only his word for that." Pearl stopped, half turning to show Stone her profile, as if she was reluctant to confront him. "What did you have to give him to bring him here?"

That was another slap. Moon gritted his teeth, looking away. Everything he had taken from them—food, the clothes he was wearing, even Stone's protection while he was poisoned—flashed through his head. He had accepted it all with the idea that he would act as one of their warriors; Pearl had to know that. She wanted to drive him away, and he knew why.

That Moon was here as a potential consort for Jade somehow gave the younger queen power, taking it away from Pearl. Moon hissed under his breath. If Pearl wanted to drive him out, she was going to have to try a lot harder than this.

As if called by his thought, another voice, sharp with irony, said, "I've left gifts. He's taken none of them." The warriors on the ledge parted abruptly for a light blue form, the only other Raksura in the room who hadn't shifted to groundling. She stepped off the ledge and landed lightly on the paving. She was smaller than Pearl, the same height as the other warriors. The silver-gray pattern overlaying her scales was less complex than Pearl's brilliant indigo, and the frilly spines of her mane weren't as elaborate. Her jewelry was silver, rings, armbands, and bracelets, and a belt worn low above the hips with polished ovals of amethyst and opal. Moon had only caught two glimpses of her before, but this was clearly Jade.

She stalked forward, radiating barely contained irritation, her gaze on Pearl. "The things he accepted from the Arbora are only what they would give in hospitality to any visitor." Her voice hardened into a snarl. "Try your claws on me, why don't you."

Pearl moved away from her, her lip curling in contempt. "You're a child. You have no responsibility in this court and you've made no attempt to assume any."

Jade's laugh held little amusement. "You say that as if it's what you want."

Stone broke the moment. "That isn't what we came here to discuss. The Arbora want to go to a new colony. Our lines haven't flourished here, and you know it as well as the rest of us do. All the consorts of my line are dead, Rain is dead, and your last clutch didn't survive to—"

Pearl rounded on him, hissing. "I don't need you to remind me of that!"

Evenly, unaffected by her anger, Stone said, "Then what do you need?"

After a moment she stepped away from him, shaking her head. "We have too many Arbora and too few Aeriat. We can't leave this place, not now." Her hands curled into fists. "I've waited too long. I take the blame for that."

Flower stepped forward and suddenly had the attention of the entire room. It gave Moon some insight into just how much power the mentors actually held. Among all the larger Arbora and the tall warriors, Flower should have been a slight, insignificant figure, but every Raksura here turned to listen. She said, "It's not too late. There are ways around the lack of Aeriat. We don't all have to go at once. We can make the journey in stages."

Pearl hesitated, though Moon couldn't tell if she was giving the suggestion serious thought or not. Then she paced away. "It's too dangerous. We would die in stages."

His voice tight with irony, Stone said, "We're dying here, and that started before you let the Fell in."

Pearl turned toward him, her mane flaring in challenge. "What do you want from me?"

"You know what I want." Stone let the words hang in a fraught silence. When Pearl looked away, he said, "I'll settle for your word that you'll agree to move the court if I can get the means to transport the Arbora safely."

Pearl laughed, more annoyed than amused. "Your plan is ridiculous," she said, sounding exasperated. "I think your mind has finally turned."

Stone smiled, showing his teeth. It was somehow a far more threatening gesture than it should have been, and a ripple of unease went through the ranks of warriors. But he only said, "Then you have nothing to worry about."

Pearl watched him a moment more, then she turned her gaze to Moon, contempt in every line of her body. "I want your solitary gone from this court."

Moon glared narrowly back at her and tried to shift, tried it with everything he had. He felt the change gather in his body, felt it burn in his chest, but he couldn't push past whatever power Pearl still held over him. But when he said, "Then make me leave," it came out in the deeper rasp of his shifted voice.

Pearl's face twisted into a snarl. "Get out of my sight!"

That he was willing to do. Moon snarled and turned for the door, barely noticing as the Arbora scattered out of his way. He strode down the passage to the landing, every step further away from Pearl's presence a relief. The others came out behind him, and he pounded down the stairs until he felt the pressure in his chest ease and knew he could shift again.

He left the stairs at the next landing, and headed blindly down a corridor until he found an opening to the outside. He shifted and jumped out, meaning to glide down to the foot of the pyramid. His head still swam from the effort of trying to shift against Pearl's restraint, his heart pounded with rage.

Distracted, he sensed something above him and snapped into a sideways roll. A dark green warrior shot past him, his stooping dive turning into an awkward tumble. Moon felt his lips pull back from his fangs in a silent snarl. They weren't high enough in the air to play this game.

He turned back toward the pyramid and landed on a broad ledge. Hissing angrily, the warrior banked around and tried to angle in at him, his wings beating hard. *Idiot,* Moon thought.

Moon leapt up, caught the warrior's ankle and yanked him out of the air. The hissing turned into an outraged yowl, cut off abruptly as Moon swung him against the upper ledge. The warrior snapped his wings in to protect them and tried to dig his claws into the stone to scrabble away. Moon pulled him down, caught him by the throat, and pinned him to the wall. The warrior bared his fangs; he could have sunk his claws into Moon's wrists, or lifted a foot and tried to disembowel him. Moon should have torn his throat out.

Instead, he followed an instinct he didn't know he had, and drew himself up, flared his spines out, and leaned in. The warrior's eyes went narrow as he tried to avoid Moon's gaze. Then his spines, crushed against the stone, began to wilt as the furious resistance leaked out of his body. Knowing his point was made, Moon said softly, "Don't do that again."

The warrior jerked his head in response. Moon released his throat and stepped back. He half-expected to be tackled off the ledge and for it all to start over again, but instead the warrior shifted to groundling. He was a lanky boy, turns younger than Moon, with a shock of red hair, dark copper skin, and a deeply embarrassed expression.

Several warriors circled the air above them, and Moon was sure two of them were River and Drift. No one else dove for him. Moon turned and leapt off the ledge again.

He glided down toward the teachers' court. As he landed on the soft grass, he startled a flock of tiny flying lizards. They burst into alarmed retreat in a flurry of gold and violet wings.

Moon shifted back to groundling, and there he stopped, leaning one hand against the gritty, moss-covered stone of a pillar. He wanted to get out of this place. He wanted to fly in the cool air or float in the river, but he didn't want anyone to think for one heartbeat that he had run away. *At least there's no question of fitting in anymore,* he told himself bitterly. That bird had flown a long time ago.

Stone's great dark form landed in the center of the court, crushing some flowering bushes and almost flattening a small tree. He set Flower on her feet and then shifted to groundling.

"That went well," Flower said dryly, as they started toward Moon. She winced. "Moon, you're still bleeding."

"Let me see." Stone reached for him. Moon jerked away with a half-voiced snarl. Stone cuffed him in the head so hard Moon stumbled into the pillar. "Stop that. And don't shift," Stone snapped.

Moon subsided, unwillingly, remembering that he really didn't want to fight Stone. Flower hurried away, disappearing through the archway into the common room. Stone took Moon's shoulder and turned him around, pushing his head down to look at the cuts.

"Ow," Moon muttered.

"You shut up. Flower—"

"Here." Flower was back, handing Stone a wet cloth that smelled of something earthy.

Stone pressed it to the back of Moon's neck. Whatever was on it stung at first, then cooled the cuts. Stone said, quietly, "Pearl isn't... It's not supposed to be that way."

Moon set his jaw. "You said she was sick, not..." So bitterly angry that she was blind to everything. "What's wrong with her?"

"We don't know." Flower leaned on the pillar, looking up at him, a sad twist to her mouth. Other Arbora had reached the court, gathering in the common room and talking in soft, worried voices. "It could be disease, or just all the loss. Her last two queens' clutches, the ones that should have given Jade consorts and sister queens, were stillborn. Then Rain died. He was the last of the consorts of her generation."

"It isn't always this bad." Stone sounded weary. "She was better yesterday." To Flower, he said, "We need to make plans. Send someone to get the maps."

"Petal already has." Flower tugged on Stone's arm. "That should be enough. The grenilvine works quickly."

Stone pulled the cloth away and stepped back. Moon turned around, feeling the back of his neck, startled to find scabs instead of open cuts. Flower took the blood-stained cloth away from Stone and stood on her tiptoes to look at the wound. She nodded to herself, patted Moon on the arm, and walked back inside.

Stone watched him, giving nothing away. "Are you staying?"

Moon had regained enough self-control not to snarl the answer. "I said I would."

Stone's smile was a thin line. "Yes, you did." He turned away, and Moon followed him into the common room.

He caught many sideways glances, worried, uncomfortable, unreadable. Petal, Rill, and several others pulled cushions and mats out of the way, clearing a large space on the floor. More Arbora came in; Moon recognized Knell, the leader of the soldiers, and Bone and some of the other hunters. Balm and several other warriors followed them in; they looked uneasy, but no one objected to their presence.

Then Chime and Bell carried in a big, rolled-up hide, nearly twelve paces long. They put it down on the floor and unrolled it, pulling the edges to spread it out.

Moon stepped closer, unwillingly interested. It was a map, carefully drawn in black, blue, green, and red inks on the soft surface of the hide. Everything was drawn in broad strokes, with mountains, rivers, and coastlines sketched in lightly. He had never seen a map this large, showing such a vast area of the Three Worlds.

"We're here." Stone stepped out onto the map and tapped a spot with his foot. It was a star shape next to the blue line of a river. "From here, I could get across and out of the river valleys in three or four days." His brows drew together as he studied the faded ink below his feet. "That's eleven or twelve days for our warriors, more when they're carrying Arbora. And we still have a long way to go after that."

"Eleven?" Distracted, Moon padded across the map, looking for the Cordans' valley so he could trace their route here. Stone's pace, judging by the trip from Sky Copper, was one day to what would have been three at Moon's pace. "You mean nine."

"I mean eleven," Stone said. "Consorts and queens fly faster than full grown warriors. And I wouldn't be pushing them as hard as I pushed you. You'll get faster as you get older and bigger; they won't."

Moon grimaced—something else he hadn't realized. He had noticed that Chime and Balm flew at a more leisurely pace, but had thought that was just because they hadn't been in a hurry. He found the spot that might be the Cordans' river and followed it up into the vague outlines of a mountain range.

Balm said, "But Pearl was right. We have more Arbora than Aeriat, plus we'd have to carry supplies for the journey, and everything we'll need at the new colony. It would be taking an awful chance to split up the court like that."

Knell the soldier seconded that with a grim nod. He was powerfully built like Bone, but not nearly as grizzled and scarred. "It would take several trips, and we'd be vulnerable both here and at the new place. It would give the Fell plenty of time to attack."

Bone scratched the scar on his chest. "You could abandon most of us."

Several people hissed at him, Aeriat and Arbora. Stone gave him a bored look. "And we could all eat each other before the Fell arrive. That would solve our problems, too."

"Now that we're done with the daft suggestions," Flower prompted. "Anyone have anything sensible to say?"

Moon crouched to examine the area where he thought Star Aster might be, but the places indicated were all marked with glyphs in a language he couldn't read. He said to Stone, "So you're thinking of something to transport everyone in. Like a boat?" Though navigating an unknown river could be almost as slow and dangerous as walking.

One of the smaller Arbora, sitting at the edge of the map, asked, "What's a boat?"

"It's a thing some races of groundlings use to travel on water," Petal explained.

And there's that, Moon thought wryly. None of the Raksura would know how to sail or navigate a river.

But Stone said, "Like a boat." He turned, taking another pace across the map. "Have you ever heard of the Yellow Sea?"

Moon watched him, frowning. "No."

Flower walked over to stand next to Stone, thoughtfully twisting a lock of her hair. "It's a shallow sea, very shallow, barely a few paces deep in some stretches. Something in the water makes everything yellow—the sand, the plants."

Stone nudged a spot on the map with his foot. "There's a groundling kingdom out there, a remnant of one of the flying island empires. They have flying boats. Raksura have treated with them before, and I've been out there a few times."

Flower nodded slowly. "That could work, if the boats are large enough." She lifted a brow, giving Stone an annoyed look. "How long have you had this in mind?"

"Not long." He nodded to Moon. "When I went back to your flying island, I looked at the books you found. That got me thinking about other possibilities than just carrying the Arbora."

Moon shrugged noncommittally. He remembered the pictures of the people with tentacles. If the flying boats were more manageable than carriages on the backs of giant birds, it might work.

"You want to transport the Arbora in a flying boat?" Knell said, staring at Stone as if he had shifted and managed to end up with a second head.

Stone lifted his gray brows, fixing a concentrated stare on Knell. "Why not?"

"I don't know." Knell stepped back off the map, making a helpless gesture. "It sounds crazy."

"We could still be attacked while we're moving," one of the other soldiers said uncertainly.

Flower still stared down at the blot of delicate color that marked the Yellow Sea, brows knit in concentration. "We could be attacked while moving in the conventional way. With these flying boats, we could move all at once, and perhaps faster, and the warriors would be free to fight."

"And we could bring more of our belongings," Petal said. She had taken a seat at the edge of the map, her arms wrapped around her knees. "Like the anvils for metal-working. I couldn't think how we were going to move those."

There was a murmur of agreement from around the room.

"How do we get their boats?" a younger male warrior asked, sounding baffled by the whole idea. "Steal them?"

"You could buy them," Moon pointed out, exasperated. These people were hopeless. "You've got silk cloth, furs, metals, gems. You could buy anything you wanted in most of the civilized cities in the Three Worlds."

Stone gave the young warrior the *I can't be bothered to deal with your stupidity* look Moon knew well from their travels together, then said to the rest of the gathering, "We could bargain to use the boats just for the journey. It's not like we'll need the things once we get where we're going. Like Moon said, we have goods we can offer them in exchange."

"We have to try." Flower glanced at Stone. "Will you go to speak to them?"

"I'll go," a new voice said. It was Jade, standing in the outer doorway. She was still in her other form, her wings folded, so weary that her mane was nearly flat. Moon felt everyone looking at him, or trying not to look at him, and tried not to react. Jade continued, "Stone should be here if the Fell return. And I've heard the stories about the Yellow Sea. Solace and Sable and a flight of warriors first visited the groundlings there." She lowered her head, the scales on her forehead rippling as she frowned. "They were a sister queen and her consort, from an earlier generation."

Moon knew she was talking to him; everyone else had to know the story already. Before he could decide whether to reply, Flower cleared her throat and said, "You'll need to take some warriors, so that would make it a two day flight, but we still need time to pack up the colony. Historically, we're supposed to be able to migrate at a moment's notice, but I think that's a bit optimistic since we haven't actually had to do it for generations."

Jade nodded. "And we are asking the Yellow Sea groundlings to trust us with their boats, even though we're going to offer them payment. The request will sound better coming from a queen." She added, more grimly, "And it will get me out of Pearl's way."

"There's a thought." Stone eyed Moon in a way Moon didn't like. He wasn't surprised when Stone said, "I want you to go with her."

The room was very quiet. Moon knew he didn't have a choice. Refusing would mean embarrassing Jade in front of her people. Considering his own recent public humiliation, he had no intention of inflicting that on anyone else. Especially since she had defended him to Pearl. Moon said, "I'll go."

There was a collective breath of relief.

Chime, who had managed to keep quiet up to this point, said, "Has anyone thought about the fact that even if we get the boats, Pearl didn't agree to leave?"

"Yes, we've thought of that." Stone's gaze was on the map. "I'll deal with it."

Moon thought that sounded like a threat, but he admitted that he wasn't the best judge.

After that, the talk turned to the details of the journey, who else Jade would take with her, what Stone had found the last time he had visited there, the possible dangers along the way, and what they would offer the Yellow Sea groundlings. Clouds had come in from the north, and a light rain had started, pattering the leaves in the court. Moon sat beside the archway, just out of reach of the rain, and worked on listening unobtrusively, something he thought he hadn't done enough of lately.

Finally Jade and the other Aeriat left for the upper levels of the colony, Stone disappeared, and the Arbora broke up into groups to talk about moving the court. Moon slipped away, going back up the stairs to the bowers.

There were still too many people around, so he went up to one of the less-occupied halls, where a doorway to the outside overlooked the river. He shifted and climbed up the wall above the archway, looped his tail around one of the stone projections there and hung upside down from it, coiling up to wrap his wings around himself. He needed to think, and had always found this a particularly restful position to do it in. He had no idea if this was acceptable Raksuran behavior, not that it mattered. *Practically spitting in the queen's face probably isn't acceptable either.* He was also well above eye level here, and in the shadow above the doorway; if she sent any warriors to force him to leave the court, it was just as well if they couldn't find him. He didn't want to kill anybody and interfere with Stone's plans.

The journey tomorrow with Jade would be an uncomfortable experience. He didn't know if she could do to him what Pearl had done—draw him into that bond—or if it was only something that the reigning queen could do. He had no intention of ever being within Pearl's reach again, and Jade… now he knew to be wary. He didn't think either one of them could keep him in that state against his will, but Pearl had seduced him so easily. He didn't want to fall into that trap again.

After a time, he realized someone was nearby. He pulled the edge of his wing down to see Flower sitting cross-legged on the floor below him, looking out at the river. Without looking up, she said, "Don't mind me. I use this window for augury when the wind is from the south. I doubt anyone else would have seen you up there."

Moon twisted around to look out. The plume trees along the river bank waved slightly in the breeze, and higher up above the valley a small flock of yellow birds swooped and dived, bright against the gray clouds. "What are you auguring?"

"The prospects for your trip to the Golden Isles. I'm trying to read it out of the effect of the wind on those birds."

A bird swooped low, catching an updraft to soar back up to where the others circled. The only portent Moon could read was a bad one for the insects caught in the breeze. "Does it look good?"

"It says that the journey should be made, but then we knew that already. It says that Stone is right, that the Islanders are likely to listen to Jade's request. What it says about the outcome of the journey… is confusing, and useless." Flower frowned absently. "Can I ask you a question?"

This is why you should keep your mouth shut, Moon told himself, but fair was fair. "Yes."

Her eyes still on the birds, she said, "When did you stop looking for others?"

Moon couldn't pretend not to know what she meant. "A long time ago." He wondered if she could read the truth of his answers in the wind, in the way the birds banked and tilted their wings. To deflect further questions on that topic, he added, "I lived in a lot of groundling cities."

She nodded slowly. "Most groundlings aren't meant to live alone either, I suppose. But then we're born in fives, and clutches are always raised together. Or at least, that's the way it's supposed to work."

"So we are born like groundlings. Not in… eggs." Moon had been wondering. Five births at once seemed a lot for a groundling woman.

Flower did him the courtesy of not looking incredulous at his ignorance. "Yes, we are born like groundlings. But our young are smaller, though they do grow more quickly, and can walk and climb much faster than most groundlings." She smiled. "It's why the teachers always look so tired."

Moon let his wings unfurl and hang down, stretching. The scratches from Pearl's claws had nearly vanished, and barely pulled at his scales. "So why is it such a terrible thing to be a solitary?"

She lifted her brows, considering the question. "We're not meant to live alone. It's generally assumed that Raksura who do were forced to leave their court because of fighting or other unwanted behavior." She leaned back to look up at him. "Since young consorts are prized above any other birth except for queens, it just makes it look worse."

Well, that figures, Moon thought dryly. He had, after all, no proof whatsoever that he hadn't been thrown out of a court—except for his encompassing lack of knowledge about all things Raksuran, which Stone at least could vouch for.

Flower's mouth was a rueful line. "Stone said there were four Arbora with you that didn't survive. I suppose, if the warrior did steal you, she might have brought the others along to keep you company. But if she was escaping some disaster, she might have just grabbed you and as many other children as she could manage."

Not that that was any better. "So if we're born in fives, there was at least one more of their clutch that she left behind to die so she could bring me."

"I was actually trying to be comforting." Flower sighed, and there was something far away in her eyes. "Moon, there's something I don't think you know. Queens are born with power, but a consort's power comes with age. When you spoke in your shifted voice to Pearl—Only a consort coming into maturity could have done that."

Moon felt mature already. Most days, he felt elderly. "It doesn't matter."

"It does matter." Flower stood, her shabby skirt falling into place around her. "We don't use magic; we're made of magic, and you can't run away from that."

Watching her walk away, Moon thought, *I can try.*

CHAPTER
SEVEN

⁂

They were to start for the Yellow Sea at dawn the next morning.

Moon didn't have much in the way of preparations to make. He borrowed a small cloth pack from Petal, just large enough to carry his old clothes and some dried meat and fruit she insisted he take. He didn't have anything else to carry, though he was starting to covet the knife and belt, still in the pile of refused gifts outside his bower. It wasn't as if he needed a knife in his shifted form, but he was used to having one as a groundling, and you never knew when it would come in handy. But he didn't weaken enough to take it.

Before first light, Moon flew far enough away to be out of the hunters' range and took a kill, a small grasseater. He purposefully overate, knowing he would need it for two long days of flight.

It was still dark when he got back to the colony, so he stretched out on a ledge, pillowed his head on his pack, and napped.

The gray dawn light roused him, and he woke to see a group gathering on one of the terraced platforms below the pyramid. Stone and Flower were there in groundling form, plus Chime, Balm, and Jade, and three of the warriors who had come to the teachers' common room with her yesterday.

Moon jumped off the ledge and glided down toward the platform. He landed just in time to hear one of the warriors say, "He's probably run off. How long are we supposed to…" The words trailed off as Moon touched down on the paving and folded his wings.

"Wait?" Stone finished mercilessly. Chime gave the offender a derisive smile, Flower winced, Jade kept her expression blank, and everyone else looked uncomfortable. Impervious, Stone asked Moon, "You ready?"

Moon shifted to groundling, since everyone else was, and shrugged. Flower gave Stone a repressive look and introduced the three other warriors. "Moon, this is Branch, Root, and Song."

Song was female, younger and a little smaller than Balm, but she had the same warm, dark skin and curling honey hair, as if they might be related. Root was the one who had speculated that Moon had run off, and also the one who had asked yesterday about stealing the flying boats from their groundling owners. He and Branch looked enough alike to be clutch-mates. Both had reddish-brown hair and copper skin, not unlike the young warrior who had attacked Moon yesterday, but in more subdued shades. If they were from a related clutch, that was just Moon's luck. Root was typically slender but Branch had a bigger, broader build, which might mean his shifted form was larger. *That could be a problem,* Moon thought, resigned to trouble.

Moon had no idea what his chances were in a fight against a larger male warrior, or a group of warriors. What worried him the most was that he had never had a real fight in his shifted form that wasn't to the death. Play-wrestling his Arbora siblings with claws carefully sheathed had been his last experience with it, and he had never fought just for dominance or to make a point.

But he had no intention of letting anyone else use him to make a point.

Jade told Stone and Flower, "We'll be back as soon as possible. If we're delayed more than a few days, I'll send someone as messenger."

"Take care," Flower said, with a worried smile.

Everyone shifted, Moon following a beat behind the others. Stone didn't say anything, but Moon was aware that he watched them, long after they leapt into the air and flew toward the west.

They flew all day, passing the point where the hilly jungle gradually gave way to flat coastal plain. As the afternoon became evening, Moon saw the plain had turned to marshland, with bright green grass and tall elegant birds undisturbed by their passage high overhead. In the distance the sea was a yellow haze.

When they reached it, the setting sun made the yellow of the water even more brilliant. The waves rolled up a wide beach bordered by low dunes and a band of yellow vegetation. The sand glinted with metallic and crystalline reflections. Jade had followed Stone's directions well, and they reached the coast only a short distance away from the first landmark: a ruin rising up from the water, about a hundred paces out from the land.

Moon landed on the beach, shifted, and stretched. He wasn't that tired; he had grown used to keeping up with Stone, and this hadn't been very strenuous flying. It was also warmer here, despite the strong wind off the sea, and the sand was hot under his feet. He walked toward the waves as the others landed a short distance away.

From the look of this ruin, the groundlings who had built the blocky pyramid and the statues in the valley hadn't made it as far as this coast. The structure was a series of big platforms, placed as if forming a circular stairway up to the sky, each roofless but ringed by tall thin columns linked by delicate arches. It was all made of metal and covered with verdigris, and the supporting posts in the water were heavily encrusted with little yellow barnacles. Moon reached the waterline and stepped onto the wet sand, letting the frothy edge of the waves run over his feet. The sky was tossed with clouds; a haze of rain fell far off to the south.

A little way up the beach, the others had gathered into a group to talk. Moon kept part of his attention on them, while he watched the waves suck sand from around his toes.

Chime came over to Moon, slogging through the loose sand. He stopped a few paces away and said abruptly, "Are you speaking to me?"

"What?" Moon stared at him, startled out of his mood. "Yes."

"You've barely spoken to anyone except Stone since what happened with Pearl."

Moon scratched his head, watching the last of the light glitter on the water. That wasn't quite true, but he could see how it would look that way to Chime. "I didn't have anything to say."

"Somehow I find that hard to believe." Chime folded his arms, rolling his shoulders uncomfortably. "What Pearl did was unacceptable, even if you're a…"

"Groundling-eating solitary," Moon supplied.

"Groundling-eating solitary, she shouldn't have behaved that way. Since you were brought to the court by Stone… The groundling-eating part was sarcasm, yes?"

Moon gave in. Chime seemed to be offering friendship, in his own way, and he wasn't going to turn that down. They were both outsiders among the Aeriat, and Chime seemed more out of place at times than Moon did. He just said,

"Speaking of eating, let's go look for dinner."

They found tidal pools farther up the beach, in the rocky flats at the edge of the yellow scrub. The shallow pools had trapped fish, crabs, and other shelled creatures, and some water lizards, coming in to feed. The fish were too small to be more than a snack, but the lizards would make a more substantial meal. Moon shifted and slipped from pool to pool, catching surprised lizards, breaking their necks, and tossing them out for Chime to collect. They also found small patches of metal-mud, which Chime had heard about but never seen before. It was good for making colors for pottery, and Moon's favorite groundlings, the Hassi, had also used it when they hunted on the forest floor. Once it dried on skin or scales, the metallic odor disguised your own scent. It also burned easily, something that Chime seemed to find fascinating.

The others all explored the ruin or the beach. They were divided into two camps, with Moon on one side, and everybody else on the other. Or two and a half camps, since Chime hovered in the middle.

When Root and Song wandered over to try their luck in the pools, Moon and Chime carried their catch over to the ruin, landing on a platform about halfway up the structure. As a place to camp it wasn't ideal. There was no real shelter; the slender pillars didn't provide any windbreak. But the metal was hot from the day's sun and felt pleasant on Moon's scales, and the elevation made it difficult for anything to come at them from the shore. For one night, it wouldn't be a problem.

"These are a little chewy," Chime commented.

"Save the guts," Moon told him, "If we throw them in the water, they might attract something bigger."

Chime glanced warily down at the waves washing against the pillars. "How big?"

Jade dropped onto the platform. Moon embarrassed himself dramatically by scrambling sideways and almost leaping off into the water before he could stop himself. It wasn't that it was her; he had never reacted well to being startled while eating. When he was alone, it was when he was at his most vulnerable.

Jade stared at him warily. When he self-consciously sat down again, she said, "I wanted to ask you something." She knelt gracefully and unfolded a leather packet. "I know all groundling cities are different, but do you have any idea how many of these I should offer?"

Moon leaned forward, frowning in consternation as big, lumpy, white objects spilled out of the packet. It took him a moment to realize they were pearls, huge ones. He flicked one with a claw, and it caught the light, reflecting soft iridescent blues, reds, greens. They had to be from the deepwater kingdoms, further out into the seas than Moon had ever ventured. "It'll depend," he told her. If the Yellow

Sea groundlings traded with any waterlings, they might already have access to pearls like these. But this was still something they could trade anywhere along the Crescent Coast, to the Kish empire, the Hurrians. He was trying to remember the prices in Kishan coin that the Abascene traders had charged for passage on their ships, and mentally convert it to what the pearls were probably worth. And account for the fact that they were bargaining for flying boats that had to be worth more than any ordinary barge. "Start with five of the medium-sized ones. That's probably low, but not insulting."

Jade had begun to look impatient, but now her expression cleared. "I see. Thank you."

Still chewing on lizard meat, Chime asked her, "What if they don't want to trust us with their boats? If they say no, we're stuck."

Jade weighed the pearls in her hand thoughtfully. "Stone doesn't think they will."

Stone isn't always right, Moon thought, but kept it to himself. If this didn't work, they would have to move the court the hard way, and he wondered if Jade had thought about that. Moving a large group over land wasn't impossible, just difficult and dangerous; groundlings did it all the time. He was about to say this when he caught something on the wind.

It was just a faint trace of other, of something that wasn't sand, salt, or dead fish and lizards. Moon pushed to his feet, just as Jade said, "Did you smell that?"

Moon took a deep breath, his mouth open to draw the air past the sensitive spots in his cheeks and throat. "It's gone now."

Jade stood, the strong wind catching at her frills. "At least there's no mistaking the direction."

Chime twisted around, looking worriedly out to sea. "Was it Fell?"

"Probably," Moon said, at the same time Jade answered, "Maybe." Moon turned to look inland. With the wind off the sea so strong, anything could come at them from the land. His eyes caught movement against the darkening sky, but it was only Branch and Balm, circling high above the beach.

Jade said, "Fell wouldn't be out at sea, not unless there was something they really wanted." She was right about that; Fell would be just as vulnerable on long flights over water as Raksura.

"So they're after us?" Chime looked up at her, his face uneasy. "Pearl wouldn't tell them where we were going. Would she?"

"She's not that far gone." Jade sounded weary and disgusted. "And Stone wouldn't let them in to speak to her. It has to be a coincidence."

"A coincidence." Moon couldn't help himself. "Like Sky Copper being destroyed before they could accept Stone's offer of alliance."

Jade's frills stiffened and she said, flatly, "I didn't know you took that much of an interest."

I didn't know I did, either, Moon thought. He didn't have another answer. He looked back toward the beach, watching the waves rolling up. After a moment, Jade hissed, picked up her bundle of pearls, and jumped off the platform.

Chime sighed pointedly, as if the effort of putting up with them was almost too much. "I'm not going to say anything," he began, "But—"

"Don't," Moon said. "Just don't."

Something woke Moon, late into the night. He opened his eyes and didn't move, trying to sense what it was. He was on the middle platform, lying on his side in groundling form to conserve his strength. The wind was cool, the dark sky streaked with clouds. Something warm leaned against his back, and something heavy lay across his waist. It took him a moment to identify it as Chime's tail. Bemused, he thought, *That's... different.*

Moon was fairly certain Chime had gone to sleep as a groundling and, from his steady breathing, Moon could tell he wasn't awake. *He shifted in his sleep?* Moon had never done that, but then, much of the time his survival had depended on not doing that.

Chime was also still partly a mentor. *He sensed something that made him shift in his sleep.*

Moon eased up on one elbow. He hadn't been included in the discussion about who stood guard when, and so had left the others to it. Now he saw Balm perched on the edge of the highest platform in her shifted form, leaning against one of the slender pillars, looking out to sea. The line of her body was tense, as if she searched the sky for something.

Clouds covered the waning moon, reflecting some of its light. The constant motion of the waves made it hard to pick out movement. Moon couldn't scent Fell, but there was a strange odor on the wind, a slightly bitter tang.

Balm hissed a warning, flattening herself to the platform. An instant later a dark shape moved across the clouds. Moon dropped flat, and felt Chime jerk awake beside him. Moon squeezed his tail, whispering, "Don't move." Chime went still.

Moon didn't shift, afraid it would draw the thing's attention. Upper air predators often had frighteningly accurate eyesight, good enough to pick out a small loper in tall grass. If this thing was nocturnal, it might hunt by sound, movement, or strange senses unique to itself.

Time stretched, made more painful by the fact that flattened to the metal platform, Moon couldn't see where the thing was. But it must be moving away. The strange scent slowly faded out of the wind.

Finally, Balm called, "It's gone. It went north."

Chime slumped in relief. Moon sat up and took a deep breath, rolled his shoulders to ease the tension. He heard the others moving, a rustle of wings as someone shifted. A head peered down at them from the platform just above, and Chime waved at it to show they were all right. Sounding shaken, he asked, "Did you see what it was?"

"Not a Fell." Balm leaned down from the higher platform to answer him. "The body was long and narrow, like a snake. A big snake."

"Stone didn't say anything about big predators," Jade's voice came from above, more thoughtful than worried. "Maybe it's only here during the warm season."

Moon tugged on Chime's tail, which at some point had wrapped firmly around his waist. "Could you...?"

Chime twitched in embarrassment. "Oh." He let go of Moon and shifted back to groundling. "Sorry."

Moon shrugged off the apology. "You shifted in your sleep. Is that normal?"

"No, not that I know of." Chime looked warily out to sea. "You think I shifted because I felt it out there? Because I'm a mentor?" He lifted his shoulders uncomfortably. "But it was just an animal—albeit a big animal. I don't know why it would cause that reaction, unless there was something magical about it."

Moon nodded. "That's mostly what I was worried about."

"I don't know," Chime said again, sounding testy about it. "I'll have to ask Flower, if we get back alive."

"Get back alive?" Moon echoed, startled. It wasn't a long trip, and Stone hadn't indicated that it was a dangerous one. Granted, Stone had different standards for danger, but still. He took a wild guess. "How many times before this have you left the colony?"

Chime's glare was palpable even in the dark. He lowered his voice and glanced warily at the upper platforms. "All right, yes, this is the first night I've ever spent away." He shrugged uneasily. "I didn't realize it would be this..."

"Dark?" Moon suggested.

The sound of gritted teeth was obvious. "That's not funny."

Moon heard the others settling down again. Song took Balm's place as guard. There wasn't anything Moon could say to Chime that wouldn't be either pointless or patronizing. He just said, "Don't put your tail on me," and lay back down, pillowing his head on his arm. After some fidgeting and hesitation, Chime curled up behind him again.

The rest of the night was uneventful.

They reached the Golden Isles the next afternoon.

Moon saw the crops first: forests of short, ferny trees rising up out of the sea bottom, and beds of floating moss, planted with bushy root vegetables. Further in toward the islands, groundlings in small reed boats paddled swiftly between the thick clumps of foliage, tending it with long rods. They wore big, conical straw hats, and at first didn't see the Raksura flying over them. Then Moon heard a thin shout distorted by the wind, and all the straw hats tipped upward. They seemed to be small people, their skin a honey-gold, their hair light-colored.

Just beyond the floating fields, the flying islands hovered high above the sea. Most were fairly large, though smaller chunks drifted in their wake. Some were high in the air, but others were only twenty or thirty paces above the water. They were all covered with conical towers and domed structures made of a white clay and roofed with reeds, connected by bridges and long galleries.

The flying boats were everywhere, docked at round wooden platforms stuck out into the air from the edges of the islands. They looked like ocean-going sailing ships, except the hulls were slimmer, less substantial, made of light lacquered wood or reeds. They were all sizes, from tiny rafts that could only hold a few people to double-hulled cargo craft more than three hundred paces long. Most had one or two masts, but they must be there for some reason other than sails, since there were no spars to support them.

Below the lowest island, floating on the water's surface, was a large wooden platform built as a docking place for conventional sea-going craft. It was connected to the island above it by long wooden stairways. Two big flat cargo barges were moored at it, and a group of Islanders, in the midst of unloading clay jars from a third barge, pointed and stared and called out to one another.

Stone had said that they should land on the lowest platform, as it was the formal entrance to the city. Jade led the way as they glided down toward it, and Moon landed on the battered boards with the others.

The Islanders stared and scrambled around the stacks of clay pots and baskets to get a better view, or rushed to the railings of the nearby cargo barge. They seemed avid with curiosity and confusion, but not much afraid. They were short, the tops of their heads barely reaching Moon's shoulder, most dressed for work in little but brief wraps around their waists. Most of them wore the straw hats. This close, he could see they had golden skin and golden eyes, and their hair was white, silky as floss.

More Islanders clattered down the steps from the upper island. This group seemed more intent, as if they meant to officially greet or repel strangers. They wore short robes, belted at the waist, and some wore lacquered armor pieces that protected chest and back. Their weapons were staves made of reeds wrapped together and lacquered hard. Still, Moon had the impression they didn't encounter much serious fighting, and probably spent more time breaking up brawls on the docks.

The armed group reached the platform and approached cautiously. At some signal from Jade, the warriors shifted to groundling. Their audience exclaimed in astonishment.

After a moment of indecision, Moon shifted, too. He stood on the platform under that startled gaze, the sun warm on his skin, the strong wind off the water pulling at his hair and clothes. Every nerve itched; he felt horribly exposed. He had never shifted in front of groundlings unless he was in the midst of a last-ditch escape. This just felt… wrong.

The leader of the Islanders stepped forward, her expression wary. Her age was hard to tell; the fine lines at her eyes and mouth could easily have been from the sun and the omnipresent glare off the water. She spread her hands, saying, "I greet you on behalf of the Golden Isles… in peace?" She spoke Altanic, which was a relief to Moon.

Jade copied her gesture. "I am Jade, of the Indigo Cloud Court, sent by our line-grandfather, Stone. We seek to treat with you, to discuss a trade."

"Oh, good." The woman's relief was obvious. "I'm Endell-liani, the overseer of cargo and trade. Will you come with me to talk with our Gerent? He is the elected leader of our trade guilds and speaker for our people."

Jade inclined her head, the breeze making her spines flutter. "We would be honored."

They followed her up the steps to the first island. The stair, supported by stone pillars with heavy wooden beams as cross-braces, was broad and steady. Along-side it, sharing the stone supports, was a pulley system for lifting small loads of cargo. Moon supposed large loads just went up in a flying boat.

As they climbed, Moon braced himself against the new array of curious stares from the Islanders on the next level; maybe it would be better when they went inside, where he wouldn't feel so exposed. He thought he wasn't betraying his nerves, but Jade kept glancing back at him with an air of suspicion, as if she thought he was doing something embarrassing.

Then Root, climbing the steps behind Moon, grumbled, "Why do we have to walk? Why can't we fly?"

Or maybe Jade had been looking past Moon at Root, waiting for him to do something embarrassing. At least he had spoken the Raksuran tongue and not the trade Altanic the Islanders were using. Further down the steps, Song hissed at him and said, "Because it would be rude to the groundlings."

Root laughed. "They don't care. They want to see us fly. They stare like—"

Moon's last nerve snapped. He stopped and turned abruptly back to Root. "I care."

Root bristled, but Moon stood a step or two above him, looking down—a dominant position. Root gave in, twitching his shoulders in an unconscious at-tempt to lower the spines he didn't have in his groundling form. He muttered, "Sorry." Song emphasized the rebuke by slapping him in the back of the head.

Moon turned back, avoided Jade's gaze, and kept climbing.

They reached the first island, where the stairs gave way to a paved plaza sur-rounded by white clay towers. Market stalls built of reeds or shaded with bright cloth canopies opened onto it. Most of the people gathered around the stalls were Islanders, though a few groundlings were of obviously different races, maybe traders from the barges. Moon smelled fish frying in sweet spices, and hoped the Islanders' idea of hospitality included offering food.

Then Song said, "Jade, what's that?"

Moon turned to look. Song pointed to the sky, squinting to see past the glare. Moon found the object immediately, a light-colored shape against the clouds. At this distance, it had to be something large. Very large.

Their Islander escort stopped and watched them uneasily. All the other Raksura had gone still, staring up at the sky. Peering up as well, Endell-liani said, "What is it?"

"There's something up there, heading this way," Jade answered.

It had a long snake-like body, white or pale yellow, and blended into the clouds it had dropped out of. The wings were huge, rounded like a water-skating insect's, translucent in the sunlight. A slight acrid scent tainted the air. Moon said, "Balm, this is what you saw last night?"

She glanced uneasily at him. "It's the same shape, same scent."

It drew closer and closer, past the point where Moon hoped they were all mistaken and that it wasn't heading toward the islands and would turn away. It grew larger and more distinct, causing a bewildered stir among the watching Islanders. The hum of its wings was audible now, and growing louder.

"I see it now. It's a cloud-walker." Endell-liani waved a hand, baffled. "But they're harmless. They live very high in the air, and come down only to feed on a certain plant that lies across the surface, much further out to sea. They don't even bother our ships."

That explained why Stone hadn't warned them about it. A plant-eating upper air skyling wasn't much of a threat. Except this one headed down, straight toward the Islanders' harbor.

"It doesn't look harmless," Chime said, his voice low. "It looks like it's coming down here for a reason."

Moon had to agree. The creature plunged toward the harbor area just below this island, still not veering from its course. Sentries on the upper island shouted alarms; on the lower docks, Islanders backed away, scattered up the stairs and ladders onto the first island. Little skiffs in the water paddled rapidly away in all directions. One of the trade barges tried to cast off, though it was pitifully slow.

"This is so strange." Endell-liani shook her head in horrified disbelief. "Perhaps it's injured, ill, and it's —"

The cloud-walker's plunge turned into a spiral, its translucent wings a blur of movement. The head was big and round, the crystalline eyes multi-faceted; Moon couldn't tell if it was focused on the harbor or the small floating island to one side of it. A cluster of flying boats hung off a platform on the island. The wind from the creature's wings caused them to rock and clatter against each other.

For a moment it seemed as if the cloud-walker would do nothing, its shadow falling over the barges and docks while the Islanders froze in horror. Then the long, heavy length of its tail whipped around and struck the nearest cluster of flying boats. Moon flinched back as the hulls shattered. The platform broke in half, crashing down into a water-barge below. Wood cracked and groundlings screamed as the barge's big mast shattered.

Endell-liani turned and ran for the end of the plaza, shouting, "Harbormen, assemble!"

The cloud-walker writhed in the air, as if the contact had been as painful for it as it was for the boats, the barge, and crew. It pushed upward, circling the upper island, knocking the roof off a tower with one casual blow of a foreleg.

"This can't be a coincidence," Chime said, turning urgently to Jade. "It's here for us."

He had to be right. Unless this giant plant-eater had suddenly developed a taste for groundlings, this attack was aimed at the Raksura. And the Islanders, their ships, the helpless groundlings on the trade barges, were going to take the brunt of it. Moon looked at Jade and demanded, "Are you just going to let this happen?"

She turned to him, her spines flaring out in anger. She said, "Then stop it."

It was equal parts challenge and order.

Moon shifted and leapt into the air, hard beats of his wings taking him up. He needed to get above the thing as it swung around to take another dive.

It came around the top of the highest island and, instead of diving again, it veered off.

It's heading for—Moon snapped his wings shut and dropped, the skyling's swipe missing him by a bare wingspan.

Moon spread his wings again, catching himself on the wind as the cloud-walker overshot him. *This is a problem,* he thought, twisting in midair to follow its progress. He had expected it to ignore him in favor of the flying boats or the running Islanders. But if he couldn't get on top of it, at least he could keep it moving, maybe tire it out.

It circled again and headed back for him, and he saw that it didn't have claws. Its hands had stick-like fingers covered with flat pads, each capable of easily squeezing Moon to pieces. He banked and flew away from the islands, leading it out over the open sea.

It was fast, too fast. Moon was barely past the outer edge of the moored barges before its shadow fell over him. He dove, down and to the side. The displaced air as it rushed past him nearly sent him tumbling.

It circled again. Moon had no idea how he could keep this up much longer.

Then he caught movement from the corner of his eye. Root and Song were in the air, arrowing straight in toward the thing. He looked for the others and saw Jade, Chime, Balm, and Branch high overhead, angling to try to hit it from above.

The cloud-walker spotted Root and Song, and veered toward them. Moon drove himself upward, hard and high, reaching the others just in time to join their dive for the cloud-walker's head.

From this angle Moon could see how the long snake-like body was articulated; he aimed for the joint just below the round head, hoping for a soft spot.

He struck the body, found the rim of the shell, and sunk his claws into the tough gray hide just under it, furling his wings to keep from being blown off. Jade slammed down just past him and hooked her claws over the edge of the shell. The others hit further up or down. The cloud-walker abruptly bucked, its body contracting hard enough to knock Moon's feet loose. For an instant he was almost standing on his head. Exerting every ounce of his strength, he dragged himself down and landed again. Jade still held on, her spines flat with the effort, but the others were gone.

Moon didn't have time to worry about whether they were still alive. He looked down the cloud-walker's back to get his bearings, then did a double-take. *That can't be right.*

Midway down the length of the creature's body was a huge, discolored lump of flesh, a growth as big as a small hut. It glistened unpleasantly in the light, so mottled it was hard to tell if had once been the same color as the cloud-walker's hide or not. *Maybe we're wrong. Maybe it's not Fell-sent.* Maybe the creature had just been maddened by illness.

Moon slapped Jade with his tail to get her attention. Jade tried to hit him back with her own tail, missed, then finally twitched around to look. She stared at the horrible thing, then turned to Moon. Instead of disgust, her expression held startled comprehension. She leaned over to shout in Moon's ear, "Fell, in there!"

"What?" Moon shouted back. He looked at the tumor again. Fell were capable of some strange things, but this… "How can—Are you sure?"

Jade glared, and made a series of incomprehensible gestures with her free hand. She seemed sure.

The cloud-walker swung around to begin another dive, and there was no more time to discuss it. Moon motioned for Jade to stay back, and climbed toward the mass, hooking his claws around the edges of the cloud-walker's chitonous plates to haul himself along.

Drawing closer, he thought he saw a dark shape inside the semi-translucent growth. Holding on to a plate with one hand, he poked the tumor cautiously. The texture was softer than he had expected, almost rubbery. He was glad the pads on his scaled hands weren't very sensitive; he would have hated to touch this thing with his groundling skin. Moon braced himself and swiped his claws across the mass.

The surface split, but the cloud-walker didn't react. The big body tipped down, diving toward another target. Moon clawed and tore at the mass. It split further, releasing an acrid stench he could scent even in this harsh wind. It abruptly collapsed, revealing the dark shape that lay inside. Moon stared in shock. *Jade was right.* Hidden inside the growth was a Fell ruler.

Unconscious, cradled in what was left of the tumor, it looked even more like a Raksura—a consort—than the minor dakti. Like them, it had webbed, leathery wings, but its dark scales were smoother, its face less animal and more Raksuran. Instead of spines, it had a rigid bone crest fanning out from its head. Moon surged forward. He had to kill this thing, now, before—

Its eyes snapped open, dark with feral rage. It leapt at him.

It hit Moon and bowled him backwards. He lost his grip on the cloud-walker's plate and tumbled right off its back with the ruler on top of him. Moon caught its wrists, keeping its claws away from his throat, and jammed one foot against its stomach to hold it off. It whipped its tail around and caught him across the back, the sharp barb barely deflected by his spines. It laughed in his face, knowing if Moon let go, it would have him. The only safe way to kill a ruler was to catch it while it was asleep or drop on it from behind, and Moon had missed those chances.

Past the edge of the ruler's spread wings, Moon saw movement, a flash of blue and gray Raksuran scales. *I hope that means what I think it means.* He snarled at the ruler, wrenched free, and fell away.

It howled with amusement and angled its wings to dive at him. Just as Jade hit it from behind.

There was a confused flurry of wings and tails, a spray of black Fell blood. The stench of the blood went straight to Moon's head; he lost all caution and flapped to get up to them to re-join the fight.

Something slammed into his back, a wing beat hard enough to stun him. Moon plummeted, unable to catch himself. A heartbeat later he slammed into water, the force of his fall sending him straight down to strike the shallow, sandy bottom. The impact knocked the air out of his lungs and he flailed for the surface. But his claws caught in a soft mesh, like a net threaded with layers of filmy cloth. *Not cloth, moss and water plants.* He had hit the water in one of the Islanders' floating fields.

He tore at the strands wrapping his arms, trying to rip the soft fibers away and fight to the surface. While the moss shredded easily, the net itself wouldn't tear.

Moon thrashed toward the surface. The stuff wrapped around his wings, his tail, as if it were alive; the weight dragged him down. *Don't panic,* he thought, his heart pounding frantically. He couldn't go up so he tried to go down, struggling to get below the net so he could swim out from under it. He scraped the bottom, sand and shells scratching against his scales, but the whole mass moved down with him, twisting around him. He hadn't had a chance to take a deep breath before he went under. His lungs burned as he ripped at the net, fighting the drag of his own trapped wings. He knew he had only one choice left: he shifted.

Much of the weight dragging at him vanished but water flooded his lungs. The net still wrapped his body. Blind, choking, he tore upward but the moss and netting closed over him, blocking his way to the surface. He thought, *You should have taken the knife. Happy now?*

Then everything went dark and drifting.

The next thing he knew, someone pounded him on the back. Moon choked and coughed until he got a ragged breath of air.

An arm around his chest held him up just above the moss-clotted water, an arm with scales. In instinctive reflex he tried to shift again, but nothing happened. He thought woozily, *That's either very bad or*—He let his head drop back and saw the person holding him was Jade.

She hung off the side of a big flying boat, clinging with one hand to a rope. Above her, Chime gripped the side of the boat with his claws, one hand wrapped around Jade's wrist to keep her from falling. An Islander woman suspended beside them wore a roped harness that let her hang nearly head-down in the water. She sawed at the net with a long blade. Moon didn't know if Jade had really killed the Fell, if the others had survived the fight. "Where—" It came out in a barely audible rasp.

"Hold still," Jade said, her voice gritty with the effort of holding up his groundling form plus the water-logged weight of the net and the moss. He wanted to tell her to let go. The only thing supporting her was Chime's grip on the boat; if she fell, they would both be trapped in the net.

The weight dropped away abruptly, and Jade gasped in relief. The Islander woman leaned back in the harness, shouting, "He's free! Pull, pull!"

Chime hauled at Jade, and Jade dragged Moon up. He held on, watching the water and the sinking tangle of net and moss recede, until Jade pulled him over a wooden railing.

Moon grabbed it and hung on, determined not to collapse. Several Islanders retreated to the central mast, where they hauled on the ropes attached to it. The sails unfolded from the sides of the mast in a light wooden framework, extending out like giant fans.

The deck swayed under Moon, and he thought his head was swimming. Then he realized the boat was lifting up from the water, heeling over as it rose in the air and turned back toward the city. "Did you kill the Fell?" he croaked.

"It's in pieces," Chime told him, jittery with relief. "The others are looking for its head. The cloud-walker just flew away, as fast as it could."

Jade added, "The Fell was controlling it." She turned abruptly to the Islander woman, who was being helped out of her harness by two sailors. "Anything you want, anything in our power to give, just ask."

The woman was startled, looking from Jade to Moon. "It isn't necessary. You drove the cloud-walker away."

"It is necessary," Chime hissed in Raksuran, and turned half away to look out over the sea. "That Fell was after us. It caught the cloud-walker last night, and followed us. Once it realized we must be here for the boats—"

"Yes, it followed us." Jade turned back to him, her voice a low growl. "Pearl didn't send it here."

Moon wanted to argue, but just held on to the railing. A Fell ruler hadn't decided to follow them on an off chance; it had known they had an important task, even if it wasn't certain just what the task was. And someone had told it.

CHAPTER EIGHT

The flying boat took them up to the highest island, to a building of sun-warmed clay and reed-thatched roofs, made up of dozens of slim towers, balconies, and domed turrets. Moon was too sick to investigate how the boat worked, or enjoy the novel sensation of flying in comfort with something else to do all the work. The craft swung close to the turrets and dropped a gangplank.

Moon followed Chime and Jade as Endell-liani led them down onto the wide circle of the tower's docking platform. The fresh wind was the only thing keeping him on his feet. Endell-liani told Jade, "This is the palace of the Gerent and the trading guilds. The rooms in this tower are for your use. You are our honored guests."

As Jade thanked her, Balm, Branch,

Root, and Song arrived in a noisy rush, landing on the platform with a clatter of claws against wood. Jade hissed them quiet and spoke to them in Altanic, so Endell-liani could follow the conversation. "Was that the only one?"

Balm shifted to groundling, the others following belatedly. "There was nothing else as far as we could see," she said, breathless. "The cloud-walker is still heading out to sea, so fast we couldn't catch up to it."

"The cloud-walker was just a prisoner," Jade told her. "The Fell had made a sac on its back, and a ruler was inside. He must have taken control of the cloud-walker's mind somehow."

Chime twitched uneasily. "I know the kethel grow sacs like that so they can carry dakti more easily. I didn't know rulers would get inside one."

"They're getting inventive." Jade's spines relaxed as the tension went out of her shoulders. "Hopefully they only caught one cloud-walker."

"One would have been enough," Chime pointed out. "It could have destroyed this place."

Branch held up the ruler's head. The jaws hung open, and one eye was torn out. "What should we do with this?"

Moon tried to croak out an answer, but Jade turned to Endell-liani, asking her, "Do you know about the Fell rulers? The head has to be—"

"Yes, we know." Endell-liani turned back to the flying ship and waved imperatively at someone onboard. "It should be placed in a cask of salt and buried on land."

Moon didn't need to hear anymore; the cask of salt wasn't necessary, but the head did need to be concealed under a layer of earth, otherwise it would draw more rulers.

The wooden door into the tower stood open, and he went inside. A short passage led to a big round room with high windows that let in light and air, the walls and floor rubbed smooth with white clay. He staggered through the first inner doorway, then the second, until he found a room with big water jars and tile basins and drains. He dropped to his knees beside a basin and retched into it.

"Are you all right?" Chime asked from a safe distance behind him. "We didn't see where you fell at first, and we kept expecting you to come back up."

"Thanks," Moon managed to croak. Aside from having half the Yellow Sea and all its plant life in his stomach, he was fine.

When he finished, he felt hollowed out, and it hurt to take a deep breath. His clothes dripped and he still had strands of moss wrapped around him. He had no idea where his pack had ended up.

He wandered out the nearest door and found a small, open court, its smooth white clay reflecting the sun. Most groundlings would have found it too hot for comfort; it was probably meant more to allow light and air into the windows and doorways of the rooms around it. A few chairs of light, delicately carved, ivory-colored wood were scattered about, along with a couch draped with gauzy white fabric. Moon peeled his wet shirt off and collapsed on the couch, stretching out face down and pillowing his head on his arms. It was Islander-sized and too short for him, his feet hanging off the end, but it was far more comfortable than the floor.

He heard Jade and Chime come out into the court. One of them, he wasn't sure which, brushed the hair off his temple, then laid a cool hand on his back to feel his breathing. He made an "umph" noise to show he was still alive. Chime said, "Better to let him sleep."

They left. Moon lay there and listened to the others talk and move in and out of the court and the rooms around it. The baking sun lulled him into a half-drowse.

Sometime later he heard unfamiliar footsteps and smelled groundling tinged with salt and sun and sweet oil, the scent he was learning to associate with the Islanders. He turned his head, squinting. The sun had moved enough for shade to fall across half the court, and an old Islander man stood in it, watching Moon. His hair, beard, and mustache were as silky white as gossamer, a startling contrast against his weathered gold skin. He held a large book with wooden covers.

"I wanted to show you something," he said, as if this were the middle of a conversation they had been having. He stepped closer and crouched down to set the book on the paving. He flipped it open and paged through it. Moon pushed himself up a little more and leaned over to see. He had slept long enough for his clothes to dry, for the sun to bake most of the sickness out of him.

The paper was white, some kind of pounded reed, and it was filled with squiggly writing in different hands and inks, in a language with curving characters that Moon couldn't read. The old man found the page he wanted and turned the book so Moon could see.

It was a sketch, an Aeriat in his shifted form, wings and spines flared. Scribbled notes trailed down the page. The old man tapped it. "This is correct? This is a young consort, like you?"

Moon touched the page. The sketch didn't indicate what color the scales were, unless it was in the notes. But he thought the spines went further down the back than a warrior's, that the wings were proportionally larger.

"If—" His voice came out as a croak and he had to clear his throat. "— the scales are black, yes." His throat was dry and sore. He would have to go in search of water soon, but he didn't want to drag himself up yet.

"I've seen the old consort who came here, but only from a distance. He spoke only to some traders and the Gerent." He opened a wooden case that hung at his belt and took out some loose sheets of paper and a writing instrument that appeared to be a charcoal stick in an ivory holder. He peered closely at Moon; his golden eyes were a little filmy. "Always black?"

"I think so." It occurred to Moon that he really should know these things. He turned the page, where he found a sketch of a male warrior balanced on the piling of a pier.

The man smoothed the paper on the clay floor. "You don't grow a beard?"

"Lots of groundling races don't," Moon said, before he remembered he didn't have to justify it. These people already knew he was different. Nobody was going to ask those questions that had once been impossible to answer, like, *What are your people called?* and *Where do you come from?* The old man grunted thoughtfully and scribbled a note.

Chime walked into the court. He stood next to the couch, directing a puzzled frown down at the old man. In Raksuran, he said, "Their leader is here, talking to Jade."

"He came here?" That was a little surprising. Moon had assumed the negotiation would take place in some council room somewhere in the palace below them. Maybe it was a good sign.

"They're being polite." Chime stepped sideways, angling his head, trying to read over the old man's shoulder. "They knew Jade didn't want to leave you."

That was more surprising. "Me? Why?"

Chime's expression suggested that the question could be more idiotic, but he wasn't sure how. "You're her consort. Everyone realizes that but you."

Not having spines that he could flare threateningly at Chime at the moment, Moon settled for ignoring him. He leaned over the book again and turned more pages. Towards the back was a drawing of Stone in his shifted form, but it was from a distance, with the roof of a tower to give perspective. That was the last drawing, and Moon turned back to the front, finding older sketches of female warriors and Arbora. He paused at a more detailed drawing of a queen curled up on a broad windowsill, so unexpectedly sensual it made him blink. He switched back to Altanic to ask the old man, "Is this whole book about Raksura?"

"Yes. It goes back several generations, copied from older documents." The old man turned the pages back to the beginning, where the ink was a little faded. "It begins with the first sighting of Raksura by an expedition to the interior."

In exasperation, Chime pointed down at the old man. "Who is this?"

"I don't know." Preoccupied, Moon studied the drawing. It was blocky and not as skilled as the later sketches, showing a flying boat with little winged figures around it.

"This wasn't done at the time." The man sniffed disparagingly. "Inaccurate."

Chime sat down and leaned in to look at the scene. "How do you know it's inaccurate?"

"It doesn't match the account of the starguider Kilen-vanyi-atar, who wrote of meeting the Raksura, and treating with their court." The man traced his finger over the writing, found a passage, and read, "'As our craft sailed over the clearing, we saw an outcrop of stone, and on it, lying full in the fierce sunlight, were eight or so people. My first fear was that they were dead, but they lay more in the attitude of sleep, and showed no wounds. Their clothing was as bright as the plumage of birds.'" He looked up. "He goes on to say that they woke as the ship drew closer, transformed, and flew swiftly away. It took some time for him to convince one to speak to him, let alone to come near his ship."

Moon thought that if the boat could get so close without waking them, then the whole group was lucky not to have been eaten by something before the Islanders happened along. "They were probably humiliated at being caught in the open."

Chime turned his head to study the drawing, saying absently, "They sound almost as twitchy as you."

Moon thought Chime needed to visit a lake bottom again, and made a mental note to arrange that as soon as possible.

The old man squinted at Chime. "You are a warrior?"

"No," Chime said. Moon cocked an eyebrow at him, and Chime gave him a thin-lipped glare. "Well, yes," Chime told the old man grudgingly.

"There are differences between you?"

"He's moody," Chime offered, leaning over to frown at the writing. "More than anyone I know, actually."

Trying to page to the back of the book to see if there were any more drawings of queens, Moon snorted derisively. "Meeting the people you know would make anybody moody." Then he heard voices from the other room, and a small commotion of footsteps. He rolled onto his side in time to see Jade, Balm, Endell-liani, and several other Islanders come through the nearest doorway. A young Islander man pushed past Endell-liani to burst into the court, only to stop abruptly. He stared at Moon's old man, and said, nonplussed, "Grandfather."

"I'm busy," Grandfather said, still writing.

Endell-liani gave the young man a look of marked disapproval. "Niran, I told you everything would be well."

The other Islanders stood there awkwardly. Moon picked out the one that must be the leader: an older man, polished stone beads braided into his straight white hair, wearing a robe dyed a rich blue. The leader turned to Jade and said, "My apologies for Niran's impulsiveness."

Niran looked uncertain, but not particularly guilty. It was obvious that Grandfather had heard there was a consort here and slipped away from the Gerent's party in search of him. Apparently, finding him missing, Niran had come to the conclusion that he had been eaten.

Jade's expression was ironic. "There is no need for you to apologize."

It was a deliberate hint. Niran must have been less than tactful in his search, and Jade couldn't let the insult go by. Moon approved; he was a rank amateur at Raksuran relations with groundlings, but it had to be made clear that the implication that any of them would even consider hurting a harmless elder was a serious insult. Everybody looked expectantly at Niran, who said, stiffly, "I apologize."

The Gerent gave him a long look, then turned back to Jade. He inclined his head to her. "You are gracious. Please, let us continue our talk."

Jade resettled her wings and led the way back inside. The Islanders followed her, with only Niran and Endell-liani remaining. Niran hesitated, saying, "Grandfather, you should leave them alone."

Grandfather fixed a sharp gaze on Moon. "Do you want to be left alone?"

"No," Moon said, too caught by surprise to lie. The question had more weight than Grandfather realized.

The sharp gaze was transferred to Niran. "Now go home. I'll come when I'm finished here."

Niran lingered, frustrated, but Endell-liani took his arm, tugging him away, and finally he went with her. Chime watched them go, frowning. "That's not a good sign."

Moon shrugged. Niran had a right to be cautious, but this would teach him to be subtle about it next time. Moon asked Grandfather, "Will you read this book to us?"

"Yes." Grandfather tugged it away from Chime. "I will read you Kilen-vanyi-atar's observations."

With the negotiations going on in the inner room, they settled in for a long wait. When Moon tried to drag himself up to go in search of water, Chime refused to let him. Chime found Root in the next room and sent him to get water and tea, then sent him back after that for cushions and a chair for Grandfather, whose name turned out to be Delin-Evran-lindel. Apparently the more names you had, the higher your rank, and Delin was an important scholar.

The book was fascinating. It told the history of all the interactions the Islanders had ever had with Raksura, and legends about them collected from other races. "This scholar actually spoke to the Ghobin?" Chime asked at one point, incredulous and impressed. "How? And more importantly, why?"

"Venar-Inram-Alil was a very determined man," Delin admitted. "Also something of an ass."

"Did they kill him?" Moon asked. He had never seen the Ghobin before, but they were a persistent threat in the forested hills much further inland. They lived underground, tunneling under other species' dwellings to attack them, or stealing their young as food.

Delin turned the page with decision. "Eventually."

Some of the information collected in the book was wrong, which Chime pointed out immediately. Delin made careful corrections. There were also myths and fragments of the Islanders' own lore, stories about where their flying islands had come from and how they had been made. Moon found it all interesting. Balm stayed with Jade, but Branch and Song drifted in to listen, with Root wandering in and out, pretending to be bored.

After the request for tea, the Islanders sent in food, and after a while Moon felt like eating again. They provided fish, roasted whole or baked in clay pots with spices, yellow squash-like things that grew in the water-garden plots below the islands, and raw yellow clams and shellfish from the sea bottom. The others balked at the cooked fish, which just left more for Moon. The Islanders sent wine as well, but Moon preferred the delicate green and yellow teas. Fermented or distilled liquids had never had much effect on him, and it was interesting to see it was the same with the other Raksura.

Late in the afternoon, Delin found a story in the book that said Raksura could be captured by a ring of jien powder. Since there happened to be some available in the palace larder, Chime insisted they make the experiment. Moon thought it unlikely; jien was a popular spice in the east, and since it was often sprinkled on top of pastries and dumplings, he had gotten it on himself on many occasions. It had never had any ill effect on him, if he didn't count sneezing, but saying so would have ruined the fun. The others picked Root to experiment on, but apparently convinced this was a trick, he retreated to sulk in a doorway. They finally tried it on Song, who stepped in and out of the circle of spice with no difficulty, saying, "I think we're doing it wrong."

Branch and Root got a little rowdy afterward, teasing that threatened to escalate into a fight. After the Niran incident, two young warriors in a loud and violent play-fight would be the last thing Jade needed. Moon said, "Branch. Root," and then stared at them, communicating that if he had to get up off his couch, someone was going to get hurt.

They both subsided; Branch looked guilty.

Moon remembered thinking that Branch might be trouble, and knew he had been wrong. Branch was good-natured and quiet. Root was loud and annoying because he was young. Song was sweet and fierce, and shoved both bigger males around like a miniature queen.

Moon reminded himself that this was just a temporary place for him. If he wanted to stay with Indigo Cloud, he would have to keep defying Pearl, and sooner or later that would throw the whole court into chaos. From what he could tell, the court couldn't stand any more chaos. But it was seductive, this easy comradeship. It might be easy, but it wasn't uncomplicated.

The day wore on toward evening, and the shadows grew deep enough that Chime went to light the bronze oil lamps that hung around the court. Not long after that, Moon had to tell the others that groundlings didn't get stronger as

THE CLOUD ROADS · 111

they got older, and that Delin needed rest. Delin claimed that he was well able to continue as long as they wanted, then fell asleep in his chair.

Chime sat at Delin's feet, paging through the book, while the others talked or curled up to nap. Moon just enjoyed the quiet.

Then Song said, "Moon, is it true you don't know what court you came from? That you were alone until Stone found you?"

Moon lay on his back, watching the sky turn orange and violet with sunset. "I wasn't alone. I lived with groundlings, off and on."

Root stirred. "What was that like?"

Moon hesitated. He had no idea what to say. *When I was too small to live in the forest without getting eaten, I went to a groundling town. It was terrifying.* Or *I had to teach myself their languages. I picked through garbage for food. I didn't know how to fit in, what to do.* That wasn't the whole truth, though. *I loved living with the Hassi, but the Fell came. I had friends, but I always had to leave them, before anyone found out.*

Branch snorted, and from the sound, gave Root a shove to the head. "Idiot. Can you think of a harder question?"

"What?" Root demanded.

"What's the wind like?" Chime said dryly.

"You mean, right now, or—" Root subsided, disgruntled. "All right, all right, I see."

Balm walked into the court. One look at her expression, discouraged and angry, told Moon all he needed to know even before she spoke. "They said no." She sat down on a chair, burying her face in her hands.

Chime stared. "What, just like that?"

"No, not just like that. That's what we've been arguing about all day." Balm rubbed her eyes. "If they do it, they think the Fell would take more cloud-walkers captive and send them out here. Or the boats will be destroyed along the way, when the Fell attack us."

They could still move the court, but flying in stages or going on foot would take longer and leave them open to more Fell attacks. Moon hadn't realized until this moment just how much he had counted on this trip being successful.

"What are we going to do?" Root asked uneasily.

"Go back," Branch said. He sighed. "Think of something else. Or do it the hard way."

Song got up, took Balm's wrist and tugged her to her feet. "Come and get something to eat."

Branch and Root trailed after her. Chime and Moon sat there for a moment in silence. Then Chime stood. Sounding resigned, he said, "I'm going in to light the lamps. I can't think when it's dark."

Moon nodded. As Chime went inside, Moon got up to look for his shirt and found that someone had rinsed out the saltwater and moss and left it draped over a chair to dry. He pulled it on and went back to sit on the couch, depressed. He had counted on this working, counted on the court being able to move relatively quickly, so he would be free to leave them and the Fell and his own confusion behind.

A blue Arbora walked into the court. Moon stared, then realized it was Jade. This was the first time he had seen her other form. She was still tall and slim, and her scales had the same blue and gray pattern, but they looked softer, closer to groundling skin than Raksuran hide, though that might have been a trick of the shadow. Her wings were gone and her mane was smaller, not reaching much past her shoulders, and was more soft frills than spines. She hesitated, then said glumly, "I suppose Balm told you."

He nodded, uncomfortable. "You did all you could. They still might not have agreed, even without the Fell."

"I know." She came over to sit on the end of the couch, adding with rueful sarcasm, "I pointed out that if we hadn't been here when the Fell attacked, the damage would have been much worse. But I think they saw the flaw in my logic."

Moon looked away, a wry twist to his mouth. "It's just a little flaw." He hesitated, absently rubbed at a spot on the cushion. "I wanted to thank you for pulling me out of the sea."

He had meant it to be friendly, but Jade's whole body stiffened. "I would have done it for any member of the court."

Well, fine, Moon thought. He had been hoping for an actual conversation; he wasn't even sure why. But he needed to make sure of one more thing. "Did she ask for anything? The Islander woman who helped us." If Jade hadn't followed through on that promise, Moon needed to find the woman and make good on it—and hope she didn't ask for anything complicated so that he could fulfill the obligation before they had to leave.

But Jade said, "She didn't ask, so I gave her one of the pearls, a small one. Endell-liani said it was enough for her to buy her own garden mats, and a new house for her family. I gave another one to the master of the flying boat, to sell and divide among the crew."

So that was taken care of. Moon should just shut up now, but he said, "That was generous."

Jade gave him a look he couldn't read. "You're a consort."

If they were going to have a fight, they might as well get on with it. He said, tightly, "I'm a feral solitary with a bad bloodline."

"Pearl said that, I didn't. I—" She seemed to steel herself. "Would be honored to take you as consort, except, apparently, I have no idea how."

Nonplussed, Moon stared at her. "Uh."

Jade shook her head in frustration. "I know in theory. I tried the gifts; that's what all the traditions say to do, but they didn't say what to do if you didn't accept them." She waved her hands helplessly. "Look, even now, look what you're doing—"

Moon realized he had been unconsciously edging down the couch away from her. "I don't—" He knew he owed her an explanation, but it was hard to put his instinctive response into words. "The way I've lived, it's not a good idea to accept gifts. In a strange situation, you don't know what it's obligating you to do. Especially anything relating to—" He discarded several different words and finally settled on, "—mating."

Jade absorbed that in silence. Finally she said, "I know I should have waited. Stone told me that you'd never even heard of Raksura before he found you." She sighed. "In a strong court, there would be clutches of consorts and sister queens, and we would all have been raised together. I'd know which one I wanted, and if he'd accept me. And I'd know what to do, even if I had to fight the other queens for him. And at least I'd have someone to go to for advice." She shook her head, exasperated. "I haven't been able to talk to Pearl about anything, for turns and turns." With rueful resignation, she added, "Stone said I should just take you, fight it out, and get it over with."

That was typical. "He gives me lousy advice, too."

"Stone feels responsible. We lost too many warriors and consorts in the fighting, when the Gathen tried to take our territory, then the Sardis attacked the Sky Copper Court and we went to defend them. The consorts that were left… I was just a child, and Pearl didn't want them because they had all belonged to Amber, so they went to other courts. Flower said things happened so gradually— sickness and dead clutches, and one thing going wrong after another, and they were so busy worrying about the latest disaster—that no one looked at the whole. Stone had left the court by that point, flying off alone, exploring. He didn't come back until Rain, Pearl's last consort, died, and after that, it was too late." She looked at Moon for a long moment. "I know I haven't made it sound particularly inviting, but… Do you want to join Indigo Cloud?"

Moon shrugged uneasily, reluctant to speak. But he thought she had been honest with him, and it seemed wrong not to be honest in return. "I don't think I can fit in." There were those words again. It would be a good day if he never had to hear or say them again.

"You'd rather live with groundlings?" she asked, then than added quickly, "Not that that's a bad thing. It's just… unusual."

"I want to live where I don't have to hide." That was about all the honesty Moon could take for the moment. "And does it matter what I want? Pearl ordered me to leave."

With an edge to her voice, Jade said, "And you refused."

"I told Stone I'd stay until after the court moved." Moon let his breath out.

They could talk about this all night, and it wouldn't change anything. "If I can make it that long. The warriors aren't going to just let me ignore her, and I can't fight all of them."

Jade growled low in her throat. He didn't think it was directed at him, but it sent a weird tingle up his spine.

It also woke Delin, who sat up, blinking uncertainly. He looked around for his book and found it where Chime had left it, tucked under the cushion at his feet.

Glad for the interruption, Moon said, "Sorry we woke you."

Delin cleared his throat. "I wasn't asleep, only resting. Your voices are pleasant to listen to."

Moon hadn't had a chance to observe much about Islander manners, but he already knew Delin was no stickler for formality. Settling for a simple introduction, he said, "Jade, this is Delin-Evran-lindel."

Delin nodded formally to her. "Was your business with the Gerent successful?"

"Not really." Jade poked at the couch cushion with one claw, looking oddly young.

Moon explained, "They wouldn't agree to trade us the use of the flying boats."

Delin rested the book on his lap. "Why do you need wind-ships when you have wings of your own?"

"We don't all have wings," Moon told him. "We need a way to move the Arbora, before the Fell attack the colony."

Jade stirred, but didn't protest. Moon doubted their purpose here was a secret to anyone; the Fell had made sure of that.

Delin scratched his chin thoughtfully. "The Gerent is not the only one who owns wind-ships."

Jade lifted her head, frowning at him. "He and Endell-liani said that all the ships were controlled by the trading guilds."

"Not all. Only the primary cargo vessels. There are many families who own ships for the purpose of exploration, or trade in small luxury goods." Delin glanced toward the lamplit doorway. "We should speak to my daughter. But it would be better if those in the palace did not see us go."

That was one problem Moon could solve. He said, "We can do that."

It was full dark by then, so after a quick scout around the rooms to find an unobserved window, Moon, Jade, and Delin set out for his home. Chime saw them off with a hissed, "Be careful. And don't drop him." At least he had said it in Raksuran.

Delin's family home was on one of the smaller islands that floated a few hundred paces above the water. Lamplight shone from the windows of towers and lit little courts and gardens. Moon carried Delin and kept his pace to a slow glide, hoping to keep the old man from getting sick. But Delin was well accustomed to travel on flying boats and he seemed to enjoy it. He tapped Moon on the chest, pointing toward a balcony on a large tower on the narrow end of the island. Moon glided down toward it, Jade barely a beat behind him.

Jade had left Balm to guard the entrance to their rooms and to cover their absence. If the Gerent or anyone else asked for Jade, Balm would say that she was with her consort and couldn't be disturbed. If someone asked for Delin, she would say that he and Chime were consulting over Delin's book, and anxious to finish before Delin left for the evening. Everyone else had been ordered to stay out of sight and keep their mouths shut.

The balcony was dimly lit by a lamp inside the room, half-shielded by the white curtains across the doorway. The space was also just wide enough for Moon to land without fouling a wing. He saw why Delin had picked this balcony; it faced out toward the sea, away from any docks or the windows of near neighbors. He managed the landing, then set Delin on his feet and shifted to give Jade room. Jade lit neatly on the railing, folded her wings, and stepped down onto the balcony.

A young woman pulled the curtain aside, then jerked back with a startled yelp.

"Quiet!" Delin hushed her hurriedly. "It's me."

She hesitated uncertainly, staring. "Grandfather?"

Delin waved an imperative hand. "These are my guests. Now go find your mother."

The room just inside the balcony was Delin's study. It was smaller than their rooms in the palace, and the cushions and hangings had faded from the sun. Books and unbound rolls of paper crammed the shelves, as well as trade pottery and carvings from far away in the Three Worlds. Moon recognized figured blackware from Kish, a delicately enameled vase from Cient, polished shells that might be from a sea kingdom. Delin's entire family seemed to be here, the adults sitting on the floor mats to listen to Jade, and the adolescents and younger children hanging back in the doorways, watching curiously.

Jade sat in front of the balcony door, with Moon a little behind her. It still made him deeply uncomfortable that these people knew what he was; he knew it didn't make sense, it was irrational, but he couldn't help it. It hadn't bothered him with Delin, but then Delin was unusual for a groundling.

Jade explained their request plainly, leaving out only the fact that Pearl might be treating with the Fell. Moon couldn't fault her for omitting it. He wasn't sure how much Jade knew, past vague suspicions, and she seemed reluctant to believe even those. And after hearing it, the Islanders would have to be crazy to agree to this.

As it was, it was hard to tell what they thought of the proposal. Delin's eldest daughter, Elen-danar, was the head of the family, an older woman who bore some resemblance to him in the quick intelligence in her golden eyes. She asked careful questions, and seemed hesitant but willing to listen. Niran, unsurprisingly, was obviously against it.

"You brought them here?" he said, too horrified to dissemble, when Delin led them into the room. The other adults had been obviously embarrassed by his reaction and anxious to make up for it, so Moon thought it might have done them more good than harm.

Elen-danar tapped her fingers on the clay floor, frowning in thought. "With so many aboard, there would be little room for food or water. We usually bring large stores so we don't have to land in dangerous country."

"You wouldn't have to land," Moon put in. He felt he had to say something before anyone decided to interpret his silence as guilt or deception. "The warriors could refill the water containers and bring food to the ships."

"That would let the ships travel much faster," one of the younger men said. "If we don't have to stop at all—"

"We could supply you for the trip back as well," Jade added.

"But what would the Gerent and the trade council say?" Niran said, exasperated. "They've already decided this is too dangerous."

"We are not in the trade council. They don't speak for us," Delin said firmly. There was a murmur of agreement from a few of the others.

Still thoughtful, Elen-danar said, "I think you've told us all we need to know. We'll have to discuss it among ourselves."

Jade inclined her head, accepting the answer. "We will leave your islands tomorrow. If you decide in our favor, send someone to us in the morning." She opened the fold of leather, spilling out seven of the large pearls. "If you decide against us, send someone to return these."

As they flew back up to the palace towers, Moon saw activity on the platform docks directly below the structure. A small flying boat, lanterns hanging from its prow and stern, was coming in to dock. A dozen or so Islanders cast lines to haul it in. Occupied as the men were, Moon didn't think they had been seen, but Jade's colors did catch the light.

They both landed on the roof above the inner open court. Moon crouched, listening for a moment. The lamps in the court had been put out, though light shone from the doorways, and he heard Chime's voice, and Song's. He nodded to Jade, then leapt down onto the court below.

Jade landed beside him and folded her wings, shaking her frills back into place. "What do you think the chances are?" she asked, keeping her voice low.

Moon shifted to groundling. "It was hard to tell." He thought it depended on who had the most influence in the family, who marshaled the best arguments. Delin was obviously for them, Niran against, but it was impossible to tell about the others. "It could go either way."

She folded her arms, twitching her spines in frustration. "Stone thinks it's our only chance. Flower said he never wanted the court to move to this colony in the first place."

Moon hesitated to ask, but Stone was such an enigma that he couldn't pass up the chance. "Is that why he left the court for so long? He didn't like the colony?"

Jade shook her head. "No, he left because his queen died. Her name was Azure. I don't remember her. It was before I was born." Her shoulders tensed, and he saw her claws flex against her scales. Not looking at him, she said abruptly, "I know you want to leave the court. I would ask you, that if you do… you would consider leaving me with a clutch."

Moon went still. It should have been a terrible idea. But the first thing that flashed through his mind was to wonder if he could make it a condition that he keep one of the babies—or two. It would have to be two, to keep each other company. But he couldn't raise them alone, and the moment of wild hope was abruptly over. He thought, *Don't be stupid.* Even if it were possible, raising two fledglings outside a court would just brand them as solitaries, to live alone or try to beg their way into a colony.

No, it was impossible. His heart sank and he wondered if this was what Sorrow had felt, this need to have companionship so intense it made you willing to do anything. *Almost anything.* It wasn't a comfortable thought.

But leaving a clutch behind to be raised in Indigo Cloud wasn't a much better prospect. The court would eventually manage to negotiate for more consorts, and Moon's clutch would become less important. If anything happened to Jade, the clutch would be left to Pearl's mercy.

It clarified the situation completely, to realize that he didn't want to father any children unless he could be there to kill anything that threatened them.

He could try to explain that to Jade, but after what had happened the last time he had refused a request for a baby… "I'll think about it," he finished, and knew he sounded guilty.

"No, you don't have to answer—" Jade began, then abruptly cut herself off.

There was a new voice from inside. Listening hard, Moon realized it was Endell-liani. *That's not a coincidence.* He whispered, "They saw us."

Jade hissed in annoyance. "Let's hope they saw us on the way back." She caught his wrist and pulled him along, across the court and through the doorway.

All the others were there: Balm and Chime stood in the inner doorway with Endell-liani as if they had just stepped in, Song and Branch sat on the floor cushions, Root was in his Raksuran form, hanging from the ceiling. He saw them, dropped to the floor, and shifted back to groundling; he left huge gouges in the clay ceiling.

Endell-liani didn't look startled to see them. She said, "I'm sorry to disturb you. The sentry on the docking platform thought he saw something in the air, and I wanted to make certain it was one of you."

"Yes, we, ah, felt the urge to fly." Jade smiled, careful not to show her teeth. "We're newly mated."

Moon didn't have to fake looking flustered. He tugged his wrist free and went over to sit on a bench. Jade's remark had been calculated to cut off any further request for explanation. With some groundling races the ploy wouldn't have worked but, for the Islanders, it was evidently perfect. Endell-liani apologized again, already backing out of the room. Balm threw a startled look at Jade, and then followed Endell-liani out.

The others were quiet, and Moon realized they were staring at him. Chime craned his neck, making sure Endell-liani was out of earshot. Then he turned hopefully to Moon. "Did you really?"

Jade flared her spines, and Moon fled the room.

Moon climbed out a window and went up to sit on the roof. He watched the clouds travel across the night sky and the endless motion of the sea. The wind was turning cool, and the reed roof didn't hold the day's heat. When he heard the others settling down to sleep, he gave in to impulse and climbed back down the wall to go inside.

They had put all the lamps out, but he could see only one sleeping body in the room off the court, in a nest made up of floor cushions. Moon heard the others, and thought it was Branch on guard in the passage to the dock platform, while everyone else was in the next room.

Chime sat up and said, "Here."

Moon hesitated. Chime should be with the other warriors and Moon shouldn't be encouraging him to separate himself like this. Then he thought, *Forget it.* He didn't know where he was going when he left Indigo Cloud and he wasn't going to give up even one night of comfort and company. He shifted to groundling as Chime moved over.

As Moon stretched out on the cushions, Chime whispered, "Sorry about earlier. I realize I shouldn't have said that."

Moon settled on his side, wriggling to find a spot for his hipbone. "It's all right."

"I just… We've all been hoping—"

Moon set his jaw, exasperated. "You don't have to hope. Once the court moves you can get a consort from Star Aster."

Chime whispered harshly, "I don't want a stuck-up consort from Star Aster acting as if he's condescending to do us a huge favor. I want you."

Moon rolled over and sat up. He leaned over Chime and hissed, "You're not going to get me."

Chime hadn't been raised to be a warrior and didn't give way as easily as Root and Branch. He shrank back a little in token submission, but immediately demanded, "Why not?"

With an annoyed growl, Moon gave up and lay back down. The others might not be able to hear what they were talking about, but everyone might wonder why they were snarling at each other. "Stone never thought this would work. He just needed a consort so the others would agree to move the court. You and Flower know that."

Chime persisted, "We don't know that, and you don't know what Stone thinks. Nobody knows what Stone thinks."

Moon gritted his teeth. "If you don't be quiet, I'm going to bite you."

He didn't know if Chime believed him, but at least he stopped talking.

CHAPTER
NINE

M oon woke to early dawn light
and the cool air from the open
door to the court. Chime,
completely undeterred by their argument, was a warm presence against his
back. Moon pushed himself up on one
elbow and groaned under his breath. If
Delin's family decided against them, this
was going to be an interesting day—interesting in the sense that he would like
to just fly off and enjoy it in an entirely
different part of the Three Worlds.

He could hear the others already stirring; Jade walked out into the main room
first. She went to the doorway and glared
out at the sky, already lightening to a
clear blue. "It could have rained," she said
under her breath. "We've got no reason
to stay here now."

"It's going to look suspicious." Balm
followed her and leaned in the doorway

to look worriedly at the sky. She told the others, "The Gerent gave us a firm answer last night, and we'd already said we needed to return to the court as quickly as possible."

She was right. The sky was almost cloudless. Everyone had eaten heavily yesterday, more than enough for the flight to the mainland; they should already be in the air. If the Islanders asked what they were waiting for, Moon didn't know how Jade would explain it.

Root wandered over to the doorway and looked out uncertainly. "What do we do if they don't come?"

"They'll be here," Jade said, turning away from the door. It was hard to tell if she was reassuring Root or herself.

Chime got the brazier lit in the main room and made tea. It gave them something to do, which helped a little, but Jade and Balm still stalked the empty rooms. The others were restive. Root kept climbing the walls and trying to hang off the doorframes, and Song and Branch bickered like bored children. After a while, Moon felt he had to do something with the younger warriors. Jade was so tense she hadn't been able to get her spines down for half the morning. "Maybe I should take them fishing?" he said to Chime. He thought it was either that or kill them.

"You almost drowned yesterday," Chime said, banging the iron kettle onto the holder. "You want to go out there again?"

"Yes." Moon had been almost killed too many times to develop an aversion to anything. "I wasn't planning to go fishing under the moss net."

He looked up to find Jade standing over him, her frills stiff with exasperation. "If you would take them out of here for a while, I'd be grateful—"

Then Balm ducked through the doorway from the entrance hall. "Someone's coming," she whispered anxiously. "I think this is it."

"Tell them to come in." Jade turned to the younger warriors. "Go out to the court! Don't make it look as if we're waiting for something."

Song, Branch, and Root scrambled to obey. Moon stayed where he was, sitting beside the brazier. After a moment of twitching uncertainly, Chime settled back down on his cushion. Jade shifted to Arbora, probably to get rid of most of her spines so they couldn't flare out in agitation.

Then Balm walked in with Delin, Niran, and Endell-liani. Endell-liani inclined her head in greeting and said, "Forgive the intrusion, but Delin-Evran-lindel said that you were expecting him?"

Delin said, "We were invited for breakfast," and winked at Moon. Niran flushed dark with mortification.

"What if they don't come?" Root said. "What if they keep the pearls and cheat us?"

Moon, stretched out in the sun and trying to nap, hissed under his breath. They were at the metal ruin on the shore of the Yellow Sea, up on the top platform. They had arrived yesterday evening and stayed the night. It was now afternoon, another clear day with a bright sun and a good, cool wind off the water. With a dry edge to her voice, Jade told Root, "Then we go back home empty-handed and I look like a fool. Now be quiet."

Delin had arranged to meet them here with three of his family's wind-ships. The other Islanders might guess that the departure of the ships only a day after the Raksura had left had something to do with an arrangement to help move the court, but they wouldn't be able to prove it. Delin seemed to think that was all that mattered. He had explained, "They may talk, but that's all. We have always been explorers. We make the connections with other races that allow the trading guilds to open new markets and prosper, to let our scholars increase their knowledge. We go as we will and have never been under their direction."

Moon hoped he was right.

At dawn this morning, Jade had sent Balm and Branch on ahead to the court, to let them know that the boats were coming. It was hard to believe that the entire court could make ready to move in just these few days, but Moon was willing to be surprised.

He had spent a lot of time last evening and this morning out scouting, going alone so he could stretch his wings and cover more distance. He had looked for signs that they had been followed by Fell or suspiciously low-flying cloud-walkers or anything else out of the ordinary, but he had found nothing. Just sea and dunes and salt marsh.

Some distance to the north, he did stumble on a small camp of groundlings who were following a narrow river inland. They had white silky fur that rippled in the wind, and bony crests like sea birds. They also had good eyesight; they spotted Moon at a higher altitude than most groundlings could have managed, and stared with interest and not much apparent fear, shielding their eyes against the sun. Moon supposed that if he had been Stone he would have taken the chance to stop and chat—but he wasn't, and he didn't.

He had returned to find Chime hunting among the tidal pools, and Song and Root playing in the surf. Jade sat on the beach, her blue and gray colors vivid against the golden sand. As he landed next to her, she asked, "Any sign?"

"Nothing." He shifted to groundling, feeling uneasy. The ruler who had taken control of the cloud-walker would have known they had reached the Islanders, but not what they had done there. If they were lucky, it hadn't had a chance to pass on even that much information to the others. But Moon wasn't willing to trust to luck. He said, "Fell don't give up."

"I know," she said, absently drawing her claws through the sand. "They should be here looking for us. I'd worry less if they were."

They had all eaten. Root and Song had played in the waves until they were half-drowned. Moon felt he knew every pace of the surrounding marshland. At this point, there wasn't anything to do but sleep in the sun and wait. The metal of the platform was baking hot, and lying on it in groundling form felt like a luxury. Groundlings with skin unprotected by scales or fur shouldn't be able to touch metal this hot without burns, so Moon had always been careful not to indulge in it in front of anyone.

"But what's to stop them from keeping the pearls?" Root persisted. He was on watch, and he, at least, was wide awake.

Chime and Song, sprawled near Moon on the platform, both snarled in chorus. But with weary patience, Jade said, "Their people are traders. For them, baubles like that are a measure of trust."

Baubles, Moon thought, grimly amused. There had been times when a few baubles would have made all the difference in the world.

At least it gave Root something to think about. He was quiet long enough that the sun lulled Moon to sleep again. The next time Root spoke, it was to say, "Something's coming in from the sea."

Moon rolled to his feet, almost shoulder to shoulder with Jade. In the distance, a shape danced on the horizon, but he couldn't tell if it was on the surface of the water or flying above it. There was no distinctive scent in the wind, animal or otherwise.

"Wait here." Moon shifted and jumped off the platform.

He had only made a third of the distance before he could see it wasn't one shape but three: three long wind-ships, their fan-like sails spread, making their way towards the shore.

Moon had been on boats that sailed on the water, but he had never had the freedom to climb all over one in his shifted form and see how it worked. The wind-ship was bigger and more interesting than any he had been on before. Under the main deck toward the bow were two large holds, empty except for food stores for the crew and clay water jars. The holds took up most of the room, but toward the stern there were smaller cabins for sleeping and eating, and one solely for the storage of maps, drawn on thick reed paper and rolled into lacquered wood cases.

The wind-ship's sails were like giant fans, unfolding out from the large mast when the sailors pulled and adjusted the ropes. A ladder on the mast ascended to a little wooden box at the very top.

"What's in here?" Chime asked, leaning over to look in. "Oh, sorry," he added in Altanic.

An Islander woman was inside, apparently acting as look-out. She was very young, dressed like the other sailors in pants cropped at the knee and a loose shirt, her white hair kept off her face by a patterned scarf. She looked startled by their sudden appearance, but not panicked or upset.

"Will these ships hold the entire court?" Moon asked, boosting himself up to cling to one side of the box. Up here, the view was unobstructed by the sails or the bulk of the ship below. The marshland spread out below them like a green carpet, the hills a brown and gold haze in the distance.

"It'll be crowded, but I think we can do it." Chime hung on to the other side of the box, lifting his head so the wind stirred his spines. "If they have to, the warriors can spend most of their time in the air."

Jade was over on the second ship with Root and Song, speaking to Diar, who was in command of the expedition. Ten Islander sailors crewed each ship, most members of Delin's extended family. Niran was in charge of this vessel, and hadn't made any effort to speak to them. His attitude still made it plain that he would rather not be here at all.

Moon felt a light touch and looked down to see the look-out run her finger down one of his claws, as if fascinated by the smooth texture and the bronze and black banding. He didn't move, too bemused to react.

"Delin's waving at us," Chime said, leaning out to peer down at the deck. "I think he wants us to come down."

Delin stood on the deck with Niran. Moon let go of the box, leapt out, and cleared the sail to glide down to the deck. Chime landed beside him a moment later and they both shifted to groundling. Niran's jaw was set and his golden skin flushed with irritation. *That's going to be a problem,* Moon thought. It was also going to become annoying. Both he and Chime knew better than to pull on ropes or touch anything else that looked delicate; if Niran had difficulty dealing with them, it was going to be interesting to see how he handled it when curious Arbora were climbing all over the place.

Delin just smiled. "You like our ship? It is the *Valendera,* the oldest of our craft, built by my father's father. The others are the *Dathea* and the *Indala.*"

Chime said, "Yes, but how do they fly?" Earlier, he had climbed over the side and down under the hull, trying to see what kept the ship in the air. Moon had just figured that some things flew and some didn't, and since the ship was from a flying island, its chances of doing so were better than most.

But Delin said, "I'll show you," and led them back toward a small deck cabin in the stern. Niran followed with an air of unspoken protest.

When Delin opened the heavy door, Moon saw that crystals in the walls and roof allowed in light while blocking the weather. Built-in benches along the wall doubled as storage chests. A shelf held lacquered map cases. But in the center of the cabin was a wooden pedestal with a heavy metal lid. It was etched with glyphs in the Islander language, and other symbols Moon hadn't seen before. Metal handles stood out from the top of the pedestal, apparently so it could be turned, allowing the symbols to point to different directions.

Delin touched the lid, smiling reverently. "This contains the sustainer, the engine which controls the ship's speed and direction." He slid a bolt aside and opened the top of the pedestal. Inside was a chunk of gray rock, shot through with glittering metallic elements. He looked at them, brows lifted inquiringly. "Do you know what this is?"

Moon had no idea. He guessed, "A magic rock."

Chime's face was rapt. He looked up at Delin, smiling. "A piece of a flying island."

Delin nodded. "A small piece, a very important piece, from the heart of an island. One of the things we search for in our explorations are fragments of islands, uninhabited and too small to be of use. We excavate and look for these rocks, which are buried throughout them."

Chime looked like he desperately wanted to touch the rock, but knew he shouldn't. "So you turn the case—"

"And the ship turns with it." Delin carefully closed the lid again. "The force of the sustainer propels us. It allows the ship to float on the waves of invisible force that cross the Three Worlds. The sails are only to take advantage of the wind for extra speed. We can't be becalmed like an ocean-going ship."

It was probably a stupid question, but Moon couldn't help himself. He asked, "When you take the rocks out, do the islands sink?"

"If we take too many, yes," Delin told him. "There is a plateau in the north that is said to be a large flying island that fell to the ground. They believe several civilizations fought over possession of it, and that their attempts to drive each other away caused the power inside the rock to stop working."

Chime stepped around the pedestal, examining the rest of the cabin. In the back wall, a small compartment held a heavy bowl of water with a sliver of metal shaped like a fish floating in it. Chime touched the bowl. "What's this?"

That one Moon recognized. "It always points to south, so they can navigate." He touched the fish, making it spin and bob.

"How do you navigate when you fly?" Delin asked.

"I always know which way south is." The words were out before Moon remembered that he didn't actually know if that was a Raksuran trait or not. He slid a glance at Chime.

But Chime nodded as he leaned down to study the little metal fish. He said absently, "It's a pull toward the heart point of the Three Worlds. We all feel it, including the Arbora."

Delin was already opening his writing box, but Niran stared, disbelieving. He repeated, "You always know where south is."

Moon and Chime both pointed. A moment later the metal fish steadied in its bowl, seconding their opinion. Niran folded his arms, his face still skeptical. Exasperated, Moon had to ask, "Why would we lie about that?"

Delin sat down on one of the benches built into the wall, smiling mildly as he got out his writing instrument. "I'm sure a test could be arranged."

That took up the rest of the afternoon.

Below them, the marshes gave way to plains studded with scrubby trees. The wind changed as they traveled further inland, and the sailors folded the sails up; the ships then moved with only the sustainer to power them. It was slower, but they still made good progress. Another benefit of traveling on a flying boat was that you didn't have to stop to sleep or eat; Moon thought the steady progress of the ships would come close to making up for their slower speed.

In the early evening, Moon took Root and Song hunting, and they brought back a couple of big flightless birds, similar to vargit, for the Islanders. By the time they got back, the setting sun was turning the sky a warm gold.

Diar, on the *Dathea*, thanked them with genuine enthusiasm. "We usually live off grain porridge and dried root crops on these trips, and at home every meat other than fish is imported, costly, and not fresh." She was older than her brother Niran, short and strongly built. She didn't seem to share Niran's reservations or, if she did, she hid it better.

While the crew carried their catch away, Moon remembered something he had meant to tell the younger warriors. "Don't eat in your shifted form in front of the Islanders." Some of the crew were openly nervous of them, some curious, and others cautious. Watching warriors eat would appall most groundlings, and it was too easy to imagine Root dragging a fresh kill up onto the ship's deck.

Song nodded understanding, but Root had to ask, "Why not?"

"Because you're disgusting," Chime told him. "Even we think so." Moon didn't think he was exaggerating; Chime had been an Arbora for most of his life, and the mentors and teachers ate more like groundlings than Raksura.

Root bristled, then looked at Moon, and meekly lowered his spines.

Each ship had a special room below for cooking, with a fire in a heavy metal container. The Islanders cut the birds up, mixed them with root vegetables from their stores, and cooked it all in clay pots. Moon was still full from eating this morning, but it smelled so appetizing that accepting a bowl to be polite was no hardship.

Afterwards, he went up on the deck. Big lanterns were lit on the prow, but most of the ship was in shadow. Many of the Islanders on the *Valendera* had gone below to sleep or sit at the long table in the crew's common room. The decks of the other two ships were empty except for a couple of sailors on watch. Root and Song were over on the *Dathea*, and Chime had gone up on top of the steering cabin to sleep. Moon didn't know where Jade was until he caught a glimpse of blue and gray in the light of the bow lantern.

He took a step in that direction, then made himself turn back. He was leaving after they moved the court, and there was no point in… There was just no point.

He wandered back down the deck, to a platform where coils of rope were stacked. Sitting there, he had a good view over the railing.

The night air was like cool silk against his skin. The other two ships were half-lit shapes to either side, moving in near silence. When he flew under his own power, the terrain flashed by; at the slower pace and lower altitude of the ship it was much easier to see and oddly fascinating to watch. He caught flickers of movement in the tall grass and the trees, and hints of scent in the breeze, but he was too well fed to feel any urge to obey the reflexive impulse to hunt.

Then he heard a light step on the boards. Jade climbed onto the platform and sat near him. She wore her Arbora form, her colors soft and muted in the shadow. She curled up her tail, wrapped her arms around her knees, and said, "If you stand by the ladder, you can hear them talking below. I was listening to what they said about us."

Moon lifted his brows. It was always a good idea to be cautious, but her expression didn't seem urgent, so she must not have heard anyone plotting against them.

Jade continued, "They say we're not nearly as savage as Niran led them to believe." One corner of her mouth lifted in a smile. "They think Root is cute."

Moon twisted around to look over at the *Dathea*. The moonlight illuminated Root and Song sitting on the railing in groundling form. Root flicked at Song's hair, apparently in an attempt to get her to shift and rip his head off. Moon considered intervening, but he figured the situation would work itself out in a moment. "Would they like to keep him?"

"I may ask." Jade sounded amused. "They call you 'the quiet one.'"

Moon supposed it was true. Over on the other ship, Song pushed Root off the railing. He tumbled, shifting in mid-air, and caught himself before he crashed into a tree. As he flapped back up to the ship, Moon said, "It's hard to believe he's related to Branch."

"He isn't. Though they've always been close. Root's other clutch-mates were all Arbora." She absently rubbed at the polished wooden boards, looking thoughtful. "Sometimes there's a division, among the warriors, between those whose mothers were Arbora and those whose mothers were queens. Branch's clutch-brother is a good example of that." Her voice turned dry. "He's too clever to push me, so I have no excuse to give him the beating he deserves."

Moon turned back to look at her, frowning. If Branch wasn't related to Root, then his name might not mean tree branch, but... He said, warily, "Branch's clutch-brother is River? And there's another warrior called Drift?"

Jade nodded absently. "They were one of Amber's clutches. The other two clutch-mates were consorts, but they didn't survive. Why do you ask?"

Moon considered not answering, but he didn't owe River any favors. "My first day at the colony, River and Drift told me to leave."

Jade tilted her head, eyes narrowing in annoyance. "Did they." She looked out across the dark forest. "River is one of the warriors who sleeps with Pearl."

That... somehow isn't a surprise, Moon thought. It certainly explained River's attitude.

Still sounding irritated, Jade said, "Queens and consorts always have warrior and Arbora lovers; that's not the problem. And it isn't as if I think she should be alone. But with Pearl's consort dead, it's as if River thinks he's taken that place. He's not a consort, and sleeping in her bower doesn't give him a higher place in the court."

Moon had noticed that sex among the Arbora seemed informal, and he had assumed it was that way among the Aeriat as well. When Moon was younger, he had always made it a point to try to figure out the local customs. It had taken him some time to realize that just because someone offered to have sex with you didn't mean he or she was supposed to or that accepting wouldn't get you killed. But every groundling settlement had different rules, and often there were different customs even within individual tribes and cities, and after a time he had just given up on it. It was something else that had made the Cordans' camp an easy place to live; it had all been decided for him.

"The last place I lived, the elders chose who lived together. People didn't always listen," he added, remembering the rumor about Kavath and Selis' cousin. "But it mostly worked out."

Jade hesitated, her claws working absently on the wooden platform. "Stone told me he found you living in a groundling settlement." She tilted her head, watching him directly. "Was it very hard to leave?"

"In a way." Moon couldn't keep the irony out of his voice; Stone obviously hadn't told her the whole story. "One of the women I was living with saw me shift, and thought I was a Fell. She poisoned me and told the others. They took me up into the jungle and staked me out to die." He heard her startled hiss, and finished, grimly, "They were Cordans. The Fell moved across their land, from city to city, town to town, killing and eating and moving on. They have reason to be afraid."

She was still a moment, watching him. "You're defending them."

Moon bit his lip and said nothing. He couldn't defend them, but he didn't want to listen to anyone else condemn them, either. Until you had seen a groundling settlement ravaged by the Fell, you couldn't understand. "If she hadn't seen me, I'd still be living there."

Jade shook her head a little. "But would you be happy?"

When Moon left the Indigo Cloud court, it would be so people wouldn't ask him questions like this anymore. Being warm, dry, able to find food, shelter, in friendly or at least not openly hostile company, were the only things that had ever mattered. He said, "That was never the point."

She was quiet for so long he thought she would leave. Moon couldn't see the point in talking to him, either. Then he felt a gentle touch, as Jade drew her fingers through his hair.

The touch moved to the back of his neck, drifting over the vulnerable skin that Pearl had scratched. Her hand slid down his back, and he realized she was giving him time to escape. But when she pressed against his side, he leaned into her warmth.

She brushed her cheek against his. In Arbora form her softer scales had the texture of rough velvet. Every muscle in his body went tense, heat coiling through him. *You told yourself you weren't going to do this,* he thought. Except it was hard to hold to that with Jade's arm around his waist, her breath in his ear, her teeth gently nipping the back of his neck. And if he didn't stop now, he wasn't going to stop.

He jerked away from her, scrambling to his feet. He rasped out, "I can't," and shifted. He leapt up and away, clinging to the mast for a moment before pushing off.

He landed on the cabin roof with a loud thump. Chime, lying on the warm wood in groundling form, started and blinked at him. "What's wrong?" he asked sleepily.

"Nothing." Moon folded his wings and started to sit down.

Then Jade thumped down onto the planks. Badly startled, Moon went into a defensive crouch. Chime yelped and curled into a ball, arms over his head. Jade whispered rapidly, "I'm sorry, I didn't mean to do that. But it's just that you're *here.*" She hissed in frustration and leapt into the air.

Moon eased back to sit down and shifted to groundling. Chime sat up, breathing hard, one hand pressed to his chest. He gasped, "I thought you were going to fight."

"No. Not fight." Moon didn't intend to explain further.

From somewhere below, he heard Niran's voice, demanding wearily, "What are they doing up there?"

After a time, Chime grumbled and lay back down, moving around, trying to get comfortable again. He had just settled down when Moon heard a rush through the air as someone glided over. Root landed lightly on the cabin roof and folded his wings. Sounding embarrassed, he said, "Jade threw me off the other boat. Can I stay here with you?"

"No," Chime snapped.

"If you're quiet," Moon told him.

Root shifted to groundling and curled up on Chime's other side, despite Chime's hissing at him. Moon wasn't sure if Jade was fed up with Root or just fed up with male Raksura in general.

His reaction to her had caught him off guard, frightened him. Self-control, making decisions and sticking to them, had always been important to his survival.

Since the moment he had met Stone, he felt like he didn't know what he was doing. He couldn't afford to be like this.

The ship was quiet, nothing moving near them except the wind, but it was a long time before Moon could relax enough to lie down and sleep.

The next day dawned cool and damp, with gray clouds obscuring the sky and ground mist winding through the trees below. Moon managed to communicate to the others, even Chime, that he preferred to be alone, and went up to sit on the railing of the prow. From there he could watch the forested valleys roll by under the ship.

The trees were tall with heavy foliage at the very top, with clumps of dark blue fruit. Big crab-like creatures with colorful shells clung to the top branches, eating the fruit. They were smaller than branch-spiders, but Moon found the resemblance close enough. They might be good to eat, though.

Absorbed in the view, he was still aware that one of the Islanders had come to sit on the deck ten paces or so behind him. He didn't realize it was Delin until he heard the rustle of paper. He looked to see the old man sitting cross-legged, a light wooden tablet braced on his knees, sketching something with close concentration.

Moon hopped down to go look at it. He could scratch out the characters for Altanic and Kedaic in ways that were readable, but he had never been able to draw an image that even he could recognize. He crouched beside Delin, studying the sketch. It was the ship's prow, with someone perched on it, and it took him a long moment to realize who it was. "That's me?" He had seen his groundling form in clear water or glass or polished metal, but never from the side like this. Stone was right—he was all skin and bones.

"It is." Delin smiled, adding a last few strokes with the charcoal stick. "I will add it to the book, and title it 'Moon, Consort of Indigo Cloud.'"

He wanted to be in the book, but it should be the truth. "Maybe just title it 'Moon.'"

Delin's look was thoughtful. "You are not of the same court as the others?"

"No. I'm just… visiting." There was no reason to say anything more, but Moon found himself admitting, "I don't have a court."

"I thought your people did not live alone."

Moon shrugged. "They don't, apparently."

Delin nodded, taking that in. "I have read that young consorts are usually shy creatures, who do not venture far from their homes." Moon couldn't help a derisive snort. Delin added, with a touch of irony in his expression, "Perhaps they do not understand you."

He was probably right, and it probably worked both ways.

After a while Delin went below, and Moon went back to the view.

Towards afternoon they were over the hills and the heavier jungle. Moon thought they were nearly to the river, with only a short distance to go.

Then Chime, who was taking in the view from the top of the mast, called out, "Someone's coming!" Moon snapped around to look, and saw Chime pointed towards something ahead of them in the distance. A shape in the air headed their way. Moon shifted, standing up to taste the air. It was a Raksura.

Chime glided down from the mast to land next to Moon. "I can't tell who it is yet." He squinted into the distance, frowning. "I don't know why they're sending someone to us. They should know we're on the way."

Good question, Moon thought. Either Balm and Branch hadn't arrived, or... something else had.

The warrior finally drew close enough for Chime to identify him as a young male called Sand. Jade, Root, and Song were waiting with Moon and Chime by the time Sand landed on the *Valendera*'s deck. He shifted to groundling, breathing hard from what must have been a hard, fast flight, and said to Jade, "Stone said not to bring the groundling boats any closer. The Fell have been to the colony again."

Jade's spines were already flared with agitation. At this she went deadly still. "What do you mean 'been to the colony?' They attacked?"

Sand shook his head hurriedly. "No, no. A ruler came again, with dakti. Pearl wanted to let them in to talk, but they wouldn't. Flower said it was because they knew Stone was there. Then they left."

Chime hissed; he looked sick. "You could have said that first."

Moon looked away, keeping the relief off his face. *Not too late; just hovering on the edge of disaster. As usual.* He turned back to Sand. "Who knows about the wind-ships? Who did Balm and Branch tell?"

Sand looked uncertainly from Jade to Moon. "Just Stone and Flower, and me, so I could carry the message. They said not to tell anyone else." He turned back to Jade. "Stone wants you to leave the boats out here and come in to meet him at the Blue Stone Temple."

Chime told Moon, "That's near the valley where we went hunting."

Jade's tail lashed. "Good. We'll need a chance to make plans." Moon hoped she meant, *make plans so that we can load the ships without giving Pearl a chance to tell the Fell about it.*

"What are we going to tell the Islanders?" Song asked, looking around the deck. They had been speaking in the Raksuran language, so no one had overheard. All three ships had stopped, and the *Dathea* and the *Indala* had drawn up alongside the *Valendera*. The crews were out on deck, waiting for news.

"The truth," Jade said. She turned to where Delin, Niran, and Diar waited near the deck cabin.

They took the news well, though Niran folded his arms and looked as if this was no more than he had expected. But as Delin pointed out, if there were no danger from the Fell, then none of them would be here in the first place.

Diar seemed undisturbed as well. She said, "We can rig the ships the same way we do for storms. We find a clearing and tie off to sturdy trees or rocks, then winch the ships down out of the wind."

"We'll send someone to you soon," Jade told her.

The Blue Stone Temple lay in the forest, just over the hills from the plain with the statues. It was a big square structure buried in the trees and half-covered by flowering vines. Made from solid slabs of stone, it was open on all four sides, with a large skylight in the flat roof. The large pool it was built over was its most unique feature. Its square edges had been softened by the forest's mossy carpet. The blue-tinted stone blended into the shadows under the trees, and Moon would have been hard pressed to find it on his own.

As they circled down to it, Moon caught a strong stench of death; a large bloated carcass of a waterbeast floated in the pool.

As they landed on the temple's roof, Moon spotted Stone's distinctive shape dropping down out of the clouds. Two smaller shapes accompanied him.

"That's Balm and Branch," Jade said, sounding preoccupied. "If we can start the journey tomorrow…" She turned away and dropped down through the skylight into the temple.

Jumping down after her, Chime said, "I was thinking, if we can use the ships to cache some of our supplies away from the colony, then come back later—"

Root, Song, and Sand followed and Moon stood there a moment, shaking his head. None of them seemed to be thinking about what they were going to do about Pearl. They seemed to believe she would snap out of it once they got her away from the colony and her visits with the Fell.

He stepped over the edge of the opening and dropped down into the temple. Inside it was just a big empty space supported by square pillars, high-ceilinged and open. The light was tinted green by the screens of foliage, the stone stained dark with moss. The reliefs on the walls had been rubbed away by time and weather. Chime, shifted to groundling, was crouched on the paving, sketching out a map in the leaf mold while Jade, Song, Sand, and Root watched.

Moon walked toward the open side that faced the pool and stood at the edge of the platform. The water was dark green, thick with scum, the bloated waterbeast lying at the far edge. It looked as if something had killed it, dragged it here, then discarded it, and their arrival had driven away any scavengers. Insects skated across the water, but nothing else moved. The stench of the carcass was worse than the hunters' tanning court.

Moon shifted to groundling so his sense of smell wouldn't be as acute. If they were going to spend much time here, it might be worth it to try to move the thing, but if it fell apart it would be worse.

He heard the rush of air above as Stone arrived, and turned to see the dark shape dropping through the skylight. He carried Flower in one big talon. He set her down and shifted to groundling. As Flower shook her hair out of her eyes and straightened her smock, Balm landed beside her. "I'll keep watch up here," Branch called to them, looking down through the skylight.

"You've done it," Flower said to Jade, smiling. "We knew you would."

Jade smiled back. She had tried to seem matter-of-fact about all this, but now she couldn't help betraying a little pride over their achievement. She said, "So far. Now we're trying to think how to get everyone on the ships as quickly as possible, before the Fell return."

Chime looked up at Flower. "I thought we could get the hunters to cache the heavier supplies, maybe in the upper river caves. Then—"

Flower sat down opposite Chime to examine his map. Balm shifted to groundling and looked over her shoulder.

Stone stood apart, and Moon went over to him. He said, low-voiced, "They told you about the cloud-walker?"

"Yes." Stone kept his eyes on the others. "The Fell didn't come anywhere near the court until yesterday, and Pearl never left while you were gone."

Moon couldn't help feeling relieved. At least someone else was thinking about this. "But others did."

"Yes. A third of the warriors and probably half the Arbora, like they do every day." Stone's expression was ironic. "But most of them didn't know Jade was going to the Yellow Sea."

"And you trust the ones who did?" Moon persisted.

Stone admitted, "I used to."

Moon hissed in frustration. This wasn't going to work, no matter how clever Chime, Flower and Jade's plans were, unless they dealt with Pearl. And no one seemed to want to admit that Pearl needed dealing with. "When you get to the new colony she'll just—"

"Wait." Stone tilted his head, frowning. "Do you smell that?"

"Of course I smell that. Will you listen to me—"

"No, there's something else—"

Moon heard a rush of wings overhead and spun around, looking toward the skylight. It sounded like a number of Raksura, but Branch hadn't given a warning. He tried to shift... and nothing happened.

Startled, he looked at Stone. Stone muttered, "Oh, no. This is all we need."

Pearl dropped through the skylight and landed on the stone floor, her scales a burst of brilliant gold and indigo against the stained paving.

CHAPTER
TEN

cx

P earl stalked forward, her spines flaring. Half a dozen warriors landed behind her, shifting to groundling as they settled on the paving. Branch stood among them, as well as River and Drift.

Chime shoved to his feet, fell back a step, and threw a worried glance at Jade and Flower. Root and Song just looked confused. Everyone had shifted to groundling. Moon couldn't tell if that was automatic deference to Pearl or if she had used her queen's power to make them do it, the way she was keeping Moon from shifting back to Raksura. Jade just folded her arms and looked frustrated.

Pearl bared her teeth. "So here you all are, speaking in secret."

Stone growled in pure exasperation. "Pearl, what are you doing?"

Desperate, Balm turned to Jade. "I didn't tell—"

"I know it wasn't you," Jade said quietly.

That was when Moon registered the guilt on Branch's young face. *Stupid, stupid little...* This was like a bad joke.

"Branch." Flower didn't raise her voice, but Branch flinched. "It was your idea to come here. Balm said we should meet at the cave above the Bird Valley, but you said this was better because it was further away." She lifted a brow. "You fooled us very easily. We didn't suspect a thing."

Helplessly, Branch turned to Pearl. The queen said, "He was being loyal."

"Loyal?" Jade's spines flared. "We have to speak in secret because you keep telling the Fell everything we do!"

Pearl rounded on her in fury. "I've told the Fell nothing!" she snapped. "I'm trying to buy time." She turned to glare at Stone. "By not letting them in to talk you've made them suspicious and more likely to attack." Her gaze went to Moon. Her lips drew back in a sneer as she paced toward him.

Moon circled warily away from her, knowing better than to let her get within arm's reach. His skin itched with the urge to shift, but he was trapped in groundling form. He saw River, standing back with Branch and the other warriors, smile derisively. Pearl stopped as Moon backed away. She tilted her head at Jade, saying, "So you didn't take him yet. Having second thoughts about polluting our bloodline with a stray?"

Jade hissed between her teeth. *How does she know that?* Moon thought incredulously, torn between humiliation on his part and fury on Jade's. It wasn't as if she hadn't tried.

"Buy time?" Stone repeated. "How? The Fell want to kill us all—"

Pearl shook her head. "That's not what they want."

In pointed disbelief, Jade said, "Then what do they want? Tell us. I'm sure we'll be fascinated."

"Fascinated isn't the word." Pearl hesitated, then drew in a sharp breath. "They want to *join* with us."

Everyone stood there for a moment, still with surprise. A rustle of confusion flitted through the warriors, though none of them dared to speak. Even River and Branch and the others closest to Pearl looked uncertain, as if they hadn't heard this before, and wished they weren't hearing it now. Moon thought, *That can't mean what I think it means.*

Flower stepped up to stand next to Jade, her expression caught between incredulity and dismay. She said, "The Fell told you this? When?"

"Not long ago. The first time they came to the colony," Pearl said. Under the concentrated stares of Stone, Jade, and Flower, her spines seemed to droop a little. River and her other warriors didn't look so confident anymore. Branch looked sick.

Stone shook his head, unwilling to understand. "By join, do you mean eat? Because…"

"No." Pearl lifted a hand to her head, and for a heartbeat she looked exhausted. "Their flight is failing too. They said their progenitor died a few months ago. That's when they first approached me."

Before this, Moon would have given a lot to see something that shocked Stone, but he didn't want it to be *this* something. Stone said, "You're saying they want to breed with us."

Pearl looked away.

The temple was quiet except for the buzz of flies from the pool. Even the trilling birdcalls from the forest seemed distant. Chime was the first to break the silence.

"That's not possible," he said, his voice thick with horror. He turned to Flower. "Is it?"

Everybody turned to Flower. She wet her lips, and said reluctantly, "It might be. The mentors who study the Fell have always believed that we came from the same source. That the similarities between us and the rulers are too pronounced to be coincidence."

Moon had a terrible realization, and he had to ask, "Stone, at Sky Copper, you said the clutches were missing?" Though he kept his voice low, it snapped everyone's attention to him as if he had shouted.

"I couldn't find the bodies of the royal clutch in the nursery," Stone answered, and rubbed his eyes. "The Fell took them."

Took them alive, Moon thought, sick. Alive as prisoners of the Fell.

"How could you… how could you conceal this?" Jade stared at Pearl, and her voice came out in a low hiss. "I should rip your heart out."

"I didn't say yes, you stupid little child. I'm not insane." Pearl bared her teeth. "But I didn't say no, either. I knew what would happen if I did." She stepped back, her tail lashing uneasily. "I didn't expect them to attack Sky Copper. I thought they just wanted us."

"Our nursery has Arbora and warriors, babies and fledglings." Flower looked ill and old, the skin of her face so pale and translucent Moon thought he could see her bones. She pushed her hair off of her forehead and paced away a few steps. "Sky Copper has… had at least one fledgling queen, and probably two younger consorts."

"Why didn't the Fell join with them then, if that's what they wanted?" Chime burst out. "They must need Arbora, too. Why destroy…" He hesitated uneasily. "Unless they made Sky Copper the same offer."

"And their queen said no," Pearl finished, watching them. "That's what I believe happened."

Stone stared at her in helpless dismay. "Why didn't you tell me this, Pearl? Or tell Flower or Jade, or Petal or Bone or Knell? You didn't think we had a right to know?"

"Because I knew you didn't trust me," she said wearily. "You'd just accuse me of treating with the Fell again."

Flower flung her hands in the air. "Pearl, I didn't accuse you of that until you let a Fell ruler into the colony to speak to you. You told me nothing!"

Pearl hissed at her. "There was nothing you could do. Nothing to be done. This was my burden to bear. You've said your scrying is useless. You can't see anything. None of the mentors can."

Flower turned away from her with an angry shake of her head.

"You could set a trap!" Moon shouted, unable to stand it a moment more. "You have something they want, so you make them think they have you and then you kill them. You don't negotiate, you don't let them…"

Pearl snapped around to face him, the barely restrained violence making him fall back a step. "You little idiot, you don't know anything!"

"Stop it!" Flower held up her hand. "All of you be quiet." Her head was cocked, as if she was listening intently. "Stone, there's something here."

Stone turned away from Pearl, scanning the empty temple. "Where?"

Moon looked around too, hampered by trying to keep Pearl in his peripheral vision. Nothing moved in the still air. Through the archway he could see the pool, a cloud of insects humming above the scummy surface and the carcass. "The water." The words came out before he finished the thought. The opaque water, that might be a pace deep, or twenty paces, thirty paces. The stench that concealed any trace of what might have passed through the temple…

Green water erupted from the pool as something huge burst up out of it. Moon dove sideways and shifted in mid-motion, even before he realized it was a major kethel.

It plunged up the steps, charging under the archway, and headed straight for Stone. Stone shifted into his Raksuran form just before it struck him, bowling him over backwards. Moon lunged for it as it passed, but a casual blow from the kethel's tail sent him flying, bouncing off the paving before he skidded to a stop. He lifted his head in time to see the kethel pin Stone against a pillar, and thought, *Pearl let us shift; she didn't know the Fell were here.*

Heart pounding, Moon rolled to his feet. Bodies sprawled on the ground; the kethel had knocked everyone across the temple, and some of them hadn't been quick enough to shift. He started toward Stone but someone shrieked a warning and he spun back to face the pool.

A second, smaller kethel heaved up out of the water and surged up the stairs into the temple. It ducked under the square archway and stopped. The horns studding its head were draped in fragments of the grasseater corpse that had concealed the Fell's distinctive odor.

Moon braced himself to leap for its throat, for the thinner scaled skin at the edge of its armored collar. He had to slow it down, give the others a chance to get away. Then he froze in shock. There was something on its chest, a bulbous, dark tumor, like the sac that had been attached to the cloud-walker's back. He had a heartbeat for the horrified thought, *Oh, tell me that's not...*

The sac split open as if sliced from the inside and dakti spilled out, ten or more. They dropped to the floor and bolted into the temple. The kethel grinned, the long jaw revealing a double row of fangs, and charged.

Then Jade hit the paving beside Moon, landing in a crouch. As the kethel lowered its head, sliding to a halt across the mossy stone, Moon darted to the left and Jade dove right. The kethel made a grab for Moon, whipping its head down, but he twisted away, feeling its talons brush against his furled wings.

Moon saw a flash of blue and gray pass over the kethel's armored forehead. The instant of distraction had allowed Jade to leap atop the creature's back. Snarling in fury, the kethel forgot Moon and reached up to claw at her. Moon lunged in, getting under its head, clawing up past the heavy armored plates on its chest. He ripped and tore at the softer scales of its throat. It shrieked in pain, but the wash of blood and ichor that flowed down its hide from above told Moon that Jade had just ripped out one of its eyes.

The big claws scraped at Moon from behind, catching in his wings and dragging him away. But Balm shot past him, leapt up to the kethel's throat to claw at the same spot, and tore at the jagged wounds Moon had left.

Moon ripped the disemboweling claws on his heels across the kethel's palm as he tore himself free. He leapt to the creature's shoulder, dodged a snap of its jaws, then swung atop its head.

He landed low on its skull and saw Jade climb back up the kethel's back; one of its wild blows must have knocked her off. Moon scrambled higher up the skull and got a precarious hold on the armored brow ridge, his claws slipping on the impervious scales. Looking down, he saw one of its eyes was half shut and leaking blood and pus, the lid ripped through. Keening in pain, the kethel twisted around to reach for Jade. Moon stretched forward and stabbed his hand into the remaining eye.

The convulsion flung him off. He slammed into the pavement. Stunned, he lifted his head to see the kethel reeling away, staggering back toward the archways out of the temple. *That's one,* he thought, and shoved to his feet.

Warriors were scattered around, locked in bloody fights with dakti. Others lay unmoving on the pavement. He saw a dakti tackle Song, but Chime leapt on it from behind, tearing it off her. The kethel still fought Stone, the two big bodies writhing in combat, black and red blood running over the temple floor. Pearl, atop the kethel's head, tried to rip at its eyes, but it kept its head down, its jaw buried in Stone's throat. Pearl couldn't get purchase. She must have worked a claw in somewhere, because the kethel let go of Stone to fling its head back and knock her away.

Moon lunged forward to take advantage of the opening, but something beat him to it, the white form of an Arbora. *Flower?* he thought in dismay, as she leapt straight into the kethel's jaws. It snapped down on her, then reared back. Convulsing, it flopped over backward.

Moon made the distance to it in two long bounds and landed beside it as the big creature stiffened and went still. Not quite still—the pockets of loose skin in its cheeks moved, as if something inside was trying to get out.

Moon yelled in alarm, grabbed the lower jaw, planted his foot on the upper, and shoved. With a crack, the stiff jaw unlocked and Flower spilled out of the kethel's mouth in her groundling form. She landed on her hands and knees, gasping. The jagged end of a long piece of wood had been driven into the soft flesh at the back of the kethel's throat.

Moon released the jaw and leaned over Flower. He had to take a harsh breath before he could speak. The stench coming from the dead kethel's gullet made his throat raw. He couldn't imagine how Flower felt after much closer exposure to it.

"Are you all right?" He hadn't seen the stick in her hands in Arbora form, and obviously, neither had the kethel. She must have snatched it up in groundling form and shifted with it, hiding it with the same magic that hid groundling clothes and weapons, then shifted back in the kethel's mouth. Moon didn't know whether to be impressed or horrified.

She nodded, gripping his arm for support and letting him help her stand. "I haven't done that in a while." She choked and leaned over to spit. "It's not a good idea. Stone?"

Moon turned, looking back, expecting to see Stone dragging himself upright. But he still lay where the kethel had dropped him, sprawled on his side on the temple floor. The kethel had torn rents in his scaled hide, and there was a bloody bite in his throat.

"Oh no," Flower whispered. Moon's heart contracted. He ran to Stone, barely pausing to rip apart a last wounded dakti that blundered into his way. He flung himself down, eye level with Stone.

This was the first time Moon had clearly seen Stone's face in his other form, without the blurring effect that he wore like a cloak. His eyes were as big around as Moon's head, slit in pain, and he panted through clenched fangs, a rough, desperate sound. Moon couldn't tell if Stone saw him or not.

Moon heard a step behind him and twitched around. It was Jade. She knelt beside him, laid a hand on Stone's cheek.

"His wings?" she asked, waiting tensely for the answer.

Flower had hurried around to Stone's back.

"Not broken," she reported. "He kept them folded."

Moon was relieved. If Stone had given in to the impulse to use his wings to try to lever himself up under the kethel's weight, it would have probably broken both, and that would have made his injuries even more devastating. If Stone hadn't been an experienced and canny fighter, he would be dead.

Flower circled back around Stone's body, anxiously looking over his wounds. "It's bad, but he can heal. He'll have to stay in this form. If he shifts, these wounds will kill him."

Jade started to speak but a sound shattered the air, a wail of heart-deep loss and pain. It froze Moon in place for an instant, sliced open a buried memory of blood and broken bodies.

Not far away, River knelt over a body, Drift crouched next to him. The figure was in groundling form, twisted and broken. Moon pushed to his feet and moved close enough to see the face. It was Branch.

The others gathered around. Root was limping. Song, Sand, and a couple of Pearl's warriors had bites and claw marks from the dakti. Chime had a gash across his chest, and Balm was so covered with kethel blood that Moon couldn't tell if she was injured or not. Pearl stepped in, knelt beside River, and carefully touched Branch's neck and face. Almost gently, she said, "He's dead, River. I think the first kethel struck him."

River made a noise again, a low moan of pain.

Jade hissed out a harsh breath. "Branch told you our plans, Pearl. What else did he do?"

Pearl stood, her claws working as if she wanted to use them on Jade. But she said reluctantly, "Branch was the one who brought me the first message from the Fell."

That's convenient, Moon thought, giving her a sideways look. But if Pearl had planned this trap, she wouldn't have let them shift to their Raksuran forms to fight. Much as he would like to suspect her, he couldn't get around that fact.

"Someone told the Fell we were meeting here," Jade said, a growl in her voice. "If it was Branch—"

"No!" River snarled at her. "Not Branch."

"After we got back to the colony and talked to Stone and Flower, I don't know where he went." Balm shook her head, appalled. "I went to rest... He could have left again..."

Pearl glared at Jade. "We'll deal with this later. We have to get back to the court. The Fell will already be there. All this was a ruse to get Stone and me away from the colony so they could attack."

"I know that," Jade snapped. She turned to Flower, who still sat beside Stone. "You'll stay with him?"

"I will." Flower nodded. "Send help when you can."

"The Islanders," Chime said suddenly. He turned to Moon. "If Branch was the one who betrayed us to the Fell—"

River rounded on him furiously. "It wasn't him!"

Moon ignored him. Chime was right. If Branch had told the Fell about the meeting here, then he would have told them about the flying boats. The Fell would know that groundlings were nearby and would search the area for them. He said, "I'll warn them."

"No." Pearl gave the order sharply, not bothering to look at him. "We need everyone to defend the court."

Moon tensed in rebellion. Pearl could mate with herself; he wasn't letting the Islanders die for her stubbornness and Branch's perfidy. But Flower said, "Let him go."

Moon turned to her. She was crouched on the floor, and her eyes were like mirrors, blind and opaque. She shook her head, suddenly normal again, the moment passing so quickly Moon thought he imagined it. She said again, "Let him go."

Pearl spat. "You're finally having a vision? Now?"

Jade just said, "Chime, go with Moon to warn the Islanders. Come to the colony as soon as you can."

Moon flew back to the ships at Chime's fastest pace. There was no sign of the Fell in this direction, but that didn't mean they were safe.

Against his will, he was seeing Pearl's situation from a different perspective now. He was beginning to think this had been the Fell's plan all along, to make the other leaders of the court distrust her. Stone, Flower, and Jade hadn't completely fallen for it, though Moon certainly had. But it had made them doubt her, perhaps kept Pearl from speaking to them until it was too late. It didn't mean Moon trusted her any more than before, but it would be a relief if she wasn't actively in the power of the Fell.

The tips of the ships' masts came into sight, barely distinguishable among the trees. Moon slowed and circled in. All three vessels were moored to the ground with heavy ropes, about forty paces above the jungle floor.

Moon landed on the deck of the *Valendera*, Chime not far behind him. As startled sailors hurried toward them, Moon shifted to groundling. They halted around him, staring. The Fell blood that had been on Moon's scales transferred to his clothes and skin. He felt punctures on his back and sides from the kethel's claws, sharp pain in his ribs from slamming into the temple's floor. Chime shifted, then winced and rubbed at the claw-slash on his chest.

Delin, Diar, and Niran pushed through the other Islanders, and Delin stopped, staring at the blood. The others looked aghast, but Delin only furrowed his brow. He said, "We were too late."

Chime flinched at that accurate assessment of the situation. "Yes. And the Fell know you're here. You have to run."

There were shocked exclamations from the crew gathered around. Delin swore in the Islander language, then said, "We must abandon the ships and hide. We can't outrun them."

That was what the Fell would expect, and that was what Moon was counting on. "The one who betrayed us never saw how many ships you brought. Take the fastest, put everyone on it, and run for the coast."

Delin's expression cleared. "Excellent."

"Oh, that's good," Chime said in relief. "When the Fell find the two empty ships they'll search the forest for the crew, and not look for a third."

Diar nodded agreement, obviously thankful to have an option that didn't mean certain death. "It's worth the chance. We'll take the *Dathea*." She turned away, shouting to the others. The crew scrambled to obey, some running for the ladders to the holds.

Niran drew breath to speak, and Moon knew he was going to say it was a trick to keep the boats. Moon was prepared to throw him onto the *Dathea;* they didn't have time for an argument. But what Niran said was, "I'll stay behind. If the Fell don't destroy the ships, I can try to take one back and—"

Delin turned to him in exasperation. "The Fell will search for us, and when they find you they will force you to reveal where we've gone. Then they will know to look for a third ship, and they will catch us all. And you will be dead for nothing!"

"We can't lose these ships!" Niran folded his arms, as if determined not to budge. "We can't afford to, and you know it."

"Can you even make it work by yourself?" Chime asked, waving a hand toward the mast and the complicated array of ropes.

Delin answered, "It's possible, but difficult and dangerous. He wouldn't be able to use the sails, only the forward motion of the sustainer, so progress would be slow. And if a storm came up, he wouldn't be able to drop the anchors and crank the ship down to the ground or tie it off, so it would surely be damaged by the wind."

"It's worth the chance," Niran said, stubborn as a rock. "If I can return with one—"

Moon barely managed not to hiss in frustration. "The Fell will eat you alive, and that's if you're lucky. Keeping your people away from them is the only thing that matters."

The Islanders, carrying packs and bags brought up from below, climbed over the railings onto the *Dathea*, while several men stood ready to cut it free from the other two ships. Diar turned back to listen to the argument, and said, "He's right, Niran, we must leave. We can build new ships."

"Not if we can't pay our debts." Niran shook his head. "I have to stay behind. Once they see we aren't here, they may leave."

Chime stared at him incredulously. "The Fell will find you, and even if they didn't, you couldn't survive on the ground in this forest, not alone."

Niran still looked unmoved, so Moon added, "If you stay behind, you'll have to come with us." There was no way Niran was going to agree to that.

Niran said, "All right, if I have to."

Before Moon knew it, it was settled. Delin hurried off to make sure his books and writing materials were moved onto the other ship, Niran went with him, and Moon cursed his own stupidity. Chime snorted and said in Raksuran, "Pearl's going to love this. She doesn't like groundlings."

"Pearl doesn't like anything," Moon pointed out. Maybe the Fell wouldn't destroy the ships once they found the Islanders gone. Anything was possible.

As the crews readied the *Dathea* to leave, Diar arranged a few details for verisimilitude. They hung a long rope ladder from the railing of the *Valendera* that dangled all the way down to the ground, as if this was the route the crew had used to flee. A few sailors climbed down and ran around in the ferny growth below the ships, breaking branches, leaving tracks and trampled plants. They also dropped a hastily gathered bag of bread and dried fruit, left a torn head cloth behind on a thorn bush, and pitched a couple of sandals down the hill into the thicker trees. Moon thought it would work. The Fell weren't ground trackers; they hunted almost exclusively by air, and since their prey was nearly always groundlings trapped inside buildings or on the open streets of towns or cities, he thought they would be fooled. He hoped they would give up quickly when they couldn't find the Islanders in the surrounding jungle.

It all took only a few moments, and they were done by the time Niran returned. He wore a sturdy cloth jacket and carried a pack. "I'm ready," he said. He looked more determined and angry than nervous.

The *Dathea* was casting off, and Delin waved from the deck. "Take care!" he shouted. "Send word to us when you can!"

Moon waved back, watching as the ship lifted up, turned, and headed back toward the coast.

Sounding miserable, Chime said, "The boats were a good idea. It would have worked. We could have moved the whole court. If we'd been a day sooner—"

"Then the Fell would have attacked a day sooner, or come after us," Moon said. There was no point in what-ifs. He turned to Niran. "You're going to have to trust us."

"I know." Niran sounded like he would rather do anything but.

As they flew over the jungle toward the colony, Moon knew it must already be under attack. They were flying into the wind and the stench of Fell was laced all through it, mingled with blood and dirt and the clean scent of the river.

They passed over a clearing, an area where a large fallen tree had flattened the other growth around it, and on impulse Moon circled back to land. Chime followed him, alighting on the piles of broken deadfall, setting Niran on his feet. Niran staggered sideways and sat down on a heavy branch, holding his head. "You fly much faster than I thought," he gasped.

Chime ignored him. "You smell it?" he asked Moon, twitching with worry. "We're too late."

Moon turned to Niran, speaking in Altanic. "The Fell are at our colony, we can scent them. I don't want them to see you; if they do it might make them look harder for the others."

Niran looked up at him, nodding ruefully. Even if he was still suspicious, he couldn't argue with this. "I'll wait here for you."

It was the best solution, but Moon didn't want to leave Niran on the ground alone. The Islander didn't know this territory, and if they couldn't return for him, he would be helplessly lost.

"Stay with him," he said to Chime. That solved a second problem. Moon had a bad feeling about what they would find at the colony, and maybe Chime didn't need to see it.

"What, you don't want me in the battle?" Chime said, uneasily.

That was part of it, too. "Just stay here," Moon said, and leapt into the air.

Past the next set of hills, the valley came within sight, and then the big step pyramid where it straddled the shallow river. Large, dark shapes flew in steady circles around it, like carrion birds over a dying grasseater—major kethel.

He had known they were too late, but it was still a sight to make his blood curdle.

Jade, Pearl, and the warriors stood on a bare hilltop, looking toward the colony. With them was a group of Arbora, a small group, only forty or so. *They can't be the only survivors.* Moon banked to land near Jade.

"Were you in time?" she asked, her eyes still on the kethel circling the colony.

"Yes." He didn't want to tell her the plan, not where others could hear. Moon looked over the Arbora, and his throat tightened. There was Bone, the old hunter with the scar around his neck, but he didn't see Petal, Bell, Rill, Knell or any of the others he knew. There were no children, and they didn't look as if they had been in a fight. Most of them were hunters, still carrying rolled nets and short spears.

"Good." Jade hissed through her teeth. "Where's Chime?"

"I told him to wait for me. Do you know what happened?"

Sounding sick, Balm answered, "Bone and the others were in the forest when they saw the kethel fly in. They ran back to the river, but they met Braid and Salt and a few others who had been in the gardens, close enough to the colony to see what happened. They said that the first kethel brought smaller Fell, rulers or dakti, to the top of the colony. They started back inside to try to fight, but suddenly no one could shift. Knell was outside on the lower terrace. He shouted at them to run. Knell didn't follow. He must have stayed to try to gather the soldiers." Her voice was choked. "It doesn't make sense. They should have fought. Even if they were taken by surprise—"

"They couldn't fight, if they couldn't shift," Jade told her. "And the Fell would take hostages."

A few paces away Pearl stirred, her spines lifting uneasily. "Keeping them from shifting is a queen's power," she said. "How could the Fell have it?"

Jade shook her head slightly, the shocked stillness of her expression turning thoughtful. "They could have a queen. They could have the queen from Sky Copper. Stone said he never found her body, or any trace of her."

"Even a reigning queen couldn't keep the entire colony from shifting, not unless they were all together in the same room. It wouldn't affect the Arbora on the lower levels."

Balm's indrawn breath wasn't quite a hiss. "A ruler is coming this way."

A shape flew toward them. Behind him, Moon heard Root make a faint, frightened noise.

Jade said, with deadly emphasis, "Friend of yours, Pearl?"

Pearl's tail lashed once. "It's Kathras, the one that came to the court while you were wasting time on your pointless journey."

With a growl in his voice, Bone said, "You want to fight each other or face this thing?"

The ruler drew closer, riding the wind to land lightly only a short distance away. He folded leathery wings, and paced toward them through the tall grass, picking his way almost delicately.

"Kathras." Pearl greeted it, calm and even. "How did you do this?"

"They wanted to join us," he said. "We hold no one prisoner." He spoke the Raksuran language, like the dakti at Sky Copper. Moon had never heard a Fell ruler speak anything but Altanic before. The rigid bone crest behind the ruler's head didn't betray emotion the way spines or frills did.

His gaze moved over them, resting for a moment on Moon. Moon felt the scales on his back itch, the urge to raise his spines, the nearly overpowering need to rip the creature apart.

Jade watched Kathras with predatory calm. She said, "Who was your spy?"

Kathras inclined his head toward her. "Your new consort."

Moon hissed in pure surprise, then felt like a fool. He should have expected this; he was the obvious choice, the only newcomer to the court. He felt the others staring at him, but Jade just sighed.

"Predictable," she said, and added acidly, "I'm surprised you didn't say it was me."

Pearl ignored it all, her attention focused only on the ruler. "What do you want from us, Kathras?"

The cold eyes turned back to Pearl. "We have what we want."

"Arbora, sterile Aeriat. That's not what you want," Pearl said. Her voice took on a different tone, warm and low. She eased forward, focused on Kathras, and Moon felt intense heat brush past him, even though she was more than six paces away. It was a faint echo of the connection he had felt when he had first seen Pearl. She was trying to use it on Kathras, trying to pull him in, seduce him, the way she had Moon.

Pearl said, "You want a queen. You need a queen. Let the others in the colony leave, and you'll have one."

Kathras cocked his head. "They don't want to leave. Come into our colony. You will see that all is well."

Drift stirred, uncertain. "If one of us has to go—"

"No." Jade cut him off, not taking her gaze away from the ruler. "If you go inside, you won't be able to shift, and they'll have you, too."

Drift shook his head, helpless, anguished. "How do we know?"

"It's a trick, a Fell trick. It's what they do," Balm added in a hiss. "You think the others want to be trapped in there with them?"

"Drift, be quiet," Pearl said. Her eyes were still on Kathras. "Your plan won't work without a queen. You know you need me. Let the others go."

"When we seek a Raksuran queen," Kathras said, his fangs showing, "we will seek one of strong mind and body, fertile, and not so easily fooled."

Pearl lunged at Kathras, but he darted backward, avoiding her claws by a hairsbreadth. As if nothing had happened, he said, "Come whenever you wish. You will all be welcomed." Then he turned and leapt back into the air.

The warriors and hunters snarled. River crouched to launch himself after Kathras, but Jade said sharply, "No, idiot. We can't fight them now."

"She's right." Pearl watched Kathras fly away. She breathed as hard as if she had just been in a fight. "They can threaten to kill the clutches and fledglings, or just send a few kethel against us.

"We need to go, before they come after us."

CHAPTER ELEVEN

‌⁊

The hunters made a sling big enough for Stone's Raksuran form, and Moon and several Aeriat and Arbora carried him out of the temple and into the deep forest. They stayed on the ground, which made the going slow and difficult, but would make it harder for the Fell to track them. Two hunters followed the group, covering any sign of their passage, and another led the way, picking the best route through the undergrowth.

Dim and green, the failing light filtered through the heavy fronds forming the forest canopy, and the ground was thick with moss and tall ferns. The spiral trees curved up, more than a hundred paces high, their roots taller than Moon's head. It was quiet except for the distant birdcalls, the treelings chattering at each other. The others had all gone ahead to make a blind, something else the hunters were expert at.

Stone was still unconscious, his breathing almost too slow to detect. His wounds had stopped bleeding, but Flower had nothing with her, no medicines or even simples to help him.

Root, on the opposite side of the sling towards the back, stumbled on something and it jostled Stone. Moon hissed randomly at all of them. Stone being hurt had created a cold lump of fear in Moon's chest that had taken him by surprise. It wasn't just losing his best ally, or that Stone had seemed indestructible. Moon might not have been Stone's first choice to bring back to the court, but Stone had plenty of time to lose him along the way to Indigo Cloud if he had wanted to. It was a shock to realize just how much it meant that he hadn't.

"He'll be all right," Flower said, though Moon hadn't asked. She picked her way along beside him in her groundling form. "He'll heal faster while he sleeps like this."

"How long before he can shift?" If Stone shifted into groundling now, his wounds would kill him instantly.

"Several days, at least." She added, "We're going to need your help."

He glanced down to see her watching him intently. "I said I'd stay until you moved the court."

Moon was getting tired of having to repeat that promise. He had come here knowing he would have to fight Fell at some point, but that wasn't what frightened him. It was the other Raksura—they frightened him, confused him, made him feel threatened in vague ways he couldn't articulate even to himself. "Nothing's changed."

"That's good to know. But we're also going to need your help with Pearl and Jade." Flower's expression suggested that what she was about to say left a bad taste in her mouth. "If you could try not to provoke anything between them. There's a time for Jade to challenge Pearl's reign, but this isn't it."

"That's funny." It wasn't funny, though Moon was willing to admit to a certain bitter amusement. "Because I'm pretty certain Stone brought me here to do exactly that."

"We did have something like that in mind," Flower admitted. "And I, at least, was foolish enough to think that Pearl might be ready to end her reign and give way to Jade, once she was made to see that Jade was ready. That may be one of the reasons why she didn't tell me what the Fell wanted." Her tone turned rueful. "What a burden that must have been on her. And I just thought she was ill." She looked up at him again. "We didn't expect Pearl to want you, but then Stone and I are old enough to be long past that sort of thing. If the court had a clutch of young consorts, if Pearl was still used to having them around, your sudden arrival wouldn't have had that effect on her."

She had that wrong. Moon found it highly unlikely that Pearl wanted him for anything other than dinner. And if they had a clutch of consorts, he wouldn't be here. He would be picked-over, vargit-chewed bones. But arguing about it wouldn't help, and there was something else he wanted to know.

"Did you really have a vision that I should go warn the groundlings?"

"I don't make visions up, Moon," Flower said with some irritation. After a moment, she shook her head. "I'm not sure it was about letting you go to warn the groundlings. Visions aren't that specific, even mine."

Ahead, their Arbora guide swung down from a tree and motioned anxiously for them to follow. "It's this way."

As they wound through the trees, Moon was glad of the guide. The blind was hard to make out, even this close. The Arbora had used a low spot overhung by trees, and weaved deadfall branches and fresh greenery to make a roof and walls. They had moved rocks, and used large sections of the moss carpet, until the whole thing looked like a hillock buried in the forest.

Niran helped two female Arbora gather greenery for more concealment. He looked up as they approached, staring at Stone with wary curiosity.

The waiting hunters lifted a section of brush, and Moon and the others carried Stone into the shadowy interior. Flower slipped in ahead of them and, after some rustling, a fall of moss hanging from the roof branches started to glow, giving them enough light to set the sling down. The ground had been carefully cleared, scraped down to bare dirt. The Arbora had methodically removed the top layer of moss and ferns, and used it to conceal the roof of the blind.

The Arbora pulled the open section back into place, restoring it with quick adjustments and repairs to the dislodged greenery. The only light was the dim white glow of the spelled moss. Moon knelt beside Stone's head, making sure he was still breathing. He thought he saw the dark eyelid shiver, but couldn't be sure.

Flower crouched beside him and tugged at his arm. "Come on, the others are making plans. We need to be there."

Moon didn't think Pearl and her supporters would feel that he needed to be there at all, but he had thought of something he needed to tell them. He hesitated. "Who'll stay with him?"

"Blossom and Bead." She nodded to the two female Arbora who were showing Niran how to wind greenery into the blind. Bead was young, but Blossom showed some signs of age, with threads of gray in her dark hair. "The only teachers to escape. And we'll put the older hunters in here. They're experienced at tending the wounded."

Moon followed her reluctantly.

The blind already had partitions, screens of woven fronds, dividing it into chambers. As Flower led the way through, Moon's spines kept catching on the woven branches and vines, so he shifted to groundling.

Somewhere nearby, Chime said impatiently, "No, that won't work. If we try to get inside the colony, we'll be caught by the same power that's keeping the others from shifting."

Balm's voice was tense with frustration. "Even if we could shift once we were inside, there's just not enough of us to fight all those Fell. We need help."

Flower stepped through an opening small enough that Moon had to duck to follow her. This part of the blind was still partially open to the outside and braced against the rough gray wall of a plume tree's trunk. Besides Chime and Balm, Jade, Pearl, Bone, and River sat on the bare ground. The others were in groundling form, and Jade and Pearl had shifted to Arbora. Pearl sat back against the wide column of a root, her body tense, her tail wrapped around her feet. Her usually brilliant blue and gold scales seemed dimmed, muted. Jade sat across from her, and Moon was struck by the sight of her face in profile, her long jaw tight with tension, her eyes narrowed. She sat with her arms propped on her knees, every muscle coiled with seething frustration. She wanted to challenge Pearl. That was obvious to him, and had to be obvious to everyone here. But she knew this was no time or place for it. The court had to be united under one queen and Pearl was it, whether they liked it or not.

Jade looked up and their eyes met. Moon was caught for an instant, then managed to look away. After a moment, she asked, "How is Stone?"

"Still the same." Flower stepped around to sit next to Chime, tugging her skirt over her moss-stained feet. "We just need to keep him still and warm, until he heals."

Moon sat next to Flower, hoping Pearl would just pretend he didn't exist. But she watched him, her blue eyes cold. With an ironic air, she said, "So tell us. How did the Fell know you were new to the court?"

Moon considered pointing out that one of Pearl's warrior friends who was a Fell spy could have reported it. Instead he said, "They saw me at Sky Copper, with Stone. A ruler spoke through one of the dakti."

Bone nodded. "Stone told us of that. These must be the same rulers that destroyed Sky Copper, not that there was much doubt about it."

"And we know the Fell share memories." Flower leaned forward, flattening her hands on the ground. "The ability seems to come from the way they breed. There are only a few females, progenitors, who mate with the rulers. Rulers born of the same progenitor have a close connection to each other. They can speak through each other, see through each other's eyes." She looked at Moon, lifting her pale brows. "The rulers are said to be able to influence some groundlings. Have you seen that before?"

"Yes." Moon rolled his shoulders uncomfortably. He had seen it from far too close. "Do you think that's what this ruler did to Branch?"

Flower started to answer, then flicked a look at Pearl. "Maybe."

River snarled, a full-throated sound despite his groundling form. "It wasn't Branch."

That was actually what Moon was most afraid of. He told River, "If it wasn't him, then whoever it was is still with us."

River tilted his head, leaning forward. "The Fell said it was you."

Bone snorted. "'The Fell said.' Warrior, listening to anything the Fell say will get you killed."

Moon pointedly turned to Jade, hoping River would go for his throat and give Moon the excuse to kill him.

"The poison I told you about, that the Cordans gave me—it kept me from shifting until it wore off. They said it was for Fell. Have you ever heard of anything like that?"

"No." Jade looked startled. "You think this poison is how the Fell kept the court from shifting?"

"Maybe. The hunters said Knell called a warning. When the Cordans gave it to me, I didn't even remember falling unconscious." Moon couldn't think of a way that the poison could be spread through water or air that wouldn't have affected the Arbora working just outside the colony as well. "Stone said he had never heard of it either."

"You brought a groundling here," River said, making it sound like an accusation. "Does he know of this mythical poison?"

Moon had to let a little of his derision show. "All groundlings don't know each other."

"We can ask," Jade cut across River's reply. "But it's doubtful. When I spoke to the Islanders' leader, the only defense they seemed to have against the Fell was the distance the islands lay from shore."

Balm watched Moon carefully. "Why did these Cordans poison you?"

Well, somebody would have to ask. Moon shrugged, as if it barely mattered. "One of them saw me shift. She thought I was a Fell."

"There's a coincidence," River put in sourly.

Chime leaned forward. "To untutored groundlings, our consorts look like Fell rulers." He added, pointedly, to River, "You may not have realized this, since you aren't actually a consort, despite your sleeping habits."

"Chime." Balm reached over and caught his wrist, giving him a meaningful look. Chime pressed his lips together and sat back reluctantly. Bone passed a hand over his face and looked away. Jade just lifted a brow.

River ignored it all, looking at Pearl. "He could be lying. It could be as the Fell ruler said."

Moon was tired of hearing it at this point. "Of course it could. That's why the Fell said it."

River started to reply, but with a growl in her voice, Pearl said, "That's enough."

River looked as if he might argue, but after a moment, subsided uneasily.

Jade drew a claw through the dirt. "I'm wondering, if the Fell had this power to stop an entire colony from shifting, why haven't they used it before now? Raksura have fought Fell off and on since the Three Worlds first turned. Weakened courts have always had to be wary of attacks, but nothing in our histories has ever mentioned anything like this."

"Because it must be something new," Flower said, quietly.

"But they didn't try to use it on us at the temple," Balm said, with a glance at Jade. "So whatever it is, maybe there's only one of it?"

Pearl eyed Flower. "Too bad there was no warning of this new thing. No visions, no augury…"

Yes, that's helpful, Moon thought. *Let's share out the blame.* But with effort he managed to keep his mouth shut.

Flower's attention appeared to be on her toes, peeping out from under the ragged hem of her skirt. "For the past turn, my augury has said to follow Stone, to leave the colony and seek another to the west." She lifted her head and deliberately met Pearl's gaze. "Too bad no one listened."

The silence grew tight as wire, then Pearl looked away, her lips peeled back in a grimace. "I did listen. I didn't heed. That's on my head."

After a moment, Bone stirred. He said, bleakly, "We have a scatter of Arbora and a bare handful of Aeriat, to go against an entire flight of Fell who can keep us from shifting. If we attack as we are, we'll die." He looked from Pearl to Jade. "What about sending to another court for help?"

Jade flicked her claws. "It's probably not worth asking Star Aster, and they're the largest court we have contact with." She took a deep breath. "Sky Copper was our only close ally."

Bone grunted in agreement, but added, "We have blood relations with Wind Sun and Mist Silver."

Pearl's eyes went hooded. "Both are small, and too far away."

With more than a trace of irony, Jade said, "And both are unlikely to want to help us, especially Wind Sun."

Pearl's voice was icy. "Dust is second consort to a reigning queen. He has nothing to complain of."

Jade bared her teeth in something that wasn't a smile. "And if we ask Wind Sun's queen for warriors, whose voice will she give weight to: the consort who fathered two of her clutches or the queen who forced him out of his birthcourt for no reason?"

Pearl avoided her gaze, and said tightly, "I knew he would find a place there."

Jade persisted, "He was young and inexperienced and not as sure of that as you were. Now when we could use the help—"

With a hint of a growl in his voice, Bone interrupted, "You've made your point, Jade."

Jade ruffled her spines, but subsided.

After an uncomfortable moment, Pearl said, "But I think Wind Sun would give us refuge for the Arbora and the warriors, if asked."

Everyone went still, startled. Then Flower said slowly, "You think it's come to that?"

That it's come to giving up, Moon thought. Going away and leaving the Raksura trapped in the colony with the Fell, the Arbora and warriors, the clutches of babies, the fledglings. *Don't,* he wanted to say, *somebody will think of something. Give it time.* But he knew he couldn't say it in any way that wouldn't antagonize Pearl.

Pearl hesitated, then shook her head. "Not yet. Not until we know if the Fell are lying, if the others are already dead."

It was deep twilight when Moon left the blind. Two of the warriors, Drift and Coil, were on watch up in the trees, along with several hunters on the ground, but he wanted to take a look around the area himself. He shifted but didn't take to the air, walking among the ferns, tasting the breeze. He passed Root and Song under some tree roots, wrapped together while Root sobbed quietly on her shoulder. He must be mourning Branch, and the others trapped in the colony. Moon winced in sympathy, but didn't pause.

He made his way through the undergrowth, while the birdcalls and buzz of insects faded away with the green-tinged light. He stepped over a group of small, bright-colored lumps that looked like mushrooms. They all stood up and ran away on stubby little legs.

They had talked about a plan for one of the young hunters to try to get in through the openings under the colony's platform, where the structure crossed the river. That would at least tell them if the others still lived. If the hunter could bring someone out, or get some idea of what had stopped the court from shifting to fight or escape, it would be even more useful. Of course, if the young hunter vanished into the colony and never came back, it would tell them nothing, and they would lose yet another Arbora.

As Moon circled around to the west, he was conscious of the warriors up in the trees, of Drift's gaze following him, resentful and suspicious. Moon passed a hunter crouched among tree roots, the dark brown of his scales fading to invisibility against the wood. The hunter made a clicking noise in his throat. Moon nodded to him, not sure how to respond. A few steps later, a slight deliberate swish against the undergrowth told Moon another hunter was nearby. Then Bone stepped out of the ferns.

Bone walked along with Moon for a few paces. He looked up into the trees and said, deliberately, "We need everyone. Can't waste our blood fighting among ourselves."

Up in the branches, Drift tried to stare Bone down, failed, and retreated with a resentful hiss. Moon wouldn't want to fight Bone either, at least on the ground; though short, he was twice the width of the other Arbora and his throat scar showed just how tough he was.

"Can't argue with that," Moon said dryly.

Bone walked with Moon most of the way around the area then, with a grunt of acknowledgement, split off to rejoin the other hunters. Heading back toward the blind, Moon caught Jade's scent, and found her waiting impatiently just past a stand of reed-trees.

"You need a bath," she said, and motioned for him to follow her.

Moon had dried kethel blood on his scales, as well as the accumulated sweat and dirt of his groundling form, but he was sure there was a little more to her request than that. He followed her down the slope of the hill, through the trees to a little spring. Barely three paces wide and probably not more than knee deep, it cut through the forest floor among mossy rocks and waterweeds. Flower sat on the bank, leaning over the water to wash out a shirt.

Jade sat down near her, and Moon stepped past them into the stream. He scooped up the cool water and scrubbed it against his scales, aware someone else was nearby. Then leaves whispered overhead and Pearl climbed down the trunk of the nearest tree like a great gold insect, moving deliberately, in near silence.

She took a seat on the bank and coiled herself up. Moon gauged the distance between them and decided he was safe enough for the moment. Jade said softly, "We've agreed that we need to keep this conversation away from the others. We wanted to talk more about the poison."

Moon nodded. It might mean Pearl wasn't as sure of River and her other warriors as she pretended, or that she suspected they were somehow inadvertently betraying her. This way, it would at least narrow the suspects down to... *Me,* Moon realized. Well, the solution had the virtue of being multi-purpose. It lessened the chances that the Fell would find out about any plan involving the poison, and it gave Pearl the opportunity to get rid of him, both at once.

"I asked Niran about the poison," Flower said, frowning as she wrung water out of the cloth. "He had never heard of it. He said their exploring ships are always on the look out for such things, but that they haven't gone toward the far east for generations."

Flicking her tail in agitation, Jade asked Moon, "Did it work on all the Fell, rulers as well as dakti and kethel?"

"I don't know." Moon crouched down to splash water on his face, tipping his head back to let it trickle down through his spines and frills. He was too conscious of just how much he didn't know about the poison. "I didn't even know they had it until they used it on me."

Pearl's expression was opaque. "You said the Fell destroyed their lands. How well could this poison have worked?"

But Flower shook her head. "It depends on when they first started using it. Were the Fell still pursuing them?"

"Not while I was there." Moon hesitated, dripping, trying to remember the stories the Cordans had told about Kiaspur and the Fell attacks. "They had to abandon their cities, but the Fell didn't follow the refugees."

"Fell don't like to give up on prey, as we well know." Flower sat back to add the shirt to a pile of wet clothes on the bank. "If these groundlings didn't discover the poison themselves until the Fell had destroyed most of their territory, it may be what let them escape."

Jade leaned forward, her face intent, looking from Flower to Pearl. "We could put it into the river, so it's drawn up into the colony's water supply. Then we could go through and kill all the Fell."

Flower asked Moon, "I don't suppose you know how to make it?"

"No. If I brought some to you, could you make it?"

"I'd be able to tell what was in it. It just depends if we can get the ingredients." Flower squeezed the water out of her own skirt. "How far away is this place?"

"Stone and I flew from there in nine days, but he carried me the last day." Moon closed his eyes, trying to call up an image of the map they had looked at when they planned the journey to the Yellow Sea. On the way to Indigo Cloud, he and Stone had cut sharply north to stop at Sky Copper. A more direct route would save some time, avoiding the plains and taking them straight back to the Cordans' valley. *Call it eleven days.* "I can go there and bring some back."

Flower bit her lip, and said to Pearl, "This fits the vision I had, better than sending him to warn the groundlings. I think we have to do this."

Pearl said skeptically, "We're supposed to trust him to come back with this poison? How do we know he won't take the opportunity to run away?"

Moon controlled a hiss. "You don't. You just have to trust me."

Pearl turned her head to regard him coldly. "You haven't earned our trust."

Moon set his jaw. "You're the one who told me to leave."

Flower lifted a brow, and said pointedly, "Queens have a right to change their minds."

Pearl fixed an angry glare on Flower.

Moon hissed in annoyance. This was pointless. He would have liked to take Chime, both for the company on the journey and the help when it came time to figure out how to get the poison from the Cordans, but that wasn't possible. He would be flying at his fastest pace, and none of the warriors could keep up with him. "If I take a warrior, it would make the trip nearly twice as long."

Flower said, "But it would be safer to send someone with you. If you fail just because you needed another pair of hands—"

"Then we won't send him alone," Jade said, tense and frustrated. "I'll go with him."

From what Stone had said, a queen should easily be able to keep up with a consort. But her offer still gave Moon pause. He wondered if she suspected him of wanting to run away, or if the Fell Kathras' accusation had had more effect on her than it had seemed.

Pearl gave her a withering look. "So we should send the only other queen away?"

Jade bared her fangs in a grimace. "If we don't drive out the Fell and free the others, there's no court for either of us to be queen of. And yes, you mean to ask Wind Sun for help, but we both know how unlikely it is that they'll answer." She settled back on the bank, coiling her tail around, and added almost wearily, "I'm the sister queen. It's my task."

Pearl hissed out a breath, turning away. After a long moment, she said, "Our only other choice is to attack the colony now and die, or be caught like the rest of the court. That's what the Fell want us to do." She looked at Jade. "Go with him."

After they had talked out all the details, Moon crawled under some tree roots near the blind and shifted to groundling to try to sleep for a while. There weren't any more preparations to make. Flower had collected a pack for them containing a few supplies donated by the hunters, but all the collection amounted to was some fruit and dried meat, flints, and a couple of blankets. He was too jumpy to get much rest, and woke instantly when he sensed someone approach.

It was still dark, though he could feel dawn gathering on the horizon. It was nearly time to leave. He eased out of the roots and made out Jade's distinctive shape stepping silently through the moss and leaf loam. She paused to whisper, "I'll tell Flower we're leaving."

"I'll be here," he told her.

Jade vanished into the dark, and Moon made his way to the blind, easing between the bundles of brush.

The small knot of glow moss strung from the roof showed him Stone's still shape, the slow, deep rasp of his breath the only sign of life. Chime, several hunters, and the two teachers slept in here. Niran was against the far wall, wrapped in a blanket and snoring quietly. Fortunately, Chime was in the outer row of bodies, and Moon didn't have to step over anybody to get to him.

When Moon squeezed his shoulder, Chime snapped awake immediately, blinking nervously up at him. Moon put a hand over his mouth before he could speak, and nodded for Chime to follow him outside.

Some of the Arbora stirred sleepily, but no one sat up as they slipped out between the walls of brush. Picking his way through the dark, Moon found his hollow in the tree roots again, sat, and drew Chime down next to him. It was too dark to make out expressions, but maybe that was a good thing.

Moon knew the sentries were too far away to hear, but he still kept his voice to a low whisper.

"I need you to look after Niran. Make sure he has food he can eat and that, if you have to move, he's not left behind."

"I will, I'll make certain." Chime hesitated, his shoulder brushing against Moon's as he twitched uneasily. "There's been whispering that you and Jade are going to go somewhere, to get help. If that's not it, don't tell me. Then I can't be made to... If the Fell catch us..."

"The Fell aren't good ground trackers. They won't find you here." Moon hoped that was true, but showing doubt to Chime wouldn't help anything.

Chime slumped a little. "That's what Pearl is saying."

"She's not always wrong," Moon admitted, trying not to sound sour about it.

"We can hope." Chime took a sharp breath. Then he leaned close, and Moon felt warm breath and a sharp nip under his ear. Chime whispered, "Be careful," and scrambled away.

Moon listened to him make his way back to the blind. *This has to work,* he thought. *It has to.*

CHAPTER
TWELVE

Moon and Jade left before dawn broke and flew through the day like arrows.

They flew over the jungle, then hills, then the edge of the grass plains, heading toward the mountains. They pushed themselves hard, stopping only briefly to rest, and at the end of each day they were too exhausted to talk about anything except whose turn it was to hunt. Moon thought that was probably a large factor in how well they were getting along.

They were one day into the mountains when Moon started to have some concern about their route. They settled for the night on a ledge on a gentle slope, sheltered by trees made of hundreds of vines, winding around themselves to form tall straggly bundles.

Moon and Stone had come through these ranges at a different point, and the cold, the strong winds and the lack of game had made it a rough crossing. Now the view of the terrain that lay before them was nothing but endless, barren slopes, snow-capped peaks, and sharp cliffs. This way was more direct, but Moon thought that maybe they should have taken an extra day and entered the mountains further south, that maybe Stone had chosen that route for a reason. But it was too late now.

He was about to tell Jade his concerns when she lifted her head, tasting the air. "Fell." She snarled. "How are they following us? This is ridiculous."

Moon stood and took a deep breath, holding it to examine the scents. She was right, not that he had doubted; mixed in with rock, damp, the rank odor of the predators that prowled the nearby canyon, was the distinctive taint of Fell. He suppressed a growl, since Jade was doing enough of that for both of them. "They must have seen or scented us when we left the valley."

Except that didn't seem possible. The Fell shouldn't be able to track them by scent; they were flying downwind. And no one could have betrayed them. The others hadn't seen them leave, and Flower and Pearl didn't even know which way the Cordans' settlement lay.

Jade tapped her claws on the rock. "Or..." She grimaced. "The Fell seemed to have a queen's power over the court. They couldn't shift to fight or run. This is like a mentor's power, the power to point the Fell in the right direction to find us, to see us in visions."

That idea made Moon's skin crawl. But he didn't want to give up. For one thing, he still hadn't thought of any better way to attack the Fell in the colony than the poison. And it wasn't just the Indigo Cloud court that needed saving. He thought about all the groundlings he had met over the turns, all the cities and settlements. The Fell had already caused enough death and destruction. If they were actually getting worse, somehow becoming more powerful, he couldn't imagine what that would be like. "We're close. Once we get past the mountains, we're there."

"Yes, I think we should go on." Jade rolled her shoulders and settled her frills. "Maybe I'm wrong. Maybe the Fell just saw us leave, and have been lucky enough to track us. If that's so, we should be able to lose them in the mountain currents."

Moon hoped she was right.

They were only halfway through the mountains when the sky turned against them. They had to fight the wind, and the clouds closed in to weep cold rain and ice. Moon thought this was probably the reason Stone had taken the more southern route. Their only hope was that the Fell following them was something less than a major kethel. If that were the case, then it would be just as affected as they were.

After two more days fighting the cold and the wet, they were both exhausted. Then in the late afternoon, Moon caught the hint of wood smoke, and a more acrid scent of hot metal, as if there was a large working forge somewhere upwind. On impulse he followed it. The slopes below them were all barren rock, and wood smoke meant trees and a sheltered valley that might give them some relief for the night.

It was nearly evening when the smoke led them over a pass, and Moon was startled to see the source. Between two peaks, ringed by crags and cliffs, was a groundling city.

It was like a small mountain itself, but made of metal as well as stone, built on a giant circular plateau that seemed suspended in the pass. The buildings were made of heaps of raw stone, forming odd-sized towers, supported by discolored metal beams. In the failing daylight, lamps glittered from windows, and smoke and white steam drifted up from hundreds of chimneys. Moon could make out the shapes of groundlings moving in the narrow streets, but he thought his eyes betrayed him because the city, the whole giant plateau, seemed to be slowly turning.

Moon cut in toward the nearest crag and landed on a ledge where he could get a good view. From this angle, he could see that the plateau beneath the city was probably two or three hundred paces tall, and the edge was studded by thick, heavy pillars, like the spokes of a wheel. Water rushed out from under it, a great torrent falling down to a narrow lake below. The platform wasn't a natural plateau but a giant wheel lying on its side, turned by the force of the water. *That's new,* Moon thought, impressed with the groundlings' ingenuity.

Jade landed next to him, breathing hard from the icy wind.

"What is this place?" She leaned forward, squinting. "And why is it moving?"

Moon shook his head. "I don't know. I've never heard of it."

The city lay right in the path of a pass, and a wide road led up to it, carved out of the rocky side of the cliff. The bulk of the city kept Moon from seeing exactly how the road reached the platform, but there must be some sort of bridge or stair. Several parties of groundlings made their way up the road, probably trying to reach the city before nightfall. A dark shape moving along resolved itself into a blocky, square wagon drawn by furry draughtbeasts, not unlike the ones the Sericans had used to travel the grass plains. Then Moon caught a flash of dark blue from the wagon box and thought they must be Sericans, or a race very similar.

Despite its odd situation, every indication suggested this was a trading city, where travelers felt safe taking shelter. Moon let his breath out in frustration, his bones aching from the damp cold. If they could go down there, buy food and a place to sleep for the night, they might be able to fly far enough to make it out of the mountains and into the warmer valleys by evening tomorrow. But

Jade could only shift to Arbora, not groundling like Moon and the others. He stared at her, realizing, "You don't look like a Fell."

She eyed him. "Thank you."

"I mean, it's me that's the problem." Moon's black scales made him resemble a Fell too closely for groundling comfort. Jade's scales were blue and gray, and in her Arbora form, without her wings and most of her spines, she would just look like a groundling from another race. Granted, most groundlings didn't have scales and tails, but at least no one could point and say, "Fell." All she had to do was not shift where anyone could see her. He took her hand, looking at her rings. "Would you trade one of these for food and a warm place to sleep tonight?"

Her brow furrowed in surprise. "I'd love to. Is that possible?"

Moon looked down at the city again. "Probably."

They waited until night filled the valley before they flew down to land among the rocky outcrops below the road. Moon shifted to groundling and Jade to Arbora, and they walked up the steep path, the lights of the city guiding them in.

The ice-laden wind was biting and the frozen mud and loose rock crunched underfoot. Moon carried their pack, and Jade wore a blanket as a wrap, tied at her shoulder. Some groundlings had nudity taboos, some didn't, but wearing nothing in this weather would attract unwanted attention. He had also had her take off all her jewelry, her rings, bracelets, and belt, and bury it in the bottom of the pack, except for the amethyst ring they meant to trade. There was no point in attracting trouble.

As the road curved around, they passed metal stands supporting torches that hissed and steamed from the ice in the air, the warm light illuminating the road ahead. Drawing closer to the edge of the platform, Moon heard the massive creak of gears, audible even over the rush of the waterfall below. The pillars supporting the city platform were huge, but mostly lost in shadow. Moon and Jade were too far below it to see much of the city itself, except for the looming columns of rock towers. Once they climbed high enough, Moon could see that the road continued on through the pass, disappearing into the dark. But at the top of the slope, a wide metal bridge, supported with stone columns, crossed a narrow gorge to the platform.

It didn't go all the way across; it stopped just before the edge of the platform, which was protected by a stone and metal wall. Apparently you had to wait until the platform rotated around to an opening in the wall before you could cross over to the city. A group of groundlings waited on the bridge. A man at the end acted as gatekeeper.

The groundlings were all bundled up in furred hides or heavy knitted cloth, waiting with varying degrees of impatience or resignation for the next gate to come around. They were tall people, heavily built, with frizzy gray-brown hair not much distinguishable from their fur hoods and cloaks. They also had heavy tusks or horns curving down below their chins.

The bridge was wide and spacious, so Moon walked out onto it. Jade followed him. It was sheltered from the wind, though not from the icy drizzle. The torch-stands lit the rocky gorge below, the silver-gray curtain of water tumbling down. The other travelers huddled in on themselves against the cold and didn't take much notice of the new arrivals.

Moon walked up to stand beside the gatekeeper to get a better look. The platform moved with grating slowness, but he saw an opening in the outer wall rotating toward them. There must be many openings, otherwise the city's platform wouldn't be accessible for half the night. The gatekeeper, bundled against the cold, waited patiently. Moon had to ask, "The water makes it turn?"

Jade leaned in to listen as the man, with the air of replying by rote, said, "There's a special sort of rock in this pass. The water turns the wheels, grinding the rock, and the movement makes the rock give off heat, and the heat is used to make steam." Like most of the others, he had smooth brown skin, deep-set eyes, a heavy forehead ridge, and bushy brows. His tusks were very white, yellowed only on the ends. He turned toward them and did a slightly startled double-take at their appearance. But they must not have seemed too out of the ordinary, because he added, again by rote, "To find the caravanserai, follow the outer ring around to the wagon path, then head in toward the center of the city. It's the widest path. You can't miss it."

"Thank you," Jade told him. She added, in Raksuran to Moon, "What's a caravanserai?"

"A place we can pay to stay the night," Moon told her absently. This close to the city, he was beginning to feel jumpy. He had been around Raksura long enough to fall into their habits: shifting whenever he felt like it, hissing when he was startled or angry. He hoped it hadn't hurt his ability to pretend to be a groundling.

They waited, and finally the opening in the outer ring grated into place, matching platforms with the bridge. The keeper opened the gate, saying, "Hurry now, step carefully!" and everyone moved across.

Moon and Jade followed the others. The outer ring was just inside the platform wall, a wide corridor along the edge of the city paved with stone and metal squares. Narrow streets led off into the interior, all lined with the tall rock buildings supported by metal girders, discolored with rust. More torch-stands lit the streets. The buildings had little round windows sealed with thin hide or what might be paper. Firelight shined through, giving the houses a lively look even though most of the inhabitants must be huddled inside against the cold. Moon caught enticing scents of cooked meat and boiled roots as they walked past.

The other travelers all took the narrower streets, but none seemed to be the wagon path the gatekeeper had described. Finally Moon spotted it, a wide opening more than large enough for the big Serican wagon he had seen earlier.

As they turned down the street, Moon saw a number of people ahead gathered around a doorway, a cave-like opening into a dim, smoky chamber. As they reached it, Moon paused, catching a glimpse inside. A groundling was sprawled on the floor, another was drinking from a ceramic bottle, and more forms were lost in the dimness. "In there?" Jade asked, eyeing the place doubtfully. "It stinks."

It did stink, of some kind of drugged smoke, and it looked like it was a place for locals. "No, not there."

As they moved on, the street got busier, with more lighted doorways, more groundlings moving from one place to the other, talking and laughing. Moon and Jade weren't the only strangers. Almost everyone was bundled up against the cold, but Moon caught sight of groundlings with bright green skin, and a whole group whose heavy fur coverings appeared to be at least partially attached to their bodies.

A few people glanced at them as they passed, but the looks seemed more curious than hostile. Music came from the windows above them, drums and something that made a high-pitched wailing noise. As they passed some of the doorways Moon felt rushes of warm, steamy air, heady promises of comfort, if the gatekeeper was right about the caravanserai.

Then at the next bend, a big, tusked groundling lurched out in front of them. Thinking it was an accident, Moon moved to step around him. But the man shoved forward, barring his way.

Moon didn't flinch, just met the man's belligerent gaze and snarled under his breath. The man's tusks had a complicated design carved into them, the shallow grooves filled in with black ink, and his fur coat gave off a smoky, sweet stink. More groundlings gathered around the nearest doorway, watching with suppressed laughter.

The man faltered when Moon didn't give way, then glared and rocked forward, lifting a hand.

Jade stepped forward and caught his arm, effortlessly shoving him back. Her fangs were slightly bared, just the tips showing over lips curled with contempt. The groundling stumbled, staring blankly, bewildered by her strength. Moon snorted, partly in bitter amusement; the groundling would have been even more startled if she had ripped his guts out. Before anything else could happen, Moon caught Jade's wrist, shouldered past the groundling, and tugged her after him.

No one followed. Tracking the movement behind them, Moon heard laughter and some imprecations, but most of it seemed to be directed at the groundling man for being stupid enough to test strange travelers.

Jade bristled and walked like she wanted a fight. After a moment, she rolled her shoulders, making her spines and frills relax. Reluctantly, she asked, "Was that the wrong thing to do?"

Moon shrugged a little. "Maybe, maybe not." It was always hard to tell if it was better to meet a challenge like that and fight, or give way. "We won't be staying long enough to find out."

The street widened out into a round plaza, with more passages leading off between the tall rock towers. The Serican wagon stood parked to one side, a few Sericans in heavy embroidered coats wearily unloading it, their indigo skin and dark hair catching reflections from the firelight. The furry draughtbeasts had been released from their harnesses and lay beside the wagon in a comfortable huddle. One of them lifted its massive head, and the beady eyes half-buried in fur glared warily at Moon and Jade.

The Sericans carried bags and bales through a low doorway into the biggest building, a rambling structure with odd corners and overhangs, at least four levels tall. It had several open doors, and many windows flickering with light.

Tattered flags hung outside the main door, the same system Moon had seen used in Viridian Coast trading cities. The red one meant provisions were sold here, the blue that there was space for travelers to sleep, and the others all had various meanings for the storage of wagons, draft animals, and whether trade was done there. Moon fell in behind one of the Sericans, following him under the heavy doorway and down a corridor that was angled to keep out the wind. The air was heavy with the scent of cooked meat, the sounds of talking and laughter. Then they walked into a wave of steamy warmth. Behind Moon, Jade hissed in relief.

The corridor widened into a foyer, one passage angling off to a room where Moon heard someone moving barrels around, and the other heading further in. Moon followed it as it wound deeper into the building, past little rooms or cubbies, each furnished with hide rugs and cushions. A variety of people sat in them, talking, or eating and drinking from copper dishes. Many were the locals with the bushy hair and tusks, but Moon saw more Sericans, some short groundlings with small brown horns peeking out from under their hooded jackets, and the people with the bright green skin.

Moon made his way along, hoping to find a proprietor somewhere, the ice melting in his hair and dripping coldly down the back of his shirt. The heavy scent of meat, even cooked, had caused a clawing sensation in his stomach. He could also smell boiled roots, and something sweet and salty-spicy. People glanced up as they passed but, again, with idle curiosity, not hostility.

By luck they stumbled onto a larger room, mostly occupied by a big stove of gold-colored ceramic, the source of the steam heat. Pipes led up from it into the ceiling and down through the stone floor, and it clanked and hissed and emitted heat like a bonfire. A waist-high section extended out, apparently for cooking.

A local woman stood at it, stirring something in a big pot that breathed sweet-scented steam. She had white beads braided into her long, curly hair and red curlicues incised on her tusks. Two children bundled up in knitted wool played on the floor, then stopped to stare up at the newcomers with big eyes. The woman looked up, and smiled. "Travelers? You want to buy food?"

"Yes, with this." Moon showed her Jade's ring.

She leaned in to look, lifting a finger to touch it carefully. Her fingernails were of rough horn, almost claw-like. She nodded approvingly. "White metal and a nice stone. That'll buy a lot of food."

Some of the tension uncoiled in Moon's spine. He would have hated to walk out of here empty-handed; remembering what it was like to be warm made the freezing wet night seem all the worse. "And a place to sleep."

The woman frowned and looked thoughtfully around the room, but apparently only because she was trying to sort out where to put them. "There's an empty crib at the top, but the wind-shield is broken and no one else wants it." She peered down at their bare feet. "You two might not mind it."

Moon and the woman negotiated, while Jade flicked her tail for the entertainment of the two children. They settled on a hot meal now and in the morning, space for the night, plus a sack of dried meat strips and other provisions to take with them when they left. The woman also threw in a flask of whatever was in the pot, which turned out to be a meat broth with dried berries in it. Jade looked mildly horrified, but Moon was happy with it. Altogether, the amount of food wasn't the equivalent of a whole herdbeast buck, but it would be enough to keep both of them flying all day tomorrow.

Following her instructions and carrying the blankets that came with the room, a lamp, and the basket of food, they followed a passage to stairs so narrow that Moon didn't know how wider groundlings could fit through. On each level, oddly shaped doorways led off to low-ceilinged passages divided up into cubbies, most of them blocked off by leather curtains. The Serican women seemed to have most of the second floor, and were busy hanging up icy coats and cloaks to drip in the passage. One did a double take as Jade went past, but then smiled and shook her head. Moon realized she must have caught a glimpse of Jade's blue scales and thought she was a stray Serican.

The room at the very top was theirs, the only one on that level. They both had to duck to get through the doorway. Light from the passage showed that the space was a little bigger than the cubbies below. It had a round window and, as the woman had said, the thin hide frame stretched over it was torn, letting in a cold draft. The only furniture was a hide to warm the stone floor and a thick sleeping mat stuffed with grasses. But a couple of the stove pipes came through the floor here, winding up and away into the wall, emitting heat and little traces of steam. Having direct access to the outside in case they needed to escape wasn't a bad thing, either.

"This," Jade said, with conviction, "was a wonderful idea." She tossed the blankets onto the sleeping mat and shed her wrap, shaking the melting ice out of her frills. "I would've given her that ring to sleep in a corner downstairs."

"That would have been bad bargaining," Moon informed her, setting the basket down.

While Jade hung her wrap over the window to block the worst of the drafts, Moon used flint and tinder to get the lamp lit. Instead of oil or a candle, it had a solid block of squishy material that the woman had said would burn most of the night, though not very brightly.

Once it was lit, the warm glow made the room cozy. Moon unpacked the basket of food, taking out the pleasantly warm clay pot first. Lifting the lid showed it was filled with meat in a thick, spice-scented sauce. Jade sat down across from him and took a piece from the pot, sniffing at it doubtfully. "Are you sure this doesn't spoil the meat?"

"It keeps it from spoiling." Moon ate a piece, licking the sauce off his fingers. There were also rounds of brown bread, another pot filled with bulbous purple roots and boiled greens, and sweet pastries with nuts and dried berries. They ate in companionable silence while the room grew warmer.

So far, they hadn't made anything but vague plans for what they would do when they arrived at the Cordans' valley. On their long flights, Moon had thought of a number of bad ideas, the worst of which was that they might try to steal someone, hopefully one of the elders, and convince him to reveal the location of the poison. Every idea seemed awkward at best, dangerous, and destined for failure. But until now he hadn't thought of the simplest solution, that Jade could pass as a groundling. She might be able to walk into the camp and ask for the poison, or at least for the knowledge to make it.

Jade bit into one of the purple roots and blinked at the taste, but still swallowed it. "You lived in places like this?"

Her tone made him look up, frowning.

"It's not that bad."

A lot of different groundlings must pass through here, and no one had taken much notice of them. It wouldn't make a good place to live; the terrain around the city was too barren to easily conceal shifting. And it was just too cold. She was still staring at him. He said, "Why?"

She shook her head. "Just trying to understand."

"Understand what?" Just to be an ass, he offered her the flask of fruit and meat soup.

She gave him a look, ignoring the flask. "Understand you."

Moon couldn't think why she would want to. He hadn't been making an effort to understand her, and had done everything he could to keep her at arm's length.

He broke the last round of bread apart, and tried not to ask; he didn't really want to know. But he found himself saying reluctantly, "And do you?"

She watched him long enough for him to have to fight the impulse to shift. Finally she said, "You're angry that we didn't find you sooner."

She was right about that, but it wasn't a revelation. It had been wearing on him since he had first arrived at Indigo Cloud. It made no sense, it wasn't logical or fair, by any stretch of the imagination, but he couldn't help feeling it. He shrugged, and bit into a chunk of bread.

Jade took her time as she finished a last strip of meat, then licked her fingers. Right at the moment when Moon thought he might be safe, she added, "And you're afraid, now that you've seen what your life with a court might have been like, that you'll have a harder time feeling contented in any place you settle."

That one was wide of the mark. Moon had seen close-knit communities before, had lived in beautiful places while knowing he didn't belong and couldn't risk remaining. He thought of the Hassi and their city above the link-trees. Not bothering to keep the sarcastic edge out of his voice, he said, "If I'd been able to choose what I was born as, I'd have picked something different." *As long as it was something that could still fly.*

She tilted her head thoughtfully. With real curiosity, she said, "If Pearl had accepted you from the first, would it have been different? Would you have wanted to stay?"

Moon looked away, his jaw tightening. There had been a moment when, if Pearl had asked nicely, she could have had him on the floor of the gathering hall in front of the entire court, and he knew it. He was afraid everyone else had known it, too. He didn't know whether to be angry at the rejection or relieved at the close call.

"You were expecting a consort from Star Aster," he said, "a sheltered, spoiled consort with a perfect bloodline. Are you asking me to believe that it wasn't a shock when Stone showed up with me?"

"I've known Stone all my life. I'm not surprised at anything he shows up with. You can't have come from a bad bloodline; you're strong, healthy, and your conformation is perfect." Jade lifted her brows. "And you're high-strung, shy, and have the same delicate sensibilities of every gently bred and sheltered consort I've ever met."

Moon knocked back the last of the fruit soup, and set the flask aside. "We need to sleep." He didn't know why he was angry with her, why he felt exposed to the bone. *I am not high-strung.*

Jade didn't pursue the argument or comment on his retreat, which just made Moon more irritated with her. When she started to push the blankets into a nest on the sleeping mat, Moon took one and retreated to the far edge. But he wasn't angry enough at her to sleep on the cold floor.

CHAPTER
THIRTEEN

cᴥව

Moon snapped awake with the
conviction that a Fell ruler
stood over him. Beside him,
Jade twitched upright, snarling. The
faint lamplight showed the room was
empty, but Fell scent hung in the air.

"Not here. It's in the wind!" Jade
threw blankets aside as she scrambled
upright.

Appalled, Moon rolled to his feet. A
Fell ruler flew somewhere nearby, over
the pass or the valley, and the wind had
carried the scent to them. Jade was already at the window, pulling the blanket
and the torn wind-shield aside. Cold
air blasted in as Moon leaned past her
to see out.

The plaza below was empty, except for
the wagons and the huddle of draughtbeasts. Few windows were still lit, and
the torch stands in the streets were dark.

Heavy clouds cut off any glimpse of starlight. Moon could barely see. The night would be nearly impenetrable to most groundling eyes.

"It's somewhere close," Jade growled, and shifted to her winged form. She hooked her claws over the stone window sill and pulled herself up to climb out. "We have to kill it."

"I know," he snapped. The ruler couldn't be allowed to follow them toward a Cordan camp. If the Cordans really had used their poison in the fighting in Kiaspur, the Fell could know about it, could realize that Moon and Jade meant to get it to use at the colony. Moon shifted and followed as Jade slid out the window.

Moon sunk his claws into the stone as the wind tore at him, threatening to rip him right off the wall. It was laden with ice sharp as needles, peppering his scales. He followed Jade up the side of the building, and dragged himself up onto the rounded roof.

They both crouched there, tasting the wind. Around the caravanserai was a dark sea of rocky rooftops, with chimneys releasing gusts of white steam. The sky was a featureless curve of solid cloud, the mountains visible only in outline. Sight was almost useless, and scent wasn't much better; the wind gusted in all directions, making the Ruler's trace seem to come from everywhere. Jade scanned the sky, snarling in irritation. "I can't tell the direction. We'll have to search."

And we have to split up, Moon thought. If they didn't find the ruler now, all it had to do was hide and wait for them to move on. "You take the north side. I'll take the south," he said, and let himself fall into the wind.

He flapped to get higher, banking toward the north peak and away from the city. He flew a hunting pattern over the dark slopes of the valley, following the wind currents and trying to pinpoint the Fell taint. Tantalizing him, it came and went.

The clouds drifted apart, allowing starlight to fall through, making it a little easier to see. Moon had covered half the valley when he sensed movement in the darkness above him. Knowing it wasn't Jade, he twisted sideways in one sharp motion. The dark shape of a Fell ruler plunged past him.

Hah! Finally. Moon dove after it, angling his wings for the least resistance. The ruler flapped frantically, trying to correct its out of control plunge. Before it could get its balance, Moon struck its back, using the claws on his feet to rake down the join of its wings.

The ruler rolled and made a wild grab for him but Moon dove past. Then he caught an updraft and rode it back up.

The ruler floundered in the air, shouting after him, "Did you think you could run from us? That I wouldn't follow you wherever you went?"

With a shock Moon recognized the voice. It was Kathras, the ruler who had come out of the colony to taunt Pearl. *He thinks we were running?* Moon banked around for another strike. As he dove, Kathras rolled to claw at him but Moon hit him hard, raked him across the belly with his feet and twisted away again. Kathras fell, extending his wings to save himself. Moon slipped sideways and hit Kathras at the wing join a third time. He felt something snap under his claws.

Kathras slashed up at him, then fell away, tumbling down toward the rocks below.

The ruler bounced off a crag, then fell down into a gorge. Moon spiraled down, mindful of the gusty wind. He spotted Kathras sprawled on a rocky ledge and landed on an outcrop just above him. He crouched to peer cautiously down at the ruler.

Kathras shoved unsteadily to his feet, his crumpled wing hanging limp. This close, Moon could see light-colored patches in the ruler's scales, raw spots. Kathras quivered with weakness, and Moon scented blood, dried as well as fresh. *He flew himself ragged to catch up with us. He did think we were running.* Moon felt a surge of hope. If that was true, then the Fell didn't know about the Cordans or the poison; they believed Moon and Jade were trying to escape.

Looking up at him, Kathras whipped his tail, rage in every line of his body. He spat the words, "I thought we could speak in private. We have so much to say to one another."

"The only Fell I know are dead." Moon had never seen a ruler angry before, never seen one show any real emotion except amused contempt. That he had provoked it was a heady sensation, but not one he meant to enjoy for long.

Moon leapt down to the ledge and landed a few paces away from Kathras. He started forward. He needed to finish this and then find Jade, to tell her they didn't have to worry.

Then Kathras said, "You knew me in Saraseil."

Moon halted, shock freezing him into place. *It's a trick,* he reminded himself. *It's always a trick.* But he had never told anyone about Saraseil. There was no one left alive who knew he had ever been there. He managed to say, "That's a lie. He's dead."

"That was Liheas, blood of our blood. He thought he would bring you to us, to please us. But you betrayed us." Kathras hissed, bitter and reproachful. "Did you think we would forget?"

Liheas. It was eighteen turns ago and far across the Three Worlds, more than half his life ago, but the name was like a knife in his chest. Moon shook his head, furious, horrified. He couldn't believe this was happening; it had to be a nightmare. "Betrayed you? You—He lied to me, told me... I knew he was lying, he would have killed me."

Kathras shouted, "We would have given you what you wanted! We would have loved you, given you a place."

Moon surged forward to tear him apart. His claws were a hairsbreadth away from Kathras' throat, when Kathras shifted.

It didn't look as it did when Raksura shifted; there was no blurring of vision, no illusion of mist or smoke. It was as if Kathras' body became liquid and flowed into another shape.

He looked like the groundling form of an Aeriat, tall and slim. But instead of a copper or dark tone, his skin was as white as alabaster, gleaming faintly in the starlight. His black hair was long and fine, and he had a straight nose and wide-set eyes. He was dressed in dark, silky garments, torn and ragged in the wind. Kathras was a beautiful groundling, but no more so than Balm or Chime or any of the other young Aeriat. But there was something that pulled at Moon, an uncanny attraction, an empty beauty that drew him in to fill the void.

Moon looked into those eyes, and knew whatever had lived in them, whoever it was who had spoken to him, was already gone. He ripped his claws across Kathras' throat.

He tore the flesh open to the bone, blood gushing over his hand. Kathras' head tipped back and he collapsed like an empty sack.

Breathing hard, Moon backed away, shaking the blood off his claws. It didn't help.

Then he felt something watching him. He looked up.

Jade perched on the crag just above him.

For a heartbeat, Moon had a stupid hope that she hadn't heard them. Then she leapt down onto the ledge, and he knew she had heard, and that she was going to kill him. And he was going to let her.

Jade looked at him for a long moment, while the cold wind pulled at them and shock froze Moon into a statue. He couldn't read her expression.

Then Jade hissed and turned away. She put a foot on Kathras' chest, reached down, and laced her claws through his hair. With one sharp jerk, she ripped his head off. Moon watched her scrape at the gravel at the base of the rock, carving out a hollow to drop the head into. She pushed the gravel back over it, covering the white face. Moon knew earth was better, but the ground was frozen, and the pebbles would make enough of a barrier to keep the other Fell from being drawn to Kathras' body.

Jade caught his shoulder and shook him. Moon flinched away, but she just said, "Can you hear me?"

He realized she had been speaking while he had stood there staring at Kathras' corpse. "What?"

"We're going back to the city." She took his chin, and turned his head to face her, making him meet her eyes. "Follow me. You understand?"

He nodded and followed when she leapt up to the crag, and then into the air.

They flew back to the city through the darkness and the icy wind, spiraling down to land on the round roof of the caravanserai. Crouched on the rocky tiles, Jade pointed for Moon to go first. He climbed down the wall to crawl in through the window.

Inside, the lamp still burned, throwing warm yellow light over the sleeping mat, the tumbled blankets, their pack, and the basket and pots from their meal. Automatically, Moon shifted back to groundling. The melting ice on his scales immediately soaked his clothes. Sheltered from the freezing wind, the room should be warm, but he couldn't feel anything. His legs gave out and he sank down to sit on the floor.

Jade climbed in through the window and shifted back to Arbora, her frills dripping ice. She picked up the wooden frame of the wind-shield and jammed it back into the window with one violent shove. Then she turned and sat down, facing Moon. Her face intent, she leaned forward, bracing her hands on the floor and spreading her claws. "Tell me."

Moon stared at her, then took a sharp breath. It took effort to get the words out.

"Saraseil was a city on the gulf of Abascene. I was there when the Fell passed through it, about eighteen turns ago. I'd never seen Fell before." He shook his head slowly, trying to think how to explain. "They were shifters that flew."

Jade hissed under her breath, something in Raksuran Moon had never heard before. She flicked her claws impatiently. "I see. Go on."

"The Fell took the citadel first, in the center of the city, and the groundlings were all running away, or trying to. Everything was falling apart. The dakti and kethel were killing people in the streets, digging through the walls of the houses to get to them. I didn't want to think I was a Fell, that I came from things that would do that. But I had to know." He realized he was shivering, and rubbed his hands on his damp shirt. He felt an incredible distance between then and now, as if he were telling a story that had happened to someone else. Maybe he had been someone else then, the way he had been someone else before Sorrow and the others died. "I flew to the roof of the citadel and got inside through a window. But I couldn't get close enough to see anything, so I let the dakti catch me, and they took me to the ruler in the council hall. I asked what I was."

Jade's expression could have been carved out of the mountain's bedrock. He couldn't tell what she thought. She said, "Did it tell you that you were a Fell?"

"Yes."

Jade's eyes narrowed. "And you believed it?"

"No. I knew it was lying. As soon as I saw it…" Moon tried to think how to describe that moment of realization, of relief and horror all mixed together. As soon as he had looked into the ruler's eyes, he had recognized the lie. That whatever he was, it wasn't this. And he had understood just how big a mistake he had made in going to the citadel and drawing the Fell's attention. "I knew it would never tell me what I was."

Jade looked away, the tense lines of her shoulders and spines relaxing minutely. "How did you escape?"

"The ruler took me up to the rooms where the Saraseil lords lived. Everything was torn apart, like they had looted the place but hadn't taken anything. There was a dead woman there, a groundling woman. Everything smelled like death." The memory was like a particularly vivid dream image: the torn silk drapes, the fine glitter of shattered wood and ivory, the woman's blood on the bed cushions.

"I went out on the balcony, and the city was burning." He had liked that city, too. It had had a busy port, and drew groundlings from far across the Three Worlds. Moon had blended right in, and he had done well there. "The ruler said I belonged with him, that he was going to keep me forever."

Like Kathras, Liheas' groundling form had been beautiful, dark hair like silk and unmarked skin and eyes such a deep, vivid blue. Moon had known then why so many groundlings let the Fell in. The beauty of the rulers, and their power to influence, hid the horror of the kethel and the dakti until it was too late.

Liheas had said he loved him. Moon hadn't believed it, but he had been caught enough in the spell to let the creature take him, out there on the balcony while Saraseil burned.

"I waited until he went to sleep. Then I snapped his neck and set the room on fire, and then I flew away."

Jade stared, startled, then shook her head. Her voice dry, she said, "That must have been a shock for the Fell. That's usually their role." She sat back, watching him thoughtfully. "And you didn't tell us because...?"

"How could it matter? It was turns ago." It wasn't that he hadn't thought about Saraseil in a long time; it was that he hadn't thought about it ever, except to take it as a lesson to stop looking for his past. The whole thing had been a nightmare. "I never thought about it."

She was giving him that look again; he couldn't tell if she believed him or not. She said, "So if you don't think about it, it's as if it never happened?"

Moon shrugged helplessly. "It worked until now."

Jade sighed, obviously giving up on that point. "So that ruler is dead, but before you killed it, it must have... shared the memory."

"I didn't know they could do that, then. I found out more about them afterward, by talking to groundlings in Kish." Moon rubbed his face, trying to banish the images. His hands were still painfully numb and his skin felt like ice.

Jade nodded understanding. "When you were looking for us."

"I stopped looking for what I was. After that, I just didn't care anymore. It didn't seem as if there was any point." The room must be warm. Wisps of steam still came from the heating pipes. But the bone-chilling cold had settled into his body to stay. At least it made it easier to think. "This can't be the same Fell flight that attacked Saraseil. It was too long ago, on the far coast."

Jade waved a hand, her mouth set in a rueful line. "Their bloodlines range far across the Three Worlds. If it was a related flight, they could still share memories."

That was a frightening thought, but it was the only thing that made sense, the only explanation for how Kathras could know Moon. He protested, "But the Fell couldn't have come to Indigo Cloud because of me. They were talking to Pearl before Stone found me."

Jade didn't look convinced. She said, "If it is you they came for, they would've had to know that you would eventually come to Indigo Cloud, that if they waited long enough, they would find you there. That's a mentor's power again."

If the Fell had come to Indigo Cloud because they had somehow known that Moon would eventually go there... *They could have been following me for turns and turns.* The thought made him sick. All the places he had been, where Fell or rumors of Fell had followed him. *If they were looking for me... No, that can't be true.* They would have found him before now. They would have found him when he had come out of Kish again and gone back toward the east. He had enough trouble. He didn't need to borrow more.

He looked up to see Jade watching him with a frown. She said, "You're still shaking."

"I can't get warm." The ice was inside his skin, in his thoughts. He supposed if Jade was going to kill him, she would have done it by now. If he was going to be alive in the morning, he needed to be able to fly. "I'll go downstairs." He started to push to his feet.

Jade caught his arm and pulled him back down beside her. He twitched in a half-hearted attempt to escape, but she wrapped a strong arm around his waist, pulling him back against her chest.

"No, just stay," she said, but her voice was gentle. He was so cold and tense that his body felt brittle, and her hands, even through his damp clothes, were pure heat. Then he realized the cloud of warmth enfolding him was from her half-furled wings, that she had just shifted out of her Arbora form. "No, if anybody sees—"

"Everyone's asleep," she said into his ear. She waited patiently until he subsided, then gave him a reassuring squeeze. Moon gave in, sinking back against her.

She held him close, and ran her palm over his arms, his chest, soothing his shivers away. Her scales caught against his groundling skin, and the effect was hypnotic. Then she nuzzled his ear, soft and warm, and her teeth grazed the back of his neck. The gentle bite sent a shock right down his spine. Moon made a noise embarrassingly close to a squeak.

Jade pulled back, startled. "Sorry."

After everything that had happened tonight, he hadn't thought he could feel anything. Suddenly he could feel everything, everywhere. Something had broken free inside him. He said, "No, don't... don't stop."

She gripped his shoulders and turned him around to face her, moving him as if he didn't weigh anything. He had never been more vulnerable. He was in groundling form, and she could keep him from shifting. It should have been frightening, but it just made him want to wrap himself around her and bite her neck. "Moon, do you know what you're saying?"

"Yes. What?" His senses had been stifled by the cold but her scent was suddenly overwhelming. He tried to lean in toward her.

Jade held him back, her frills twitching in frustration. She tried again, "Why now?"

It took an effort, but he made himself articulate his racing thoughts. "Because you know everything, and you still want me."

Jade growled, in a deep tone he hadn't heard before. She pushed him down, flattening him to the pallet.

Before this, Moon had always had to hold back, to be careful. It wasn't just that most groundlings were weaker and more fragile than he was. He had always been afraid that something would happen at a vulnerable moment, that if he let himself relax completely, he might just shift. This time he didn't hold back at all, and it felt so right it left him dazed.

Afterward, he lay on the pallet with Jade wrapped around him, sated and content and pleasantly achy in just the right places. He listened to the low buzzing growl of satisfaction in her chest and thought, *Stone was right. The bastard.* Moon was terrified of not fitting into the court, so afraid that he was willing to let Pearl force him out, when instinct said to fight to stay.

After tonight, spending his life defying Pearl and watching his back in Indigo Cloud didn't seem so much worse than lying his way into another groundling settlement, or moving aimlessly from one trade city to another. The first option might be just as fraught, but it came with companionship and sex and not having to hide what he was. At least he could just give it some time and see what happened.

With more than a tinge of irony, he told himself, *You've got that settled. Now you just need to get the court away from the Fell.* If they couldn't, if their plans failed...

He tugged one of Jade's frills. "Pearl said if we gave up, the Wind Sun Court would take in the Arbora and the warriors. She didn't say what would happen to you."

He felt her shake her head. "Pearl and I won't leave the court."

She was telling him that she and Pearl would stay to fight the Fell to the death. It shouldn't surprise him; it was what he had seen groundlings do. He hesitated longer over the next question. He knew most groundling women couldn't tell right

away, but if there was a chance, he wanted to know. "Did you get a clutch?"
She nuzzled his temple. "No."

That was fast. "How do you know?" he said suspiciously.

She sounded wry. "We're not like groundlings, Moon. It's not random chance."
Her voice turned grim. "I won't have a clutch until the court is free."

He had to admit that was probably for the best. He thought about the others,
trapped with the Fell, and reminded himself, *We're nearly there.* One more day's
flight and they would be past the mountains and over the jungle valleys where
the Cordans' camp lay.

Jade sat up a little, looking down at him, her eyes serious. "I want you to
promise me that if we fail, you'll lead the survivors to Wind Sun."

Moon fought the urge to argue. He didn't want her to think about giving up.
But he knew she had to face all the possibilities. Reluctantly, he said, "I'll do it.
If it comes to that."

He felt the tension in her body ease a little. She added, "The second consort
there is Dust, one of the consorts Pearl sent away when Rain died. He may be
able to get you a place in their court. Promise me you'll try."

Because begging a place in Indigo Cloud has turned out so well, Moon thought,
that I should try it again with another court. That he wouldn't promise. "No."

"Moon." She set her jaw in exasperation. "Do you have any idea what it costs
me to tell you to seek another queen?"

"I won't seek another queen." He buried his face against her neck. "So that's
settled."

"Moon." Jade growled, and shook him a little. "For once in your life, listen to
someone."

"Ow. No."

"Moon." She gritted her teeth, then hissed in frustration, settling down and
curling around him. "Just... go to sleep."

That he could do.

CHAPTER
FOURTEEN

"Just be careful." Moon was having second and third thoughts about this plan.

"I know." Jade, in her Arbora form, took the pack and slung it over her shoulder. They were in a small clearing in the jungle, on the slopes above the Cordan camp. The warm damp air and bright sun were a welcome relief after the cold of the mountains. Tall trees heavy with vines overhung the clearing.

They had flown through the day and most of the night to get here, arriving in the valley with just enough strength left to collapse. Moon had led the way to a large tree he had occasionally used for naps while he was out hunting. They had tucked themselves in between two branches and slept curled in each other's arms. The next morning they had cautiously scouted the area on foot, finding a vantage point where they could observe the camp from a distance. From what Moon could tell, little seemed to have changed, though the flying island had drifted further down the valley. He reminded himself he hadn't been gone long; it only felt like a lifetime ago.

Now Jade tugged at the neck of her smock. "Do I look enough like a groundling woman for them?"

Before leaving the mountain town, they had bought a brown cotton garment from the woman who ran the caravanserai. It wasn't much different from what the Cordan women wore, and hung down to Jade's knees, tied at the waist. With the pack and a length of wood as a staff, she did look as if she could have been traveling on foot. They had decided she would tell the Cordans that she came from the south, and that her settlement was in danger of attack by Fell, that she had heard about the poison from rumors brought by travelers from Kiaspur. Moon had heard enough about the Cordans' homeland to give her convincing secondhand detail about it, things she would have been told by people who had been there. And he had also given her every detail about how to pretend to be a groundling that he could remember. There was only one problem.

"Can you hide your tail?" he asked.

She tilted her head in mock inquiry. "Hide it where?"

"Tuck it up around your waist."

She folded her arms, eyeing him warily. "Are you serious?"

He caught her tail and pointed to the spade shape on the end. "This is distinctive. If Ilane sees this—"

"All right, all right." She pulled it out of his hand, and pushed it under her skirt, frowning in concentration as she coiled it around her waist. "There."

"Just be—"

She caught his shirt, pulled him in, and nipped his ear. "I'll be careful. I'll meet you at the river at nightfall."

He watched her walk away through the trees, picking her way down the slope. He told himself she looked like a groundling; no one in the mountain city had noticed anything out of the ordinary. *But they aren't as hysterical about Fell as the Cordans,* he thought, and ran a hand through his hair in frustration. It was going to be a long day.

Taking the opposite direction, Moon shifted and climbed the nearest tree, their vantage point on the river flat. He climbed high enough that he had a good view of the fields that led down to the river, and the camp.

It still looked much the same; the fence of bundled sticks enclosing the conical tents, the greenroot plantings at the edge of the river, smoke rising up from cooking fires. At this time of day the river bank was busy: children swam, women washed clothing or carried water jars back up to the tents.

Moon perched on a branch and waited nervously as he watched Jade walk out of the edge of the forest, cross the open field, then arrive at the camp's makeshift gate. It still stood open for the hunters who would trickle back in groups before sunset. She spoke to the gate guard, who was not Hac, fortunately. Fortunately for Hac, at any rate; Moon didn't think Jade would be as patient as he had been.

More Cordans gathered round, drawn by the appearance of a stranger, but no one seemed agitated or upset. After a short time, Jade walked with them into the camp, heading toward the elders' tent.

Moon settled back, hissing in anxious frustration. He had nothing to do but wait.

The afternoon wore on, and Moon watched the hunters return, recognizing Kavath from a distance by his pale blue skin and crest. There had been no unusual disturbance in the camp. He caught the occasional glimpse of Jade, walking between the tents. It was too far away to recognize anyone else. He would have liked to know where Selis was living, if she had found a better place. He wondered how he would feel if he saw Ilane, and twitched uncomfortably.

When night gathered in the valley, Moon uncoiled out of the branches and jumped to the next tree, and the next, working his way through the forest, down the hills and toward the river. It helped that he knew where all the Cordans' hunting trails lay so there was little chance of encountering anyone. It was dark by the time he reached the river bank, well above the Cordan camp.

Still in his Raksuran form, he slipped down into the water and let the current carry him along, just a dark, drifting shape. As he drew near the camp, he went under, swimming into the thick reeds. In that concealment, he surfaced just enough so that his ears, eyes, and nose were above the water.

He heard the normal evening sounds of the camp, conversations, children shouting and laughing as they played. He smelled wood smoke and once-familiar people, and the greenroot they boiled or baked for dinner. A few women came down the sandy bank to wash cooking pans, but the time for bathing and swimming was past, and most of the camp would be sitting outside their tents to eat.

Then he caught Jade's scent. Unexpectedly, it stirred sudden heat in his belly. He told himself not to be an idiot. He had only been away from her half a day.

A few moments later, she appeared over the top of the bank. She moved idly, as if she was only here to enjoy the cool breeze off the river. Moon splashed, just loud enough for her to hear.

She walked down the sand to the shallows, wetting her feet, then wandered casually toward the reeds. When she was close enough, she whispered, "I assume that's you."

Moon swam a little closer, lying flat in the shallows, still mostly concealed by the reeds. "Well?"

She hissed between her teeth, controlled and angry. "We have a problem. I don't think they'll give it to me."

Moon was so startled he almost sat up. "What? Why not?"

"I've told them our settlement is under attack by the Fell, that we need the poison to help fight them off. I offered to buy it, I tried to give them my rings, but they wouldn't take them. They seem sympathetic, they told me stories of what happened to their cities, but they say the poison won't help me. They keep hinting that I should stay here and join them." She kicked at a clump of weeds, every line of her body tense with frustration. "It's partly the timing. They know there are no other groundling tribes or settlements close by. I've had to make them think I've been walking for days and days, over dangerous territory. They think it will be too late by the time I get back."

"Stupid bastards." Moon sunk under the water to keep from growling. Even if they thought Jade would be too late to help her people, withholding the poison just seemed cruel. Better to let her have it and at least try to get back in time. And it was for their own damn good; killing Fell benefited everybody. Especially these Fell, with the odd abilities they seemed to have. He surfaced again. "Damn it."

"I'd try to steal some, but I can't get them to give me any clue where they keep it, or how they make it, or even if they have any on hand." Jade shook her head frills. "Any ideas?"

Moon could only think of one possibility. "There's a woman named Selis. I lived with her, and she knew what I was. If you can talk to her alone, tell her... Tell her the truth."

Jade hesitated, drawing her toes through the sand. "Are you certain? If she betrays us to the others, there's no chance left of getting it by stealth. We'd have to fight them for it."

"I don't know," Moon had to admit. Anything was possible. Especially with Selis. But she had been openly contemptuous of the elders and pretty much everyone else in the camp. And she had had plenty of opportunity to betray him before, and hadn't. "She's the only one who might be willing to help us. If she wants to talk to me, tell her to come out to the forest tomorrow morning." Women often went outside the camp in the mornings to pick bandan leaves, dig roots, and collect whatever nuts and fruit were ripe. It was the best opportunity to speak unobserved.

Jade thought about it a moment more, staring thoughtfully off across the river. "All right," she said finally. "I'll find her."

"I'll watch for you. Good luck." Moon slipped under again, and pulled himself along the bottom until he could swim upstream.

Moon caught his own dinner in the river, since it was easier than hunting the forest in the dark. After that he went back through the trees to his perch, watched the dark camp, and slept in snatches. It was a nerve-racking wait.

Finally, just before dawn grayed the sky, Hac pushed the gate open and stood in the gap, scratching himself. The hunters left first, a long straggling column of men taking the trail that led up the slopes into the forest. Then, as the morning light grew brighter, the women and older children started to come out.

They were in small groups of three or four, carrying baskets, wandering across the field to the fringes of the forest. Trailing after one group was Jade, taller than the others and distinctive even in the brown smock. Beside her was a short, sturdy Cordan woman with a basket on her hip.

They let the others draw ahead, then angled toward the fringe of the forest. Careful not to rustle the branches, Moon climbed down the tree, and made his way through the forest toward the point where they would enter it.

He waited for them a couple of hundred paces into the trees, screened by the tall fronds of the ground plants. He finally heard footsteps in the bracken: Selis' steps. Jade, even in Arbora form, moved in near silence. He shifted to groundling.

As they drew closer, Moon heard Selis say, "Are you sure he's here? He's not reliable."

Moon stepped out of concealment, and Selis stopped short. Moon made himself stand still, though he was suddenly aware that his heart pounded with tension. Seeing Selis again was stranger than he had thought it would be.

They stared at each other. Then Selis said, with deliberate irony, "It's all right. I made sure Ilane didn't follow me."

It caught Moon by surprise, and he snorted in bitter amusement. "That makes one of us."

"It's not funny." She took a few steps closer. "I'm living with my sister now."

Moon winced sympathetically, for the sister and for Selis. Selis hated her family and, from what he had been able to tell, the feeling was mutual.

Making it sound like an accusation, she said, "They said you were dead, that you got carried away by a Fell."

"It wasn't a Fell."

Her expression suggested he was still just as stupid as she remembered. "That I figured out for myself." She sniffed and added, "Ilane is living with Ildras."

Moon folded his arms, feeling his jaw tighten. Ildras, the chief hunter, had been a friend. And he had already been living with two women. Somehow Moon didn't see Ilane taking third place. "What about Fianis and Elene?"

"They're practically her servants now." Selis and Moon shared a look of mutual disgust. A little tension went out of Selis' shoulders, and she tossed her basket on the ground. "So you want the poison."

He nodded. "Jade told you why?"

Selis sighed, and scratched at a bug bite on her arm. "It's been used in the east, down in the peninsula, for a long time. It's not as good a weapon as they tell each other. You have to get it inside the Fell or it's useless. The story says that the last garrison of Borani in Kiaspur drank it." She rolled her eyes. "A seer told them it would save them. It didn't do anything to the men, but the Fell ate them, then sickened and couldn't pursue the refugees."

Jade lifted her brows, startled. "I can see why it's a last resort."

Selis threw her a dark look. "A last resort for fools."

"We know where these Fell are living," Moon told Selis. "We can get it into their water."

Selis' permanent frown turned thoughtful. "That could work," she admitted grudgingly. "I've never heard that done before, but then all we know are rumors. They say the Duazi, a wild tribe down in the moss forests, found it by accident. It was in their food, and they've never been attacked by the Fell since."

"Do you know what's in it?" Jade asked, watching her sharply.

"No. But it must be things that are easily found or we wouldn't have it. I know they keep it in the elders' meeting tent." Selis lifted her chin and looked hard at Moon. "I want to see you."

Moon knew what she meant, but it felt like a strangely intimate thing to do. He had always had two lives, one as a groundling and one as something else. Once he met Stone, the two lives had come together, but Selis had only known him as a groundling. "You've seen me."

She took another step forward, determined. "Not up close. Change."

It was a challenge, and he didn't want to show his reluctance. Moon shifted, on impulse making it happen slowly. Selis, being Selis, didn't flinch. He settled into his Raksuran form, and she studied him, leaning in. He raised the frills and spines around his head, showing his mane. After a moment, she reached up and touched his nose. She said, "It still looks like you."

"It is me."

She blinked at his voice, then stepped back. "I'll get the poison for you. I'll try to copy the ingredients out of the elders' simple book, or get one of the vials they keep already made up."

Jade closed her eyes briefly in relief, then asked Selis, "What do you want in exchange?" She turned to reach into her pack. "We have gems and metal."

Selis shook her head impatiently. "I've no use for it. There's no one to trade it to. And what else would I do with it? Wear it?" Her laugh was abrupt and bitter. "I'm doing this for myself, to spite Ilane and the elders."

Moon shifted back to groundling, finding it easier to argue with her that way. "Then let us take you somewhere, another settlement. There's one on our way back, a trading city in the mountains. A lot of travelers go through there. You could get passage down into Kish."

Selis looked as if that was the worst idea she had ever heard, but that was nothing new. "I couldn't leave the camp."

Impatiently, Moon demanded, "Why not? You hate everybody here."

Selis folded her arms stubbornly. "It's what I'm used to."

Moon knew all about that. He said, "You can get used to something else."

Selis looked, if anything, more stubborn, and Jade put in quickly, "You don't have to decide now. Think about it, and tell us what you want when you bring us the poison."

Selis shrugged. She leaned down to reach for the basket, but Moon beat her to it, picking it up to hand to her. She snatched it, glared at him, and stamped away.

Jade shouldered her pack and moved to follow Selis, saying, "I'll meet you after dark at the river."

Moon watched them go. *This should work.* If the Cordans had really believed Jade's story, if Selis didn't get caught searching for the poison. *Those are big ifs.* And he had another long day of waiting ahead.

At dusk, Moon slipped into the river again and drifted downstream. He arrived a little early, and though the shadows were heavy, a few women still rinsed out the big clay jars used to store seed flour, and their children splashed in the shallows. Moon stayed away from the bank, hooking his claws around a rock and letting his face break the surface just enough to let him breathe. The water pulled at his spines and frills as if he was a drifting weed.

Finally the women carried the jars away and the children reluctantly followed. Moon let go of the rock and drifted closer, fetching up in the reeds where he had waited for Jade last night.

Darkness fell, and he caught faint, distant voices from the camp, though he couldn't make out the words. Time crept on and Moon started to fidget, absently ripping up weeds from the sandy bottom. *Where are they?*

Then he heard feet pounding on packed earth, and a moment later Selis ran over the top of the bank. She reached the shallows, hastily wading out until she was knee-deep. "Moon!" she whispered harshly. "Are you—yah!"

Selis hopped sideways, cursing, as Moon stood up out of the water. He shifted to groundling and demanded, "What's wrong?"

"They must have been suspicious of her all along, and then they saw her talk to me," Selis explained rapidly. She waved her hands in frustration. "They never pay heed to me. Why should they do it now?"

Moon felt his heart nearly stop. "They caught her?" He started for shore. "They saw her shift?"

"No, I think it was Ilane." Selis splashed after him. "Fianis said Ilane saw something about Jade, something that reminded her of you. She said Ilane told the elders about it and made them suspicious."

Moon ran up the bank and through the greenroot plantings, Selis hurrying after him. It was dark between the tents ahead, but the common spaces were all lit by cooking fires and torches. And he could hear voices raised in argument. Jade said in exasperation, "Why do you think I want it? I want to kill Fell! That's the only thing it's good for, isn't it?"

Slipping through the first few rows of tents, Moon saw that Jade stood in the center of the camp with a milling crowd of Cordans gathered around. Most seemed more confused than angry. Jade faced the elders Dargan and Tacras, with Ildras, Kavath, and some of the other hunters surrounding her. And Ilane stood behind Ildras, watching with wide-eyed concern. She was also the only Cordan woman toward the front of the crowd. The others had all drawn back out of the conflict.

She's behind this, Moon thought, torn between anger and exasperation. *Of course.* Selis and Fianis were right; Ilane had seen something about Jade. Something that had told her that Jade was like Moon.

Grimly determined, Dargan told Jade, "We know you are lying to us! There is no settlement near here, no place you could walk from in the time you say."

Moon stopped at the edge of the communal space, catching Selis' arm. The elders' tent was a large conical structure on the far side of the open area. The flaps were drawn back and a couple of lamps were lit inside. A few people sat in front of it, watching the confrontation. He told her, "When they're distracted, go get the poison."

Selis threw him a dark look. "Make it a good distraction."

Selis slipped into the shadows, circling around the crowd. Moon started forward. Between the confusion and fitful light of the torches, no one had noticed him yet. Many of the hunters still carried their weapons, long spears for killing the smaller vargits, bows with bone-tipped arrows.

"Tell us who you are!" Tacras faced Jade, angry and a little frightened. "Are you Fell?"

"Of course not," Jade snapped, and Moon could hear the frustrated growl under her voice. "My people have been attacked by the Fell. We need help, help that you can provide! That should be the only thing that matters!"

Tacras fell back a step and Dargan looked uncertain. The other Cordans stirred uneasily. Moon knew one reason why they were suspicious. To their eyes, Jade was a woman alone facing an angry crowd, but she wasn't the least bit afraid of them.

Almost sounding as if he were trying to be reasonable, Dargan said, "But you aren't telling us everything. Even if there was a settlement nearby, why would they send only one of their number on such a dangerous journey?"

Jade started to answer, but Ilane shouted, "She lies! I told you, she looks like him. Her skin has the same pattern as the Fell that was among us."

"You should know!" someone in the back of the crowd yelled. Moon was pretty certain that was Fianis, who Ilane had replaced in Ildras' tent.

Ilane tossed her head, angry at the barb. "I speak the truth!"

Jade grimaced, and Moon snarled under his breath, annoyed at himself. *Damn, didn't think of that.* He and Jade had the same pattern to their scales, but he hadn't thought Ilane had caught more than a glimpse of him in his other form. *But she saw you after she gave you the poison.* She must have sat there in the tent and watched him, while Selis slept and Moon lay in a drugged stupor, the pattern appearing on his skin. It made his flesh creep.

"I don't know what you're talking about," Jade tried, folding her arms. "I think that woman's mad with... something."

Dargan didn't seem pleased by Ilane's interruption, but he said to Jade, "Then tell us why you came here alone."

Selis had reached the side of the elders' tent, waiting for a chance to slip through the entrance. The people sitting outside it hadn't moved. Moon stepped forward. Letting his voice carry, he said, "She's not alone."

Everyone turned. A confused murmur rose from the people on the far edge of the crowd who couldn't see. But the group around the elders stood still, stunned into silence.

"It's him!" Ilane shouted, ducking behind Ildras. "I told you!"

Moon shifted and leapt into the air. Everybody screamed and scrambled to get away. He spread his wings, flaring his spines and frills, and landed next to Jade. She gave him an annoyed look and said in Raksuran, "I assume this is a plan."

"Selis is in the elders' tent," he told her.

"Good." Jade shifted and flared her wings out with a violent snap.

More Cordans screamed and ran. Arrows flew, but Moon ducked and twisted away. Jade charged the archers and they scattered. She leapt to the top of a tent, flaring her wings again to draw everyone's gaze.

Ildras ran at Moon with a barbed spear. Moon caught the weapon and yanked it out of his hands. Careful to pull the blow, he used the hilt to slam Ildras in the head. Ildras staggered backward and collapsed.

Selis bolted out of the elders' tent. Moon shouted, "You've got it?"

"Yes!" She held up a woven bag.

Moon shot forward, caught her around the waist and jumped into the air, snapping his wings out to take flight. Jade followed right behind him.

Selis shrieked and grabbed his shoulders, her face buried against the flanges protecting his collarbone. Moon said in her ear, "Wrap your arms around my neck."

After a moment she loosened her grip enough to do it, winding her arms carefully between his spines.

Moon banked toward the flying island, its shape outlined against the starlit sky. They needed a chance to talk and to look at what Selis had managed to steal.

If the Cordans were still watching, they might see them land there, but there wasn't anything they could do about it.

He lighted in an open court, with a long, vine-choked pool and crumbling pillars. He set Selis down. She stumbled to the pool, sitting heavily on the edge to splash the stale water on her face.

Jade landed beside Moon, folding her wings. "You enjoyed that, didn't you?"

"No. Maybe." He had to point out, "You're a terrible liar."

"Yes, I realize that." She shook her ruffled frills, still irritated. "I was going to leave them a ring to make up for it, but if that's the way they're going to behave, forget it."

Still leaning over the water, Selis waved a hand at her. "Don't waste your gems. Those dungheads aren't worth it." She sat up, dug in the bag, and pulled out a rolled bandan leaf and a small wooden jug with a clay stopper. "I hope this is what you need. I just pulled the page out of their simple book. They had jugs of the stuff all made up, a dozen or more."

Moon shifted to groundling, and sat down on the moss-stained paving as Jade took the leaf. Jade unrolled it, angling it so the faint starlight would fall on it. In Altanic, it read, *Three-leafed purple bow, boil until blue, strain liquid, boil again...*

"Can we get this in the west?" he said. He had never heard of purple bow, three-leafed or not.

Jade thought for a moment. "If it's what I think it is. A flower that grows inside the boles of spiral trees?" she asked Selis.

"Yes." Selis frowned at the leaf, squinting to see it in the dark. "From what I could tell, it's just a simple, boiled down over and over again."

Moon took the stopper out of the jug and cautiously sniffed it. It had only a faint, weedy odor, but a familiar one that he was unlikely to forget. "This is what they gave me."

"Good." Jade sighed in relief, resting her head in her hand. She looked at Selis. "I take it you don't want to go back to your camp."

"No." Selis shrugged, resigned. "I suppose I should take this as a sign. I'll go to that mountain city you mentioned." She stopped, suddenly appalled. "By go there, you mean fly there, don't you?"

Moon gave her a look. "No, we're going to walk. It'll take half a turn, at least, and—"

"Fine." Disgruntled, Selis flicked a hand at him. "Just don't drop me."

Because time was short, they left that night, taking Selis with them and flying toward the mountain city. Moon had a few ideas about preparing Selis for the flight, from his experience of being carried in groundling form by Stone. They cut up a blanket to wrap inside her Cordan sandals, turning them into warmer boots, and cut another piece for her to use as a hood and scarf. Since all Selis had was a light cotton tunic, they gave her all their clothes, which amounted to Moon's pants and shirt, and the rough smock Jade had gotten at the caravanserai. The woven silk of the Raksuran fabric did the most to protect her from the cold wind during flight, but it still wasn't easy for her, and they stopped periodically to rest and let her recover a little.

It was late afternoon when they arrived on the opposite side of the pass from the city. Moon and Jade shifted to their other forms, took their clothes back, and Selis bundled up in the remaining blankets. Then they walked up the road to the city's bridge. Selis was exhausted and pale under her light green skin, but triumphant at making it there alive.

They took a space at the caravanserai for Selis. Moon and Jade meant to stay there only long enough to rest and stock up on food for the balance of the flight through the mountains. Moon had been trying to think of a story to explain their reappearance with Selis, but Selis had supplanted anything he could have come up with by airily telling the proprietor, "They're helping me leave my family, who are all dungheads."

They had arrived in time to catch the Serican traders before they started their journey back down the pass toward the Kishan territories. The Sericans were taking several passengers already, including a local family, and two women of the small-statured groundling race with the little horns. Moon sat with Selis while she bargained for her passage, but she did a good job of it, especially considering it was her first time.

Jade had already given Selis the rest of her jewelry—rings, necklace, and belt—which would be a small fortune in Kish. The caravanserai keeper had helped her convert one of the rings into little lumps of white metal, which were currency here and in Kish, so she could pay for her passage and supplies.

After the passage was arranged, Moon and Selis walked out into the plaza outside the caravanserai. It was still cold, but the morning was bright and sunny, the sky a deep, cloudless blue, promising better weather for Moon and Jade's journey back through the mountains. Since they had arrived, a little market had sprung up in the plaza, with hides spread out on the paving where the locals sold metalwork, leather, furs, and knitted wool clothing. Inside an open tent, a young woman carved tusk tattoos for the local men.

The Sericans had advised Selis on what supplies she would need for the journey, and Moon followed her around while she bought real boots and a fur-lined coat. Jade was asleep up in their cubby, and Moon knew he should join her. His back ached, and he was so tired that everything—the rock towers that loomed over them, the wagon the Sericans loaded, the awnings and wares of the market—had taken on a bright edge.

Selis pulled on the coat she had just bought, which was a little too big for her.

Once she was down in the Kishan valleys, it could easily be re-sold to traders going up the mountain route. She smoothed a hand over the leather, and not looking at Moon, said, "You were right. About leaving. Every moment away from those people is a relief. It's been so long since Kiaspur was destroyed, I forgot what a city was like. I thought I'd be afraid to be alone, but…" She shrugged, obviously uncomfortable expressing herself. "I want to see Kish."

Moon didn't need Selis to thank him, or to tell him he was right. She had trusted him when she didn't have to, helped him and Jade when it would have been easier and safer to do nothing. He just said, "There's lots of different travelers and traders in Kish. It's easy to blend in."

She watched him a moment. "And you're going to help these people kill Fell."

"They're my people." It felt strange to say it. He had only admitted it to himself a few days ago, and it still didn't feel quite real.

Selis snorted. "You're in love with that woman."

"No." At her skeptical expression, he gave in and added, "Maybe."

"You're stupid about women." After a moment of thought, she added, "You're stupid about men, too."

Moon couldn't argue with that. "I know."

"She treats you better than Ilane did, at least."

Moon started to protest, then subsided. Ilane had treated him well. She just hadn't cared about him beyond his ability to give her what she wanted and please her in bed. At the time, it had been enough, but then he had never known anyone who had actually seen him for what he was. He pointed out, "Jade hasn't tried to kill me yet." Despite all the provocation he had given her.

Selis made a noise of grudging agreement. "Just be careful."

Moon shrugged. That was something else he couldn't promise.

CHAPTER
FIFTEEN

⤢

They said goodbye to Selis in the mountain city, and flew day and night, stopping to rest as infrequently as possible. The wind was with them and the weather stayed fair, speeding their flight out of the mountains.

Once they were over the warmer forests they pushed even harder and didn't stop at all for the last two days. Just before sunset, they reached the valley where the others had taken shelter.

While the Fell stench lingered in the direction of the colony, no taint drifted through the grove where the blind lay. Moon was so exhausted he flew through a plume tree while trying to land and reached the ground in an uncontrolled tumble.

As he sprawled in the moss, Jade dropped through the canopy in an anxious rush, landing on her feet beside him.

"Moon, are you all right?"

He stifled a groan. "Yes. I meant to do that."

He had a few new bruises, but the plume tree's branches were too soft to cause any real damage. He shifted to groundling and nearly collapsed again when he shed the weight of his wings. It was a relief, even when it meant trading them for aching muscles and an encompassing weariness. He staggered unsteadily to his feet.

He caught a scent of Raksura, just before three hunters darted out of the undergrowth. They stood for a heartbeat in frozen shock.

Then the smallest one shouted, "You're back!" He shifted to groundling, turning into a slight boy, and threw himself at Jade to hug her awkwardly.

She returned the hug for a moment, her shoulders tense. "We're back," she said, her voice suddenly thick. "It's all right."

"We're so glad to see you," one of the others said. She tugged at the boy's shirt. "Strike, let go of the queen. Let her go into the blind. Bramble, go find Bone and—"

A violent rustle through the trees interrupted her and then Chime, Balm, and Root dropped to the ground. As all three shifted to groundling, Chime turned triumphantly to Root. "I told you they'd come back!"

"I didn't say they wouldn't," Root protested, and Moon lost the rest as Chime flung himself into his arms.

Moon stumbled and almost fell under the onslaught, flustered and self-conscious as Chime hugged him. He hadn't expected a greeting like this from anybody. Balm and Root fell on Jade just as enthusiastically, and as more hunters arrived, they all practically tumbled into the blind.

Inside, glowing moss strung from the woven branches gave wan light, and a small rock hearth was piled with stones spelled to give off warmth. Seated near it were Flower, the two teachers, Bead and Blossom, more hunters, and Niran. They all came to their feet with startled exclamations. Flower held her hands out for quiet, staring intently at Jade. "You've got the poison?" she demanded.

"Yes." Jade lifted her pack, pulling out the bag with the flask. "And we know how to make it."

Flower hissed in satisfaction, taking the bag.

"Poison?" Balm turned to her, startled. "What poison?"

"It's the poison that Moon knew of, that keeps Fell from shifting," Jade explained, looking around at the others. "We went to get it from some groundlings."

Ignoring the chorus of questions, Moon looked for Stone, and for a moment thought he was gone. His dark form didn't fill the back half of the chamber; Moon couldn't hear the slow rasp of his breath. Then, back against a partition, he saw a pallet made up of cut branches and woven plume fronds, with someone lying on it in groundling form.

Behind Moon, Bone and more of the hunters pushed through the branches into the blind, greeting Jade warmly, but Moon barely noticed. He went to the pallet and dropped to his knees. Stone's skin was ashen, and big gray-green bruises spread across his face, neck, his chest. Under the edge of his shirt was the seam of a half-healed wound, the skin puckered and raw.

Flower took out the poison flask and opened it to sniff cautiously at the contents. She looked up, telling Moon, "He was able to shift to groundling yesterday, but he's still not recovered. It'll be a few more days, at least."

Stone's eyes were half-open, but when Moon leaned over him, his good eye focused and he took a sharp breath. In a voice weak and grating with pain, he said, "It's you, good. Give me a hand."

Moon got an arm under him and helped him sit up. Stone's grip on him was strong, but he leaned on Moon's shoulder as if that was as far as he could get. He smelled of dried blood and sickness. Flower said hastily, "Don't let him stand. He thinks he's healed, the stubborn idiot."

Stone cleared his throat. His voice was uneven, and he didn't lift his head from Moon's shoulder. "Did you get it?"

"Yes." Moon frowned down at him. "How'd you know?"

"They said you and Jade went to get help from another court." Stone snorted in derision, then flinched, as if it had pulled at his wounds. "I knew that was useless. When they told me what happened, I figured you'd try for the poison the groundlings used on you."

Jade knelt beside them, touching Stone's shoulder gently. She asked the others, "What about Pearl, and the other Aeriat? Are they watching the colony?"

"Yes. Not that there's been much to watch," Bone told her, sinking down beside the hearth with a weary grunt. The others were settling down, taking seats around the chamber, crowding together, listening anxiously. He added, "We've counted at least five kethel, but we're not certain how many dakti or rulers."

Jade nodded. "What about the rest of the court?" No one answered immediately and her voice tightened. "They're alive?"

Moon waited for the answer, tensing. This can't be for nothing. *If we're too late...*

Flower had unrolled the leaf with the boiling instructions for the poison; she looked up with a grim expression. "As far as we know."

Someone in the back added bleakly, "As far as we hope."

Jade's spines lifted in agitation. "You haven't been able to get anyone inside the colony?"

"No." Balm's jaw tightened as she admitted the failure. "We could never get anyone in through the water channels under the platform, the way we planned before you left. They keep a kethel lying in the river down there."

Moon slumped, a little relieved. At least they hadn't found proof that the others were all dead.

Chime added, "We even thought of trying to get Niran inside, since he doesn't need to shift, but the more we talked about it…" He turned to Niran with a shrug.

"The more foolish it sounded," Niran finished, sounding ironic. He looked better than Moon would have expected for a groundling living rough in the forest with Raksura. His white hair was tied tightly back and he wore an oversized silk shirt over his own clothes, probably borrowed from one of the Arbora. "It was getting near the place at all that was the stumbling block, not what one could or couldn't do once inside."

"But we have seen the dakti bring in food," Balm said. "Grasseater carcasses, and melon and roots from our own plantings: that's food for Arbora and Aeriat, not Fell."

So what are the Fell eating? Moon thought, sickened, but managed not to say it aloud.

Jade's jaw tightened, as if the same thought had crossed her mind. She asked, "So there's been no sign of anyone inside trying to escape?"

Bone lifted his hands, helpless and frustrated, and Moon had the feeling he and the others must have talked of little else while they waited here, debating the question from every angle.

"If no one in the court can shift," Bone said, "they wouldn't have any chance to run. The major kethel are always on the terraces and in the river."

"In short, we don't know anything," Chime said with a wince.

Distracted, Flower shook the flask again. "How much of this do we need to make?" she asked. "Moon, how much did they give you?"

Moon thought back to that night with Ilane. Distance and a little revenge had made that memory less painful. "There couldn't have been much, at first. It was in a small cup, and the odor wasn't strong. I don't remember anything after I drank it. It was morning when I started to come to, but I could hardly move. Then they forced some more down my throat." He looked up to see they were all staring at him. "What?"

Appalled, Blossom said, "It sounds horrible. You lived with these people and they did this to you, just like that?"

Moon didn't have an answer for her. It had been horrible, but after stealing the poison and scaring the Cordans all to pieces, he didn't have much to complain about.

"We all thought you went to Star Aster to ask for help," Balm told Jade. "Pearl sent Vine and me to Wind Sun. We only got back two days ago."

"I don't suppose they offered any?" Jade didn't look particularly hopeful.

"No. It's as we thought before you left. They said the survivors would be welcome to take refuge, but they wouldn't send warriors." Balm lifted a hand, frustrated. "They didn't say so in so many words, but it was obvious they thought we brought this on ourselves."

"Yes. We were certain Star Aster would say the same, so we tried for the poison instead." Jade sounded grimly resigned. "And I don't blame Wind Sun. We had no formal alliance, and they're a small court. And they know if they had asked for our help, we would have said no."

There was an uncomfortable moment as everyone absorbed that. In a small voice, one of the younger hunters said, "So we did bring it on ourselves?"

Stone stirred, lifting his head enough to say in a raw croak, "No. Nobody asks for something like this."

Flower stoppered the poison flask and set it aside, saying in exasperation, "Stone, damn you, lie down or you'll never get better."

"I feel fine," Stone insisted faintly, slumping back against Moon's shoulder.

"We can tell," Moon said, making his voice dry to hide his relief. If Stone felt well enough to argue, he couldn't be as weak as he looked.

"Why isn't he in a healing sleep?" Jade asked, moving around to help Moon lower Stone to the pallet again.

"With a consort, that's easier said than done," Flower told her. "He has to cooperate with me, and he won't."

Moon heard a rush of wings outside, like wind through the trees.

"That's Pearl and the others," Bone said, cocking his head to listen.

Moon flicked a quick look at Jade. This could still go badly wrong, if Pearl had changed her mind about their plan to use the poison. *She's been here all this time and hasn't come up with any better idea.*

A hunter ducked into the blind and said, "The queen's back." He pulled the branches aside and Pearl stepped in. She was still in her winged form, and her expression gave no hint to her mood. Moon caught a glimpse of the other Aeriat behind her, with River pushing forward to get a look into the blind.

Without glancing back at him, Pearl flared her spines to keep him out. She said, coolly, "We need to speak in private."

Still sitting beside Stone, Jade inclined her head. "With the leaders of the Arbora."

Flower exchanged a look with Bone, and told the others, "The rest of you start collecting this plant. It's three-leafed purple bow, that grows in and near spiral tree boles. Chime and Blossom, organize everyone into groups. Salt and Strike, make sure nothing eats Niran."

Niran snorted, as if this was a running joke. He got to his feet, telling Flower, "Thank you for your consideration."

"Wait." Jade held Pearl's gaze. "Send two hunters back to watch the colony. Keep the Aeriat here."

That was only good sense. Branch might have been the traitor, but Moon still had doubts. And if he wasn't the traitor, it could be someone else here, especially the Aeriat who had come to the Blue Stone Temple with Pearl.

Pearl's eyes narrowed, but she didn't question it. She turned her head to tell the Aeriat, "Do as she says. No one else is to leave this grove."

Flower and Bone stayed where they sat. The other Arbora got up to leave the blind, some casting uneasy glances back. Moon started to get up, and Jade shook her head slightly. He eased back down, not sure if this was a good idea. It seemed a bad time to antagonize Pearl, when they should be focused on how best to get the poison into the Fell. But sitting here for this long had given his exhausted body a chance to stiffen up. He felt heavy, as if he was going to sink right into the earth.

Chime and Balm went last, and reluctantly. Moon heard the other Aeriat outside asking frustrated questions before Balm drove them off.

Pearl waited until the voices faded, then sat down, curling her tail around neatly. She didn't look at Moon. He thought that was just as well. She said to Jade, "I take it you were successful."

"We brought some of the poison and the knowledge to make it." Jade flicked her tail restlessly and added, "We can't risk anyone going near the colony. If Branch wasn't the traitor, whoever it is—"

"I did follow that." Pearl's voice was acid. "Even if your poison works as it should, there's still the power that kept the court from shifting. If it forces us into groundling form—"

"Then we'll fight that way," Jade finished tightly.

Pearl lifted a brow. "That's easily said."

Bone leaned forward. "We've got some skinning knives, and javelins, to use as weapons. If the dakti are sick and forced to shift to groundling, we'll have a chance." He hesitated. "We've sat here for days trying to think of a better plan, or how to seek help. We can't leave the others to the Fell, even if it kills us all."

"He's right." Flower hugged herself, tucking her hands under the sleeves of her smock. "We've discussed it at length, all of us. We won't abandon the rest of the court."

Pearl tapped her claws on the dirt, and added deliberately, "There's something else to consider. All these days, the Fell haven't bothered to search the valleys for us." She fixed her gaze on Jade. "Why is that, do you think?"

Flower and Bone both started to speak, but Jade's voice cut across theirs. "Wait." Watching Pearl, Jade said, "The queen is about to tell us."

Pearl tilted her head. "I think it's because they want something very specific from us, and until now, that something hasn't been here."

Moon felt his skin start to crawl. *It's not me,* he thought. It couldn't be. *This is not my fault.*

Jade met her gaze, then let her breath out in a hiss. "It's a possibility." Pearl lifted a brow and Jade added, reluctantly, "Kathras followed us."

Bone frowned, and Flower stared at Jade, blank with surprise. She said, "The ruler who came out to speak to Pearl?"

Jade didn't look at Moon. "He followed us as far as the mountains. Moon killed him, but before he died he said enough to tell us that the Fell thought we were fleeing. The other rulers must have felt his death, seen something of what he saw, at least."

Moon looked down at Stone, keeping his expression still. Maybe she wouldn't have to tell the whole story. Stone was still conscious, and squinting at him suspiciously. That didn't help.

"But how did Kathras follow you?" Flower asked. "By scent? Surely if he was that close…"

Jade spread her hands on the packed earth. "We didn't scent him until we reached the mountains. And he must have started after we left, because he near flew himself to death to catch up with us. A more powerful ruler or group of rulers must have been forcing him on." She shrugged uneasily. "It's as if they have a mentor, whose augury can point them in the right direction. Kathras knew nothing of our plans, or the poison, but he knew which way to fly to find us."

Flower hissed in anger, and rubbed her face. "I don't understand this. There's something we're missing."

"Are we missing something, Jade?" Pearl asked with deceptive lightness.

Jade hesitated, drawing her claws through the dirt. "There's one more thing."

Moon tensed, suddenly cold with dread. She hadn't said she wouldn't tell them. He reminded himself he hadn't done anything wrong, he hadn't betrayed anyone except himself, turns ago in Saraseil.

Reluctantly, Jade said, "This Fell flight knows Moon. A long time ago, in a groundling city, he killed a ruler they were related to. That's why Kathras said he followed us."

Flower and Bone stared at Moon. Stone groaned under his breath. Pearl just looked grimly satisfied.

She's going to use this against us, Moon thought. He couldn't let it look like Jade was shielding him. He said, "It was eighteen turns ago, when I didn't know what I was. I let them catch me, then when I realized I wasn't one of them, I killed a ruler and escaped." He was a little startled at how easy it was to tell the story now. "Kathras sounded like he—they—felt betrayed."

The two Arbora were quiet long enough to painfully stretch Moon's nerves. Then Flower exchanged a rueful look with Bone, and said, "Well, I know what River would say to that."

Jade cocked her head, a mild challenge. "Then let's save the delight of hearing it now."

"What does Stone say?" Bone asked soberly.

Stone's eyes were closed now, but he said, "If he's a Fell ally, he's doing a bad job of it. He keeps killing them. He killed a bunch of dakti at Sky Copper." With a grunt, he added, "Said we should eat them."

"I did not, you sick bastard," Moon snapped.

Flower shook her head, and the harsh line of Bone's mouth tugged upward in a reluctant smile. He said, "That's well enough for now, then."

"We can talk about this later," Jade told Pearl. "We need to start work on the poison."

Pearl stood, looking down at them. "As you say. But we will talk of it." She gave Jade an ironic nod, and walked out of the blind.

Jade twitched her spines and turned away, hissing to herself.

Bone got to his feet, saying, "When we free the court, we can settle all this. Until then—"

"I know," Jade snarled. She shook herself, and added, more softly, "I know."

Bone shook his head and followed Pearl outside.

Flower sighed and gave Moon a wry look. "You're certainly a handful, aren't you?"

He shrugged, defensive and uneasy. "I can't help it."

Jade settled her spines with difficulty, then turned back to face them. "Flower, have you been able to scry anything?"

Flower gave her a glare of pure frustration. "I only get asked that question ten times a day." She carefully tucked the poison flask and the leaf back into the bag. "We know someone told the Fell we were meeting you at the Blue Stone Temple. I've bent my scrying on that, trying to make certain it was Branch. But all I see is an image of the colony."

Jade frowned, thinking it over. "As if the one who actually betrayed us is trapped with the others?"

"Or something." Flower shook her head wearily. "For a while now we've thought something was wrong in the colony, but no matter how hard the mentors looked, we never found any real sign of it. There was nothing solid, nothing but feelings, bad luck, bad omens. I'm starting to wonder." She sighed. "I don't know."

"We'll know more when we get back inside." Jade sounded grimly certain.

"We can hope." Flower pushed to her feet. "Now you two rest while we get this poison started."

Flower slipped out through the woven branches, leaving them alone except for Stone, who was breathing deeply again. Moon could hear the Arbora moving around outside. They talked quietly, with hope and excitement about the plan.

There was a patch of bare dirt at his feet that looked very comfortable, so

Moon lay down on it. Jade still sat there, staring grimly at nothing. He reached out to her, tugging on one of her frills. "Sleep."

She growled, but came over to lie beside him, wrapped an arm around his waist, and pulled him against her. Moon tucked his head under her chin. It might have been easier when it was just the two of them, alone in the vast distances of the Three Worlds, but he had missed Chime and Flower and Balm and the Arbora. After a moment, Jade sighed and said, "It's for the best."

Moon knew she meant it was for the best that he had told them about Saraseil. He wasn't so sure. It was something Pearl could use against him, and now that he had decided to stay, that mattered a great deal more. "Will she tell the others?"

He felt her stir uneasily. "Not the Arbora. Not at first." She wove her fingers through his hair. "They'll have to know sometime. It's better if it comes from you."

"I know." And it was painful how much it mattered.

"When this is over, we'll worry about it," she said, unconsciously echoing Bone.

Moon woke surrounded by sleeping Arbora, several of whom were using him to keep their feet warm. Late morning light came through the woven branches of the blind, and Niran rustled around near the hearth.

Moon didn't feel like he had slept very long. He had been dimly aware of the Arbora coming and going all night, as they collected the plant and brought it back to the blind. Just before dawn, some hunters had brought in a couple of kills. Rested just enough to feel hungry again, Moon had crawled out to take his share, then crawled back to the blind. Jade had gone off with Flower at that point, to check on the progress with the poison.

Now he sat up, propping himself on his arms, still feeling bleary and vague. He had discovered something else about Raksura: they weren't meant to fly for days on end without sleeping or eating. He was coming around to the idea that he had been born to do nothing more than lie around in the forest and eat and nap.

Sitting at the hearth, Niran glanced up. "Sorry. I didn't mean to wake you." He had a blanket wrapped around his shoulders and was trying to balance a water gourd in the heating stones. He looked bleary-eyed and vague, too.

"It's all right," Moon said around a yawn. He craned his neck to see Stone, still lying on the pallet. It didn't look as if he had moved, but his breathing was deep and even. "Did you find enough of the plant?"

"Not nearby. We had to go a little further up the valley, but there it was plentiful." Niran hesitated, as if he found what he was about to say awkward. "I realized I hadn't—I wanted to thank you, for taking the time to warn my family. If you hadn't, they would surely have been killed."

Moon shrugged, a little uncomfortable with the gratitude. It would have been pointlessly cruel not to warn them; there was no reason the Islanders should suffer just because the Raksura were trapped. "Did the Fell find the flying boats?"

"They went right to them." Niran shook his head, resigned. "They climbed over everything, damaged the decks somewhat, and searched the surrounding forest, but Bone said he didn't think they looked any further."

Moon had thought the Fell would surely destroy both boats, but it was hard to tell if the Fell understood how important property could be to groundlings. Since the boats seemed abandoned, the Fell might just have forgotten about them altogether.

"When this is over," he said, "maybe you can still get them back to the islands."

Moon had wondered how Niran had been getting along, but if he could casually mention Bone, by far the most frightening Arbora here, then he had probably gotten over his dislike and suspicion.

Niran admitted, "I've thought about trying to take one back now, but it seems certain the Fell would notice and pursue me. Even if they didn't, there's the danger of storms, and I can't secure the ship against one alone. Balm said that if possible, after this is over, some of you will help me return." He took a deep breath. "I hope to find out more about these Fell before I go. If, as you all fear, they have some new power, they could become even more virulent than ever."

That was what Moon was afraid of. And he wasn't sure that any amount of warning could help vulnerable groundlings. "At least you could tell your people how to make the poison."

Niran snorted. "I am practically an expert at it now." He nodded toward the east wall of the blind. "The others are brewing it over by the stream. Flower thinks it will take at least half a day."

Moon should go see if they needed any help. He climbed to his feet, carefully stepped over the sleeping bodies of the hunters, and made his way outside.

He pushed through the screen of branches and out into the cool morning air, following the scent of the poison through the trees. He caught a glimpse of someone moving in the foliage overhead, but assumed it was a warrior or hunter. Then Pearl dropped lightly to the ground.

Caught in groundling form, Moon didn't try to shift; he just stopped, watching her warily. Hunters slept in the blind barely thirty paces away, and he could hear faint sound from ahead, toward the stream, so if she wanted to kill him she had to do it in front of witnesses.

Pearl folded her wings, taking her time about it. With more than a trace of irony, she said, "I admit I'm surprised you returned."

Moon made his expression just a little bored. "If you thought I was lying about the poison, why did you agree to let Jade go with me?"

"I didn't think you were lying," she corrected. "I just didn't believe you'd return to fight for the court. And that was before we found out about your earlier adventure with the Fell."

He had known that was coming. He set his jaw. "It was a long time ago, and it has nothing to do with this." He reminded himself he didn't have to justify anything to her.

She eyed him deliberately. That cold gaze that made him feel as if his skin was inside out. "You deliberately drew their attention. Even the groundlings you were living with would have known better."

Yes, the groundlings had known better, but Moon had been young and half out of his head with fear that he was somehow related to these murdering mindless predators. He knew that now, but hindsight didn't help. "What do you want from me?"

Pearl seemed to find that question grimly amusing. She gave him a long look. "I want to know if you've told us everything."

"I've told Jade everything."

"And she seems to believe you." She flicked her tail thoughtfully. "But she hasn't been foolish enough to take you as consort yet."

"Yes, she did. On the way to the east." As soon as the words were out, Moon cursed himself and thought, *That was stupid.* He didn't know how it worked, but it had to be Jade's place to tell the court, especially Pearl.

Pearl seemed to freeze for a moment, her expression hardening. Then she looked away with a slight smile that just barely revealed her fangs. "Even if you gave her a clutch, that doesn't make you her consort."

Walk away, Moon told himself, *just walk away.* He had made a mistake and he didn't need to aggravate it. But he had to know, and he couldn't help himself. "What do you mean?"

Pearl said, "When a queen takes a consort, she puts a marker in his scent. Only other queens can detect it, but it gives you a status in the court that nothing can take away." She looked at him again and laughed. "You should have bargained for that before you bred with her."

Stung, he said, "She doesn't have a clutch." *And it wasn't a bargain.*

Pearl cocked her head, as if honestly curious. "That's what she told you?"

Moon stood there, unable to speak, furious with himself for letting her do this to him. *She's lying.* That seemed obvious. *To drive you away from Jade.* Of course she was lying.

Behind him, two half-asleep hunters stumbled out of the blind. They stopped when they saw Pearl and Moon.

Pearl turned away without another word and moved off through the green shadows toward the stream.

Embarrassed, one of the hunters said, "Sorry. Didn't mean to interrupt."

Moon swallowed his anger. It wasn't exactly an unwelcome interruption.

"It's all right."

He plunged into the undergrowth and went on toward the stream. He reached a clearing where the Arbora had scraped the moss back to bare dirt, but built a canopy of branches and fronds overhead. From the air, the open space would appear to be just another stand of trees. Jade, Flower, Balm, and some of the hunters sat on fallen logs and rocks.

In the center of the cleared space, they had dug a large pit in the forest floor. It was partially covered with tree fronds, and Flower stood over the open side, using a stick to poke dubiously at the dark contents. Waterskins, round river rocks, broken water reeds, and a pile of dark foliage that must be the three-leafed purple bow lay nearby. Steam was rising off the pit, leaking between the fronds; Flower must have used her magic to heat stones, dropping them in to boil the water. The weedy odor of the poison hung damply in the air.

Jade and Balm sat on a fallen log, talking to Bone who, even in groundling form, looked almost toad-like compared to the more delicate Aeriat. River and Drift sprawled on the ground nearby, bored and restless. Song, Root, Sand, and the other warriors slept under the tree roots.

Chime sat a little apart, near Flower's pile of ingredients, studying the poison-making instructions. Moon took a seat next to him, and Chime glanced up, then frowned. "Are you all right?"

"Sure, just… tired." Moon self-consciously avoided looking toward Jade. Across the clearing, Pearl stepped out of the ferns. Showing absolutely no interest in Moon, she walked over to sit down near Bone.

Chime grunted and went back to the leaf. "Don't breathe the fumes. If anyone stands too close, it makes them woozy."

No one else seemed to be listening, so Moon asked, "Is it true that queens mark their consorts?"

Chime nodded. "It's something only other queens can scent." He peered at Moon a little uncertainly. "Are you worried about that? I mean, it wouldn't hurt. It just tells other queens that you're taken, so they don't fight over you."

"I just wondered." If Pearl wasn't lying, it meant that Moon had given up his only advantage, that there would be no reason now for the others to stop Pearl from driving him out. He didn't even blame Jade. Not much, anyway. He had refused her gifts, and after that she had asked him for a clutch, not to be her consort. It was just that after hearing about the other queens and consorts, he had assumed it was the same thing.

But it didn't change anything. He had known that he would have to fight Pearl and her allies if he wanted to stay. Now it would be harder. *If it's true,* he reminded himself.

He glanced up to find Pearl watching him, and looked away, resisting the urge to bare his teeth at her. Then he found himself staring at Chime. Under the bronze of Chime's skin, on his forehead and cheek, there were green-black discolorations, bruises on top of bruises. In the shadows last night, Moon hadn't noticed, but in the daylight it was obvious. "Did you have another bad landing?"

"What? Oh." Chime frowned at the ground, scratching absently at the moss with his heel, as if he had forgotten he was in groundling form and didn't have a claw there. "No."

"Somebody hit you." Moon felt a growl building in his chest. "Pearl?"

Chime snorted. "Pearl doesn't know I'm alive." He twitched uncomfortably under Moon's continued stare, and finally admitted, "It was River."

"Balm didn't help you?" Moon looked across the clearing. He had thought Balm and Chime were friends, at least from the way they had played together in the lake. She sat near Jade, her chin propped on her hand, listening to the others talk. Her expression was glum and her body drooped with exhaustion.

Chime shrugged wearily. "When she's around. But she and Vine were gone to Wind Sun for days, and… I don't want to ask her for help. I don't want them to gang up on her. She's Jade's clutch-mate, and they've always been together, and with Pearl at odds with Jade, Balm's position is hard enough. What are you doing?"

Moon stood and crossed the clearing to stand over River.

River looked up at him with a smile. "Was Chime begging you for help?" It was as if he had overheard their conversation, or been waiting for Moon to notice Chime's bruises.

"You're going to be begging for help." Moon was certain his first mistake at Indigo Cloud had been not beating River insensible at the earliest opportunity. But he had just enough sense left to know it would be better if River attacked him first.

"What do you care?" River shoved himself upright, sneering, leaning forward in challenge. "You're a mongrel solitary, acting like you think you're first consort when you're not even part of this court."

That stung more than River could know. Moon kept his voice even. "I'm still a consort. That's something you'll never have, no matter how many queens you sleep with."

River snarled, flushing a darker copper. "You're the one who came here to hide. You're the one who brought the Fell down on us. They followed you to the mountains thinking you were running away again. They came here for you, because you went to them!"

Moon fell back a step. The whole clearing went silent; even the wind stopped. The hunters exchanged uneasy looks, whispering to each other. Woken by the commotion, the Aeriat were watching, startled and wary. Flower and Bone both stared at Pearl.

Pearl's spines lifted and she snapped, "River. That's enough."

Jade came to her feet. She glanced at Pearl, her expression tight with fury. In a growl, she said, "Moon, leave it. We can't afford a fight now."

Maybe not, but they were going to have one. And if he wasn't her consort, then he had no obligation to listen to her. "Then keep us from shifting."

Jade's eyes went hooded. "Done."

"What?" River looked from Jade to Pearl. Moon saw his eyes narrow when he tried to shift and failed. He glared at Jade, hissing in annoyance.

Moon asked, "Afraid?"

"You're too much of a coward to fight in the air," River began. Moon shut him up with a punch to the face.

Moon didn't know how to have a serious fight as a Raksura without killing or crippling his opponent. But as a groundling, he knew plenty. River staggered back, then surged forward with a snarl, tackling Moon. Moon landed hard on his back but brought a knee up and rolled, throwing River to one side. They both scrambled upright and River, growling in earnest now, ducked a punch and nearly slammed a blow into Moon's throat.

They fought across the clearing, smashing into the undergrowth, slamming each other into trees, sending hunters scrambling away. Then Moon caught River with a hard punch in the gut, and kicked him in the chin when he doubled over.

River dropped in the dirt, tried to get up, but sank back down, panting with effort. Moon leaned over him, grabbing his hair to lift his head up. His voice rough from the blow to his throat, he said, "Talk all you want. But if you want to fight, you fight me."

River bared his teeth, but it was a half-hearted gesture.

Moon dropped him, turned his back, and walked away. He had no idea where he was going, just away from the clearing, away from the stares and accusations. His hands hurt, though he couldn't feel his other bruises yet; Raksuran heads were harder than groundling, so he had had to hit River hard enough to bruise his knuckles.

He was barely past the first stand of trees when Chime caught up with him. Sounding bewildered, Chime said, "Is it true?"

Moon didn't stop, didn't look at him. The hurt tone in Chime's voice just made it all the worse. "Yes. Some of it."

"But you went to the Fell?"

Moon shook his head. "Go ask Flower. She knows."

Chime stopped, and Moon kept walking, weaving away through the trees, looking for a quiet spot away from the blind.

At least Pearl wasn't holding it in reserve to use against him anymore.

CHAPTER
SIXTEEN

Moon spent the rest of the morning in a tree near the clearing in his shifted form, hanging upside down by his tail from a branch. The hunters kept watch on him, the way they kept watch on all the Aeriat on Jade's orders, but no one came after him. That was probably for the best, because he was so bitterly angry he couldn't think straight.

He knew the Fell hadn't attacked Indigo Cloud because of him; it didn't make sense. Even if the Fell had shamen that could predict where Moon would be, they had had plenty of time to come after him before this. The Fell had been moving all over the east for the past twenty turns, and so had Moon. And yes, it had been a mistake to go to the Fell in Saraseil, and no one knew that better than him. But if these Fell felt betrayed because Moon had killed the ruler Liheas there after all this time, then that was crazy.

Moon had never faced a ruler before, and he had been younger then and not as strong. He had one chance to escape, and it had been better to wait for Liheas to sleep, even if he had to pretend to believe the lies and let Liheas touch him. And he had no idea why he was trying to justify this to himself. Fell killed groundlings like cattle, tortured them for pleasure, and destroyed their homes; if the Fell didn't want to be killed in return, that was just too damn bad.

Restless, Moon gripped the branch with his tail more tightly, his scales scraping through the bark. He had no idea if Jade still wanted him after this, if she hadn't counted on having to tell the others about what he had done in Saraseil, or their reaction to it. If Pearl was telling the truth and Jade already had a clutch, she didn't need him anymore.

That hurt more than anything.

He knew that Pearl had driven off consorts that had been born into the court because they had belonged to other queens, or because she hadn't wanted to look at them after her own consort had died. He knew she wouldn't hesitate to try to drive him off, if Jade did nothing to stop her. His only option would be to fight, to hurt or kill Raksura he had no real quarrel with, to stay in a place where no one wanted him.

That's if we survive the attack tonight, he reminded himself. They still needed him for the battle at least.

After that… Jade had said that having seen what a Raksuran court was like, he wouldn't be able to settle anywhere else. *She was still wrong,* he thought, his anger tinged with that familiar sense of resignation. *I wasn't able to settle anywhere else before this, either.*

He tried to ignore the traitor voice that whispered, *And if this Fell flight is following you, for whatever insane reason of its own?* That meant no more groundling camps or cities, either.

When the shadows were lengthening toward afternoon, a hunter came to the base of the tree and said, diffidently, "Moon? They want you to come and look at the poison."

What Moon wanted was to hang in this tree until it was time to go be killed by the Fell. But he dropped to the ground, shifted to his groundling form, and followed her back to the clearing.

The others were gathered there, a cautious distance from the pit. Moon tasted the air and knew why. This close to the liquid, the weedy odor had taken on an intensity that made his stomach want to turn.

He stopped at the edge of the group. The hunters and the Aeriat flicked looks at him, and some tried to unobtrusively sidle away. Chime stood over the pit with Flower, watching her stir the contents. He saw Moon and twitched uneasily, turning his attention back to the poison. Jade turned toward him, but Moon avoided her eyes. Pearl, standing at the opposite side of the pit, ignored him.

Moon didn't see River, who was probably back at the blind, being catered to and sympathized with.

Flower looked up, her face flushed and hot. She saw him and held out one of the nut shells they were using as cups. "Moon, does this color look right? It's changed from purplish to clear, like the sample in the flask."

The group parted for him and he stepped forward, just close enough to see the contents of the cup. It had been night when Ilane had given him the poison, but he would have noticed a dark substance in the normally light green tisane. He nodded.

"Good. Now we have to test it." Flower told the others, "If it needs another boil…"

"Yes, but we can't test it on you," Chime said in frustration. "We'll need you when we enter the colony. Whoever we test it on might not recover in time."

"Yes, I know, but I always test my simples on myself, and…" Flower took a few steps back and sat down heavily. "I think the fumes are getting to me."

Chime flung his arms in the air, and Jade said, patiently, "Yes, Flower, that's what we've all been trying to tell you."

Balm said, "But we do need to test it. If we put it into the water and nothing happens, there won't be a second chance."

Behind Moon, someone cleared his throat.

"I'll do it."

Moon turned to see the youngest hunter, Strike, who had been the first to greet Jade last night. Strike said, "I want to fight in the battle, but I'm the smallest, so I'm the… most expendable?"

Bone scratched his head, and said reluctantly, "Not expendable, but… You are the smallest, and I'd thought to leave you behind anyway."

Jade grimaced, watching the boy unhappily. Moon wanted to protest, to offer himself, though that made just as little sense as using Flower to test it. But the whole idea of deliberately putting an Arbora at risk, especially a young one, felt wrong down to his bones. He wished they could catch a dakti to test it on, but there was too great a chance that the other Fell might sense what was happening.

Jade said to Strike, "If you're certain. If you're not, tell us now."

Strike twitched his spines, obviously uncomfortable with all the scrutiny, but he said, "I'm certain."

Flower took the cup of poison and poured water into it from a skin. She handed the cup to Strike. "Better sit down."

Strike took a seat on the mossy ground, careful not to spill the clear liquid. He looked down into it, biting his lip. "Should I shift to groundling?"

"Most of the Fell won't be," Bone said, crouching near the boy. "We might as well see what it does."

Jade nodded. "Go ahead, Strike."

The boy took a deep breath and downed the cup in one long gulp. Everyone watched uneasily.

Birds called in the trees, and somewhere on the far side of the stream a treeling squeaked. After a time, when nothing dramatic happened, some of the hunters started to relax, moving away a little to sit down in the dirt.

Chime began, "Maybe it's not—"

Then Strike swayed a little, his eyelids drooping. "I'm really sleepy. Is that supposed to…" Suddenly he shifted to groundling and slumped over.

Bone caught him, easing him to the ground as Flower hurried over. She held a hand in front of Strike's mouth, carefully pushed his eyelids up to look at his pupils, then put her head on his chest to listen to his heart. After a tense moment, she sat up, wiping the sweat off her forehead. "He seems well enough, just deeply asleep."

Moon stepped closer. "Look at his arms."

Bone turned Strike's arm and pushed up the sleeve of his shirt. On the boy's deep copper skin, lines were already appearing, very faint but growing darker, mimicking the scale pattern of his Raksuran form.

It had taken longer to work on Moon, but then he was bigger than Strike. He said, "That's what it did to me. That's how they knew."

Jade looked at Pearl, her spines half-lifted in challenge. "Well?"

Pearl inclined her head, as if conceding a point to Jade. "We'll go at nightfall."

Moon hung around the fringes of the clearing as the others hurried to get ready. Strike was carried back to the blind to recover. Some of the hunters left to take a kill so everyone could eat before the battle. The others organized themselves to transfer the poison to waterskins, a messy and dangerous job. After the first one got woozy and had to stagger off, they sent for Niran and reorganized, with him being the one to fill the skins from the pit. The fumes didn't seem to have any effect on him at all.

The others crouched on the ground nearby. Chime sketched a map of the river and the colony in the dirt. Moon leaned against a tree, just close enough to hear their plans. If they didn't want him there, they could tell him to leave. Chime was saying, "We need to distract the kethel guarding the river, or we won't be able to get close enough to get the poison into the channels that draw up the water."

"We still don't know if we'll be able to shift once we get near the colony," Pearl said, still sounding skeptical of the entire thing.

"We know that," Jade said, her frills ruffled with tension. She turned to Bone.

"Exactly how close were the Arbora to the colony when they realized they couldn't shift?"

Bone frowned, looking around at the others. "What did Blossom say? They were below the first terrace? Or closer?"

Balm stood. "I'll go to the blind and ask her."

Jade waved a distracted assent, and Balm headed out of the clearing.

Moon watched her go, mostly to have something to look at besides Jade. So he saw Balm glance back before she stepped into the undergrowth.

Huh, Moon thought, not sure what it was about that glance that set off a warning. As if Balm had wanted to make sure she wasn't followed. Moon was standing back against the thick trunk of the tree, at an angle, and he didn't think she had seen him watching her.

It seemed unlikely. But there was no point taking chances. He pushed off the tree and picked his way through the ferns after her.

He realized almost immediately that she wasn't walking toward the blind. She moved at an angle to it, to pass it at some distance and wind her way deeper into the forest. She avoided the sentries, the hunters posted in the trees near the blind and the clearing.

Even as he followed her, Moon couldn't believe she was doing what it looked like she was doing. She wouldn't betray Jade, let alone the rest of the court. *Not in her right mind,* he thought uneasily. There had to be another explanation.

They were perhaps a hundred paces past the blind, where the spiral and plume trees grew close together, linked by vines to form an almost impenetrable canopy overhead. She shifted, half-extending her wings to leap partway up the trunk of a plume tree.

Moon shifted too, sprinting through the undergrowth to catch up with her. He reached the base of the trunk and looked up to see her climbing rapidly; she was trying to get past the canopy to take flight. He still couldn't believe it.

"Balm," he called. "Where are you going?"

Her claws slipped on the wood as she twisted around. She stared down at him and her face was empty of expression, as if she hadn't heard him, couldn't see him.

Moon froze for one startled heartbeat. *All right, now I believe it.* He scrambled up the trunk after her. She climbed frantically, showering him with fragments of bark. She fought her way past the heavy branches, then jumped, flapping to get height. Right behind her, Moon planted both feet on the trunk and shoved off.

She rose over the trees with strong wing beats but Moon was stronger. He slammed into her from behind and caught her around the waist. She shrieked in rage, clawing at his arms, but he snapped his wings in and twisted to the side, using his weight to pull her off balance.

She flailed. A buffet from her wing caught him a stunning blow to the head, and they tumbled toward the ground.

They crashed through the leafy branches, and Moon made a desperate grab, catching hold of one. The branch bent under their weight, swinging them into the bole with a brutal thump, but it didn't break. Balm abruptly stopped fighting and pulled her wings in, survival instinct overriding everything else.

Moon kept hold of her, not sure if the fall had shocked her back to her senses enough for her to save herself. He looked down and saw flashes of color through the undergrowth and the lower branches as all the Aeriat and most of the hunters crashed through the forest toward them. *Wonderful,* Moon thought sourly. This explanation wasn't going to be easy. He picked out a mostly clear area of mossy ground, and dropped.

He extended his wings just enough to control their fall. They landed hard but intact. He let go of Balm and she stumbled away a step, then sat down on the moss, making no attempt to get away. The Aeriat and hunters arrived in a rush, surrounding them, most of them growling, others just baffled. Jade landed in front of Moon, her mane flared, and flung her arms up. "Quiet!" The others went silent. "Moon, what—"

"The Fell did something to her." Moon said it rapidly, staying focused on Jade, trying to get the words out before somebody jumped him. "She was going to them."

Balm looked up, shaking her frills back, staring at him incredulously. "How could you—I was not!"

"They must know we're back, the same way they knew we left," Moon insisted. "Now they're calling her to them to find out why."

The others muttered to each other again. Flower and Chime, at least, watched Balm worriedly. Pearl's expression was completely opaque. River stood beside her, looking confused but vindicated. Struggling to her feet, Balm shouted, "I was not going to the Fell!"

The hard part was that Moon didn't think she had any idea that she was lying. She looked more hurt and angry than anything else.

He said, "Then why didn't you go to the blind like you said? Why didn't you answer me?"

"Quiet, both of you." Jade's growl silenced the whole group again. She stepped forward, catching Moon's wrist. He flinched, almost pulling away, but she was looking at the claw marks on his arms. Balm had torn into him hard enough to pierce the tough skin between his scales, leaving long scratches deep enough to sting. Jade looked at Balm, at her golden scales, unmarked.

Balm stared down at her claws as if she had no idea how Moon's blood had gotten there. Jade asked quietly, "Where were you going, Balm?"

"I was—" Balm took a sharp breath, as if she couldn't finish the sentence and didn't know why. Her anger gave way to confusion and she shook her head. "I was just going to scout."

"You don't know where you were going," Moon said, driving the point home. If she would admit it, maybe it would help break whatever hold the Fell had on her.

"I was going to scout!" Balm snarled.

Jade watched Balm carefully. "You said you were going to the blind to speak to Blossom. And I told all the Aeriat to stay on the ground until we left for the attack."

Balm spread her hands, helpless and frustrated. "I know that, but I wasn't going far."

As an explanation, it wasn't much, and Moon saw the doubt in Jade's eyes. He said, "It's not her fault. She doesn't know they've done this to her."

Pearl turned to Flower, sounding thoughtful. "Is that possible? That she could be under the Fell's power without knowing it?"

"They do it to groundlings," Moon said in exasperation. "It doesn't look like this; it's much easier to tell. The groundlings do whatever the Fell want, and they don't know why."

Jade snapped, "Moon, quiet."

Moon shut up, unwillingly. At least they seemed willing to believe him.

"It's possible," Flower said, her eyes narrowed in speculation. "Balm has no reason to betray us."

"Of course I don't!" Balm looked ready to weep.

"Anymore than Branch did," Flower finished quietly.

Everyone was silent, watching Balm uneasily. Then River said with bitter satisfaction, "I told you it wasn't Branch."

The last place Moon wanted to be was on River's side, but he was right. All the evidence against Branch could also be leveled at Balm. She had the same opportunities to slip away from the colony as Branch had. She had known they were going to the Golden Isles, known about the meeting at the Blue Stone Temple, known that flying boats had come back with them, but not how many. And she had known that Moon and Jade had flown toward the east, but hadn't known they had gone for the poison until last night.

Flower folded her arms, still speculative. "Balm, will you let me see through your eyes?"

What? Moon thought, startled, but everyone else seemed to know what she meant. Balm looked around at them all. "Yes, I've nothing to hide."

Flower nodded. "We'll do it now. Come back to the blind."

"I'm sorry," Moon said to Jade, though he knew there was no help for it. It would have been better not to expose what had happened to Balm in front of the whole group—Moon knew that better than anybody—but that hadn't been possible.

Jade shook her head, took Balm's wrist and led her away after Flower and Pearl.

Moon followed with the others. The hunters spread out, but the Aeriat still pointedly surrounded him. He couldn't keep his spines from flaring in response. It was mildly gratifying when they backed off a little, even River and Drift.

Moon found himself walking next to Chime, though he wasn't sure if Chime had meant for it to happen or if it was just an accident. Moon had to ask, "Flower can see thoughts?"

"No, mentors can't do that." Chime frowned at the ground. "But she can see if there's anything in Balm's head that isn't supposed to be there. It's hard to describe. You look into someone's eyes, past the surface, and you can see colors, and interpret them." He added bitterly, "I did it once, before I turned into an Aeriat. It's not easy, but Flower is very strong."

They reached the blind, and a hiss from Bone sent most of the hunters scattering back to their watch positions. Niran waited at the entrance, a couple of waterskins slung over his shoulder.

"What happened?" he asked, looking around at all of them.

"It's a long story," Chime told him, nervously. "Wait out here for now."

Niran grimaced in annoyance but turned to go back to the poison clearing.

Jade had already led Balm into the blind. Moon ducked under the branches and followed the others inside. In the main area, Stone still lay on the pallet, apparently deeply unconscious. Strike, his skin now completely mottled by the poison, curled up next to him. Stone must have been awake at some point, because he had moved his hand to rest on the boy's shoulder.

Balm shifted to groundling and sat down by the hearth, as the others found places out of the way. She told Flower, "I'm ready."

Then Pearl said, "Moon first."

Moon hissed at her. Pearl tilted her head, staring at him coldly. He felt a pressure grow in his chest and behind his eyes, the pressure to shift to groundling. He resisted, too angry to give in.

It could have gone on for a while, Pearl refusing to give up and Moon trembling on the edge of shifting until he collapsed from exhaustion. But, sounding mortally exasperated, Jade said, "Moon, just do it. This won't hurt you, and it'll prove you aren't under any Fell influence."

He had to admit it sounded rational when she put it that way. His voice grating with the effort of resisting Pearl, he said, "Will Flower be able to do both of us?"

"Don't worry about me," Flower told him impatiently. "Now come on."

Moon shifted to groundling just as his legs went weak, and he sat down hard on the bare dirt. Still glaring up at Pearl, he said, "Go ahead."

The other Aeriat relaxed, and Pearl looked away. She tried to seem unaffected, but her stiff spines betrayed the effort of trying to force him to shift. He was bitterly glad to see it.

Flower knelt in front of him and tugged her smock into a more comfortable arrangement. "Now, just be still." She put her hands on his face, a light touch. Her skin felt cool and dry. Moon waited, defensive and impatient and wondering why helping these people had ever seemed like a good idea. After a moment, she said, "Moon, stop fighting me."

"I'm not fighting you," he said, gritting his teeth. *If I was fighting you, we'd all know it.*

Flower gave him a hard stare. "If you keep it up, I won't have enough strength left to look into Balm."

Moon hissed in frustration. He wasn't aware of resisting her and had no idea how to stop. "I don't know what to do."

"He's stalling," River said. "He's deliberately—"

Jade snarled at him. "River, shut your mouth or I'll shut it for you."

Vine, the biggest male warrior, and a couple of others growled in agreement; apparently River was getting on their nerves, too. River looked at Pearl for help. Pearl just stared him down, and River unwillingly subsided.

Focused on Moon, Flower ignored the others. In a soothing voice, she said, "Just relax. Look into my eyes, think about something else."

He looked into her eyes, dark brown like most of the Arbora's, the edges rimmed with green and gold. All Moon could think about was that if she saw anything that wasn't supposed to be there, the Aeriat would kill him. Or the bleak future he faced, living alone in a tree somewhere, if he survived the battle with the Fell.

Then he blinked, realizing he had lost a moment. Flower was getting to her feet. She ruffled his hair and told the others, "Clear as the day."

Moon pulled away, twitching uneasily. It would have been less strange if he felt something, if some trace of the intrusion lingered. Fighting the urge to huddle in on himself, he looked up, but the others were all watching Balm. She struggled to keep her expression calm, but she looked strained and anxious.

Flower sat in front of her. Smiling reassuringly, she put her hands on Balm's face, gently tilting her head back.

At first it didn't look any different from what Flower had done to Moon. Then Flower's eyes started to change, to turn silver and opaque, the way they had in the Blue Stone Temple. The others stirred uneasily, and Moon was unwillingly fascinated.

Suddenly Flower jerked back from Balm, sitting back on the dirt with a thump. She gasped, "It's true."

Jade hissed, her claws coming out. "The Fell? They're controlling her?"

Flower nodded. "Their taint is in her mind. And I saw something, on the queens' level of the colony." The silver sheen slowly faded from her eyes, making

Moon's skin creep.

"No," Balm protested, horrified. "I'd know. Wouldn't I know?"

"This is strong, stronger than I've seen before." Flower bared her teeth. "I couldn't find the thing that was causing us harm, because it wasn't here. It was somewhere else."

Jade dropped down beside her, saying urgently, "Flower, what do you mean? What did you see on the queens' level?"

"It's a Fell—I'm not sure what kind. Like a ruler, but not." She made an impatient gesture. "All I have is a hint of color from its mind. I'll have to see it in the flesh before I can say. But it's been watching us for turns. I saw the colony through it."

"This was the thing causing sickness in the colony?" Pearl demanded. "How?"

Flower looked up, her face flushed. "This Fell flight has been watching us through this creature."

"That's not possible," River said, sounding offended by the possibility. He looked around at the others. "It can't be… We've never heard of that before."

"Just because we've never heard of it before doesn't make it impossible," Chime said. He wrapped his arms around himself, looking deeply worried. "And we've known—everyone knows—the rulers can share their memories. They can see through the dakti, maybe the kethel too."

And speak through the dakti, Moon thought, remembering what he and Stone had seen at Sky Copper. Thinking of that, it suddenly seemed a lot less unlikely.

"But there was no Fell in the colony for a ruler to share memories with," Bone said, his voice thoughtful rather than protesting. "You mean this thing just thought about the colony and saw us, heard us?"

"Not very well," Flower admitted, "Or the Fell wouldn't have needed to get inside Balm's mind." She winced. "It must have been like a mentor's vision, just enough to give them the general idea of what we were doing."

Jade shook her head, appalled. "And it made us sick, made clutches die."

Flower let her breath out in an angry hiss. "The concentrated attention of a flight of Fell was directed on us. The Fell ruin everything they touch; that's not just willful destruction. Their magic carries a taint, even if they don't intend it. After turns of focusing on us, the taint… affected us."

Unexpectedly, Pearl said, "It makes sense." She didn't even look surprised. "If there had been anything physical inside the colony, something the Fell had managed to put there, we would have found it by now." She shook her head, the tips of her fangs showing. "We looked hard enough."

Jade nodded reluctant agreement. She asked Flower, "Is this the creature that has a queen's power over the court, that kept them from shifting to fight or escape?"

"It could be." Flower turned to her. "If it can watch us from a distance, it could have other powers." She shook her head, frustrated. "I have to find out what manner of creature this is, where it came from. If it's a new kind of Fell."

"That we can find out later." Jade's gaze turned cold. "For now, we know we have to kill this thing."

Pearl said deliberately, "After we put the poison in the water and it's had time to work, the Aeriat can fly to the top of the colony. If this creature is on the queens' level, we can find it and kill it."

Bone sounded dubious. "That's if you can keep your wings long enough to reach the top of the colony."

Jade shook her frills impatiently. "It's our best chance. And if killing this thing means we can shift inside the colony again—"

"Then we'll have that advantage," Pearl said, her expression grim. "If not, so be it."

Balm had listened to them all, stunned and sick. "Why did they choose me? Was it something I did?"

"Maybe it wasn't only you," Vine muttered uneasily. He was the one who had been sent to Wind Sun with Balm. The fact that he had spent that time alone with her, with no idea she was affected this way, must have been shocking to him. "They could have caught any warrior who ever left the colony alone. Flower will have to look into all of us."

No one looked happy about that prospect. But Chime said, "Balm's the only one who's tried to leave since we found out about the poison. If there was anyone else, they could have easily gotten away in the confusion when Moon was stopping her." He looked at Balm, wincing in sympathy. "And if the Fell were watching us, knew things about us, they may have picked her because they saw she was close to Jade."

"I'll still have to check all the warriors," Flower said, sounding grim at the prospect. "But if the Fell did this to more than one or two, it might have come to light in a mentor's augury. They may not have wanted to risk it."

"But can you make it stop?" Balm asked Flower desperately. "Make the Fell let go of me?"

Flower shook her head reluctantly, and spread her hands. "I've never had to do that before."

Balm turned to Moon. "Did the groundlings have a way to make this stop? To get the Fell taint out of their minds?"

"I don't—" Fell usually killed the groundlings they took this way when they were of no further use. He had no idea what might happen to survivors—if any. But he didn't want Balm, or the others, to get the idea that death was her only option. The only thing he could think of was to buy time until they could talk to someone who might know, like Stone or Delin. "I think it went away when the Fell who did it died." Maybe that was even true.

Jade knelt in front of Balm, taking her hands. "In that case," she said, her voice hard and fierce, "we'll just have to kill every Fell we find, to make certain we get the right one."

The others finished forming the plan, such as it was, and there was nothing to do but wait until sunset. Moon's nerves still itched and he needed to be alone for a time. He slipped out of the blind, looking for some tree roots to hide under.

He heard someone come out after him, and Jade's voice said, "Moon, wait."

He kept moving until she added, annoyed, "Moon, don't make me catch you."

He stopped, feeling tension in a tight band across his shoulders. "I'm not leaving. I'll be with you when you attack the Fell."

Jade halted just behind him. "If you hadn't caught Balm... There was no way she could reach the colony without us realizing what she'd done. The Fell would have known there was no use sending her back. They would have kept her."

"I know." Balm would have told them about the poison, and the Fell would have done to her whatever they were doing to the rest of the court. He thought of his only full day at the colony, when Balm had directed them toward the plain with the statues as a good place to hunt, and how they had caught a scent of Fell. He wondered now if she had gone there alone at some point in the past, for privacy or to explore, if that was where the Fell had caught her.

Growling with impatience, Jade took his arm and pulled him around to face her. "What is it? Pearl shouldn't have told River about what you did in the groundling city, I know. But the others would have had to hear about it eventually."

Moon hesitated. He didn't want to ask because he didn't want to hear the answer. Not knowing at least allowed some room for hope. But he made himself say, "Pearl said you had a clutch."

"What?" Jade stared, then stepped back, her eyes narrowed. "Of course she did." She folded her arms, tapping her claws. "She's lying."

Moon looked past her left shoulder. This was the other reason not to ask. Her denial didn't help at all; Pearl's lie was too insidious, there was no way to know the truth. "All right."

Her whole body went stiff with anger. "You don't trust me."

There were a number of things he could have said, but what came out was, "I wish I did."

Her spines ruffled and she hissed, turned away, and stamped back toward the blind.

CHAPTER
SEVENTEEN

❧

At sunset, Moon, his wings tightly folded, crawled on his belly through the grass toward the river. He hoped the dakti were asleep. He was going to have enough to worry about with the major kethel.

Moon had volunteered for this part of the plan, and no one had argued about it. It only made sense; if he did it wrong, he had the best chance of being able to fly fast enough to get away from the kethel.

Bone, Chime, and most of the hunters waited in the forest, on a hill where they had a good view of this side of the colony. Jade, Flower, and some of the Aeriat were further down the bank, near the terraced fields and a second set of channels for the irrigation system. Pearl and the other Aeriat were on the far side of the colony, ready to come in from that direction.

Bead and Blossom stayed behind in the blind and, with Niran's help, looked after Stone and Strike. Two older hunters, Knife and Spice, had been left behind to help restrain Balm if the Fell tried to use their hold on her again. She had been anxious and miserable the rest of the afternoon, but hadn't shown any further signs of being under their control. Moon hoped that knowing about it now gave her some ability to resist. Flower had looked into the other warriors, but no one else had shown any sign of Fell influence.

Moon had only been on the fringes of the discussion, but everybody seemed to have a different idea as to what the survivors should do if the attack failed and the combatants were all killed. They agreed that whatever happened, Stone would be ragingly angry when he woke and discovered that he had missed it.

Moon reached the bank about a hundred paces downstream from where the colony's stone platform stretched across the river. In the high grass near the water's edge, he risked lifting his head to get a look at the colony. This side was already in shadow, framed against blue sky fading into yellow and orange as the sun set past the forested hills. The light of glow moss still shone from the openings up and down the pyramid's wall, throwing yellow reflections down onto the dark surface of the water. It looked oddly normal, but then the moss would glow for a long time without help from a mentor. He couldn't hear anything, except for the occasional cackle of a dakti. He hoped the place wasn't a charnel house.

Moon slipped into the shallow water. According to the Arboras' careful scouting, a kethel lay in the water at the base of the platform, in the gap that allowed the river to flow under the structure. It had obviously been posted to keep any Raksura from swimming under the platform and entering the colony through the openings there. Fortunately, the smaller channels that fed the water system were on the far ends of the platform, and not as difficult to get to.

The trick was to attract the kethel's attention enough to get it to move, but not enough to make it tear the riverbed apart looking for intruders. It would have been safer to do this from the bank, but Moon didn't want to risk the kethel leaving the water to search for him.

He took a deep breath, sunk down, and swam underwater to the middle of the river. He surfaced behind a rock, hooking his claws on it as the current pulled at him. The air was heavy with Fell stench so he couldn't scent the individual kethel, but its presence had fouled the water, lacing it with a taste like rotted meat.

Hoping the Arbora were ready, Moon lifted one foot above the surface and brought it down sharply, making a distinct splash.

There was no response, no movement from the colony, just the faint whisper of wind in the trees. Moon gritted his teeth and forced himself to wait, counting heartbeats. Then he splashed again.

He felt the water move first, the wave as the kethel heaved its body up. Moon couldn't risk a look but the creature must have stood to stare down the length of the river. Moon sunk down under the water again and let go of the rock, allowing the current to carry him downstream a short distance. Then he kicked the surface.

He felt the vibrations as the kethel stalked forward. *That's done it,* Moon thought and, still underwater, swam for the bank. He huddled in the rocks, surfacing just enough to breathe. The kethel paced downstream, nearly to the point of Moon's first splash. It stood for a long time, then growled, a low grumble of irritation, and turned back to the colony.

Using the noise of the creature's movement as cover, Moon slung himself out of the water and scrambled up the grassy bank into the brush. Once in the shelter of the trees, he shook the water off his scales, shivering in relief. The poison should be in the river now, if the Arbora had managed to pour it in while the kethel was distracted, and it would have been flowing right toward him. *I'd rather face the kethel than the poison,* he thought.

Moon slipped back through the forest up to the low hill where the Arbora waited. Heavily cloaked with trees and ferns, it made a good vantage point to overlook the colony. Moon ghosted quietly through the foliage, passing the Arbora hidden in the grass, who acknowledged him with quiet clicks.

He found Chime and Bone crouched behind a tree and stretched out next to them. "Did they do it?" Moon whispered. If they hadn't, the plan was stuck, because there was no way the kethel would fall for that trick again.

"Yes," Bone answered. He jerked his head toward two Arbora, nearly invisible behind a bush. "Salt and Bramble got right up under the edge of the platform and poured it into the fountain channels."

"They said the smell disappeared once it was in the water," Chime said. "So maybe the Fell won't realize it's there."

That was a relief. "Good." Moon relaxed into the grass. Now they just had to wait. Flower had said that it wouldn't take long for the poison to spread into all the colony's fountains and pools. The dakti and kethel would probably drink before going to sleep, so it shouldn't be long before most were affected.

He was just settling comfortably into the moss when the kethel burst out of the water, shaking its head frantically. Startled, Moon sat up to see better.

"What's this?" Chime said, anxious.

The kethel slung itself onto the bank, and flailed in the brush, the trees waving wildly as their trunks cracked and split under its claws. It thrashed twice more, then collapsed, sliding back down the muddy bank into the river.

Bone hissed in admiration. "That was the poison?"

"It had to be." Moon eased forward, trying to see. The kethel lay on its back, one leg twisted at an odd angle, dark fluid leaking from its mouth.

"It didn't do that to Strike," Bramble whispered from somewhere behind them, sounding awed.

"Strike's not a Fell," Moon reminded him.

His voice tense with excitement, Chime whispered, "The current forms a pool right under the colony, and the kethel was lying in it. It must have gotten a big dose of whatever poison didn't get drawn up the channels."

Moon squinted, making out movement on the platform. Several dakti came out of the lower entrances and flew down over the terraces to the riverbank. The Arbora twitched in quiet excitement, whispering to each other.

The dakti clustered around the kethel's body. Moon couldn't quite see what they were doing. They seemed to be poking around the corpse, maybe trying to decide what had killed it. He cocked his head, listening hard, and heard flesh tearing. *That can't be… Oh, that's perfect.* He leaned down to whisper to the others, "They're eating it."

Chime stared, and Bone muttered, "That's typical of them."

They listened to ripping and crunching sounds as the dakti tore at the kethel's body. With no warning, another kethel appeared on the platform; it must have walked out of the colony and then shifted. It flew down and landed in the water, scattering the dakti as it sniffed at the corpse. Moon held his breath. If the kethel somehow detected the poison…

The kethel tore a huge bite out of the corpse's belly, chewing it with apparent satisfaction. Then it spoke to the dakti, a low rumble that Moon couldn't make out. It turned away from the corpse and Moon suppressed a snarl of disappointment. But instead of leaving the body, the dakti tore chunks off and leapt into the air to carry the meat back into the colony. More dakti came out to help tear the corpse apart, while the kethel climbed down the bank and walked into the water, moving upstream to the overhanging terrace. There, it slid down under the surface, taking the dead kethel's place at guard duty.

Bone stirred impatiently. "The poison will be either in the channels up inside the colony or washed away downriver."

"It ate the poisoned kethel's belly," Chime pointed out. "Just wait."

Finally, the dakti had transported most of the corpse inside, and the colony grew quiet again. Moon felt the pull of each passing moment. He reminded himself that if the Fell were eating kethel tonight, it might mean that they weren't eating Raksura. It also might mean that they had finished off all the Raksura days ago, but for the moment he could hope otherwise.

Near the platform the river bubbled and thrashed. Then the kethel lying under the water suddenly broke the surface, drifting limply.

"There we go," Moon whispered, easing to his feet. If eating from the poisoned corpse had been enough to kill a kethel, it was enough to kill the dakti.

Bone told Bramble, "Tell the others to signal the queens."

As Moon turned to creep back down the hill, one of the Arbora made a sound, a call that blended into the distant cries of the nightbirds. Following Moon, Chime whispered, "It's frightening that this was the easy part."

Moon and Chime met Jade, Song, Vine, and Sand at the edge of the forest.

"Careful," Flower whispered, sinking down into the high grass with Bone and the other hunters. For once, she was in her Arbora form, and the pure white of her scales made it harder for her to hide.

Jade led the way swiftly down through the terraced plantings. On the far side of the river, Moon caught a flash of gold as Pearl and the rest of the Aeriat approached the colony from that side. *Two queens, nine warriors, and me,* Moon thought. He hoped that was enough.

They meant to stay on the ground until they were as close to the colony as possible. Everyone had agreed that the force that had kept the court from shifting seemed to have only been in effect inside the colony itself, and not the outer terraces. But if that had changed, it would be better to find out while on the ground rather than in the air. They all had knives and short spears borrowed from the hunters to use when they were forced to shift, though Moon had no idea how good the Aeriat, used to fighting with their claws, would be with the weapons.

The colony was still quiet. No dakti had come out to see about the second dead kethel, another good sign. Jade paused at the moss-covered stone platform that crossed the river. There was no ground entrance in the wall facing this side, and fewer openings in the levels above, which was why they had chosen it. She glanced back at Moon and the others, saying in a low voice, "Everyone all right?"

Moon nodded. He didn't feel any impulse to shift to groundling. Chime whispered, "So far," and the others murmured agreement.

Jade pointed to the ledge marking the pyramid's highest level and the square opening there. Pearl's group would be heading for a similar entrance on the same level, but on the opposite face of the structure. "Go quickly," Jade whispered, then crouched to leap into the air.

Moon followed her, a few hard wing beats taking him up to the right ledge. He landed a moment after Jade and hooked his claws into a chink between the stones. Chime landed beside him; Song, Vine, and Sand lighted further along the ledge.

He didn't hear Pearl and the other Aeriat, but saw Root duck around the far corner, wave at Jade, and duck back.

"Right," Jade said under her breath, and climbed through the entrance. Moon slipped in after her, Chime and the others on his heels.

Inside was a small room with heavily carved walls, with images of giant groundlings in heavy armor glaring down at them. Jade had already reached the next doorway, which opened into a wide stairwell. Glowing moss had been knocked down and lay strewn on the steps, still giving off enough light to show balconies in the walls, all hung with the big sleeping baskets. Water ran down from a spout high in the wall, collecting at the bottom of the chamber in a pool with floating flowers. Personal possessions were tumbled everywhere, silk blankets and cushions, torn clothing, broken baskets. Behind Moon, Song hissed softly in dismay.

Jade stepped out onto the landing, and paused to taste the air. Moon couldn't smell anything but Fell stench, couldn't hear anything but the trickle of water. Jade glanced back at him, mouthing the words, "You feel anything?"

Moon shook his head. Whatever force had stopped the court from shifting, it wasn't working on them yet.

They made their way down the well, dropping from platform to platform. Jade stopped at a window in the wall and ducked to peer through it. Moon looked over her shoulder.

It opened onto a broad ledge above a large chamber, the same one where the court had gathered on Moon's first full day at the colony. It was lit by fading glow moss, and the stone platforms across the back were strewn with furs and cushions. A dozen or more dakti crouched near those platforms, picking at a carcass, gnawing bones. Jade's spines lifted, and she nudged Moon's arm, pointing to one of the dakti.

It sat a little apart from the others and, at first, he thought it was deformed. But the odd, smooth shape of its back showed that it was missing wings. *A Fell without wings?* He hadn't thought that was possible. It looked like an Arbora, short and heavily built, except its scales were black, with the heavier plates of a dakti. Whatever it was, it had to be the creature Flower had seen through Balm. There couldn't be two strange new Fell invading the colony. *I hope,* he thought.

Then, on a landing below, a dakti ducked out of a doorway. It stared up at them, aghast, for a heartbeat, then opened its jaws to shriek.

Jade launched herself down the stairwell and landed on the dakti, crushing it before it managed more than a squawk. Moon leapt after her, landing on the platform just above her.

Then Jade suddenly twitched, her spines flaring in alarm, and shifted to Arbora. An instant later, Moon's claws vanished and he was suddenly in groundling form. He swallowed back a yell, dropping to a crouch to keep from falling. On the platform above him, Song and Vine landed awkwardly, and Chime crashed into a sleeping basket; they all shifted into groundling form. Moon tried to shift back to Raksura, just in case it was still possible. He felt a pressure in his chest, behind his eyes, and nothing happened. *This is almost as bad as the poison,* he thought, shoving to his feet. At least he still had his clothes, and the long bone javelin borrowed from the hunters.

Jade shook herself, recovering from the shock, and ducked forward into the doorway the dakti had come through. Moon jumped down behind her.

In the big chamber, the cluster of startled dakti leapt up, hissing, to charge at them. Jade blocked the doorway, and the dakti hesitated, unwilling to attack a Raksuran queen even in Arbora form. One conquered its fear enough to lunge at her, and Moon dropped into a crouch, leaning under her arm to stab at it with the javelin. It jerked back, shrieking, but he didn't think he had hurt it. *Oh, we could be in trouble here,* Moon thought, ducking away from the creature's flailing claws as Jade held the others off. Fighting Fell as a groundling was going to be even less fun than it had always looked.

One dakti bounced up to the window above the ledge, flinging itself through into the stairwell and into Song and Chime. Song grabbed its wing and jumped off the platform onto the steps, using her groundling weight to yank the creature out of the air. Chime scrambled after her, swinging at it with his javelin. Vine grabbed a loose stone from a platform and whacked it in the head.

That only took three of us, Moon thought sourly, as Sand braced himself at the window to try to repel the other dakti. *This isn't going to work.*

Then Pearl and the other Aeriat burst in through the doorway on the opposite side of the chamber. The dakti scattered to face the new threat. Pearl pounced on one, ripping its head off, and River hooked one down out of the air. A heartbeat later, all the Aeriat were suddenly groundlings. River staggered and nearly fell; Root, in mid-leap, did fall. Moon looked at the wingless dakti, and saw it staring intently at Pearl, just as she shifted to Arbora.

"It is that thing; it's doing this," he told Jade.

"Get it," Jade snarled to Moon, and dove through the doorway. Chime and the others followed her, and Moon used the distraction to head for the strange dakti.

Even as an Arbora, Pearl didn't hesitate, bounding forward to slam another dakti into the wall. Jade lunged in to pull a dakti off Root, and Moon dodged around the fight.

The strange creature saw him coming and ran, scampering up the steps to the platform. Moon bolted after it. The creature scrambled away from him, huddling in on itself. It moaned and lifted its head, and he stepped back abruptly, feeling a cold chill. Its eyes had an avid expression completely at odds with its terrified posture.

Then it lunged at him. Moon swung the javelin like a club, slamming it across the creature's head. He dodged a wild blow as it fell across the steps, then slammed the point into its chest.

Its scales resisted the sharpened bone, and Moon leaned all his weight on it to drive it in. Gurgling, the creature clawed at him, tearing at his shirt and scratching his arms as he grimly forced the javelin further into its chest.

Vine ran up, grabbed the upper part of the javelin, and threw his weight on it as well. Moon felt the creature's scales give way with a crack. Dark blood gushed from the wound. Moon saw the intelligence fade from the creature's eyes, leaving them blank and gray.

The pressure in his chest lifted so abruptly that Moon stumbled down the steps. In relief, he shifted back to Raksura. Vine stepped back and shifted too, calling to the others, "That's it! We can shift!"

Bloody and ragged from the brief fight, the others all shifted and pounced on the last of the confused dakti before they could flee.

As the last of the dakti died, Jade shifted to her winged form and jumped up to the platform to land beside Moon. She said, "Song, Vine, go out and signal the Arbora." The plan was for the Arbora to climb up the outside of the colony, gather here, and then they would all fight their way down through the structure together.

As Vine turned to leap for the skylight, Jade moved forward, staring down at the strange dakti. "This has to be the thing Flower saw, but what is it?"

The others gathered around as Pearl stepped up onto the platform. She circled the dead creature, her lips curling in disgust. "A new kind of Fell? It looks oddly like an Arbora."

Chime reached down toward it. Then his spines flared and he jerked his hand back. Sounding sick, he said, "It's a mentor."

Jade shook her head, staring at him. "It can't be. It looks—"

"Like a Fell. I think it's a crossbreed, part Fell, part Raksura." Chime's face was bleak. "They weren't lying when they said they wanted to join with us."

Moon looked down at the thing, appalled. He had been hoping that the "joining" was just a Fell lie. Root eased forward to sniff at the creature; Sand grabbed his spines, dragging him back.

Chime continued, "They must have done it before. Captured Arbora, forced them to mate with rulers, until they produced a mentor." He waved a hand frantically. "They didn't need a Fell in the colony to see us through its eyes. This thing could see us because it was part of us. Not our court, not our bloodline, but still Raksura, still a mentor."

The others stirred uneasily. Pearl hissed, sounding more angry than anything else. "How did it force us to shift? That's a queen's power, not a mentor's. And even another Raksuran queen couldn't force Jade and I to shift, no matter how old or powerful she was."

Chime shook his head, baffled. "Because it's a crossbreed? I don't know. It had to know we were there before it could force us to shift, though. That's like a queen's power."

"It sees through the other dakti," Moon said, the realization turning his blood cold. "When that one saw us in the stairwell—"

"This creature knew we were there," Jade finished. She gave the mentor-dakti a kick with one clawed foot, as if she had to suppress the urge to tear the body apart. "That must be how it forced the court to shift. The kethel dropped the dakti on the colony, they ran through, finding everyone, and this creature used its power on them."

"We just have to hope it's the only one," Moon said, and looked up to see everyone staring at him. "Well, we do," he added defensively.

Song and Vine leapt back in through the skylight overhead. A moment later Bone, Flower, and the other Arbora swarmed in through the doorways. A few of the hunters carried extra waterskins filled with poison.

Still in her Arbora form, Flower climbed up to the platform to stand beside Chime, staring down at the dead crossbreed.

"It's worse than you thought," Chime told her. Flower hissed and crouched to poke at the creature.

The other Arbora gathered around the platform, watching Pearl. Pearl's spines flared, and she said, "Work your way down. Kill them all. Find our court."

Bone growled, and the hunters turned nearly as one, flowing toward the doorway out to the big central stairwell. Moon leapt over their heads to land in front, beating Bone down the passage and diving down the stairs.

The Arbora bounded after him, climbing along the walls and ceiling. Moon met a dakti, surprising it as he whipped around a corner onto a landing. He tore its head off before it could scream. The stairs divided at this point, splitting off into a wide passage that led to more Aeriat bowers and then a second stairwell. Jade leapt down to land beside him, just as Bone caught up to them. She said, "We'll take the other side."

Moon nodded. They had to move fast. "Look for the kethel."

Jade turned for the passage, hissing for the Aeriat to follow her. They flashed by in a multi-colored swarm of wings and tails. Moon turned down the stairs with Bone and the hunters.

They reached the next landing down, where three passages split off. One led forward into the pyramid's central shaft, another led to the right, turning narrow, concealing the room it opened into. Moon heard the bubble of fountains and, over the sick stench of Fell, he caught the scent of the poison. And a faint sound of movement, something like hissing, breathing.

He went down the right hand passage in a bound, the hunters right behind him. The doorway at the end opened into a long chamber with an open-roofed court in the center. It was full of dead and dying dakti.

They sprawled everywhere, smaller and shriveled in death. Chunks of bloody meat, already attracting buzzing insects, lay among them. *Kethel meat,* Moon thought, with some satisfaction. *That's what they get for eating each other.* The stench was unbelievable.

Behind him, a startled hunter asked, "Is that one of us?" In the nearest pile of dakti was a body, no scales, the naked skin light-colored but mottled with green and black. The hunter reached down for it, meaning to pull it away from the pile.

Moon lunged in and grabbed his arm before he could touch it. "No, it's a dakti!"

"He's right." Bone shoved forward, giving the white form a kick. "That's the dakti's other form. Like our groundling forms, but—" The shifted dakti writhed away from him, unable to stand but still snarling defiance, barring fangs. It had harsh features, flat empty eyes, dark hair matted and ragged. "—not much like." Bone disemboweled the creature with one swipe of his claws.

Someone in the back said, "It's killing them, not just making them sleep like it did Strike. And why did only one of them shift?"

"Only one so far," someone else answered. "Maybe that one got less than the others."

"Flower always did make strong simples," Bone said, turning away from the dying dakti. "And there's power in anything made by a mentor."

It's probably lucky we didn't kill Strike, Moon thought. But then Flower hadn't been thinking about killing Raksura when she brewed the poison. "Keep moving." He turned back to the passage.

Out in the stairwell he saw flashes of gold, copper, and blue as Aeriat dropped through the central well; a moment later dakti screamed in chorus. Moon snarled, wanting to join the fight, but he kept to Jade's instructions and led the way down the stairs to the next level.

This was the fourth level up from the river terraces, and the landing led to several doorways and passages. Moving rapidly from one to the other, Moon found nothing but empty rooms with storage baskets and cushions tumbled around, smashed pottery, and broken tools.

Then with a little cry of horror, a hunter jerked back from a doorway. Moon leapt forward and grabbed the hunter's spines to drag him out of the way, expecting a flood of dakti or the missing kethel. But the room was empty, except for bundles strewn across the floor.

Then he saw the bodies, some wrapped in blood-stained clothing.

He stepped inside, feeling the dirty floor grit under his claws. Arbora started to push in after him, and he snarled, "Stay out there!" It could be a trap. The room was empty except for the corpses, the carved figures of the ancient groundlings staring dispassionately down from the stone beams. There were no other doorways, but the dakti could swarm in through the air shafts.

The Arbora scrambled back, obeying without argument. Moon moved forward, tasting the air, but all he could smell was Fell and death. *We're too late,* he thought, sick at heart. He knew there was nothing he could have done; he and Jade had returned as fast as they could. *And the Fell didn't come to Indigo Cloud for you,* he reminded himself. That didn't help.

But as he stepped further into the room, he saw this death wasn't new. From the smell of rot, these people must have died days ago, not long after the colony had been taken. There were at least forty or fifty bodies, mostly Arbora, male and female, and a few taller, slimmer shapes that had to be Aeriat. Most were in groundling form, only a few in Raksuran. All were twisted and broken, skin or hide slashed by claws. He heard a step behind him and glanced back, baring his fangs, but it was Bone. The other hunters still held the stairwell.

Moon looked back down at the bodies again and recognized a face. It was Shell, one of the soldiers who had tried to chase him out of the colony his first day here, when Chime had hurried to defend him. Shell was in groundling form, ripped from chin to crotch, his eyes still open. His hands were curled claw-like, dark residue caught under his fingernails, in his teeth.

Moon looked away. *The Fell didn't eat them. But they ate the Raksura at Sky Copper.* He had a very vivid recollection of the dakti with the arm clutched in its jaws. And Stone had found few intact bodies when he had searched the mound. *It doesn't make sense.*

Bone circled the rows of bodies. His voice thick with misery, he said, "These are mostly soldiers. They must have fought." Then he froze, looking down, hissing in dismay.

Moon moved to his side, and found himself staring down at Petal's face. She was in her groundling form, gray and rigid in death.

He looked up. Bone's spines rippled in fury.

"We're wasting time," Moon said, and turned for the doorway.

On the next level down they found a score of dakti trying to flee down a passage, flushed out of hiding by the Aeriat on the other side of the building. Moon helped corner them, then let the Arbora thoroughly tear them apart before he made them head down the stairs again.

On the level below, Moon hissed for silence. He could hear something below, a flurry of movement, hissing. He took the last turn, coming down to where the stairs ended in a junction of two large passages. One led out to a big room with an opening to the outside, letting in cool air. But he sensed movement down the left hand passage, a lot of movement.

"That's the soldiers and hunters' bowers," Bone whispered.

That meant the hall would have many tall doorways opening to small, curtained-off rooms, some at floor level and some above it. If it followed the same plan as the other bower halls, the rooms were just stone partitions, not completely enclosed. Moon asked, "Air shafts in from the outside walls?"

"Yes!" Bone turned, signaling half the hunters to head toward to the outside opening.

Moon went down the passage to the bowers. Through the doorway ahead he could see a partition wall, and not much else. The hissing had stopped, and he was certain the dakti knew the Raksura were here.

Moon swung up to the top of the doorway and glanced inside: the hall was full of dakti, most clinging to the ceiling carvings, ready to drop on whoever walked in. They saw him and shrieked in rage.

Moon leapt into the hall and shot across the ceiling, hooking his claws into the carvings, tossing startled dakti off right and left. From their screams of alarm, they had been prepared for Arbora, but not an Aeriat. The floor was already littered with pale, mottled bodies: poisoned dakti shifted to groundling. *This flight must be huge.* Without the poison's help, the Raksura would have been easily overwhelmed.

The Arbora followed Moon in a wave. More dropped down through the air shafts from outside. A dakti landed on Moon's back and was plucked off by an Arbora before he could even reach for it.

Moon reached the far end of the hall and saw the dakti falling back, grouping around one of the bowers, protecting something inside. Renewed shrieks from the dakti made him glance back. The Aeriat had arrived, dropping down the air shafts. They must have heard the commotion and come around the outside of the colony. "Here!" he shouted. He was certain the dakti were protecting a ruler.

Moon leapt down onto the top of the wall, knocking the dakti away. Bone charged up the stairs, ripping into the dakti as those below crammed into the doorway, trying to block him. Moon still couldn't see the ruler. Two large basket beds blocked his view of part of the bower. He dropped down into it, close to the wall, and something surged out from under the nearest bed.

It was the groundling form of a kethel, big, muscular and naked. Its face was boney, eyes set back deep in their sockets, fanged teeth long and yellow. Moon ducked the wild punch aimed at his head and came up slashing, ripping open the kethel's belly. It still attacked, grabbing at his shoulders, lunging in to bite him. But his scales deflected its teeth. He got an arm around its throat and threw his weight down to snap its neck.

The kethel collapsed. Moon jumped over it and tore the beds aside. A ruler shot up at him and, unlike the kethel, it wasn't in groundling form. It knocked Moon backwards, flat on his back.

It gripped his throat, its weight pinning his legs. Desperately, he clawed at its hands, trying to get a knee up to push it off. It was too strong, it had him pinned. He could feel its claws about to pierce his scales. He saw a flash of gold and indigo from above, then Pearl landed on the ruler, straddling it. She gripped the bony crest behind its head and reached around to grab its chin with her claws and twist. The ruler's eyes turned stark with terror, right before they went blank with death.

Pearl tossed the body away, slamming it into the bower's wall, then leapt up and out of the chamber.

Moon bounced to his feet, looking around for the next Fell, but everything in the bower was dead. He swung up to the top of the partition wall for a view of the hall. Dead dakti, whole and in pieces, lay everywhere. Warriors and hunters tore through the bowers searching for more. Jade stood in the center of the hall, tail lashing, waiting for the others to finish the search.

Chime leapt up onto the wall next to Moon. He was panting and covered with Fell blood. Wild-eyed, he said, "That's two kethel dead outside and one in here. There's still at least two left."

Clinging to the stone beams above, Vine said, "This flight must have been huge! I've never seen so many dakti—"

"Back here!" Bone shouted from somewhere toward the back of the hall. "Here!"

Moon jumped to the next bower, then the next, following Bone's voice, as the Aeriat and the hunters scuttled across the walls, or leapt after him. He reached the last partition to see Bone standing at an archway that led into the next hall of bowers. He jumped down to Bone's side. Then he saw what filled the next hall, and just stood there, staring.

The room was packed with large globes of a mottled, glassy substance, each as big as a small house, crammed in between the bowers. Sacs. The sacs that kethel made, to attach to their bodies and carry dakti. They filled the entire hall.

Jade pushed through into the doorway to stand beside Moon and Bone. The others, hunters and Aeriat, crowded behind them, some hanging from the top of the archway to see inside. Everyone was silent with shock.

"Why would they keep dakti in here like this?" Jade said under her breath. She stepped cautiously up to the nearest sac. She leaned close to it, peering into the mottled surface. Then she jerked back with a hiss, slashing it open with her claws.

The mass split open and a dozen limp figures tumbled out, sprawling on the stone floor. They were Arbora and a couple of Aeriat, all in groundling form, their clothes stained, stinking of unwashed skin and fear sweat. But not rot. Jade dropped to her knees and rolled the nearest Arbora over to touch his face. She cried out, "They're alive!"

Bone and the others surged forward. Moon caught hold of the side of the archway to keep from being carried along. As they all ran to the other sacs, Pearl leapt up to the wall of a bower, snarling at them, "Look first! Make certain it's Raksura inside, not dakti!"

Then someone cried out in anguished relief, "The clutches! The clutches are in this one, back here!"

It went straight through Moon's heart, and he couldn't watch anymore. He turned back to the outer chamber, just in case there were any stray dakti survivors creeping up behind them. The others' raw emotion made him uncomfortable, and he still felt painfully like an outsider. *That's because you are an outsider,* he reminded himself. The only thing that had changed was that now he didn't want to be one any more.

Then from outside, through the air shafts, he heard a whoosh of big wings. "Kethel!" he yelled, darting to the nearest shaft. He scrambled up to reach an outside ledge. Framed against the dying sun, one kethel was already in the air, and a second launched itself up from the terrace below. A cluster of dakti rode the first, huddled down to cling to its back. Moon thought the larger figure just behind the armored crest might be a ruler. *Good, they're leaving,* he thought. As the second kethel banked away from the colony, he saw the gray, bulbous mass attached to its chest. It was carrying a sac.

It could be full of dakti, but Moon had to make certain. He jumped into the air, hard flaps carrying him up after the kethel. He got up under its belly, but couldn't get a good look at the sac from this angle. *If it's full of dakti, you're going to feel stupid,* he thought, and shot up to hook his claws into the kethel's belly plates.

He clawed his way up toward the creature's chest and swung forward, close to the sac, peering through the cloudy surface. He saw shapes, then realized he was looking at someone in groundling form, crammed against the wall of the sac, at least two other forms behind her.

Her eyes opened. Moon stared, horrified. He couldn't slash the sac open—if they were all Arbora, they would fall to their deaths, and he could only catch one.

Then the kethel's big, clawed hand came at him and he twisted away, leaping off and snapping his wings in. He slipped through the creature's fingers, falling in an uncontrolled tumble. He extended his wings, catching himself and craning his neck to see the kethel.

Both creatures flew hard, shooting swiftly away over the valley. Cursing to himself, Moon circled back toward the colony.

Jade and Pearl stood on the ledge outside the air shaft. Jade called, "Moon, what was it? What did you see?"

Moon landed on the ledge above her, leaning down. "It had one of the sacs, with Arbora trapped inside!"

Jade turned to Pearl. Pearl's spines flared out, and she said, "Go after them; take the Aeriat!"

Jade shouted back into the colony, calling the Aeriat, and Moon took to the air, chasing the kethel.

CHAPTER
EIGHTEEN

The two kethel flew at their best speed, their shapes etched against the night sky, so fast only Stone could have caught up with them. Flying full out, Moon could just keep them in sight.

He looked back to see the warriors already dropping back. No matter how hard they flew, the younger and smaller fell the farthest behind. *This isn't going to work,* Moon thought desperately. He slowed to fly level with Jade, circling her to shout, "You stay with them. I'll follow the kethel!"

Jade circled with him, looking back at the warriors, grimacing in despair. The Aeriat were strung out in a long line, with only Vine and River coming close to keeping up. "Are you sure? If they stop—"

"This could be what they want. If you

don't stay in a group, they could send dakti back to swarm the stragglers." The danger would just increase as the night wore on.

Jade growled in reluctant agreement. "Leave us markers so we won't lose your trail."

"Wait, wait!" That was Chime, flying full out to catch up with them. He slowed into a circle, panting, and said, "Here, take this, just in case you can use it."

It was one of the waterskins of poison. Chime held it out and Moon caught it, slinging it over his shoulder.

"Be careful!" Jade called. As she and Chime banked to turn back, Moon flew ahead to catch up with the kethel.

All too soon he lost sight of the others, and it was just him and the kethel, alone under the vault of stars. The kethel slowed their pace a little, and Moon hung back as far as he dared, both to conserve his strength and to stay at the far end of their range of vision. He hoped that if they looked back, he would just blend in to the night sky.

They headed mostly northwest, with no abrupt changes of direction. Moon stopped briefly at likely outcrops to pile up stones pointing the way. He hoped that was what Jade had meant when she said to leave markers; he had no idea what other kind of markers to leave. Whenever he landed, he noticed how awkwardly heavy the waterskin of poison was, and he didn't think he would be able to use it. If the rulers killed at the colony hadn't managed to pass on a warning about poisoned water, then the kethel certainly would. But he might find something to do with it. It was too valuable a weapon to just abandon.

As dawn broke, the forested valleys came to an abrupt halt, giving way to a flat plain of yellow grass crossed by shallow streams and dotted with trees. *There's no cover*, Moon thought, cursing the Fell. *None. A baby treeling couldn't hide in that.* They had probably chosen this path deliberately, knowing that any pursuers would be completely exposed.

The grass was sparse, barely knee-high. Trees as slender as rods stood as much as two hundred paces high. Their canopies fanned out like round sunshades, the light green leaves providing little barrier to the eyes of anything flying over. The rocky streams were nearly flat too, barely a few fingers deep, the water glittering in the sunlight. It would be a perfect hunting ground for the major kethel.

Moon landed long enough to make another arrow out of rocks, pointing the way across the plain.

By late evening, the stench of Fell was heavy on the wind, and Moon thought the kethel must be close to their destination. The streams winding through the plain had coalesced into a broad river running toward a series of ridges and the foot of a distant escarpment. Moon spotted some hopping grasseaters near the river and made a snap decision to take one. He had no idea how much longer the kethel meant to fly, and he couldn't keep up this pace on an empty stomach.

He stooped on a hopper before the herd knew he was there, killed it, and ate nearly fast enough to make himself sick. Then he flew to the river to drink and quickly wash the blood off. There, he discovered the banks were dark with what looked like metal-mud. *Hah, finally, a little luck.* Moon scraped his claws through the mud to make certain, then dropped and rolled in it, wincing at the metallic odor, extending his wings to thoroughly coat his whole body.

Once it dried on his scales, the odor would disguise his natural scent. The fact that it also burned easily was worrisome, though he would have to pass close to a flame for the dried mud to catch. Though he suspected that once he found the kethel's destination, accidentally burning to death would be the least of his worries.

He quickly made two more rock arrows, one pointing in the direction the kethel had taken and the other toward his mud-wallow; he hoped the others found it and got the idea.

He took flight and, after a burst of speed, came within sight of the kethel again. He settled in for a long steady haul.

The sun set, and the kethel continued more than halfway through the night until they reached the rocky outline of the escarpment. Moon had been flying so long by that point that he stared in shock when the kethel suddenly banked and circled for a landing.

Moon dropped toward the ground, seeking cover in the rocky hills on this side of the river. He landed amid boulders and old rock falls covering a steep hillside, under the partial cover of tall spreading trees, and crept up to the top to try to see where the kethel had gone.

Moon's namesake had waned to nothing and the only light came from the stars. It was too dark to make out much but the vague shape of the escarpment. That whole side of the cliff was in deep shadow. But the kethel had settled somewhere over there, and the stench of Fell was intense. This had to be more than just a rest stop. Watching intently, Moon caught flickers of movement and thought it must be dakti, flying above the cliffs. *The kethel met up with another flight, or the rest of their own flight.* He hesitated, but there was nothing he could do. He couldn't fly over there blind. He hissed in frustration, and dumped the heavy waterskin of poison off his shoulder.

Moon shifted to groundling form to conserve his strength; the dried metal-mud settled on his skin and clothes, gritty and itching. Then he tucked himself into a hollow in the rock, and waited, watching and dozing off and on.

Finally the sky lightened with the leading edge of dawn, and the shadows gradually turned from dark to gray, revealing the valley and the cliff face.

The river curved there, gleaming silver in its sandy bed. At the base of the cliff was the ruin of a groundling city. A great city, with two vast levels of pillared porticos that flanked arched gateways, leading back into the rock. Above, the cliff face, hundreds of paces high, swelled out like a ball.

No, I'm looking at it wrong, Moon thought, as the light grew brighter. *That's not part of the cliff.* It was two cities, not one. A groundling ruin with a giant Dwei hive built on top of it.

Squinting, he could see the difference between the golden stone of the cliffs and the gold-tinged dust covering the rough material of the hive. The groundling city had been built at the entrance to a gorge. The groundlings must have carved out the gorge for more room, perhaps bent the flow of the river away from it, and used the rock to build their city. Turns and turns later, with the groundlings gone and the city fallen to ruin, the Dwei had constructed their hive, using the sides of the gorge to brace the enormous structure, and sitting it firmly atop the ruined city, filling the gorge from one side to the other.

The Dwei were skylings, something like insects, something like lizards. Moon didn't know much about them except that they didn't seem to prey on groundlings or other races. They made their hives with a substance that looked like clay, secreted out of their bodies somehow. He didn't think they would voluntarily share their hive with Fell, or anything else. *The Fell must have kept the hive and ate the Dwei.*

Dakti circled above the top of the hive, and one dropped down to vanish somewhere inside it. There had to be an entrance up there; that had to be where the kethel had gone. Trying to follow them would be instant suicide.

Moon had never been inside a Dwei hive before, but he had seen drawings. The inside of the hive should be hollow, with plenty of room for the kethel to fly and climb around in their shifted forms. But the gates and doorways he could see in the groundling city's long portico looked like they were meant for normal, Moon-sized groundlings. If the hallways and corridors further inside were comparable, the kethel wouldn't be able to fit down there unless they shifted to groundling. The ruin didn't have to be attached to the hive, but it might be, and if he could find the way in before Jade and the others arrived, it would save time and argument.

He needed to see how far into the gorge the city extended. If there was a way in through the back somewhere, it would be easier to avoid the circling dakti sentries. And if he got killed in the attempt, he needed to leave some sort of message for the others.

His markers and the scent of the metal-mud would point the way here. This was a good, concealed vantage point, and it was unlikely that the dakti would stumble on it; they didn't seem to be scouting any distance from the hive. *Of course, they wanted us to follow them, and they're hoping we'll attack like crazy idiots,* he thought sourly, picking out a good flat rock face. The only thing they could do was attack like sane idiots, and hope that worked.

He scratched out a brief message in Altanic, explaining what he was about to do. If he found he couldn't approach the hive from cover, he would come back here to wait for the others.

Moon shifted back to Raksura, shouldered the waterskin, and started down the slope.

Moon flew the long way around, careful to stay out of sight of the hive, and stopped upriver to renew his coating of metal-mud. Then he found the other end of the gorge, which wound snake-like through the bulk of the escarpment, a long distance from the Dwei hive. He followed it back, staying cautiously low, finding the ruins of small, roofless stone buildings with crumbling walls, the remains of a road, and stairways carved into the cliffs.

Finally, as the gorge curved again, Moon found the beginning of the main ruin. He landed, blending into the shadows at the base of a rock fall. *This could work,* he thought, encouraged.

A sloping wall blocked the gorge from one cliff to the other, carved with worn figures of giant grasseaters. It had a gate, blocked by piles of old rubble and guarded only by two slim obelisks. Beyond it was a long, mostly-intact colonnade, and a maze of crumbling walls. Over the top of the cliff, he could just see the rounded dome of the Dwei hive where it sat further up the gorge. Dakti still lazily circled above it.

Moon slipped forward, moving quickly over the dusty ground, between the obelisks and over the rubble of the gate.

The partly-intact roof of the colonnade provided cover from anything flying overhead. The shade sheltered sand-colored lizards and green beetles that fled as he ran past. The colonnade ended in a long rambling building, still mostly roofed over, and he went from it to the next, and the next. Among the ruins were empty pools and fountains choked with sand, broken statues, and thornvines shrouding empty archways. The inner walls were painted with scenes of barges moving along a broad river, and desert plains, all in delicate faded colors. Some rooms were still packed with large clay storage jars, each taller than he was. At any other time, this place would have been a pleasure to explore, to poke into all its secrets.

Soon he passed through the sandy corridors of buildings darkened by the shadow of the hive. Then he reached an archway blocked by a solid wall of dusty gold-brown stone. He ran his hand over it and realized he had found the outer wall of the hive. The texture of the material was grainy, rubbery in places and stiff, almost brittle in others. *All right, you got here, now look for a way in,* he told himself.

He worked his way back through the building, finding steps that led down to what might have been a large, open plaza at one time, littered with broken stone columns. Now the hive sat atop it, forming a heavy roof over the paved space. *They must have used this building to brace the hive,* Moon thought, moving forward cautiously.

Small holes punctured the bottom of the hive, but he could see a much larger one ahead, maybe twenty paces across. Dim daylight fell through it to illuminate a circle of the worn paving.

That opening might be for ventilation, or to give access to the ruin as an escape route. Or to dump trash, because as he drew closer he could see the section of plaza beneath it was littered with big shells.

He reached one and crouched to examine it. It was curved and nearly four paces across, the iridescent surfaces scarred with recent claw marks.

Oh. I think I found the Dwei.

Moon had only seen Dwei from a distance, but he knew they had shells like these across their backs. He sniffed at the inside and winced. It smelled of recently dead flesh, and it had been scraped out with claws. Unless the Dwei ate their own dead and cast the remnants away like trash, which was possible but not likely, then the Fell had cleaned out the hive.

From somewhere far above his head, up inside the shaft, he heard a low, reverberating grumble. Moon froze until it faded into silence, then carefully eased back away from the pile of shells. Somewhere at the top of that shaft, a kethel lay sleeping.

So that's not going to work, Moon thought, retreating quietly. But if there was one shaft up into the hive, there might be others.

After a little searching, he found one toward the far side of the plaza. No daylight fell through, but no Dwei shells littered the stone beneath it either. Moon jumped up to catch the edge and hoisted himself up.

The climb was much longer than he had expected, and also uncomfortable, with the waterskin bumping heavily against his side. The shaft led up a long distance, maybe a fourth of the way into the hive, then finally opened into a dark chamber.

Moon crawled out of the shaft to crouch on the edge, all his senses alert. The cave-like space was empty of anything but dust, and smelled of Fell mixed with a musty acrid odor. Dark openings in the far wall led deeper into the hive's interior. He stood and crossed the floor to investigate.

Halfway across his foot slipped, and he stumbled on a suddenly uneven surface. It was a grate, a big one, made of the same material as the rest of the hive. Moon crouched and tasted the air. The acrid odor was stronger here.

Then a large clawed hand shot up through the grate to wrap around his lower leg. Moon nearly yelled in panic, managed to turn it into a low hiss, and tried to wrench free. The hand yanked at him, hard enough to drag him down between the bars. The waterskin of poison slipped off his shoulder. Desperate, he scrabbled for purchase on the bar, but the weight dragging him down increased a hundredfold and his claws slipped off the slick surface.

He fell down into a dark space and landed hard on rubbery ground. Something slammed down top of him, a big hand pinning his chest. A creature with a large round head with bulbous, multi-faceted eyes loomed over him. Its skin was dull green, with a soft slick texture.

A deep, raspy voice from somewhere to the left said, "What is it?"

"It's a Fell," another voice replied.

"I'm not a Fell!" Moon glared up at the creature looming over him. They were speaking something close to Kedaic, and he answered in that language. "I'm a Raksura, a consort. Look at the back of my head!"

There was a startled pause. His eyes adjusted, and he could see they were all around him, looming shapes. One said, "There are Raksura to the south."

"Still shifters, still dangerous," another replied.

"It smells strange," someone else added.

"You stink, too," Moon said, suppressing a snarl. They meant the metal-mud, but at the moment it was adding insult to injury.

Then the first voice said, "Let it up."

The creature let go of him, and Moon rolled away, getting to his feet. He looked around, but there was nowhere to go.

The big chamber was full of the creatures. They were all taller and broader than he was, with heavy iridescent shells across their backs. Their wings were thin and fine, nearly translucent, and folded back along their bodies. Moon rubbed his chest where the creature had pinned him. They were strong, too. "You're Dwei?"

The one that seemed to be the leader loomed over him, demanding, "Did you see others? Others like us?"

"What?" Then he remembered the shells. "I saw shells, down below in the groundling city. The Fell ate what was in them and threw them down into the ruin."

It jerked back as if Moon had struck it, then turned away. A noise rose up from the others, like wood rattling, that resolved into a raspy groan. The sound conveyed dismay, disbelief, grief. It made Moon's scales ripple uneasily.

Still facing away from him, the leader said, "Every two days, they took five of us away. They said they took them elsewhere, that if we did not resist, we would see them again."

In the sense that eventually you'd all end up dead, Moon thought, swallowing down a hiss. The Fell were using the Dwei as a convenient food source while the flight stayed here. Some of the dakti could be left to fend for themselves or eat each other, but the kethel and the rulers had to feed at regular intervals. It made it even stranger that they hadn't done this to the Raksura at Indigo Cloud, that they had left even the dead intact. But this was typically Fell behavior, dangling hope the same way they did to their groundling prey. He just said, "They lie." The Dwei groaned again, more faintly this time, pain and grim acceptance. "What is this place?"

The leader didn't answer, but one of the others, he wasn't sure which, said hesitantly, "We kept our crops here, the dorgali and matra we grew in the cliff tunnels. The Fell forced us in here and blocked the door. They only come to take some of us away."

The leader swung back around, staring accusingly down at Moon again. "Why are you here?"

He didn't see any reason not to answer. "They attacked our colony. We drove them off, but they took some of our people. I followed them here."

One of the others held up the waterskin. The leader said, "What is this?"

Moon hesitated, but what were they going to do with it, tell the Fell?

"It's poison. It only works on Fell." He wasn't going to tell them it worked on Raksura, just in case they decided a test was necessary. "It makes them sick, keeps them from shifting."

"That doesn't exist." The leader looked at the waterskin. "No one has heard of this."

"It exists," Moon said. "Groundlings made it."

With deep skepticism, it said, "And the Fell drink it."

"No." Moon held on to his patience. "The groundlings drank it and the Fell ate them, and died. That was the only way they knew to make it work. We put it in the water in our colony." He then admitted, "I can't use it that way here. The rulers would have passed on a warning about poisoned water before they died."

The leader blinked slowly, milky membranes sliding up to cover its eyes, then sliding down again. "You killed rulers with it?"

"And kethel and dakti. I saw a kethel drink the water and die. Another kethel ate its corpse and died." He couldn't read any emotion in the Dwei's faces, couldn't tell if they believed him or not. "Show me where the door is. I'll go up through the grate and let you out." It would be easier to find where the Arbora were kept with a lot of angry Dwei rampaging through the hive.

Someone in the back said, "The door is sealed only with a stone, but a kethel guards it."

That didn't sound encouraging, but Moon wasn't ready to give up the idea of a massive distraction that would let him get further up into the hive. "Maybe I could find a way to—"

Something moved in the chamber above. Moon went still. He heard the faint clicking of dakti climbing across the grate. The Dwei made that sound again, the rattling groan. The leader cut them off with a sharp clack of its jaws. Then it called up toward the grate, "The Raksura is here!"

Moon stared at it, incredulous. "No!" He scrambled back, hissing, but the Dwei surrounded him. He made a wild leap, trying to reach the wall, but hands grabbed his legs, yanking him down again. Thrashing wildly, he clawed at their hands, flared his spines. His claws tore their thick skin, but they slammed him down to the ground. Pinned face down, heavy Dwei hands on his back, he growled, "Are you stupid? You think they'll let you go for this?"

He could already hear grating stone from the far end of the chamber; the kethel must be moving the rock away from the entrance. The Dwei in front of him moved away, clearing a path for the kethel. The leader leaned over him, saying in a raspy whisper, "We know they will not."

The floor vibrated as the kethel entered the chamber. Blood from the Dwei that he had scratched dripped on Moon's back; it was clear and smelled like jasmine. Past their legs, he caught a glimpse of the kethel, its dark armor streaked with sand, lowering its head to menace the Dwei with its horns. The Dwei scattered away, releasing Moon, but as he pushed himself up, the kethel shot out a hand and grabbed him.

Moon hissed in furious terror, digging claws into the finger that was like an iron band across his chest. The kethel stared down at him, eyes dark with malice, and Moon knew it meant to eat him right here. He bitterly promised himself to do as much damage on the way down its gullet as possible. Suddenly, pain shot up his back, his neck, snapping his head back. He yelled, heard his voice drop and change as the pain washed over him and he shifted to groundling.

The kethel dropped him, and Moon landed in an awkward sprawl, no chance to catch himself. Panting, he rolled over, suddenly hyperaware of the cool damp air clinging to his clothes and his far more vulnerable groundling skin. He braced shaky arms to lever himself up. It was the same force the mentor-dakti at the colony had used, but far more violent. *They've got another one here,* he thought, looking up blearily. A ruler, still armored in Fell form, now stood beside the kethel. It seemed smaller and younger than Kathras, but no less dangerous.

The ruler tilted its head. "A consort. Just what we wanted." He hissed out an order in the Fell language; Moon had heard it before but it had never sounded so close to Raksuran, as if he could understand it if he just listened hard enough.

A score of dakti raced around the kethel. Moon snarled, flailing away, but they swarmed him. He kicked one, managed to smash its kneecap, then got slammed back to the ground, three or four on top of him. After a second stunning clout to the head, the world swung out of focus.

The dakti lifted him up above their heads, their claws caught in his clothes, his hair, scraping at his neck, at his back where his shirt was pushed up. The oily texture of their hands on his groundling skin made him want to scratch himself bloody, fight until they killed him. He forced himself to stay limp, to play dead, and keep his eyes slitted.

They carried him out of the chamber, and he could hear the grating sound as the kethel rolled the rock back into place. It was dark. He couldn't see anything but a ridged roof overhead. He knew they were going up, through a tunnel or passage that went up in long spirals. He memorized the route as best he could.

Finally they passed into a place with fresher air and daylight. Moon let his head flop to one side, and saw one wall of the passage was open to a vast space, lit by wan daylight falling from somewhere high overhead. It had to be the open center well of the hive.

Then the dakti stopped. He caught a glimpse of a round opening in the floor, right before the dakti flung him down into it. He fell a short distance, struck the rubbery ground, and rolled to his hands and knees, prepared to be swarmed again.

The dakti had dropped him into a shadowy chamber, light falling through long horizontal slits in the far wall. He looked up to see an opening high in the ceiling, set up into a short shaft. The dakti crouched around it and pulled some kind of translucent cover into place, sealing the opening. He looked around the chamber, and caught startled movement in the shadows. He froze, tasting the air. He scented frightened Raksura. *Frightened Raksura other than me*, he thought. "Who's here?"

Someone said suspiciously, "Who are you?"

Before he could answer, a female voice said, "It's Moon, the solitary—the consort Stone brought." Arbora in groundling form edged into the faint light, watching him warily: four females, two males, all young enough to be barely out of adolescence. Their clothes were dirty and ragged, their hair lank from little access to water.

With breathless hope, another one asked, "Is Stone here?"

"No." *At least you've found them, and they're alive*, Moon told himself. It didn't feel like much of an accomplishment considering he didn't see any way he could get them out of here. He got to his feet, moving away to see more of the chamber. "They only took six of you?"

"Yes," the first woman answered. She had skin the color of dark honey, curly bronze-colored hair, and she was beautiful, even past the dirt and the fatigue. "They brought us here in a sac. We were the only ones in it. They let us out when we got here, then shoved us into this room." She added, "I'm Heart, and that's Gift, Needle, and Dream." She nodded to the other females, then to the two males, "And Snap and Merit. They're all teachers, and Merit and I are mentors."

"Not that it's done us much good," Merit said, sounding rueful. "None of us can even shift. We don't know how they're doing that."

"How'd you get here?" Snap demanded, still watching Moon suspiciously.

"I followed the kethel." He stopped, staring at them for a moment. They were all beautiful, their skin every shade from warm brown to coppery red to light amber. They were all more than a head shorter than Moon, but they were strong and well-proportioned. All young, all healthy, and two of them mentors. *They picked them for breeding stock,* he thought uneasily. The Fell still meant to make more crossbreeds. Unable to keep the whole colony, they had probably meant to take all the young Arbora, leaving the older adults and the sterile warriors behind, but they hadn't had time. "Are you all right? They didn't do anything?"

"Not yet." Heart looked up at him, brow furrowed as she read his expression far too accurately. "Why are you looking at us like that?"

"No reason." He had to get them out of here. He stepped back and jumped for the side of the shaft. He caught the ridge around the edge and dragged himself up handhold by handhold until he reached the membrane that sealed the opening. He pushed at it, but it refused to budge. The texture was stiff and slick, as impermeable as glass.

Below him, Snap said in frustration, "It's no use. We stood on each other's shoulders to get to it, but without claws we can't get through."

Moon kept prodding at the edge, looking for a weak point, but he was afraid the boy was right.

Heart asked, "But where are the others? Did the hunters get away? Knell said he saw—"

Moon's fingers slipped and he dropped back to the floor. He absently wiped his hands. *And if you got it open, what were you going to do then?* The dakti were still up there, guarding them.

"The others are fine." He gave them a meaningful look and jerked his head up toward the opening. The Fell might be listening; with Moon here they would have to realize that Jade and the other Aeriat couldn't be far behind, but he didn't want to spell it out for them.

Heart subsided, and the others held back frustrated questions.

Watching him carefully, Needle said, "At the colony, there was a ruler who said Pearl had left us, that she wouldn't be coming back. He said they were waiting for Jade to join them, then we were going to leave the colony and go somewhere else." She made a despairing gesture. "Here, I guess."

Moon paced around the chamber, investigating the shadows. It was big enough for a few Dwei to sit or sleep in comfortably, and nearly featureless. "I think I saw that ruler. Right before Pearl tore his head off."

There were some gratified hisses, and Needle hugged herself. She said, "I knew the ruler was lying." She shot a fierce look at the others. "The queens are going to save us."

They were still watching him worriedly, and Gift said, "But why did the Fell bring us here? And why us? If they just wanted to eat us. We're small, and not much of a meal."

Moon hoped to avoid that question. He stepped to the wall with the horizontal slits, and peered out. The chamber looked down on the hive's vast central well, daylight falling down from some opening high above. The curving walls were ringed with bulbous chambers like this one, and open ledges. Wedging himself into the gap, he had a good view of the floor several hundred paces below.

A big tunnel opened in the side of the hive down there, and towards the center of the floor was a round shaft, maybe the one that had led up from the groundling ruin, the one that had shone with daylight. Two kethel lay beside it, stretched out in sleep, armored sides lifting with their raspy breathing. It was probably the two who had flown here from Indigo Cloud. From the distance and turns the dakti had taken to bring him here, he thought the Dwei must be imprisoned on that bottom level, not far from where the tunnel emerged.

Merit tugged on his sleeve impatiently. He had fluffy light-colored hair and wide eyes, and made Moon think of what Chime must have looked like as an Arbora. He persisted, "You know why they brought us here, don't you?"

Maybe not knowing was worse. Moon turned back, and all their faces, staring up at him with hope and fear and dismay, made his heart hurt. He said reluctantly, "A ruler told Pearl and Jade that this flight wanted to... join with your court. We know they already had at least one crossbreed, a dakti with mentor powers. It was the reason that the court was trapped. It sees through the other dakti's eyes, and does something so you can't shift. There must be another one here; that's what's keeping us from shifting now."

"A dakti?" Heart blinked rapidly. "But..."

Dream said, "That's not even possible, is it?" She turned urgently to Heart. "We're too different from Fell. We couldn't... could we?"

Snap sank down to sit on the floor, as if his knees had gone weak. "I thought they were just going to eat us."

"Why do they want to do this?" Merit shivered. "So they can get mentor abilities? Mentors are born at random. Even when two mentors mate, it's not certain. We think it has something to do with queens and consorts mating with Arbora, but that's just an idea. Those clutches are just as likely to be warriors, or ordinary Arbora."

If Moon had to guess, which he didn't want to, he would have said that the Fell meant to get mentors the same way Raksura did, by mating the Arbora until mentors were born. Only in Raksuran courts it was all done voluntarily. He didn't answer, hoping the Arbora would leave it at that.

But Heart looked up at Moon. "But you're a consort. They must want..."

"Uh, probably." He folded his arms uncomfortably, not certain how much to tell them. They seemed perfectly capable of drawing all the terrible conclusions on their own. "That's why the Fell stayed at the colony. They were hoping Jade and I would attack with Pearl and the others, that they could trap us."

"But they didn't trap you," Dream put in. "Until now, I mean. And Jade and

Pearl are still free, right?"

"We had a weapon." Moon turned away again, knowing he was doing a bad job of reassuring them. He looked through the slit, down at the bottom of the well. The two kethel were still asleep, but some dakti flitted around down there now. "We can't use it here. The rulers know about it now." He wasn't sure what had happened to the waterskin of poison. If the Dwei had hoped to use it somehow to bargain with the Fell, they were out of luck.

The Arbora were quiet for a moment, trading uneasy glances. Then Heart asked, "What about the others trapped in the colony? Are they all right? Did you see them?"

The others chimed in with questions then and Moon ended up telling them a little about the attack on the colony. He tried to keep the explanation confined to things it wouldn't do the Fell any good to know, in case the dakti were listening or the rulers questioned them later.

Heart and the others hadn't known that Petal and so many of the soldiers were dead, believing all the missing members of the court to be imprisoned in another part of the colony. Watching them cling to each other and mourn, Moon felt terrible that he couldn't even tell them all the names of the dead.

"They kept us in those sacs," Snap said, leaning against Merit for comfort. "Sometimes they let us out and brought us food, but only a few at a time. We couldn't shift, and with the dakti and kethel there we couldn't run away."

Finally, when the Arbora had asked every question they could think of, and discussed the situation to the point where they were just repeating themselves, they settled down to try to rest, curling up against each other. Moon sat nearby, leaning back against the wall with the slits so he could look out at the central well. He wasn't certain if they trusted him completely, but his presence seemed to give them a little hope, anyway.

The dakti didn't return. Moon watched the sunlight falling through the top of the hive change from morning to early afternoon. He knew Jade and the warriors had had time to make it here by now. They should have found his trail and the metal-mud, found the message he had left on the rock, and made it into the groundling city. *And are probably sitting down there trying to think how to take on at least three kethel at once. You never did work that part out, either.* The Aeriat who had survived imprisonment in the colony were probably too weak to fly at all yet, let alone to follow Jade all the way out here.

A hollow in the back of the chamber held stale water, but the dakti hadn't dropped in any food. Moon could go another couple of days before he got desperate, but the Arbora had already been through days of privation. They also hadn't been allowed to shift in all that time, and that had to be taking its toll. Moon was thinking of food, how he could make the dakti give them some, where Jade was and what was taking so long, when a kethel growl shattered the quiet.

The Arbora all twitched awake, eyes wide with fear. Moon sat up straight, craning his neck to peer through the slat. Below on the floor of the hive, one of the kethel had heaved itself to its feet, and the other stirred in irritation. In response, dakti dropped down through the well, spiraling in flight to cling to the wall above the lowest tunnel—the tunnel that led toward the side of the hive where the Dwei were imprisoned. *And the kethel have flown a long way, and they're waking up hungry,* Moon thought, watching grimly. At least the Dwei knew what was coming now; they had a chance to fight.

Snap and Heart crept to his side to peer out, the others gathering around. "What are they doing?" Heart asked.

Moon couldn't think of any way to make it easier, and they were going to see for themselves in a moment. "They're going to eat some of the Dwei."

Merit made a noise of dismay, and Dream shuddered.

Dakti drove five Dwei out of the tunnel. The Dwei stumbled in the brighter light, their round heads turning as they looked around. They didn't fight, didn't try to escape. Moon hissed in disgusted disbelief. "I told them I found broken shells in the groundling city. They still think the Fell aren't killing the ones they take?"

"They must have thought you were lying," Snap said helpfully.

The dakti drove the five hapless Dwei across the floor of the hive, closer to the shaft that led down into the ruin. If they meant to take them somewhere else, Moon would never know; one of the kethel grew impatient and pounced.

The first Dwei went down under its claws with barely a sound. The others scattered away, keening in terror. The second kethel leapt in to slap at them, sending them rolling helplessly across the floor. The crunching and tearing as the kethel's jaws worked almost drowned out the Dwei's cries of pain.

The Arbora retreated hastily from the openings, some covering their ears. "Is that what they're going to do to us?" Needle asked in terror.

"No." Heart pulled her into a tight hug. "If they were just going to eat us, they would have done it by now."

Merit looked away, swallowing uneasily. "What they're going to do to us worse."

Any reassurance Moon could give them would be a lie or wishful thinking, so he didn't say anything. *Jade should be here by now.* He was trusting her and whoever was with her to think of something.

One Dwei made a half-hearted attempt to take flight only to be swarmed by the dakti. They forced it down into the kethel's reach again, and it batted the Dwei back and forth a little, then finally snatched it up in its jaws. The Dwei hardly struggled.

This doesn't make sense, Moon thought. On the occasions when something large had tried to eat him, he had fought harder and more frantically than that.

This behavior was at odds with everything he had seen of the Dwei. They were much stronger and meaner than this. If all five had attacked one of the kethel at once, they could have done some damage. *Unless... They had the waterskin of poison. They knew what it was.* And he had told them about the suicidal groundling method of using it.

Moon stirred impatiently. It could just be too-hopeful speculation on his part, and even if it was true, one waterskin split five ways wasn't much. And there was still one more kethel to worry about, the one guarding the Dwei prison. There was nothing to do except to wait and watch and hope.

CHAPTER
NINETEEN

e∕⊙

The Arbora drew back to huddle together again, trying to rest. Moon stayed at the wall, grimly watching the kethel finish their meal. The dakti crept in to feast on the scraps, then pushed the shells over the edge of the shaft to fall down into the ruin.

Then Moon heard movement up above, near the sealed doorway in the ceiling. He got to his feet just as the membrane peeled away and a ruler dropped into the chamber. The Arbora scrambled up with a chorus of startled snarls and hisses, and clustered behind Moon.

It wasn't the ruler who had caught Moon with the Dwei. This one was older, more heavily built, his dark armor plates scarred and chipped from many battles. He fixed a mocking gaze on Moon and said, "I am Janeas. I've seen you, through the eyes of my brother Kathras."

"Did you see me rip his throat out?" Moon asked. He didn't feel like he had much to lose at the moment.

Janeas surged forward. He grabbed Moon's arm, yanked him forward, nearly dislocating his shoulder. Moon jabbed at his eyes, the only vulnerable point he could reach. The blow he got in return rocked his head back with stunning force. The backhand follow-up made his knees buckle.

Janeas wrapped an arm around Moon's throat, dragging him toward the doorway. The Arbora flung themselves on Janeas in a hissing mob, but the ruler partially extended his wings, buffeting them back. Clawing at the scaled arm and trying to writhe free, Moon caught a glimpse of Heart, scrabbling past the wings and nearly climbing Janeas's back up onto his head. If she had been in her Arbora form, she could have done some real damage, but Janeas just shook her off with an annoyed snarl. He stepped under the doorway, then tossed Moon up through it.

Moon landed hard on the surface of the passage and rolled upright only to get slammed down again when several dakti jumped on him.

The other dakti stood around, clicking and hissing at each other in the Fell language, sounding agitated. Janeas leapt back up out of the chamber and growled an order, and they hurried to fix the membrane back over the doorway. Pinned face down on the passage floor, Moon heard the Arbora yelling furiously. At least they didn't sound hurt.

Janeas gestured and the dakti leapt off Moon. Released, Moon scrabbled back a desperate few paces before Janeas hauled him upright.

Janeas dragged him down the passage. Moon resisted hard enough to get bounced off the wall a few times. Wherever they were going, he was certain he didn't want to get there.

The passage turned and dead-ended in an opening into a bigger chamber, the ceiling curving up high overhead. Moon barely glimpsed it before Janeas shoved him face-first into the wall and pinned him there. He twisted his head to the side to get air.

Janeas was breathing harshly, though Moon didn't think his struggles had been enough to wind a Fell. Then Janeas pressed against him, the scales of his chest so cold Moon could feel the chill through his sweat-soaked shirt. The dakti retreated back down the passage, and Moon had a heartbeat to wonder if the ruler had brought him up here to rape him. Then Janeas whispered in his ear, "She's been waiting for you, little consort. Don't disappoint her."

"Who—" Moon managed to say, just before Janeas jerked him away from the wall and tossed him through the opening into the chamber below.

He closed his throat against a yell and landed an instant later in stale water. He hit the bottom of a pool that was barely waist-deep and flailed to his feet, coughing and choking.

Shaking water out of his hair, Moon looked around, relieved to see nothing was about to leap on him. The pool lay at one end of a high-ceilinged chamber that curved to follow the side of the hive. Light fell through large windows in the outer wall that faced out into the central well. There were platforms near the windows, oval and a little more than waist-high, built of the same material as the rest of the hive, that could be anything from Dwei beds to storage containers. There was also an open shaft in the center of the floor. Instinctively, Moon tasted the air, but all he could scent from here was Fell, and that wasn't helpful. The passage behind him was set nearly thirty paces up the smooth wall, not an easy climb for him in groundling form. And he had the strong sense that Janeas still waited up there. *Not that down here is much safer.*

He climbed out of the pool, dripping on the grainy floor. The dunking had washed away most of the dried remnants of the metal-mud. He moved cautiously forward, his skin prickling uneasily, trying to see further into the shadows. He knew he wasn't alone in here.

He went to the shaft first, craning his neck to peer down. It plunged straight through the hive. Dim daylight was visible down at the bottom. That would have been a help, if he had claws to climb or wings to fly.

He looked around again. By this time his eyes had adjusted and he realized the shadow in the inner wall was a large, Dwei-sized opening into another chamber or passage.

He started toward it, noticing that Dwei shells hung on the walls, polished to gleaming green-blue iridescence and etched with markings in a strange language. They appeared to commemorate something, ancestor worship or funerary tributes. Some had been knocked to the floor and broken, the pieces scattered. Other things were strewn around, things that looked like they had been looted from a groundling city. Moon picked his away around torn and stained fragments of rich cloth and fur, a broken ivory cup, all of it dropped like trash. These Fell lived like the others Moon had seen, making nothing of their own, stealing even their clothes from groundlings.

Moon reached the opening and pushed aside the drifting fragments of a torn membrane curtain.

Beyond it was another chamber. In the shadows against the far wall, something large and alive lay in a nest of torn cloth, fragments of Dwei shell scattered around it. He could see a sloping, scaled flank, the folded edge of a leathery wing, a gleam of fangs. It was breathing, but so slowly it was nearly silent. Moon's throat was already too dry to swallow, his body already cold from fear, and he had been half-expecting this. It was a Fell progenitor, the only female Fell, the ones who mated with the rulers to produce all the rest. He had never seen one before, only heard of their existence, but this had to be one.

He stepped back, away from the curtain, feeling the cold settle into his bones. *Jade is not going to be here in time.* If she was even on her way, if the court hadn't just cut its losses and given up on him and the stolen Arbora. He couldn't let the Fell have what they wanted.

Moon backed away another few steps, trying to think. *Find a weapon and kill the progenitor. Or make the progenitor kill you.* He had to admit the second option was more likely.

He looked around at the debris on the floor, hoping for something with a sharp edge. He saw a tumbled pile of dark cloth behind the nearest platform. A few steps took him close enough to see clearly. He stopped, startled.

It was a dead ruler. He was in his groundling form, pale hair fanned out behind his head, open eyes staring sightlessly up. A trail of blood leaked from his mouth, staining the waxy white skin of his cheek. His dark clothes were disarrayed, pulled open across his chest, a chain of rubies broken and scattered near his hand, but there was no visible wound. Moon took a wary step forward, taking in a breath to taste the air again. It wasn't a trick. The ruler was really dead, and had been here long enough for his blood to cool.

Behind him, a voice said, "I killed him when he arrived with the kethel."

Moon twitched around, his breath caught in his throat.

She was standing in front of the shaft, as if she had just climbed up out of it. She could have passed for a groundling, or the groundling form of an Aeriat. She was tall and slim, with gold-tinted skin and blue eyes, her hair straight and dark, falling past her waist. She was dressed like a Raksura too, in a watered gold silk wrap, leaving her arms bare. Then a dakti crept around her, peering up at Moon with wide-eyed curiosity. A dakti without wings, with the heavy build of an Arbora. *A mentor-dakti,* Moon thought. He had known there had to be at least one more here. And there were no female rulers. *She's another crossbreed, a warrior-ruler.*

Her gaze on the dead ruler, she said, "He failed me, and I was angry. To bring me only six Arbora, no queen, no consort. By the time I discovered that you had followed him, it was too late." Her voice sounded like a groundling woman's, light and warm.

She took a step toward Moon, and that was when he caught her scent. He flinched backward, nearly overpowered by the flight-urge to turn and throw himself out the window into the hive well. He conquered it with a shiver, still feeling it trickle through his veins like icy water. Her scent was foul, strange, wrong. Even the mentor-dakti just smelled like a Fell.

She said, "I won't hurt you." She tilted her head, her lips forming a smile. There was something disjointed about her face, something awry about how she wore the expression. "You saw the Arbora are well."

The Arbora. It was a reminder that Moon didn't just have himself to worry about. He felt certain he already knew, but he made himself say, "You've still got plenty of Dwei to eat. What do you want with us?"

"We need company. There's nothing like us anywhere in the Three Worlds." She touched the mentor-dakti's head. It leaned against her leg, nuzzling her. "Especially since you killed Erasus, back at your colony. But perhaps it was appropriate that he died there, after he spent so many turns watching it for us. I wanted him to stay here in safety, but he was desperate to see it with his own eyes, instead of only in his scrying. Demus here is not so accomplished, yet." She gently pushed the mentor-dakti away. Demus hissed in mild rebuke, then turned and crept away. It was smaller than the other one, and its right leg was twisted at an odd angle. She watched it retreat, then looked back at Moon. "You didn't ask my name. It's Ranea. I know yours." She lifted her hand, and her nails were almost as long as claws. "Come here, Moon."

He fell back another step. "Let the Arbora go, and I'll do what you want." He didn't think she would go for it, but it was worth a try.

"Why should I? I need them." The smile was still on her face, but it was almost as if she had forgotten it was there. He realized then what was wrong with her expression: it was like an imitation of things she had seen others do, without any real understanding of what it meant. In the same warm tone, Ranea said, "And you don't have anything I want that I can't just take."

Moon backed away from her. He told himself it didn't matter what she did to him. If she was part Raksuran warrior, then she was infertile; it was the progenitor in the other room he had to worry about. "Your ruler told the court you wanted to join with us."

"That's true." She paced forward. There was something predatory in the ease and focus of her movement, making her look even less like a groundling. "Our flight once ruled the east, all of the great peninsula. So the rulers said."

Moon backed into the platform and flinched when its brittle edge bumped him in the lower back. She stopped a few paces away, watching him, and her foul scent made the back of his throat itch.

"They told me how the groundling empires died on our whim, and prey was plentiful. But they say we fought among ourselves, broke into smaller flights, became too isolated, too inbred. Progenitors died too soon. Fewer rulers were born, but more sterile dakti and kethel. So my progenitor and her rulers made an experiment, capturing a Raksuran consort and forcibly mating with him."

Ranea paused to taste the air. Moon knew his scent must have changed. He had felt the sweat break out on his skin. She took her time, obviously relishing his fear, then continued easily, "He died soon after. She tried again, mating her first crossbreed progeny to her rulers, to captured Arbora. Eventually, this produced Erasus, then later, Demus, and I." Her voice sharpened. "Janeas, come here, I know you're watching."

After a moment of silence, Janeas jumped out of the upper passage, glided over the pool, and landed near the shaft. Demus chirped at him, a greeting that Janeas ignored. Ranea stared at him, still with that fixed smile.

After a long moment, Janeas said, stiffly, "I have done everything you asked." He didn't look at the dead ruler sprawled near the platform.

The words lingered in the damp air. Then Ranea turned back to Moon, as if Janeas hadn't spoken.

"When you came to Liheas in the groundling city," she said, "he wanted to bring you to me. He thought you were perfect. A consort who knew nothing of the Raksura, who could be molded as we wished, who could be taught to do our bidding. But it was all a trick, and you killed him."

She probably expected him to argue with her, something that would be about as pointless as arguing with the dead ruler. Moon just said, "I was lucky."

"Do you want to know why we chose Indigo Cloud?" She moved closer, within arm's reach. "We came for you."

Don't fall for this trick again, he told himself. He said, "That's a lie. I traveled across the east, if you knew where I was you could have caught me anytime."

"I wasn't ready to clutch yet," Ranea said it as if it was self-evident. "Erasus' augury said you would eventually be at Indigo Cloud, that then the time would be right."

Clutch? Moon flicked a look at the doorway to the other chamber. "I don't understand."

She followed his gaze. "That was—is—my progenitor. My mother. She's old now, and dying." She took in his expression, and this time her smile was real, a ruler's smile, a Fell's smile, cold and predatory and satisfied. "Did you think I was only a Fell-born warrior? I'm a progenitor. A Fell-born queen."

Moon couldn't answer, his throat locked with sick horror. *You should have jumped out the window when you had the chance.*

She stepped closer, a hand under his chin lifting his head. "All I have to do is breed more queens like myself, more dakti like Demus, and nothing can stop us. We can take control of every other Fell flight we touch, have all the prey we want. We can rule the Three Worlds, earth, air, and water." Her hand moved down, resting against his throat, almost absently, part caress and part menace, like a butcher petting a herdbeast to calm it. She said, "It's known that the Fell and the Aeriat came from the same source. The only difference is that the Aeriat joined with another race of shifters called Arbora." She cocked her head. "You didn't know they were two different races? Arbora build, they shape, they craft. They make images, art. All the Aeriat do is fight and eat. Two related races that combined to make something better. Why shouldn't this happen again?"

Panic abruptly overcame numb shock, and Moon knew he had to make her kill him. He couldn't let her take him, birth another clutch of half-Raksuran monsters to attack other courts, to destroy even more groundling cities, to move across the Three Worlds like a plague. *They wouldn't stop.* They didn't know how. All they knew was breeding and eating, and they would do it until they killed every living creature in their reach. "Because you're Fell. You're abominations, and you destroy everything you touch." A shadow flickered in her eyes, and he knew the strike was true. "In Saraseil, Liheas touched me, and it ruined everything. It just took turns and turns for me to know it."

She hit him, an open-handed slap that knocked him off his feet. Half-stunned, he tried to roll away from her, but she grabbed him by the hair. Moon clawed at her arm, kicked, trying to wrench away even if he lost most of his scalp, but she pulled him up onto his knees.

A dakti careened in, bounced off the ceiling, and landed near Janeas. It spat out words in the Fell language, hissing and clicking madly.

Ranea dropped Moon and turned to the dakti. Moon scrambled away, watching her warily. He saw Janeas move away as she stepped past him, as if the ruler wasn't eager to get within arm's reach of her either. Ranea grabbed the messenger dakti by the head, lifting it off the ground and shaking it, giving it a sharp order. It repeated the words, gasping this time, probably from the pressure of her hand on its skull. She dropped the dakti and strode to the nearest window.

Moon staggered to his feet and followed her at a careful distance. He wasn't sure what he was going to see, but he was hoping for an unexpectedly large number of Raksura. He caught the edge of the window and looked down.

The two kethel who had been lying on the hive floor were gone. No, not gone. He squinted, peering down. They were in groundling form, two big muscular bodies, sprawled unconscious near the shaft down into the ruin. Other smaller bodies were scattered around them. *Dakti, the dakti that ate the kethel's scraps,* Moon thought in relief. The Dwei had really done it! They had given the poison to five of their number, then sent them to be eaten by the kethel.

He looked up to see Ranea staring at him, her eyes brilliant with rage. She said, "You did this."

"No. I was here." In hindsight, he probably shouldn't have smiled when he said it.

He saw her hand lift and tried to duck away, but the blow caught his shoulder, knocking him sprawling. Tasting blood from a bitten lip, he rolled over to see her standing over him. *You got your wish. She's going to kill you.*

Behind him, Janeas said, "He must have brought some of that groundling filth here."

Ranea turned the furious glare on Janeas. "When you found him you should have searched him, searched the Dwei."

"I didn't find him; that was Venras," Janeas said, sounding bitterly pleased. "Demus saw through his eyes. Demus should have told him to search. You've put him above us all. Such things should be his decision."

She stood there a moment, fists clenched, shivering with rage, as if unable to decide who she wanted to kill more, Moon or Janeas. Then leaned down to grab Moon's arm and dragged him upright. She tossed him at Janeas.

"Watch him."

She stepped away from them and shifted. Dark mist swirled around her for a heartbeat, forming into a shape that was something out of a nightmare. Her scales were the matte black of Fell, without the colors or undersheen of Raksura, and the texture was coarse. Her wings had the leathery hide of the dakti, and her head was crowned with both an armored crest and Raksuran spines. And she was big, half again as tall as Moon's shifted form.

She stepped forward and leapt out through the window, her wings snapping out as she dropped from view. The messenger dakti struggled up and jumped after her. Janeas stared after them, gripping Moon's arm until the bones ground together.

Think of something, Moon told himself. Ranea had killed a ruler for no reason, for trying to salvage their sick plan and bring her at least some of the Arbora she wanted. Janeas had to see that his own chances of survival rested on her whim. Moon said, "You can't think this is a good idea."

Janeas said nothing, but he didn't hit Moon, either.

Moon persisted, "All the Fell at Indigo Cloud are dead. You don't have enough here to fight us off, and the Aeriat know not to get near that thing now."

The mentor-dakti chittered warningly, and Janeas snarled at it.

Moon considered that response, the fact that he had given a ruler a chance to gloat over him and the ruler hadn't taken it. He had always thought rulers only cared about themselves, that the survival of the Fell as a race wouldn't bother them as much as a threat to their own scales. Except apparently that wasn't the case at all. There weren't that many rulers in Fell flights, and what was that like, to live surrounded by dakti and kethel who differed from trained animals only by their active malice? Maybe rulers… cared about each other. *Kathras cared about Liheas, or at least cared that I killed him.*

Moon wet dry lips and said, "Kathras was dying when he found us."

Janeas made a sound, an exhalation of breath that wasn't a hiss. Moon said, "He could barely stay in the air. She made him fly himself to death to catch up with us, through mountain currents, ice storms. There were two of us. We could stop. One could rest while the other hunted."

Janeas flung him down, and Moon struck the rubbery floor face-first. Standing over him, Janeas snarled, "You killed him. I saw it."

Moon pushed himself up enough to look at him. His nose was bloody and it was hard to breathe.

"It was easy, because he was already dying." He pointed back to the dead ruler that lay rotting in the cool air. "Just like she killed him—" Janeas took a step forward and Moon shoved himself back. "—for no reason. Because he tried to obey her orders. He tried to salvage her stupid plan."

Janeas lunged forward. Moon rolled, pushed to his feet, and backed away.

"You think there's any place for you, for the other rulers, once she does this? She needs dakti and kethel for slaves, not—"

Something flashed past the window, and Moon flinched back, thinking it was Ranea returning. But whatever it was had fallen straight down past this level. Then he heard a crash from somewhere below.

Janeas froze, head cocked toward the sound. An instant later, something else fell past the window, and this time Moon saw it: a big clay jar, one of the storage jars he had seen in the ruin.

Janeas strode to the window and Moon stumbled after him.

The jars had struck the floor of the hive and somehow burst into flame. Black smoke streamed up as fire spread across the floor.

Dry metal-mud, packed into the jars, and set on fire, Moon realized, and the surge of hope was almost painful. *That has to be Chime's idea.* They would be dropping it on the outside of the hive, too, with any luck.

Another ruler flew toward them from the far side of the hive, banking in to perch in the window. It was Venras, the young ruler who had found Moon with the Dwei. He spoke to Janeas in the Fell language, and though Moon couldn't understand the words, the panic was obvious.

Moon stepped back from the window, looking at Janeas. "They're going to burn you out, kill anything that tries to escape—"

Janeas whipped around and grabbed him by the throat. His claws pricking Moon's skin, he said, "We have their Arbora, and you. They won't burn this place while you're here."

Moon couldn't help grabbing Janeas' wrist, but he forced himself to stand still, not to try to curl his body up to use the disemboweling claws he didn't have.

"There are plenty of Arbora left alive in the colony. They don't need these." It didn't matter if it was true or not, he just had to make Janeas believe it. "And they don't want me—"

Janeas stepped close, hissing into his face. "You're their only consort—"

Moon didn't have to fake the bitter amusement. "The reigning queen ordered me to leave days ago. They know what Kathras said. They know you came to Indigo Cloud because of me. They only let me stay this long to help fight you."

Janeas stared into his eyes, and must have read the truth there. He snarled, his hand closing around Moon's throat, cutting off his air. Moon frantically pried at his hand, tried to kick, then his vision went dark.

The terrible pressure stopped. He hit the floor, gasping in a breath with the jolt of impact. His throat and lungs ached, and for a moment he couldn't do anything but huddle on the floor and breathe. He managed to look up and saw Janeas coming out of the inner chamber, half-carrying the older Fell progenitor.

She was a little bigger than the ruler, but her scales looked soft, and her armored crest was much smaller, as if she hadn't been meant to fight. She leaned heavily on Janeas' shoulder, her half-furled wings drooping.

Janeas led her to the window where Venras still waited. Venras spoke again, jerking his chin at Moon. Janeas just shook his head, stepping up to the window, pulling the progenitor after him.

They're leaving, Moon thought in dizzy relief. And Janeas didn't want to kill Moon because he knew if he did, Ranea would follow him in a fury. *That part's not so good.* If the queen-progenitor returned in time, she could take Moon and still salvage her plan for a crossbreed flight. Janeas was leaving Moon behind as the distraction he needed to escape.

Venras twitched around to take the old progenitor's other arm, and the three of them dropped out of the window.

Moon staggered to his feet. Demus had crept forward to watch Janeas leave. It saw Moon looking at it and growled, flexing its claws. *That thing has to go now.*

It was smaller than a real dakti, and much scrawnier than a real Arbora, though its teeth and claws looked sharp. Moon looked around for a weapon, and spotted an unlikely one.

Watching Demus, he went to the platform where the dead ruler lay. He rolled the body over, dumping it out of the brocade coat it wore. Shaking out the heavy cloth, he paced toward Demus.

It crept backward, its spines bristling. It rasped in Raksuran, "She'll claw the skin from your body if you touch me."

"She's going to do that anyway." Moon didn't hesitate, still stalking the creature, angling to one side, forcing it to move back toward the pool of water.

"Don't kill me." The tone changed from threat to plea and Demus crouched, trying to look helpless. "Please."

"Then take the shifting geas off me and the Arbora," Moon said, still moving forward, "and run away." It seemed a rational choice to him, but then this thing was a Fell.

Demus crouched low, whining, then suddenly leapt for Moon's head. Moon lunged toward it, swinging the heavy coat up. It hit the fabric and then him, bowling him over backward. Moon wrapped his arms and legs around it and rolled, trapping it in the heavy brocade, pinning it with his weight. Demus clawed with frantic strength, its jaws clamping onto his shoulder through the fabric, but its claws caught in the heavy material, just long enough for Moon to roll them both toward the pool.

They fell into the cold water and Moon caught a breath before he went under, using his weight to shove the creature to the bottom. Desperate, Demus wrenched an arm free and clawed at his side, tearing through his shirt and the skin beneath. Moon pinned its hand with his knee and held on grimly, staying under until his lungs were about to burst. Hoping the damn thing would be too distracted to hold the geas on him, he tried to shift.

It felt like it had when he had resisted Pearl. The pressure in his chest and behind his eyes was increased a hundredfold by the pressure to breathe, the growing pain in his lungs. Then suddenly something gave way, and wings and spines formed on his back; scales spread over his skin.

Moon lifted up, getting a much-needed breath. Demus was limp in his hands. Moon pulled the coat aside and snapped Demus' neck just to make certain.

The relief of being able to shift was overwhelming; the claw scratches, bruises, everything faded into minor irritations. He shook the water off and jumped for the passage above the pool, reaching it in one long bound.

As he raced along the open passage, flames spread across the bottom floor of the hive, and thick smoke streamed upward, obscuring much of the center well. He heard the buzzing flight of Dwei below him somewhere, and the muffled roar of a kethel. The Dwei must have overwhelmed the single remaining kethel and escaped their prison.

Several dakti still guarded the doorway to the Arbora's chamber. When Moon landed among them and ripped the first two open, the others scattered, diving off the ledge into the smoky well. Moon crouched to rip open the door membrane, calling down, "Heart? Can you all shift?"

"Yes!" He saw Heart looking up at him, bright blue in her Arbora form. "Moon, did the others start the fire?"

"Yes! Come on out; we're leaving," he told her, looking warily out at the central well. Clouds of smoke obscured the view, giving him only glimpses of dakti flying wildly around.

Merit scrambled out of the shaft, followed rapidly by Needle and Gift. Crouching next to Moon, his spines bristling nervously, Merit demanded, "How do we get out?"

Good question. Moon couldn't risk trying to fly the Arbora out one at a time, and the openings in the wall made a climb up or down impossible. He would have to lead them out the way he had come in, whether it was on fire or not. Then he made out a large dark shape, banking through the smoke, heading back toward the progenitor's chamber. *Uh oh.* Ranea was returning and Moon was out of time. "Run, that way!" The startled Arbora stood and Moon gave Merit a push to get him started. "Now! Take the first turn down!"

Dream was just climbing out of the shaft with Snap and Heart behind her. Moon dragged them out and tossed them after the others. He ran after them, keeping his eyes on that dark shape.

Merit reached the open passage in the wall first, the turn into the long spiral ramp that led down through the hive, and looked back to Moon for instructions. Moon waved at him to keep going.

Then he felt a rush of air behind him. Moon somersaulted forward and landed in a crouch. Ranea was barely ten paces away, cupping her wings, coming in to land on the ledge. He shot forward, turning to rake her across the chest with his disemboweling claws. She tumbled backward off the ledge. Moon bounced off the ceiling and dove for the passage down.

It was the long spiral he remembered, leading down toward the bottom of the hive, and he could hear the Arbora about three turns ahead of him. Leaping from wall to wall, Moon felt that familiar constriction in his chest, that pressure, and thought, *It's her, she's trying to make me shift.* Ranea was part queen, and she had the Raksuran queen's power, just not as strongly as the two mentor-dakti. If she succeeded, he was done for. But he needed her to stay focused on him, and not the Arbora.

He caught up with them at the fifth turn and dropped to the floor to run beside them.

"What is that thing?" Heart asked breathlessly. "What kind of Fell is—"

"It's another crossbreed, part progenitor, part queen."

Heart threw him a horrified look. Running just ahead of her, Merit gasped, "I didn't think this could get worse."

Oh, it can get much worse, Moon thought. "Just run."

Around the next turn, a passage in the outer wall glowed with warm daylight. Needle and Dream reached it first and ducked into it; the other Arbora followed.

Moon thought, *Damn it, that's not going to work.* They were still too high. There wouldn't be a way down for the Arbora. Moon darted after them.

The passage opened out onto a broad ledge in the side of the hive that looked out over the pillars and crumbled walls of the main entrance to the ruined city. The curve of the river lay just beyond it, the canyon heavy now with the shadows of late afternoon. "Wrong way, go back!"

"No, no, look!" Needle grabbed his arm, bouncing with excitement. "It's Jade!"

"What?" Moon turned. Jade and several Aeriat were just flying over the top of the hive. Their colors were oddly mottled and it took Moon a moment to realize they were covered with metal-mud.

Dream and Snap called out in chorus, a sustained high-pitched note. Jade twisted in mid-air, turning to lead the way in a swooping dive directly toward them. The other Aeriat peeled off to circle, and she landed with a thump on the ledge. Her scales were blotchy with metal-mud. She looked exhausted, furious, and beautiful. "Moon—"

Moon hoped she didn't want a detailed explanation, because there wasn't time for one. "Quick, she's coming! Get the Arbora out of here."

Jade turned to the warriors. "Do it! Take them to our hiding place!"

Floret and Coil swept forward, snatching up Needle and Gift on the wing. Vine, Song, Sand, and Chime landed to get the others. Chime grabbed Heart and asked Moon, "Aren't you coming?" He sounded breathless with fear and excitement.

"Not yet." Moon shook his head. "Go, get her out of here."

"I'll explain on the way," Heart told Chime, wrapping her arms around his neck.

As Chime dove off the ledge, Jade said, "Who's coming?"

He said, "It's a progenitor, a crossbreed like the mentor-dakti. She's part queen. We have to kill her."

Jade hissed, spines flaring. "Did she—"

Moon heard the rush of air from behind him and dropped into a crouch. Ranea slammed through the passage, saw Jade, and leapt straight for her. Jade fell backwards, curling her body up, just as Ranea crashed into her. They tumbled across the ledge in furious struggle. Moon jumped for Ranea's back, got buffeted back by a wing and thrown against the ledge. He rolled upright just as Jade and Ranea broke apart.

Terrified, he looked at Jade, but she was crouched, hissing through barred fangs, battered but not bleeding. Ranea had rips across both shoulders, her dark scales dotted lightly with blood. She grinned at Jade, her jaw distended to show a startling array of teeth. "Come now, we're kin. We should be friends."

Jade grinned back. "I'm going to rip your womb out and eat it." Then she launched herself at Ranea's throat.

They tumbled off the ledge in a furious, snarling tangle of wings and tails. Moon dove after them, darting in to rake Ranea's wings. Ranea obviously couldn't force Jade to shift, but Pearl had said Raksuran queens couldn't do that to each other. Moon had been able to resist her so far, but he was willing to bet the warriors couldn't.

Locked in battle, Jade and Ranea fell far enough to be in danger of crashing into the walls of the ruin. Moon yelled, "Jade, break off!"

Jade tore herself free and Ranea wheeled away, knocking off the top of a pillar before catching the air and banking up. Moon stayed near Jade, circling around while she caught the air again and swooped back up. Ranea was higher in the air, but that wasn't much of an advantage; she could only close with one of them at a time, and the other could attack her from behind.

"Try to get her up to the top of the hive," Jade said, as she spiraled up toward him. "The others are—"

Moon lost the rest as Ranea rushed down at them again, heading for Jade.

Moon slipped sideways toward Ranea, taking a swipe at her face. She turned on him with a shriek, and he kicked at her stomach, trying to hook his claws under her scales. She clawed at his legs, nearly getting a grip on him, then jerked back when Jade struck at her from below. Moon twisted away, taking a painful rake across his wing. *That ought to do it,* he thought, knowing that if she hadn't been angry enough to follow him before, she was now. He broke off, heading up toward the hive, and Ranea shot after him.

The gold-brown surface of the hive raced beneath him as he streaked upward. He could feel Ranea behind him, too close, and risked a look back. She was nearly on him, but Jade was nearly on her, raking at her from behind.

Moon shot up over the curve of the hive. The surface was hundreds of paces wide, sloping dramatically toward the big opening in the center that led down into the well. *Right, where are the others?*

Then he caught sight of a familiar flash of gold and indigo. Pearl and four warriors circled away from the top of the hive, the last one dropping another pottery jar through the opening to add to the fire and confusion below.

Pearl must have spotted Moon and seen what was chasing him. She swept into a tight turn, arrowing down toward him.

Moon shouted to Pearl, "She's part queen. She can make the warriors shift!"

Pearl called out to the Aeriat, a high-pitched cry. Immediately they banked and turned away from the hive.

Ranea saw Pearl and screamed in fury, realizing she had been deliberately trapped. Pearl stooped on her, hard and fast, as Jade came at Ranea from below. Instead of heading toward either one, Ranea dipped to the side and slammed her whole bodyweight into Moon.

The impact stunned him. He fell onto the surface of the hive, then tumbled down the slope and over the edge of the opening.

For a heartbeat he was too dazed to react, then realized he was falling through smoky air right into another fight, between buzzing Dwei and a roaring kethel. He snapped his wings in and plunged past them, just missing one of the Dwei. Once safely below them, he extended his wings and caught the air to circle away. Looking up, still a little dazed, he thought, *I'm not getting out that way.*

Above him in the smoke-filled well, the Dwei attacked the kethel, darting in at it as it twisted in the air. Their wings moved so fast they were white blurs. Their buzzing was ear-piercing. Trapped in the hive's well by the Dwei, the kethel couldn't maneuver, couldn't escape. It slammed into the hive wall, sending a whole section of ledge crashing down onto the burning floor below. Its tail knocked a Dwei out of the air, but there were too many.

Moon banked down toward the side of the hive, headed for the passage he and the Arbora had used to get out. But it wasn't there. The whole section had collapsed, and he couldn't spot the passage anymore. *I'd just like something to be easy for once,* he thought in exasperation, looking for a place to land.

The window into Ranea's chamber was still intact. He twisted to avoid another angry Dwei, and landed on the window's edge. The chamber was still occupied only by the dead, a haze of smoke hanging in the air. He bounded across to the shaft and looked down. He could still see daylight coming in from somewhere below. He slung himself over the side, holding on with one set of claws, ready to drop. Then he stopped.

He scented Raksura. He tasted the air, making certain. He thought sourly, *Oh good, more crossbreeds.*

Moon climbed down the wall, digging his claws into the rubbery material, following the scent. Openings in the shaft, some large Dwei-sized doorways and some just thin slats, let in light and air, but all were empty.

He was a good hundred paces down when he heard scrabbling, a desperate panting, as if something was trapped and trying to claw its way out. It was coming from one of the chambers with a slatted opening, and he swung down to look inside.

The occupants sprang back, hissing at him.

He was so sure of seeing a mentor-dakti, or a dozen mentor-dakti, that for an instant he didn't realize what he was looking at. There were three of them, with scales, wings, and tails, like Raksuran fledglings, the biggest not more than waist-high. Two were black like Fell, but one was bright green, with a faint yellow, web-like tracery over the scales... *Idiot,* he thought. They were Raksuran fledglings. It was a baby queen and two consorts. *The royal clutch from Sky Copper. Stone said he saw they had a queen, and Flower thought there were two consorts.* "Are you from Sky Copper?"

"Maybe!" The little queen bristled her spines, glaring. The chamber was small, the doorway in the wall sealed with a heavy membrane. The queen and the larger consort had been trying to claw their way through it. "Who are you?"

"I'm Moon, from Indigo Cloud." He dug his claws into two of the slats and threw his weight back. The slats ripped loose and he tumbled a good distance down the shaft before he caught himself and climbed back up. A repeat performance made a hole large enough for him to perch in. The three fledglings huddled together, watching him warily, and he asked, "Were there any others?"

"The others went away," the queen said, still sounding furious. "There's just us now."

The consorts were miniature versions of himself, their spines bristling with terror. The little one's wings looked far too small to support him. Moon asked, "Can you all fly?"

The queen snarled, "We're not leaving Bitter!"

"I'm not leaving anybody." He just wanted to make sure which one not to drop. "Come on, we need to go."

Bitter, presumably the smaller consort, edged forward, tasting the air. Whatever he scented must have reassured him, because he suddenly jumped for Moon's chest. Moon caught him and tucked him under his wing, telling him, "Hold on." Bitter hooked his claws firmly into Moon's scales.

The queen and the older consort looked at each other, apparently came to a decision, and leapt for Moon. He gathered them against his chest and they clung to him, digging their claws in. It wasn't comfortable, but he could stand it.

He swung back out of the chamber and started to climb down, going as fast as he dared.

"Bad Arbora-thing wouldn't let us shift," the queen said resentfully, clinging to his collar flange.

"I know. It's dead now," Moon told her. "What are your names?"

She adjusted her hold on him, thought about it, and decided to admit, "I'm Frost. That's Thorn, and Bitter."

His face buried against Moon's chest, Thorn said, "Is *she* dead?" Bitter, tucked up near Moon's armpit, shivered. There was no mistaking who he meant.

"I don't know," Moon said, figuring in their situation honesty was better no matter how grim. "I hope so."

Thorn took that in silently. Bitter whispered something inaudible. Apparently translating, Thorn said, "Where's your queen?"

Frost sniffed at Moon's neck and reported, "He doesn't have a queen."

"Why? What's wrong with him?" Thorn wanted to know.

"That's still being debated," Moon said. He was climbing down out of the smoky haze and toward the scents of dust and rock, and the acrid musk of Dwei. As he looked down now, he could see the shaft ended in a chamber, lit by late afternoon daylight and strewn with drifts of sand. "Now be quiet."

Unexpectedly, they all obeyed. Moon reached the end of the shaft and hung head down to take a cautious look at the chamber. It was empty, with one passage leading into the dark interior of the hive and another leading out to daylight. Moon could just glimpse a half-demolished wall from the ruin. He just hoped there wasn't anything out there waiting for them.

Moon dropped to the floor and started for the daylit passage. He had an instant's warning, a sense of air movement behind him. He should have turned, twisted to the side, but that would have exposed his chest and he had the three fledglings to protect. He flared his spines and bolted forward instead. That was the wrong choice.

Ranea hit him from behind, with a force that flung him forward, nearly to the passage entrance. Moon caught himself on his hands and knees, the fledglings tumbling to the floor. He shouted, "Run!"

Frost grabbed Thorn and Thorn grabbed Bitter, and they shot down the passage toward daylight. Moon twisted around, but Ranea landed on him before he could get to his feet. He let her bowl him backward, tucking his head down and clawing blindly for her face, her eyes, yanking up both feet to rip at her abdomen. She ripped back at him, snarling, and they rolled across the sandy floor. He felt his heel-claw sink past her scales into softer flesh; she screamed and flung him off. He scrambled down the passage, out through the opening, and into bright sunlight and an open court surrounded by broken pillars. He couldn't see the fledglings but knew they couldn't be far away. He extended his wings and crouched for a leap, meaning to lead Ranea away.

He felt the grip on his left wing, felt something snap, as she twisted down.

He screamed, more in astonishment then pain. He dropped to the ground, hunching over, feeling bones grind together as the wing bent backward in a way it was never meant to. Then the pain hit, and he felt a pressure grow in his chest. *Oh no.* She was forcing him to shift. He resisted, digging his claws into his own palms with the effort. Then she twisted at the wing again and pain blotted out conscious thought.

And he was in groundling form, huddled on the ground, looking up at her. Agony came in shuddering waves, like half his body had been ripped away. This time his scream came out as a dry croak. The broken wing bones had transferred to his groundling form as breaks all up and down his left side, arm, collarbone, ribs, shoulder.

Ranea stood over him, dripping blood from claw-rents all over her body. She hissed in bitter amusement, and said, "What do you think your queens would say, if they knew all that I did to their court was for you?"

Through watering eyes, Moon saw the curving wall of the hive behind her, and two shapes dropping down toward them, one gold and one blue. "Ask them," he gasped.

Ranea turned. Jade and Pearl hit her as one, taking her up off the ground and over Moon's head, slamming her into a pillar. Pearl got knocked away by the impact but Jade held on as she and Ranea fell to the ground. Jade landed on her back, Ranea atop her. But the Fell queen fought to get away, keening, and he could see Jade's claws sunk into her back, her throat. Pearl shoved to her feet, strode toward them. She slapped Ranea's wings aside, planted a foot on her back, and seized her head in both hands. The snap and the noise of ripping flesh was clearly audible.

Moon struggled to stay conscious just long enough to see Jade shove the headless body aside, and stagger to her feet, shaking blood out of her spines and head frills.

That's finished, he thought, and gave in to the darkness.

CHAPTER
TWENTY

Moon knew he was being carried, that they were in the air. He could hear vague snatches of shouts, the roar of fire, the angry buzz of the Dwei. But it was all mercifully far away.

Then they were inside somewhere, and he was being lowered to the ground, and the pull on his broken bones snapped him back to painful reality. He rode out the shuddering waves of agony, and bit his lip bloody, trying not to scream.

The room swam into focus. He lay on his back in soft sand. Above him was the arch of a golden stone ceiling, the wall just below it painted with a faded tracery of green and blue. Jade leaned over him, her eyes desperate. There was a smear of Ranea's blood on her forehead, claw-rents in her scales. "Moon, I can't let you shift. Do you understand?"

He understood. He was too weak, and shifting in this state would probably kill him. He wanted to tell her that it didn't matter, that he was dying anyway, but he remembered that she didn't know about the fledglings.

"The children?" Taking a breath to talk made his ribs grind together. "The Sky Copper clutch—"

"They're safe. Pearl has them," she said. Her hand lifted as if she wanted to touch him, but didn't dare.

Moon heard running footsteps, then Heart crouched beside him. Merit stood behind her, peering anxiously over her shoulder. Heart put her hands on Moon's face and he must have tensed, because the pain welled up and took everything away again.

He came back to dizzy consciousness, feeling as if a little time had passed. Jade was still there, sitting beside Heart, saying urgently, "Moon, just relax. She's trying to put you into a healing sleep."

Heart shook her head in despair. "I just can't do it, Jade. He's older than I am, and very strong, and I don't think he trusts me. All I can do is try to help with the pain." Heart pressed her thumb lightly on Moon's forehead, just above his nose. Warmth spread through his body and Moon felt his muscles unlock. She asked him, "Is that any better?"

"Yes…" He faded out, an inexpressible relief.

After that, everything was a blur. He slipped in and out of consciousness. His mouth was dry and sandy, and the back of his throat was on fire. Someone tried to give him water, but it hurt too much to swallow. He heard movement, footsteps, Aeriat coming and going. He wasn't certain if Jade was still here.

He heard a fragment of conversation, Chime talking to Heart and Merit about what had happened at the colony. As far as Chime knew, the Arbora and Aeriat imprisoned in the sacs were all reviving, including the fledglings and clutches, but they had been terribly weak and in need of food and clean water. After making certain there were no Fell left behind, Pearl had followed Jade and the others in pursuit of the kethel. She had caught up with Jade at the ruined city, in time to help with the plan to fill the jars with metal-mud, to set the hive on fire, and force the Fell into the open.

Then from somewhere nearby, Moon heard Root say worriedly, "What are they doing? Why are they angry at us?"

"We set their hive on fire, Root. What do you think?" That was Floret, or Coil.

"They want us to leave?" That was Song.

"They say they're going to attack if we don't go. Pearl said—"

"Quiet." That was Pearl.

But Moon had heard enough. They were taking shelter in the ruin, and the Dwei were trying to drive them off. It must mean the Fell were already gone, killed or scattered when they realized the rulers had vanished and Ranea was dead.

He opened his eyes and saw Chime sitting next to him, in groundling form. Chime leaned over him anxiously. "Moon, you're awake? Don't try to move."

"Don't…" *Don't leave,* he wanted to say, but that was pointless. They had the Arbora and the kids to worry about. He croaked out, "Before you leave, kill me, all right?"

"We're not leaving, and we're not killing anybody, except those damn Dwei, if they don't leave us alone." Chime looked up, grimacing in frustration. "Heart—"

Moon remembered something else the others didn't know. "No, I have to tell you—"

"Moon, just rest—"

"Fell crossbreeds," he managed. "There could be more." That silenced even Chime. With frequent gasps for air, he repeated what Ranea had said, told them about Janeas leaving with the old progenitor and Venras, that the other mentor-dakti was dead. He knew the others were drawing near to listen, though his vision was beginning to blur and he couldn't bear to move his head to see who was there. He finished, "And they came to Indigo Cloud for me. The mentor-dakti knew I'd be there."

He felt there should be some reaction to that, but he had closed his eyes from the effort of speaking so long, and when he opened them again everyone was gone.

Not quite everyone. Pearl sat near him. Time must have passed again because it was night, and a fire burned nearby, casting half her face in shadow. The night should be cool, but his skin felt as if it was radiating heat.

He rasped out, "Are you going to kill me?" He didn't think he was asking a lot. He was dying anyway, and they would have to leave soon; the least they could do was not leave him for the Dwei or the desert scavengers.

"It's a thought." Pearl turned her head to look down at him. She was in Aeriat form, the light catching the brilliant gold of her spines. "You've caused us enough trouble. It's either kill you or make you pay for it in clutches."

"Pick one and get it over with."

She cocked her head. "But it doesn't occur to you to call out for Jade."

"There's no one out there. The others are dead." Then Moon thought, *Wait, where am I?*

Pearl frowned, laying the back of her hand against his cheek. "Merit, go and wake Heart."

That was when Moon gave up trying to talk. Even he could tell that what he was saying didn't make sense, and it hurt too much to make the effort.

The next time he was really aware of anything, it was daylight again, and he heard Chime shouting, "Stone's here!"

Good, Moon thought. Stone was practical. *I can talk him into killing me.*

But the next person to lean over him was Flower. Her hair was tangled and wild, as if she had let Stone carry her in groundling form. She cupped her hands around his face and said, "Moon, it's all right. Just relax."

This time when he sank into darkness, it was deep and silent.

Moon dreamed he was swimming in a black sea, too far under, trying to find the surface. Something in the darkness below grabbed his ankle and yanked him down, and the dream-jolt made him twitch awake. Blinking at the dusty ceiling, he took a sharp breath, braced for pain. It came, but not in the overwhelming wave he vividly remembered.

His left arm was bent and strapped across his chest; not moving it the least little bit seemed a very good idea. His shoulder and collarbone alternately throbbed and burned, like hot metal buried beneath his skin, and the ribs on that side stabbed him every time he took a breath. His skin felt dry and too hot. His clothes were soaked with sweat. Carefully, he moved his feet, and bent one leg a little. That was probably a good sign.

"Moon, you're awake?"

That was Flower, sitting nearby. It was reassuring that he hadn't imagined her earlier. He wet his lips. "Sort of." His voice still sounded pitifully weak.

"You've been in a healing sleep for the past three days." Flower laid a cool hand on his forehead. It felt so good he closed his eyes again. Then she said, "We're getting ready to leave. The flying boats are here."

He blinked. "Our flying boats?"

"Yes. Niran is steering one, and he showed Blossom how to steer the other." She brushed the hair back from his forehead. "When Stone woke up and was able to shift, he thought it best to get the court away from the colony as quickly as possible. We loaded everyone onto the two boats, with as much of our supplies as we could salvage. Fortunately the Arbora had already started to get ready to leave before the Fell attacked. Most of the really necessary tools and things were packed in baskets in the lower part of the colony. Stone and I came ahead to see if you all had found the stolen Arbora yet."

Moon could hear the wind outside, wailing through the hollows of the ruin. "What about the Dwei? I thought they were going to attack us."

"Stone persuaded them not to," Flower said, with irony in her voice.

From somewhere behind him, Chime said, "Actually he told them they could leave us alone and we'd be gone in a few days, or he could tear what was left of their hive apart and kill them all." Chime moved into view, looking around the room. His clothes were dusty and his cheek was smeared with dirt. "Are we ready to go?"

"Very ready," Flower told him. She pulled a leather pack into her lap, sorting through it. "Is Jade on her way?"

Moon took a deep breath and rolled onto his good arm. His back protested with a stabbing sensation that took his breath away. When the room swam back into focus, he heard Flower say in exasperation, "Moon, what are you doing?"

"I'm sitting up." Gritting his teeth, he levered himself into a sitting position with his good arm. *Oh, that hurts.* Bones ground against each other in ways they weren't meant to, his vision went dark, and his stomach tried to turn. After a moment the wave passed, and he swayed, but managed to stay upright. He let out his breath, careful not to jostle his ribs. It felt odd to be sitting up, and he remembered Flower had said something about three days. The room was bigger than he had thought, with an arched doorway that looked out onto an open court strewn with rubble. The wind stirred the drifted sand up into whirling patterns.

Chime hovered over him anxiously. "Just stay still! Jade will be here any moment."

That was the point. Moon wanted to prove he could walk to the boats, even if he would need help to get up into one. He just hoped the boats were very, very close.

Then Jade landed in the sandy court with Vine, Floret, and Song. She folded her wings, stopped in the doorway to shake the sand off her scales, then strode into the room. She looked at Moon and demanded, "Why is he sitting up?"

Flower told her pointedly, "Because he's a bit too delicate at the moment for me to wrestle with." She pulled a folded drape of fabric out of the pack and handed it to Jade.

"I was going to walk to the boats," Moon said, feeling as if things were moving too fast for him. He couldn't see any remnant of the scratches Ranea had left on Jade's arms and chest.

"Of course you were." She knelt, shaking out the drape and carefully wrapping it around his shoulders. It was soft, and the scent of sweet herbs was trapped in the folds. "Put your arm around my neck."

He did, threading it through her spines. She slipped an arm under his legs, gathered him gently against her and stood up. She carried him out to the court, and murmured, "Brace yourself."

He tightened his hold on her neck and set his jaw. The jolt as she took to the air made him suck in a breath, but the flight was brief, and the light thump as she landed on the deck didn't hurt. He caught a glimpse of the fan-sails, tightly folded up against the mast, and a crowd of Arbora milling around on the deck. Claws scraped wood as they hurried to clear a path for Jade. As she carried Moon down the narrow stair below deck, he heard Niran yell instructions about casting off.

She took him into the nearest cabin and carefully put him down on a pallet of silk blankets and cushions. It was wonderfully soft, if not as warm as the sand in the ruin. The ceiling and walls were dark wood, rubbed fine until the grain showed. Glowing moss was stuffed into a clear glass lamp meant to hold a candle, and baskets, the tightly-woven ones used at the colony for storage, were packed in against the walls, taking up much of the space. Jade crouched next to him, arranging the blankets. He said, "You know the Fell came to Indigo Cloud for me."

Jade shook her head. "Don't worry about that."

That wasn't exactly an answer, and he tried to muster the strength to pursue it, but Flower came into the cabin, telling Jade, "Everyone's aboard, and they've gotten the water casks refilled." The boat trembled and swayed, and she caught hold of a basket to steady herself.

Jade bared her teeth. "If that was the Dwei, I'm going to tear their—"

Chime ducked into the cabin, dumping an armload of leather packs atop a basket. "That was Stone, trying to land on the boat without knocking the mast down."

"I need to be up there." Jade touched Moon's face. "Rest."

As if he had a choice. He watched her leave the cabin, taking the stairs up to the deck in one bound. The brief exertion of sitting up and then being carried here had already exhausted him, made him feel as if he was trapped under water again, fighting the weight of the moss nets. He managed to ask, "The boats are going to the new colony?"

"Yes, finally!" Chime waved his hands, excited. "We can't wait to see it."

He ducked out of the room and Moon sunk further down into the cushions, muttering, "Good for you."

Flower sat next to him, propping her chin on her hand. "Moon, you are going to fly again."

He hesitated. "Are you sure?"

"Yes." She put her hand on his forehead. "Now rest."

It didn't matter if Flower's "rest" had something in it other than just the word. Staying awake was too much of an effort. It was easy to just relax into sleep.

Moon woke sometime later to find a dark-haired little boy in groundling form leaning over him, staring with grave intensity. After a puzzled moment, Moon recognized Thorn, the older Sky Copper consort.

From nearby, Stone said, "See? He didn't go away." Thorn patted Moon on the nose. "Gently. Remember what I said."

Moon turned his head carefully. Stone sat on the floor a few paces away. He looked much better than the last time Moon had seen him. The bruises were gone. The edge of the claw-wound above the open collar of his shirt had lost its red, raw look and turned to scar tissue.

"We didn't believe you," Frost informed Stone, with the air of conceding a highly contested point. The fledgling queen leaned against Stone's side, and the smaller consort, Bitter, sat in his lap. The boys both wore clothes that were too big for them, and Frost wore a string of bright blue and gold beads. "The others all went away."

"I know you didn't believe me." Stone lifted Bitter out of his lap and told Moon, "They wanted to be with you, but we were afraid they would keep you awake or jostle you. The teachers have been taking care of them with the other clutches."

Bitter crawled onto the pallet next to Moon and curled up against him. Moon automatically folded his good arm around him. He noticed someone had taken his admittedly filthy clothes away and replaced them with a soft, heavy robe, and the strap around his broken arm had been changed. He hadn't had anyone take care of him since Sorrow had died, and it felt... odd. He wasn't used to depending on anybody else, for anything.

"Bitter says we're your clutch now," Thorn said to Moon. "Even if you don't have a queen." Against Moon's side, Bitter nodded confirmation.

Still half-asleep, Moon blinked at that one. He wasn't sure the court was going to go for that idea. "Uh..."

"You found us," Frost said, as if that settled the argument.

Moon decided to leave it be for now. He asked Stone, "Did they see what happened at their colony?"

"Yes." Stone ruffled Thorn's hair. "Bell said they come out with it at odd moments." He added, "And we're not calling that boy 'Bitter.'"

"It's his name," Moon said, feeling on safer ground with this one. He told Bitter, "Your name is whatever you want it to be."

Frost said, "His real name is Bitter Starshell. It's a flower that only comes out at night."

"We can call him Star," Stone said, as if that settled it.

"I'm not going to argue with you." Moon tried to make it a threat. There were more things he wanted to ask, but maybe not in front of the fledglings. Besides, it was still an effort to stay awake.

Stone took them away when Moon started to drift again. Moon spent most of the next two days unconscious, lulled by the gentle movement of the flying boat. Flower said it was the remnants of the healing sleep, but Moon couldn't stay awake long enough to get more information. Every time he asked someone a question, he fell asleep before he could hear the answer.

But then he woke one night, to cool, damp air that smelled of fresh water and green plants, and he felt more awake than he had since Ranea tried to snap his wing off. It didn't hurt to breathe, and his bones felt less mobile, more attached to each other; that had to be an improvement.

The glowing moss stuffed into the ship's candle holder showed him a pile of cushions and blankets on the other side of the room, with at least three sleeping people. Squinting, he made out Flower, Chime, and Heart.

The opportunity for escape was too tempting to pass up. Moon disentangled his robe from the blankets, rolled onto his good arm, and levered himself up. Standing, with one hand on the wall to steady himself, he still felt delicate, and his joints ached.

He made it across the floor without waking anyone, and out the open door. A narrow hall led into the small maze below decks. Other doors opened off of it, and he could hear a lot of people breathing deeply in sleep, and further away, low voices. Above his head, the hatch to the deck was open, giving a view of a star-filled night sky and letting in the cool air. The stairway was steep but narrow enough to let him brace himself against the wall as he climbed. He made it up onto the deck with only a minimum of awkward, painful bumping.

The ship sailed serenely through the night, the nearly-full moon high in the sky. The fan-sail was closed, and the breeze was light, heavily laden with the scent of fresh water. There were sleeping bodies on deck, too, most in groundling form, all wrapped in blankets. Baskets and bundles were tied off to every available spot. Far up in the bow, under the lamp, an Arbora was on watch. Looking up at the watch post at the top of the mast, Moon could see a couple of Aeriat stationed there too. The other ship was a little ahead of them, just off their port bow. Moon picked his way to the starboard rail, and leaned on it to look down.

They were passing over a vast lake, perhaps fifty paces above it, the water gleaming silver in the moonlight. Trees with delicate, feathery leaves grew up out of the lake, some nearly tall enough to brush the bottom of the hull. The water was clear enough to see brightly-colored fish flickering through it.

Moon lifted his head, the breeze tugging at his hair and his robe. He could see the distant shore, heavily forested, featureless in the dark, except for the occasional spreading shade tree taller than the rest.

He heard a quiet step behind him and glanced back. It was Niran, making his way across the deck. He leaned against the rail next to Moon. Keeping his voice low, he said, "You are feeling better, then? They said you were gravely injured."

"I was. We heal fast." Moon looked out over the lake again. He had heard enough from the others to know they had some specific destination in mind, that they were headed to an old colony somewhere that Stone knew of. "Where are we?"

The question sounded a little desperate to his ears, but Niran didn't seem to notice. "We're going southwest. That's all I can say." He shook his head. "My family has never come this far inland before, and our maps are blank, except for my track of our progress."

Moon tried to remember what Stone had said. Eleven days of fast flight, just to get out of the river valleys? "So we don't know if there are cities out here."

Niran shrugged. "Presumably there are. Somewhere."

Moon sank against the railing, wincing as his arm and shoulder throbbed. He had no idea what his status with the court was, if they were angry because he had brought the Fell down on them, or willing to forgive him because he had found Frost and her brothers, or what Pearl's attitude would be. He vaguely remembered asking Pearl to kill him, and her declining, but he wasn't sure if anything had changed. He was fairly certain Jade didn't want him dead, but there was a big difference between that and wanting him as her consort.

Niran cleared his throat. "Once we reach our destination, Stone has said that a winged group will accompany me back, so I may return with both ships at once." He paused, watching Moon thoughtfully. "My family owes you a debt, and I know my grandfather would be pleased to see you again."

"You don't owe me a debt." But having the option to return to the Golden Isles, and the extra time to recover, was a relief. A big relief. "But thank you. I'll… keep it in mind."

Niran went back to his post. Moon stayed by the railing, watching the reflections off the water, and listening to everyone sleep.

After a time, Chime wandered up out of the hatch, scratching his head. He spotted Moon at the railing and came over, saying with exasperated concern, "You're not supposed to be up. If you get sick—"

Moon had remembered one of the questions he needed an answer to. "Do you know how Petal died?"

"Oh." Chime hesitated. He stepped to the railing. "Yes, Bell told me." He fidgeted uncertainly. "Do you want to go back down?"

"No, we'll wake Flower and Heart. I want to stay up here."

They sat down on baskets against the outside wall of the steering cabin because no one was sleeping there.

Chime told him that forty-seven Raksura had died in the attack on the colony, mostly soldiers, several Aeriat, and one teacher, Petal. Chime said miserably, "Bell said they were in the nurseries when the dakti broke in, and she just flung herself at them. She thought they were going to kill the clutches, and she was trying to give the other teachers a chance to carry them away. They did get some out of the nurseries, but the kethel had blocked the way outside, and they couldn't shift, so they were trapped."

Moon leaned against the cabin wall, not sure whether he was more sad or angry. Petal hadn't had any reason to think that the dakti wouldn't kill the clutches. And if she had known what plans the Fell had had for them, she might not have acted any differently.

"Do we know why the Fell left the bodies? Why they didn't eat them?"

Chime looked troubled at the memory. "Not for certain, but Knell said the mentor-dakti was angry that so many of the court were killed. Maybe it was punishing the dakti by not letting them touch the bodies."

Ranea had said Erasus wanted to go to the colony even though it wasn't safe. "Maybe he watched you all so long he thought he was part of you."

"Ugh," Chime said, succinctly.

Moon wasn't happy with that thought either. He changed the subject. "What about Balm?"

Chime shook his head. "She's been staying on the other ship. She thinks this is all her fault."

That was ridiculous. "It's not her fault. She's not responsible for what the Fell did to her."

"Yes, and…" Chime prompted.

Moon frowned at him. "What?"

"Neither are you. I know you feel that way. You keep telling everyone that the Fell came for you. You could barely talk, and you told us that."

Moon looked out over the railing, at the slowly approaching shore. Glowing night bugs played around the tops of the water-trees, sparking in the dark. He had told them because he wanted them to know, because he didn't want their sympathy when they should be condemning him. "Chime…"

Exasperated, Chime said, "So it's your fault for being born a consort and being alone, and making a good target. It's Balm's fault for getting caught by the Fell, and Pearl's fault for trying to fend them off on her own, and Flower and the other mentors' fault for not finding out what was wrong with the colony, and Stone's fault for not coming back sooner to make us move, and Jade's fault for being too young to force Pearl to act. I can go on. Sky Copper's fault for being taken by surprise, and destroyed, and not being there to help us when we needed it."

Moon twitched uneasily, wincing when the motion pulled at his abused muscles. "All right, I see what you mean," he admitted, still begrudging it.

Chime sighed. "There's some that won't see it that way. But I don't think you should be one of them."

A low warm voice said, "Neither do I."

Moon tilted his head back, gingerly, to look up. Jade was perched on the edge of the cabin roof, looking down at them, blue and silver in the moonlight.

He was going to answer, and then he sneezed, and the jolt shot right through him. He would have fallen off the basket, but Chime lunged forward and caught him around the waist. "See, this is why we didn't want you out here. We're susceptible to lung-ailments."

Jade hopped down from the cabin roof and scooped Moon up in her arms. "I can walk," he protested, trying to make it a growl. Admittedly, it was a pitiful growl.

"I know. But you don't have to," Jade said, and carried him back down below deck.

Moon got a little more sleep that night, and did not catch a lung ailment and die immediately, despite Chime and Heart's dire predictions. But the morning seemed to stretch on forever. The good thing about being semi-conscious was that it had kept him from being bored. Now that he was alert again, there was nothing to do but sit around and wait to get well enough to shift.

In the afternoon, Stone brought Frost, Thorn, and Bitter again, which was a welcome diversion. Bitter and Thorn play-stalked each other, growling in a way that made them sound like furious bees, while Frost sat aloof and Stone said things like, "Do not flap your wings in here. You'll kill somebody."

People had been moving around up on deck all day, and Moon had mostly ignored it. From what he could glimpse, it was a bright clear day and everyone would be out enjoying it. Then he felt the boat slow, the wood creaking and groaning in protest. Moon shoved himself up on his good arm. "What's that?"

The fledglings must have heard the tension in his voice. They all froze, heads cocked to listen, but Stone looked unconcerned. "They're slowing down and pulling over to the other boat, so the whole court can have a meeting."

Reassured by Stone's attitude, Frost settled her spines. The consorts went back to their game, Thorn rolling onto his back so Bitter could pounce on him. Moon frowned at the ceiling. He was missing everything down here. "A meeting about what?"

Stone tugged on Frost's frills. Apparently feeling that her dignity was being abused, she ducked away and batted at his hand. Stone said, "About you, Moon."

"About—oh." Moon sank back into the cushions. He must have looked just as uneasy as he felt, because Frost came over and sat on the pallet next to him. Moon asked, "Why aren't you up there?"

"Everybody already knows what I think," Stone said. If Moon was supposed to know what that was, he had no idea. Stone wore his best unreadable expression. "Besides, Jade and Pearl are going to fight, and I don't want them to postpone it on my account."

"A fight?" Moon stared at him, incredulous and beginning to get mad. "And you're not going to do anything about it?"

Stone snorted. "Moon, queens fight. It's normal. And these two have a lot of disagreements to work out." He shrugged. "It'll be fine. The Arbora wouldn't like it if they went too far, and they both know it."

Moon looked at the ceiling again. He couldn't hear anything but movement, and muffled voices. "It matters that much to them what the Arbora think?"

Stone leaned over to help Bitter pry his trapped claws out of a floorboard.

"I told you, the Arbora run the court. They find food, raise the clutches, help fight, make everything we need. They don't like it if queens fight too much, or if consorts are unhappy."

Moon's shoulder was throbbing again and he made himself relax, leaning back on the cushions. "So if the Arbora wanted me to stay, Pearl couldn't force me out?"

Stone sighed in exasperation. "Moon, Pearl wants you as her consort. That's what they're going to fight about."

It was either a joke, or Stone actually was crazy. "Pearl hates me. A lot."

"She hates you as a potential consort for Jade. As her consort, it would be different," Stone explained, not patiently. "Whatever happens, you'll be first consort, the consort that speaks for the others. First consorts don't have to be mated to the reigning queen. It's just the way it usually works out." He shook his head, and admitted, "I didn't expect Pearl to want you. But after all these turns of not taking much interest in anything, including running the court, she's woken up and decided to be the reigning queen again. I guess she woke up and decided she wanted a consort, too. Jade is taking exception to that."

Moon still had trouble imagining it. But after the attack on the colony, Flower had said something about Pearl wanting him. At best, he had thought Flower was badly misreading the situation. *So maybe it was me badly misreading the situation.* That was nothing new, and it put several things in a different light. It explained River's increasing hostility. And Pearl telling Moon that Jade had lied about getting a clutch. *She was angry, because you told her you slept with Jade.* He had known Pearl was trying to divide them; he had just been wrong about why. *Idiot.*

Frost glared at Moon. "You need a queen. Otherwise you'll just cause trouble."

Stone said, "Trust me, this is a good thing. For a long time, Indigo Cloud didn't have a real queen. Now we've got Pearl back, and Jade's taking her rightful place as sister queen and heir."

Noise rose and fell up on deck. Whatever was going on, everybody seemed to have an opinion about it. Disgruntled, Moon said, "What about what I want?"

"Eventually it'll occur to them to check on that," Stone said, with irony. "It's not really about you. Like I said, they have a lot between them to work out."

Time dragged, and Moon fidgeted and tried to watch the fledglings play and ignore the urge to question Stone. Finally, Jade came down the stairs and into the cabin. Her spines were ruffled but she didn't look hurt.

"All settled?" Stone asked her.

"Yes." Jade gave him a dark look. Apparently Moon wasn't the only one half-convinced that this was somehow all Stone's fault.

Then Frost stuck her claws in Moon's sleeve and hissed at Jade. "Mine."

Jade crouched down to get eye level with her. After about three heartbeats, Frost let go of Moon and shifted to Arbora, then retreated to climb into Stone's lap. From that safe vantage point, she hissed at Jade again. Stone patted her reassuringly, saying, "I think this one's going to be a handful."

"Yes, that's all I need." Jade sat beside Moon, her thigh warm against his side.

Torn between relief and annoyance, Moon said, "I'm not going to ask if you won. Apparently it's none of my business."

"You can tell he's feeling better because he's getting all mouthy again," Stone told Jade.

Jade cocked her head at him. "Line-grandfather, could you take the clutch back to the teachers?"

"That's probably a good idea," Stone agreed. He gathered up Frost and Thorn, while Bitter climbed up to cling to his shoulder.

"You need to find queens for Thorn and Bitter, and a consort for me," Frost ordered.

"We'll worry about that a little later," Stone told her as he carried them out of the cabin.

Jade settled in comfortably next to Moon. She said, "There was talk of renaming the court, since so much has changed. Some of the hunters suggested Jade Moon, and I could see Pearl didn't like that. I, thinking I was being diplomatic, suggested Pearl Rain." Moon remembered that Rain had been Pearl's consort, who had died turns ago. He hadn't realized the courts were named after pairs of queens and consorts, but it made sense. Jade finished, "Then Pearl suggested Pearl Moon." Her spines twitched at the memory.

He wasn't going to ask if the others were going to accept him; as Chime had said, some would and some wouldn't, and that was on Moon's head, not Jade's.

"What was the final decision?" he asked.

"We decided to keep Indigo Cloud." She looked down at him, her eyes warm and serious all at once. "I can offer you the protection of a court, and hopefully a comfortable home, once we get where we're going."

After his last mistake, Moon wanted to be very specific about this. "As your consort?"

Jade sighed. "No, Moon, I thought we'd just be friends. After all, I just offered to rip Pearl's head off over you." She put her hand on his chest, warm through the silk, and it made him want to crawl into her lap. "Yes, as my consort."

He was feeling guilty about Pearl. "Is she all right?"

"She's fine," Jade said, her voice dry. "She has River and plenty of other warriors to lick her wounds." She shook her frills back. "There wasn't very much actual clawing, just screaming."

There was one thing he wanted to ask her, though now he thought he already knew the answer. He was beginning to get a better idea of how Raksuran courts worked, but he wanted to be certain. "Why didn't you do the scent-thing on me?"

"I told you I wanted you to go to Wind Sun, if we couldn't free the court. It would have been harder for them to find a queen for you if you were already taken." She eyed him. "Why?"

He wasn't going to tell her and re-start the whole fight with Pearl. "No reason." Then he realized he hadn't answered her question yet and said, "Yes."

"Yes?"

He buried his face against her neck, suddenly self-conscious. "Yes, I'll be your consort."

"Good." She sounded relieved, and a little overcome, as if there had been doubt. And there had been, but it didn't seem to matter now. She ran her fingers through his hair. "Do you want anything? Jewels, gold…"

Apparently she was serious. "Fish?"

APPENDIX I

Excerpt from *Observations of the Raksura: Volume Thirty-Seven of A Natural History* by scholar-preeminent Delin-Evran-lindel

The Two Breeds of the Raksura

Arbora: Arbora have no wings but are agile climbers, and their scales appear in a variety of colors. They have long tails, sharp retractable claws, and manes of flexible spines and soft "frills," characteristics that are common to all Raksura. They are expert artisans and are dexterous and creative in the arts they pursue for the court's greater good. In their alternate form they are shorter than Aeriat Raksura and have stocky, powerful builds. Both male and female Arbora are fertile, and sometimes may have clutches that include warrior fledglings. This is attributed to queens and consorts blending their bloodlines with Arbora over many generations.

The four castes of the Arbora are:

Teachers - They supervise the nurseries and train the young of the court. They are also the primary artisans of the court, and tend the gardens that will be seen around any Raksuran colony.

Hunters - They take primary responsibility for providing food for the court. This includes hunting for game, and gathering wild plants.

Soldiers - They "guard the ground" and protect the colony and the surrounding area.

Mentors - They are Arbora born with arcane powers, who have skill in healing and augury. They also act as historians and record-keepers for the court, and usually advise the queens.

Aeriat: The winged Raksura. Like the Arbora, they have long tails, sharp retractable claws, and manes of flexible spines and soft frills.

Warriors - They act as scouts and guardians, and defend the colony from threats from the air, such as the Fell. Warriors are sterile and cannot breed, though they appear as male and female forms. Their scales are in any number of bright colors. Female warriors are usually somewhat stronger than male warriors. In their alternate form, they are always tall and slender. They are not as long-lived generally as queens, consorts, and Arbora.

Consorts - Consorts are fertile males, and their scales are always black, though there may be a tint or "undersheen" of gold, bronze, or blood red. At maturity they are stronger than warriors, and may be the longest lived of any Raksura. They are also the fastest and most powerful flyers, and this ability increases as they grow older. There is some evidence to suggest that consorts of great age may grow as large or larger than the major kethel of the Fell.

Queens - Queens are fertile females, and are the most powerful and deadly fighters of all the Aeriat. Their scales have two brilliant colors, the second in a pattern over the first. The queens' alternate form resembles an Arbora, with no wings, but retaining the tail, and an abbreviated mane of spines and the softer frills. Queens mate with consorts to produce royal clutches, composed of queens, consorts, and warriors.

APPENDIX II

Excerpt from *Additions to the List of Predatory Species* by scholar-eminent-post-humous Venar-Inram-Alil.

Fell are migratory and prey on other intelligent species.

The Known Classes of Fell

> *Major kethel* - The largest of the Fell, sometimes called harbingers, major kethel are often the first sign that a Fell flight is approaching. Their scales are black, like that of all the Fell, and they have an array of horns around their heads. They have a low level of intelligence and are believed to be always under the control of the rulers.

> *Minor dakti* - The dakti are small, with armor plates on the back and shoulders, and webbed wings. They are somewhat cunning, but not much more intelligent than kethel, and fight in large swarms.

> *Rulers* - Rulers are intelligent creatures that are believed to have some arcane powers of entrancement over other species. Rulers related by blood are also believed to share memories and experiences through some mental bond. They have complete control of the lesser Fell in their flights, and at times can speak through dakti and see through their eyes. *(Addendum by scholar-preeminent Delin-Evran-lindel: Fell rulers in their winged form bear an unfortunate and superficial resemblance to Raksuran Consorts.)*

There is believed to be a fourth class, or possibly a female variant of the Rulers, called the *Progenitors*.

Common lore holds that if a Fell ruler is killed, its head must be removed and stored in a cask of salt or yellow mud and buried on land in order to prevent drawing other Fell rulers to the site of its death. It is possible that only removing the head from the corpse may be enough to prevent this, but burying it is held to be the safest course.

About the Author

Martha Wells was born in Fort Worth, Texas, in 1964, and has a B.A. in anthropology from Texas A&M University. She is the author of nine previous novels, including *The Element of Fire, Wheel of the Infinite,* the Fall of Ile-Rien trilogy, and the Nebula-nominated *The Death of the Necromancer.* She has also had short fiction published in *Realms of Fantasy, Black Gate Magazine, Lone Star Stories,* and the Tsunami Relief anthology, *Elemental,* and has articles in the non-fiction anthologies *Farscape Forever* and *Mapping the World of Harry Potter.* She lives in College Station, Texas, with her husband. Her web site is www.marthawells.com.